LOST & FOUND

Kitty Neale was raised in South London and this working class area became the inspiration for her novels. In the 1980s she moved to Surrey with her husband and two children, but in 1998 there was a catalyst in her life when her son died, aged just 27. After joining other bereaved parents in a support group, Kitty was inspired to take up writing and her books have been *Sunday Times* bestsellers

Kitty now lives in Spain with her husband and is working on her new novel for Avon, due to be published later this year. To find out more about Kitty go to www.kittyneale.co.uk

By the same author:

KITTY NEALE

Lost & Found

AVON

A division of HarperCollins*Publishers*
77–85 Fulham Palace Road,
London W6 8JB

www.harpercollins.co.uk

A Paperback Original 2009

1

First published in Great Britain by
HarperCollins*Publishers* 2009

A catalogue record for this book is
available from the British Library

ISBN-13: 978-1-84756-096-4

Set in Minion by Palimpsest Book Production Limited,
Grangemouth, Stirlingshire

Printed and bound in Great Britain by
Clays Ltd, St Ives plc

Mixed Sources

Product group from well-managed
forests and other controlled sources
www.fsc.org Cert no. SW-COC-1806
© 1996 Forest Stewardship Council

FSC is a non-profit international organisation established
to promote the responsible management of the world's forests.
Products carrying the FSC label are independently certified
to assure consumers that they come from forests that are managed
to meet the social, economic and ecological needs
of present and future generations.

Find out more about HarperCollins and the environment at
www.harpercollins.co.uk/green

My thanks go to a very special man, Steve Armitage of TheWebShop, who came to my rescue when I had a huge problem with my computer. Without thought of reward he kindly gave hours of his time to find my lost data and without him this book would never have been finished by the deadline.

Thanks, Steve, and may your web design business here in Spain go from strength to strength.

This one is for you, Abbie; my beautiful great-granddaughter who I feel could be destined for the stage. You are already a star that brightens our life and may all your dreams come true.

CHAPTER ONE

PART ONE
Battersea, South London, February 1954

'Where do you think you're going?'

'School.'

'Not today you ain't,' Lily Jackson told her daughter. 'Take the pram out and go over to Chelsea again. I need some decent stuff for a change and the pickings are richer there.'

'But I had two days off last week, and Dad said . . .'

'Sod what your dad said. He hardly stumped up a penny on Friday. If we want to eat, finding me some decent stuff to flog is more important than flaming school. Anyway, as you leave in just over a month, you might as well get used to doing a bit of graft for a change.'

Mavis felt the injustice of her mother's words.

For as long as she could remember, after school and every weekend, her task had been to take the pram out, begging for cast-offs. She hated it, almost as much as she hated her name. It had been her great grandmother's, but even that was better than her nickname. She knew her ears stuck out, that she wasn't clever, and every time the locals called her Dumbo, Mavis burned with shame. Oh, she'd be glad to leave school, dreamed of getting a job, of earning her own money. 'I . . . I won't mind going out to work.'

'Huh! Nobody in their right mind would employ a useless lump like you.'

'But . . . but . . .'

'But nothing. Now don't just stand there. Get a move on.'

'Can . . . can I take some grub with me?'

'Yeah, I suppose so, but there's only bread and dripping.'

Mavis hurried to cut two thick chunks of bread, spread them with dripping and, after filling an old lemonade bottle with water from the tap, she opened the back door to put them into the large Silver Cross pram. It was a cold, damp, February morning with a chill wind that penetrated her scant clothes. She hurried inside again to throw on her coat before wrapping a long, hand-knitted woollen scarf around her neck. 'I'm off, Mum.'

'It's about time too. Be careful with any glass or china, and don't show your face again until that pram's full.'

With a small nod, Mavis walked outside to the yard again and, gripping the pram handle, she wheeled it out into the back alley. It was a long walk to Chelsea, but Mavis kept her head down as she hurried along to Battersea Church Road. She was fearful of bumping into anyone she knew, especially Tommy Wilson and Larry Barnet, two boys of her own age who lived at the opposite end of the street. Tears stung her eyes. If her mother had suggested taking tomorrow off it wouldn't have been so bad, but now she'd miss one of the only lessons she looked forward to. Her art teacher, Miss Harwood, praised her work, saying she had talent and encouraged her to think seriously about going on to art college when she left school. Of course, it was a silly dream, Mavis knew that. Her mother would have her doing something to earn money and would never allow it. To her, art was a waste of time and she'd never shown interest in any work that Mavis had taken home.

Until now, Mavis thought, shivering with antici-pation. The end-of-term painting was nearly complete and when her mother saw it, instead of shame, Mavis hoped she would at last see pride on her face. It was good – in fact, according to

Miss Harwood, very good – and Mavis couldn't wait for her mother to see it.

Lily was glad to see the back of her daughter. Mavis had been a lovely baby and a pretty toddler, with dark curly hair and big blue eyes like her father. Her only flaw had been her large ears, but another one emerged soon after she started school. When other kids began to learn how to read and write, Mavis was left behind, and her clumsiness became more apparent. Simple things like catching a ball were beyond her and the only thing she was good at was drawing. What good was that when it came to earning a living?

Lily had long since accepted the truth. Her daughter might be pretty, but she was a bit simple, daft; almost as bad as her father. Ron had been an orphan, a Barnardo boy, but at least he could read. At that thought Lily scowled. Yes, Ron could read the racing form and write out a betting slip. Over the years they'd had row after row about his gambling, but nothing stopped him. In fact, it just got worse, until almost every week his wage packet ended up down the greyhound track. When he wasn't at the dogs, Ron was in the pub, blowing the last of his wages.

Lily shook her head in disgust. As always, the burden of looking after Mavis fell to her. She had to feed their daughter, clothe her, and as Ron was hardly in he took little interest in Mavis. When he had rolled home on Friday night, she had waited until he was asleep to search his pockets, hoping against hope that he hadn't blown the lot. All she'd found was a crumpled ten-bob note along with a few coppers and, knowing her stock was low, she'd felt like braining him. She was sick of flogging other people's junk to make a few bob, the old clothes being the worst. She had to wash and iron the stuff, tarting it up as best she could to sell down at the local market. Most weeks it made her enough to scrape by, but when it didn't, Lily thanked her lucky stars for her old mum. It wasn't right that she had to go to her for the occasional hand-out, but with Ron losing more than he ever won, sometimes she had no choice.

Lily took a last gulp of tea then stoically rose to her feet. What was the matter with her? She didn't have time to sit here. She had the last pile of junk to sort out, though it wasn't up to much and hardly worth the bother. She just hoped that Mavis could cadge some decent stuff this time – and that she didn't break it before fetching it home.

Ron stared at the foreman, his fists clenched in anger.

'Did you hear what I said, Jackson?'

'Yeah, I heard you.'

'Right then. Get a move on.'

'It ain't my job to dig out footings. I'm a hod carrier, not a labourer,' Ron snapped.

'Your brickie hasn't turned up, and I'm not having you standing around doing nothing. Now do as I say and get to work.'

Ron hated the way the foreman threw his weight around and he'd had enough. His voice a snarl he said, 'Fuck off!'

'You're finished, Jackson. I want you off the site. Now!'

Ron raised his fist, ready to smash it into the foreman's face, but then felt a staying hand on his arm. Pete Culling had turned up, the almost bald bricklayer urging, 'Leave it, Ron. He ain't worth it. Come on, let's go.'

His head snapped around. 'Where the hell have you been?'

'I'll tell you later. Now, are you coming?'

'Not until I've flattened this little weasel,' Ron spat, but found as he turned his attention to the foreman that the man had already moved several feet away.

Pete laughed, flashing his perfectly white teeth, but even these didn't save his acne-scarred face. He looked like a boxer, one whose nose had been flattened from too many punches as he said, 'Look at him. He's shit scared and ready to do a runner. Don't waste your energy, mate, and anyway, sod this job. I've got something better lined up: a nice little earner.'

Ron felt his anger draining away, but scowled at the foreman, unwilling to leave without a parting shot. 'I ain't finished with you yet, so watch your back. As for this job, you can stick it where the sun don't shine.'

The two men walked off the site, laughing, until Ron said to Pete, 'So, what's this nice little earner?'

'I heard about a bloke looking for teams and willing to pay top money. I went to meet up with him before I came on site this morning. He wants us now so we'll be stepping straight into another job.'

'So that's why you were late.'

'Yeah, but I didn't expect to hear you getting your marching orders when I showed up.'

'You didn't have to leave. It was me who got the sack, not you,' Ron protested.

'Leave it out, mate – we're a team. Anyway, with the money we'll be earning, I was going to tell him to stick the job anyway. Let's go to the café and I'll fill you in. Not only that, I'm starving and could do with a decent breakfast.'

'All right, but no breakfast for me. Mind you, I won't say no to a cup of char.'

'Don't tell me you're skint again.'

'Of course I ain't,' Ron lied, 'it's just that Lily made me a few sarnies for lunch and I ate them while waiting for you to turn up.'

'Don't give me that. I wasn't that late.'

Ron knew he hadn't fooled Pete. They knew each other too well and had worked together since getting demobbed. It hadn't been easy at first, coming back from the war to find half of London flattened and jobs scarce. Things had gradually improved and when at last rebuilding got underway there was a demand for bricklaying teams. Nowadays they were never out of work and it looked like Pete had come up trumps again. He grinned ruefully, 'All right, I'm skint.'

'What was it? The dogs again?'

'Yeah, but I was doing all right. I picked a couple of winners, and then got the whisper of a sure thing. I stuck the lot on Ascot Boy and he was leading the pack, but then swung wide, fell, and took another couple of dogs with him. Paul's Fun got through the gap to win by three-quarters of a length.'

'So you blew your wages again?'

'I had a few bob left, but after drowning me sorrows in the Queen's Head, I reckon Lily must have cleaned out me pockets when I rolled home.'

'Serves you right, Ron. I've said it before, gambling's a mug's game. I don't know what's the matter with you. You're good looking with a gorgeous wife and kid, yet despite Lily's threats to leave you you'd rather spend your time down the dogs or in the pub.'

'Look, I've had nothing but ear bashings from

Lily all weekend and don't need another one from you. I know I've got to knock the gambling on the head, and I will.'

'If you really mean it this time, I've got the answer,' Pete said as they walked into the café and up to the counter.

'What's that supposed to mean?'

'Watcha, Alfie. Two cups of tea please, followed by an egg and sausage with fried bread. Twice please,' Pete said, leaving Ron's question unanswered.

'Just a tea for me.'

'Ignore him, Alfie,' Pete said, and then, taking the mugs of tea, he walked over to a vacant table.

'What did you do that for? I told you I didn't want anything to eat,' Ron said as he sat down opposite.

'It's my treat, and, anyway, after hearing what I've got to say you'll need a full stomach when you tell Lily.'

'Tell her what?'

Pete took a gulp of tea, wiped the back of his hand across his mouth and then said, 'The new job's out of London.'

'Oh, yeah. How far?'

'About thirty miles.'

'What! Leave it out, Pete. That's too far to travel.'

'Before you start doing your nut, hear me out. You've heard of these new town developments?

Well, Bracknell in Berkshire is one of them. They're building houses for thousands of people, but they've got a shortage of tradesmen and it's behind schedule. That's where we come in. The bloke I met is looking for crews, and the money is top whack. If we put the hours in, it works out at almost twice what we've been earning.'

Ron pursed his lips. 'It sounds good, but there's still the problem of getting there. We'd have to be up at the crack of dawn and Gawd knows what time we'd get home.'

'There's accommodation on offer. It's only basic, but to earn that sort of money I'm willing to rough it.'

'I dunno, mate,' Ron said doubtfully.

'It's the chance we've been waiting for. We've always talked about starting up our own firm and if you're willing to give up gambling, we could pool our money, save enough to start up.'

'You'd take that risk on me?'

'We're mates, and, after what you did for me, I'd be willing to take the risk.'

Ron's head went down. During a beach landing in France he'd seen Pete pinned down by gunfire, too frightened to move. He'd run back, grabbed Pete, hauled him forward, but had taken a bullet in his leg. It had only been a skimmer, a bit of a flesh wound and, anyway, it was no more than Pete would have done for him.

Now his mate was willing to risk a partnership – but could he do it? Ron agonised. Could he give up gambling? 'I dunno, Pete. What if I let you down?'

'You won't. There isn't a dog track in Bracknell, and I reckon we'll be away long enough to get gambling out of your system. It's time to take stock, Ron. If you don't pull your socks up you'll end up with nothing. Think about the future. We ain't getting any younger, and if we don't do this now, we never will.'

Two plates were put in front of them, and Ron's mouth salivated as the smell of sausages and egg wafted up. Meat was still rationed, with only 4oz of bacon allowed a week, but there was more food available now. It was nice to have a real egg instead of that powdered muck they'd been forced to eat during the war, but as Ron picked up his knife and fork to cut into the sausage, he felt a surge of shame. Rationing or not, with most of his money going down the dogs, there wasn't much food on offer at home. He should be providing for his wife and child, but the pull of the race track always won; the thrill of watching the dogs, of picking a big winner. Some weeks he won a few bob, but then like an idiot he'd put it on another dog, only to lose it again. Pete was right. Lily was right. It was a mug's game, and he knew it.

Pete spoke and Ron was broken out of his reveries. 'Well, Ron, what do you think?'

Determined to make changes, Ron said, 'All right, let's give it a go. But Gawd knows what Lily's going to say.'

CHAPTER TWO

When Mavis had passed her gran's house in Battersea Church Road, she hadn't been able to resist popping in. Her reward was a jam sandwich that she munched as she sat by the fire.

'So, you're out with the pram again?'

'Yes. Mum needs more stock and wants me to try Chelsea.'

'And judging by the look on your face, you ain't happy about it.'

'I'd rather go to school.'

'Blame your dad. If he didn't blow all his money on gambling, she wouldn't have to flog her guts out. The least you can do is give her a hand.'

'I know,' Mavis placated, aware that Gran despised her dad, and though Mavis sort of understood why, she couldn't feel the same. She loved her dad, but just wished she saw more of him. Maybe he wouldn't go to the dogs tonight, or the pub. Maybe for once he'd come home.

'Instead of that good-for-nothing, I wish my Lily had met and married a decent man.'

Now that Gran had started, Mavis knew there'd be no stopping her. She swiftly finished her sandwich and stood up saying, 'That was lovely, Gran, but I'd better go.'

Her gran struggled to her feet, swaying a little, prompting Mavis to ask, 'Are you all right?'

'Yes, I'm fine. You're getting as bad as your mother, fussing over me all the time, but as I told her yesterday, I'm as fit as a flea.'

Mavis doubted this was true. Her gran had once been chubby and red-cheeked, but for the past six months the weight had been dropping off her. She was sixty-one, her hair speckled with grey and her skin pasty. 'Gran, you're looking really thin. Have you been to the doctor's yet?'

'No, and I don't intend to either. There's nothing wrong with losing a bit of weight. Now go on, bugger off and leave me in peace.'

The sting was taken out of this comment by a swift hug and a kiss on the cheek, which Mavis returned before asking, 'Do you need anything from the shops?'

'If you pass the pie and mash shop on your way home, I wouldn't say no to a portion of jellied eels. Hang on, I'll just get me purse.'

With the money in her pocket, Mavis waved goodbye, still worried about her gran as she pushed the pram along. Unlike her mother, Granny Doris wasn't slow in showing affection. Mavis knew she was stupid, useless, fit for nothing as her mother always said, but her gran made her feel loved. Gran would listen when she talked, whereas her mother had no patience, telling her to shut up nearly every time she opened her mouth. Mavis knew she'd be lost without her gran, and was frightened that she really was ill; tears now flooded her eyes as she turned the corner.

'Be careful, girl.'

'I . . . I'm sorry, Mrs Pugh,' Mavis stammered as she hastily veered to one side.

'You nearly barged into me. Where are you off to? It's Monday morning and surely you should be on your way to school?'

'My . . . my mum needs more stock.'

Edith Pugh's neck stretched with indignation. 'Don't your parents realise how important your education is? My son is twenty-two now, but when he was at school I made sure he never missed a day. Now look at him. Alec works in an office and is doing really well. You'll learn nothing trawling the streets. As I'm going past your house, I think I'll have a word with your mother.'

'Oh, no, please, don't do that! I leave school at Easter and . . . and it's not as if a day off will make much difference.'

The woman's face softened imperceptibly, her

tone a little kinder. 'No, I suppose not, but despite your difficulties I'm sure you're bright. I think you just need a bit of extra help and it's a shame you aren't getting it.'

Once again Mavis felt her cheeks burning. Until last year, Mrs Pugh had been the school secretary and she hated it that the woman knew of her failings. Anxious to get away, she stuttered, 'I . . . I think my English teacher has given up on me.'

'What about your parents? Have they tried to help you?'

'Er . . . yes,' Mavis lied, and to avoid any more questions, she added, 'I really must go now.'

'Very well, but watch where you're going with that pram. You nearly had me off my feet.'

With this curt comment Mrs Pugh walked away, her back bent and walking stick tapping the pavement, and Mavis too resumed her journey. She had always been in awe of Edith Pugh, and on their previous encounters when the woman had worked at her school, Mavis found her changing personality bewildering. She could be very strict, blunt, and opinionated, yet there'd been times when she'd shown kindness when questioning her absenteeism. Edith Pugh and her son lived in Ellington Avenue, only a ten-minute walk from her own home in Cullen Street, but the difference between the two was stark.

Ellington Avenue was tree lined, with bay-fronted houses that had gardens back and front. In complete contrast, the houses in Cullen Street were flat-fronted, two-up-two-down terraces, with just small, concrete backyards. There were no trees, and the only view was of the dismal houses opposite.

Mavis had been out so many times with the pram that she knew every road, lane, street and avenue in the whole area, but Ellington Avenue was one of her favourites, especially in May when the trees bloomed with froths of pink and white blossom.

At last Mavis reached Battersea Bridge, the river grey and sluggish, and the wind stinging her cheeks as she walked to the other side. On Cheyne Walk now, she hesitated while deciding which direction to take. She could try the houses facing the embankment, or those along Beaufort Street. Mavis crossed the road and turned left, a different route from her last forage. She was immune now to the looks of pity or disdain from people she passed; her one hope was that it wouldn't take all day to fill the pram.

Edith Pugh was deep in thought. Despite the girl's inability to read and write, she was sure that Mavis Jackson was bright, and not only that, the girl was pretty. Yes, but was Mavis malleable? There was

17

only one way she could think of to find out and now, raising the handle of her cane, Edith rapped loudly on the door. Despite the pain, she managed to keep her back straight and her head high when it was opened.

'Blimey, Edith Pugh. And to what do I owe this honour?'

Edith hid her feelings of disdain as she looked at Mavis's mother. Despite being pretty, with a good figure, the woman looked a mess, her peroxide blonde hair resembling straw and her clothes totally unsuitable for a woman in her mid thirties. Edith knew her own hair was mousy brown, but she kept it immaculately permed, and made sure she always looked smart, her clothes nicely tailored. Forcing a smile, she said, 'I'd like a word with you about your daughter.'

'Why? What's she been up to?'

'Nothing, other than the fact that Mavis isn't in school – but as she's leaving soon I think it's time you thought about her future.'

Lily's head reared with indignation. 'Now listen, lady, you may have been the school secretary but that doesn't give you the right to tell me what to do about my daughter.'

'No, I'm not trying to do that,' Edith said hastily. She hated that she had to affect an air of humility but nevertheless forced her tone to sound contrite. 'Oh, dear, I'm so sorry, we seem to have got off

18

on the wrong foot. You see, I came to see you about offering Mavis a job.'

'A job? What sort of job?'

'I'd rather not discuss it on the doorstep. May I come in?'

'Yeah, I suppose so,' Lily said, 'but you'll have to excuse the mess.'

Edith was unable to help her eyebrows rising as she went inside. The room was indeed a mess, with piles of junk spread over the linoleum. She could see rusted old saucepans, a frying pan black with grease, and a few odd pieces of cutlery amongst the jumble. In another heap she saw china, mostly chipped, and in her opinion only fit for the dustbin. There was a sheet of newspaper on the table on top of which Edith saw an old, dented kettle that Lily had obviously been trying to polish up.

'You'd best sit down,' Lily said.

Edith pulled out a chair and looked at it fastidiously before sitting.

'Right, what's this about a job?' Lily asked as she too sat down.

'I'm afraid it's only part time, but I'd like Mavis to work for me. You see, in my early thirties I was diagnosed with multiple sclerosis and, due to relapses, I had to give up work last year.'

'Yeah, I'd heard, but didn't know why.'

Edith ignored the interruption. She wanted to

get this over with, to leave this dirty house and its many germs behind. 'I'm only forty-three now, but my disabilities are worsening, so much so that I need help around the house and with cooking. With your agreement, I'd like Mavis for two hours a day, and an hour at weekends.'

'Two hours a day ain't much of a job and, anyway, Mavis is a clumsy cow. I don't think you could trust her not to break anything.'

'I'm sure she'd be fine with simple tasks, *and* I can teach her to be less clumsy. It's just a matter of training.'

'Leave it out. I know my daughter and gave up on her years ago.'

'I'm willing to take the risk. I'll also pay her one shilling an hour, which is a good rate for a young, unskilled domestic worker.'

'It ain't bad, but I want her to work for me when she leaves school.'

'Surely you could spare her for a couple of hours a day?'

Lily's eyes narrowed in thought, and then she began to count on her fingers. 'I make it twelve hours in total, and she'd earn twelve bob. Yeah, all right, for that money I can spare her, but I warn you, don't come complaining to me if she breaks anything.'

'I won't. I'd like to show Mavis her duties before she starts. Would you send her round to see me?'

'Yeah, but there's no hurry. She doesn't leave school until the end of term.'

'I really could do with her before then. Until she leaves, could she perhaps do an hour after school, and two on Saturdays and Sundays?'

'Yeah, but she can't start today. It'll have to be tomorrow.'

'That's fine.'

'I'll send her round to see you later.'

'Thank you,' Edith said, but as she stood up a muscle spasm caused her to gasp in pain. For a moment her vision blurred and she felt off balance, but then thankfully the moment passed. She reached out to grasp her cane and walked slowly to the door, saying as she was shown out, 'Goodbye, Mrs Jackson.'

'Bye,' Lily chirped back.

When the door closed behind her, Edith heaved in a breath of fresh air. She'd done it. The first stage of her plan was in place. She just hoped Mavis was the perfect choice.

Lily picked up the half-polished kettle, her mind full of the visit as she started to polish the other side. If Edith Pugh really could teach Mavis to be less clumsy, it would make all the difference. The woman had said she was forty-three, but dressed as though she was middle aged. Matronly, that was the only way to describe Edith Pugh; but she had sounded so sure

21

of herself when talking about Mavis. Maybe she was right – maybe it *was* down to training.

Lily knew she should have tried harder with Mavis but, busy trying to make ends meet, she just hadn't had the time, or patience. When Mavis left school, she'd planned to put her to work, sending her out most days with the pram, and using her on other days to tart up any metal stuff. More stock would increase her profits, but now Lily decided there could be an alternative. She turned the idea over in her mind. Yes, it should work, but Lily didn't want to count her chickens before they were hatched. Of course, if Ron would stop gambling they'd be in clover, but that was a pipe dream. However, if her future plans for Mavis worked out, she'd be able to take it easy – have a bit of time to put her feet up for a change.

By the end of another hour, Lily's arms were aching, but at last she had a pile of now shiny, if dented, saucepans to flog, not that she'd get much for them. Her sigh was heavy as she washed the muck off her hands, but then the door swung open and Lily spun around, her eyes widening. 'Bloody hell, Ron! What are you doing home?'

'We got laid off.'

'Why? What did you do this time?' Lily asked in exasperation as she hastily dried her hands.

'I fell out with the foreman, but before you do

22

your nut, don't worry. Pete's already found us another job and the pay's a lot better.'

'Is it now? Knowing you, I doubt I'll see any of it.'

Ron moved closer, pulling her into his arms. 'Yes you will, love. Things are going to change, you'll see.'

Lily stiffened at first as Ron's lips caressed her neck, but sixteen years of marriage hadn't dimmed her passion for this man. He might be a gambler, his wages gone most weeks before she saw a penny, but his body never failed to thrill her. She moved her hands over him, felt his muscles ripple, and melted. It was always the same. She would threaten to leave him, but then be left helpless with desire at his touch. Not this time, she thought, fighting her emotions and pulling away. 'No, Ron.'

'Come on, Lily, you know you don't mean it,' he urged, pulling her close again, the hardness of his desire obvious as he pressed against her.

It was almost her undoing, but once again she fought her feelings. 'I said no!'

'Lily . . . Lily, we should make the most of this. When I'm working away we won't see each other for months.'

Ron's words were like a dash of cold water. 'Working away! What do you mean?'

'Oh, shit, I didn't mean to blurt it out like that.

I'd planned to tell you when you were feeling all warm and cosy after a bit of slap and tickle.'

'Oh, I see, soften me up first and then break the news. Well, forget it. You can tell me now.'

Ron released her. 'All right, but you ain't gonna like it,' he said, taking a seat before going on to tell her about the job in Bracknell.

Lily sat down to hear him out, only speaking when he came to an end. 'So let me get this straight. You're saying that if you take this job you'll be able to give up gambling, and, not only that, you and Pete are going to pool your money, saving up enough to go into partnership?'

'You've got it in one. I know being apart is gonna be rotten, but I'll send you money every week.'

'That'll be a change. I get sod all off you now.'

'I know, love, I know, but I really am going to give up gambling this time. And don't forget, without me to keep, you'll be quids in.'

'Why can't you come home at weekends?'

''Cos we're going to put in as much overtime as we can. The more hours we work, the more we'll earn, and by the end of the contract Pete thinks we'll have enough to buy a van and all the stuff we'll need, mixers and such, to start up our own firm.'

Lily's mind was racing. If Ron really did mean it this time, their lives would be transformed. He'd be able to go into partnership with Pete, and the money would come rolling in . . . Oh, what was the matter with her? It was a silly dream. Ron would never give up gambling – years of broken promises were enough to prove that. 'It's all pie in the sky,' she snapped. 'As soon as you get your first pay packet you'll be down the dog track.'

'Ah, that's just it. I won't be able to. There's no greyhound racing in Bracknell.'

For a moment, Lily dared to believe that Ron could change, but then common sense prevailed. 'You'd find a track somewhere, or something else to gamble on. It's a sickness with you, Ron, and you know it.'

'Yes, but this time I really do want the cure. Pete and me will be in the same accommodation and if I'm tempted he'll keep me on the straight and narrow, you'll see.'

'So you say, but I won't be there to see it. You could be up to anything and I wouldn't know.'

'All right, you don't trust me and I can understand that, but surely you trust Pete?'

'Yes, he's a good bloke, but he ain't your keeper. If you really want to give up gambling, it's down to you.'

'Lily, I promise you, cross my heart and hope to die, I really am going to make it this time,' Ron said as he stood up to pull her into his arms again. 'I don't deserve you, I know that, but I'll make you proud this time.'

Once again his lips caressed her neck, and this time Lily didn't pull away. Ron lifted her up with ease, cupping her legs in his arms as he carried her upstairs.

CHAPTER THREE

Mavis was so tired, her feet throbbing and the pram three-quarters full as she knocked on the last door in the street. The houses were large, with several steps leading up to the front doors, but she'd had many shut in her face. She'd also narrowly avoided a copper on his beat by diving out of sight. If she got a few things from this last house, with any luck she could make her way home. Mavis waited, fingers crossed, and when the door opened, she found herself confronted by a wizened old woman bundled up in what looked like several jumpers and a cardigan.

Blimey, Mavis thought, she looks scruffier than me but, taking a deep breath, she said politely, 'I'm sorry to bother you, but have you got any household items or clothes that you want to get rid of?'

'Get rid of! Do you mean sell them to you?'

Mavis told the usual lie, the one her mother had advised. 'Oh, no, I don't want to buy anything.

I'm collecting for charity, stuff to pass on to the Salvation Army.'

'I see,' the tiny woman said. 'In that case, you'd better come in and I'll see what I can find.'

It was unusual to be invited in, but Mavis followed her into the house, along a hall and into a living room. There was no fire burning in the huge grate; the room was freezing, and she saw an old quilt draped over a chair that had been pushed to one side. Was that all she had for warmth? The room was huge, but with wallpaper peeling and an absence of any pictures or ornaments, it felt bleak.

'I haven't got much, my dear, but perhaps these candlesticks,' the woman said as she reached up to remove them from the mantelpiece, handing them to Mavis.

They weren't very large, blackened, and it was no wonder she hadn't noticed them, Mavis thought, as she took them from the woman's hands. She saw the marks through the grime but, after another swift look around the dismal room, Mavis quickly handed them back. This might be a large house, the outside appearance one of wealth, but even her small home in Cullen Street had a little more comfort. 'No, no, I can't take these. I'm sure they're made of silver.'

'Really? Are you sure?'

Mavis couldn't decipher the symbols, but knew

what they were called. 'Yes, look, you can just about see the hallmarks.'

'Oh, dear, in that case I'm afraid I can't give them to you. They're saleable, but surely I can find something for the Salvation Army. Let's have a look in the kitchen.'

Once again Mavis followed the old woman, but found the kitchen as austere as the living room. Oh, this was dreadful, she thought. The poor woman must be penniless to live like this. Cupboards were opened, most almost empty, including the pantry. Once again Mavis was swamped with guilt. She had lied to the woman and now all she wanted was to get away. 'It's all right. It doesn't matter. I've collected loads of stuff already and I really must go now.'

'But it's such a worthy cause and I'd like to help,' the woman insisted, pulling something from a bottom cupboard. 'What about this?'

Mavis carefully took the china biscuit barrel, its metal lid black with dirt. 'Thank you. This is fine and more than enough,' she said. Before the old lady could protest, Mavis fled the kitchen, ran down the hall, pulling the front door closed behind her before almost skidding down the few stairs and onto the pavement.

Full pram or not, Mavis just wanted to go home. She had looked with envy at the large houses, imagined the luxurious interiors, but seeing inside one was a revelation. That poor old woman had nothing, yet was still prepared to donate something to charity.

Mavis put the biscuit barrel in the pram. And then, deciding to risk her mother's wrath that the pram wasn't full, she started the long walk home. Oh, if only she didn't have to do this. If only she could find a job when she left school, but, as her mother always pointed out, nobody in their right mind would employ her. Downcast, she trudged along, worn out and hungry by the time she reached Cullen Street.

Lily was feeling warm and mellow. After making love they had come downstairs again and now Ron was sitting by the fire, his feet on the surround, talking so enthusiastically about his plans that Lily was beginning to feel that he really could make it this time.

The back door opened and Mavis walked in, smiling with delight when she saw her father. 'Hello, Dad.'

'How's my girl?'

'So, you're back,' Lily interrupted. 'Let's see how you got on.'

'The pram isn't full.'

'I told you not to come home until it was.'

'Lily, leave it out,' Ron protested. 'You shouldn't send her out tramping the streets; she looks frozen.'

Lily's good mood vanished. How dare Ron

criticise her? Hands on hips, she spat, 'The fact that Mavis has to go out scrounging is down to you, Ron, not me. You blow your money every week, leaving me to somehow find the rent, let alone food. I *have* to send Mavis out. If I didn't, we'd bloody well starve.'

'I know, and I'm sorry, love,' Ron said ruefully. 'I know you do your best, but things really are going to change.'

'Huh. I'll believe it when I see it.' And with that Lily marched out to the yard. She rummaged through the pram, relieved to see that Mavis hadn't broken anything, and saw a few things that would show a bit of profit. She could have done with more. It was just as well she had other plans now, but then, seeing what looked like a half-decent biscuit barrel, Lily felt a surge of pleasure, her bad mood lifting as she gave it a closer inspection. The rest of the stuff could wait until later, and Lily threw a cover over the pram in case of rain.

Mavis was sitting by the fire when Lily went back inside, smiling happily to be with her father. 'You did all right, and this is a really good find,' Lily said, holding up the biscuit barrel. 'If I'm not mistaken, it could be antique and the lid's silver.'

'Oh, no! I'll have to take it back.'

'Take it back! Are you mad?'

'But, Mum, the old lady who gave it to me lives

in this big house, but she's really poor. I only took it because I didn't think it was worth anything.'

'I can't believe I'm hearing this. If it hasn't escaped your notice, you daft cow, we're poor too.'

'But she didn't even have a fire going and there was hardly any food in her pantry.'

'Oh, and I've got a lot in mine, have I?' Lily said sarcastically. 'We're so well off that all we've got for dinner is a bit of bubble and squeak.'

'Things are gonna get better, love, you know that,' Ron cajoled.

'Yeah, so you say.'

'Lily, I promise, you'll get five pounds a week without fail.'

'Five quid! From what you said, you'll be earning nearly three times that.'

'Does that mean I can return the biscuit barrel?' Mavis asked eagerly.

'No, you bloody well can't! What your dad's talking about may never happen. In the mean-time, if we want to eat tomorrow, I'll need to sell this, and fast. In fact, you can have a go at cleaning it up while I'm cooking dinner.' Lily kept her expression stern and thankfully there were no further protests from Mavis. 'I know what a clumsy cow you are, so just polish the lid. Use a soft cloth. I don't want to see any scratches.'

While Mavis did her bidding, Lily started on their dinner, unable to help doing a mental calculation as she worked. If she really did get five quid a week from Ron, for the first time in years he'd be giving her decent money. She flicked a glance at her husband, saw that he had dozed off, and her expression hardened. What was the matter with her? Of course it wouldn't happen. She couldn't rely on Ron. As always, he'd let her down again. Still, she had the biscuit barrel and it would fetch a fair few bob, and with Mavis earning more from cleaning when she left school, things were starting to look up.

Mavis couldn't stop her mouth from salivating. She'd eaten her bread and dripping at midday and now the smell of her mother's cooking made her stomach growl with hunger. Oh, no, she'd forgotten to get jellied eels for Granny Doris! Tomorrow, she'd get them tomorrow. Her gran was sure to understand.

Gingerly Mavis picked up the ceramic biscuit barrel, and under the grime she could just about see a circle of black ponies, along with a pretty blue border top and bottom. She took off the lid, polishing it carefully, pleased to see how it began to gleam. While she worked, Mavis was unable to stop stealing glances at her father. As she'd hoped, he was home, and if he didn't go out again that evening it would be wonderful.

Ten minutes later, when Mavis thought the lid

was shiny enough to please her mother, she said, 'Look, Mum, what do you think?'

'Yeah, very nice,' Lily said, her eyes squinting to see the hallmark. 'I don't know much about date letters, but I think it's early.' She then put the lid down to pick up the barrel and, upending it, she pointed out the maker's mark on the bottom. 'Look at that, it's Royal Doulton. Well done, girl, it's as I thought. This is worth a good few bob.'

It was rare that Mavis received praise from her mother, and though unable to return the barrel, she couldn't help feeling a glow of pleasure. At least she hadn't accepted the silver candlesticks, Mavis thought, assuaging her guilt.

'Right, dinner's ready so lay the table,' her mum then ordered as she placed the barrel carefully on the dresser. 'Ron! Ron, come on, wake up.'

Mavis quickly placed cutlery on the table, smiling when her mother spoke kindly again. 'Look at him, out for the count. I've a good mind to leave him like that and it'll be all the more bubble and squeak for us.'

'I heard that,' he said, stretching his arms before standing up. He then kissed Lily on the cheek and smiled cheekily. 'Come on, woman. Feed me.'

'I'll do more than feed you if you ain't careful.'

'Is that a threat or a promise?' he asked, winking at Mavis as he took a seat at the table.

Oh, this was so nice, Mavis thought. Her mother

was in a good mood again, her father cracking jokes, and she wished it could always be like this. Mavis then saw her mother holding out two plates.

'Be careful giving this to hungry guts,' she said. 'Don't drop it, and that one's yours.'

'How's my girl then?' Ron asked again as Mavis carefully placed his dinner in front of him.

'I'm all right, Dad,' she said, loving the way her father called her his girl. She sat down to eat, the food rapidly disappearing off her plate. They were all quiet while they ate, but as Mavis finished her last mouthful her mother spoke once again.

'Right, Mavis. You've finished your dinner so get yourself round to Edith Pugh's house. You'll be working for her after school tomorrow and she wants to show you your so-called duties.'

'Mrs Pugh? I . . . I'll be working for her?' Mavis stammered. 'But . . . but what does she want me to do?'

'From what she said, a bit of cleaning, and you can get that look off your face. You ain't fit for much, even domestic work, but the woman thinks she can train you.'

'Lily, there's no need to talk to her like that.'

'Go on, jump to her defence as usual. I'm the one who has to feed her, clothe her, and do you think I like it that my daughter can't do even the simplest tasks? Mavis will bring in a few bob for a bit of cleaning, which is more than I can say for you.'

Mavis hung her head. Things were back to normal between her parents, but nevertheless her thoughts raced. She wasn't sure that she wanted to work for Mrs Pugh, yet surely it was better than taking the pram out? But would her mother expect her to do that too? 'What about stock – the pram?'

'That depends on your father. If he's true to his word, which I doubt, and sends me five quid a week, we can knock it on the head. If he doesn't, well, you'll have to keep finding me stock.'

Mavis suddenly latched on to her mother's words. 'Send it. What does that mean? Won't you be here, Dad?'

'No, from tomorrow I'll be working away. I'll have to pay a bit for lodgings, but your mother will get her money.'

'Yeah, and pigs might fly.'

'I'll make you eat your words, Lily. You'll see.'

Before her mother could respond again, Mavis hastily broke in, 'Will you be away for a long time, Dad?'

'I'm afraid so, love, at least six months, maybe more, but it's for a good cause.'

'Oh, Dad . . .'

'Mavis, that's enough. I said get yourself round to Edith Pugh's. Now!'

Desolately, Mavis pushed her chair back. She knew better than to argue with her mother, and now the only person who ever came to her defence was leaving – and from what he said, for a long time. Mavis took her coat from the hook, unable to help blurting out as she shrugged it on, 'Dad, please don't go.'

'I've got to, love. It'll be the making of us, you'll see, and when I come back things are going to be different. I'll have me own business, making a packet, and your mother will never have to work again.'

Mavis saw the look of derision on her mother's face and, like her, doubted it was true. She knew her father was a gambler, had heard so many rows, followed by his promises – ones that he never kept. Yet she loved her dad, dreaded him leaving, and tears stung her eyes as she stepped outside. What would happen to her now?

CHAPTER FOUR

Edith Pugh was struggling to wash up the dinner things when her son walked into the room.

'Leave it, Mum. I'll do it,' Alec insisted.

'I can manage.'

'No, you can't, and it's about time you listened to me. You need a bit of help, someone to take on the housework and cooking.'

'I have listened. In fact, I've taken someone on to do just that.'

He raised his eyebrows. 'Have you now? Well, that's good.'

'She'll only be working for an hour a day until she leaves school, but even that will be a help.'

'Mum, you need a mature woman with a bit of experience, not a schoolgirl. If you're taken bad again, a kid would be useless.'

'I haven't employed her as a nurse, Alec. It hasn't come to that yet.'

'All right, but when does this girl start?'

'Tomorrow, but I'm expecting her to call round soon so you'll meet her before then.'

'Good, now go and sit down. I'll finish this lot.'

Edith didn't argue this time. Her feet felt so painful, as though she was standing on broken glass, and she moved slowly across the room to sit on a fireside chair. She had done too much today, walked too far to see Mrs Jackson, but surely it had been worth it?

With a sigh, Edith closed her eyes, unaware that she had dozed off until the doorbell rang. She saw that Alec had finished washing up, that the dishes were put away, and said tiredly, 'That's probably Mavis. Let her in, Alec.'

He nodded and as he left the room, Edith managed to sit up straighter in her chair. She heard voices and soon Alec returned with Mavis behind him. 'Hello, Mavis.'

'Hello, Mrs Pugh. My mum told me to come to see you. She said I'm to work for you after school tomorrow.'

'Yes, that's right, but do sit down. You look frozen.'

'Thanks,' Mavis said, taking the chair at the other side of the hearth.

'Now then, I expect you want to know what your duties will be. I'm afraid I have rather high standards, and with only an hour each afternoon,

I think we'll concentrate on giving one room a day a thorough clean. How does that sound?'

'Er . . . it sounds fine.'

'Good, and if you have any time left, I'd like you to prepare our dinner. Peel vegetables and such, ready for me to cook. Do you think you could manage that?'

'I think so.'

Edith was so tired that she was finding it difficult to concentrate. There was something else to discuss, but what was it? Oh, yes. 'I was going to show you the house, but I'm afraid it will have to wait until tomorrow.'

'Mother, are you all right?'

When Edith turned to Alec, she saw that his expression showed conflicting emotions. He looked annoyed, probably because she had over-tired herself, but also worried. Edith adored her son. As a child she had spoiled him, but he was everything to her and they shared the same tastes in most things. They preferred classical music to modern, loved art and reading. In fact, Alec was the perfect son, so loving and caring, so, with a smile of reassurance, she said, 'Yes, I'm fine, but would you show Mavis out?'

He nodded, and as Mavis stood up, she said, 'Thanks, Mrs Pugh. I . . . I'll see you tomorrow.'

Edith nodded. 'Goodbye for now, Mavis.'

As the girl followed Alec out of the room,

Edith sagged. She heard the front door close and was about to close her eyes again, when Alec stormed back into the room.

'Mother, are you out of your mind? It's bad enough that you're employing a schoolgirl, but Mavis Jackson! You know how people gossip around here and from what I've heard she's backward.'

'Don't be cruel, Alec. Just because Mavis can't read and write, it doesn't mean she's stupid. In fact, I'm sure she's bright, and perfectly capable of doing domestic work.'

'If she can't read at the age of fifteen, there must be something wrong – and from the look of her she isn't even capable of keeping herself clean.'

Edith's mind was foggy as she struggled for a persuasive argument. 'Oh, for goodness sake, not everyone has our standards, and it would be hard to find someone willing to do things my way. Mavis is a nice, amiable girl who I'll show how to do things correctly from the start.'

'But . . .'

'Please, Alec,' Edith interrupted, 'I'm too tired to argue. If Mavis doesn't work out, I'll replace her, so please, be satisfied with that.'

'Oh, very well.'

Edith closed her eyes, hiding her relief. She couldn't tell Alec the truth – that she was doing this not only for herself, but for him too. At this moment in time, if Alec knew her plans, he'd bolt. Yet one day, when everything she intended to do was in place, her son would thank her. And on this thought, Edith finally drifted off to sleep.

Alec saw that his mother had fallen asleep and, though still annoyed, he looked at her worriedly. Without his father in his life, she was everything to him, but she was getting worse, he was sure of it. Alec looked around the room to see that as usual, everything was immaculate. The rest of the house would be the same. Obsessive, that was the word to describe his mother. She wouldn't put up with a fleck of dust, an ornament out of place and woe betide him if he left a mess in the bathroom – not that he would of course. Maybe his mother was right, Alec thought as he shifted in his chair. Maybe it would be impossible to find a woman who could work to her standards. But for goodness sake, surely she could do better than Mavis Jackson!

Yet now, as Alec recalled her face, he realised that there was indeed a spark of intelligence in the girl's eyes. Not only that, underneath the grime, he'd seen that Mavis was quite pretty too, but her dirt-encrusted fingernails had made him shudder with distaste. Like his mother, Alec knew he was fastidious, but as far as he was concerned there was nothing wrong with that. He'd been brought up to appreciate that cleanliness was close to godliness, and though he wasn't particularly religious, he liked the pleasure of a clean home, clean body, and immaculately laundered clothes.

Oh well, Alec thought as he stood up, deciding to take a look at his stamp collection. As his mother said, if Mavis didn't work out, she'd soon be given her marching orders.

Mavis hurried home, her thoughts on Alec Pugh. She'd seen him around, but knew little about him, and now, after meeting him face to face, she was frowning. Alec Pugh wasn't very tall and not much to look at, with mousy brown hair and a moustache to match. His manner had made her feel uncomfortable – the way he'd taken her in to see his mother with obvious reluctance. It had been the same when she was shown out. He'd opened the street door, and had almost slammed it behind her without saying a word. He was rude, stuck up, but at least she wouldn't see much of him, Mavis decided, consoled by the thought. If she was only working for an hour after school, she'd be long gone before Alec Pugh came home from work.

Mavis turned into her street, almost bumping into Tommy and Larry. Her stomach lurched and she immediately lowered her head. If she crossed to the other side, maybe they'd leave her alone, but before Mavis got the chance, Larry stood in front of her.

'Well, look here, it's Dumbo.'

'Leave me alone.'

'Now there's no need to be unfriendly. In fact, how about a walk on the common?'

'No, no,' Mavis gasped as she tried to step around them.

'There's no need to run away. Come on, come with us and we'll have a bit of fun.'

Mavis frantically shook her head. In her last encounter with the two boys, they had tried to do dirty things to her. She'd been too ashamed and scared to tell her parents, and though she remembered how they threatened her to keep it a secret, Mavis still grasped at the only thing she could think of to scare them off. 'If you don't go away, I'll tell my dad what you did to me.'

Larry's eyes narrowed into threatening slits. 'I wouldn't if I was you, Dumbo, 'cos if you do we'll only make it worse for you. Ain't that right, Tommy?' he added, throwing a quick glance at the boy by his side.

'Yeah,' Tommy agreed, but there was a flicker of fear in his eyes. 'Come on, Larry, let's go. I don't fancy the smelly cow anyway.'

'You're right, she ain't much,' he agreed, leaning forward until he was almost eye to eye with Mavis. 'Now listen. If you open your mouth, not only will we make it worse for you, we'll tell your dad that you asked for it, that you led us on. I bet he'd love to hear that his precious daughter's a tart.'

With that they walked off, but Larry's voice was loud enough for Mavis to hear his next comment.

'Don't worry, Tommy. It's like I said before, even if she opens her mouth, nobody would believe that thicko over us.'

Mavis hurried off, and on reaching her front door she took a gulp of air before walking into the kitchen, unaware of how pale she looked.

Her father's gaze was sharp. 'Mavis, you look like death. What's the matter?'

She was saved from answering when her mother spoke. 'What happened? Don't tell me you blew it and didn't get the job.'

'No, no, I got it. I start tomorrow.'

She saw her father frown, then he said, 'Well, my girl, something's upset you. Come on, spit it out.'

Mavis hung her head, searching for an answer and, unable to tell the truth, she said, 'It's Mrs Pugh's son. I . . . I didn't like him.'

'Why? What's wrong with him?' Lily asked.

'He . . . he was funny with me. Stuck up.'

'Well, that doesn't surprise me. Like his mother, from what I've heard – just 'cos he works in an office, Alec Pugh thinks he's a cut above the rest of us.'

Once again her father spoke. 'Are you sure that's all it is, Mavis? He was just off with you. Is that right?'

With her mind churning, Mavis knew she couldn't tell her father the truth. He'd go mad, and Larry was right, what if he didn't believe her side of the story? Had she led them on? Mavis didn't know. She'd bumped into them on the common, had been pleased that, instead of making fun of her as usual, they'd been friendly. They'd sat on a bench, both boys telling her silly jokes that made her laugh. But then the atmosphere changed, became tense and as though on cue, they fumbled with their trousers. She'd never seen willies before and was horrified when they pulled them out. Larry flaunted his, giggling, and unsure of how to react she had giggled too. Larry had told her to hold his, but suddenly frightened by the intense look in his eyes, she had said no. Larry had pounced then, pulling her from the bench and onto the grass. Tommy at first hesitated, but then joined in, both pushing her back and trying to lift up her skirt. She had screamed, kicked, and it was then the boys saw someone coming. They released her from their grip and she had scrambled away, picking herself up to run home, too sick with shame to tell her mother what had happened.

Since that day, four weeks earlier, she had avoided them, went in the other direction if she saw them coming, but she had seen them too late this time.

'Mavis, I just asked you a question.'

'Sorry, Dad. Yes, Alec Pugh was just off with me. Like I said, sort of stuck up.'

'I ain't having some jumped-up office clerk looking down on my daughter. You can get back round there and tell the woman she can stick her bloody job.'

'Leave it out, Ron,' said Lily. 'She'll do no such thing. Anyway, I don't know what all the fuss is about. It's Edith Pugh she'll be working for, not her son.'

'She's just as bad, ain't she?'

'Maybe, but she can teach Mavis a lot and it's daft to blow the girl's chances.'

'Chances! Doing flaming cleaning!'

'What else is she fit for? If Edith Pugh can teach her to clean without breaking every thing she touches, it could lead to something.'

'Huh! Like what?'

'I dunno, but it's better than learning nothing.'

'Well, I think it's up to Mavis. Now, my girl, do you want to take the job or not?'

Once again Mavis hung her head. If her father kept his word and sent five pounds every week, maybe her dream of going to art college was within reach. She daren't raise the subject yet – not until her mother had seen the painting. In the meantime she was happy to earn a few bob working for Mrs Pugh. 'I don't mind, Dad. It's only for an hour after school.'

'Are you sure?'

'You heard the girl, Ron, and, as I said, it could lead to something. Now then, Mavis, get the rest of the stuff out of the pram so I can give it a good look over.'

Mavis went into the yard, still dreaming, still hoping her dad would keep his word. With the money he sent, *and* if she carried on cleaning for Mrs Pugh when she left school, perhaps every evening and weekend, surely then her mother would be able to afford to let her go to college.

CHAPTER FIVE

Lily woke up on Tuesday morning to find that Ron had taken most of the blankets. She shivered, snuggled up to his warm body, aware that this was the last time she'd be able to do this for a long, long time. He stirred, groaned with pleasure as her hand moved down to touch him, and soon Lily was wrapped in his arms, their lovemaking passionate. Lily relished Ron's touch, his mouth as it devoured hers, and was taken to new heights, her nails raking his back.

When it was over, Ron collapsed by her side, and Lily wondered as she always did why their lovemaking had only resulted in one child – one who was nothing but a disappointment. It didn't help that her neighbour and so-called friend next door, Kate Truman, had three kids, all normal, one so good at school that she was going on to college.

Kate was always bragging about how clever her Sandra was, and how her younger daughter, Ellie,

49

was also showing signs of passing her eleven plus. Even Kate's son was doing well as an apprentice plumber, though the boy was so ugly he reminded Lily of a bulldog. Oh, what was the matter with her? It was just sour grapes, Lily knew that, but she was sick of the pitying glances Kate threw at her whenever Mavis was around. And it wasn't just Kate – others in the street were the same, proud of their kids; whereas Lily knew nothing but shame.

Lily knew that she should love Mavis, had waited for that wonderful moment that other women spoke about when their babies were first put into their arms, but for her there had been nothing. She had looked at her baby and felt nothing! And all these years later, she still didn't. It added to her shame, made her sharp with Mavis but, unlike Kate, she had nothing to be proud about in her daughter. Was the fault hers? Was there something wrong with her? Did she lack maternal instincts? No, no, if Mavis had been normal, surely she would have grown to love her? Her thoughts making her restless, Lily threw the blankets to one side, but Ron turned to grab her, holding her fast.

'Don't get up yet, love.'

'I've got work to do, and if you want to be away by eight, you'd better sort your stuff out.'

'What's to sort? I packed my case last night. Come on, let's make the most of this last morning.'

Unable to resist, Lily turned into his arms again, their lovemaking slower this time. Like her, Ron knew that this would be the last time, his touch tender, caressing, until unable to hold back any longer they became frenzied: so in tune with each other's bodies that they both climaxed at the same time.

Lily lay for a moment, panting, but knew that like it or not she had to get up. With a swift kiss she pushed Ron off and then clambered out of bed, quickly wrapping her old, fleecy dressing gown around her.

'Lily, I don't think I want to go. How about I get another job locally?'

'Why the sudden change of heart?'

'It's you, love. I don't think I can stand to be away from you for months on end.'

Lily was tempted to agree, but common sense took over. If Ron worked locally he'd be down the dog track as soon as he got his first wage packet and, as usual, she'd be left with hardly a penny. At least if he was working away, and *if* he stuck to his promise, the future would be rosy. Yes, she'd miss him too – well, she thought, smiling wryly, she'd miss the sex – but it wasn't forever.

'Yeah, it's gonna be rotten,' she placated, 'but if you don't go in with Pete, there'll be no chance of your own business. Not only that, it's a bit late now to let him down.'

Ron scratched his head, and then ran a hand around the stubble on his chin. 'Yeah, I suppose you're right.'

'Of course I am. Now come on, get yourself up, and I'll see what I can rustle up for your breakfast.'

'A nice bit of bacon would be nice.'

'Bacon! Leave it out, Ron. I've got ration points for four ounces, but no money to buy any. There's an egg and I'll fry that with a couple of bits of toast.' And with that remark Lily left the bedroom to hurry downstairs.

Ron lay back on his pillow, flooded with shame. What was the matter with him? He'd asked for bacon, spoken without thought, and now Lily was going to fry him their last egg. What would that leave for her and Mavis? Sod all!

He'd been a shit of a husband, a shit of a father, but he really was going to change now. Lily deserved better. Mavis deserved better. Thinking about his daughter now, Ron frowned. He didn't know why Lily was so hard on the girl, and when he got the chance he tried to intervene, yet somehow that only made things worse. Mavis might not be bright, but she was beautiful, with a personality to match, and surely she could do better than domestic work?

Ron dressed before he picked up the bucket to

take downstairs to the outside lavatory. He emptied it first then sat down on the wooden seat, shivering with cold. Christ, to have an inside bog would be heaven, and once again he burned with shame. If he didn't blow his wages every week they could rent a better house, one with a bit of comfort for Lily and Mavis.

Still, he thought, assuaging his guilt. Things were going to change. He'd send Lily five quid a week without fail and she could start looking for somewhere decent to live.

Still shivering, Ron headed for the tiny outhouse where he dashed cold water over his face, then shaved. When he at last entered the warmth of the kitchen, he found Lily had a pot of tea made, and said as he sat at the table, 'Pete will be here in half an hour.'

Lily poured the tea, only saying, 'It's a bit weak. I had to use the same tea leaves again, and there's no milk.'

'It's fine and I hope you haven't cooked my breakfast.'

'I was just about to.'

'No, love, I'm not hungry,' he lied. 'We'll have a bit of breakfast on the way to Bracknell. I'm just sorry I can't give you any money before I go, but by the end of the week I'll be able to put something in the post.'

'Yeah, right,' Lily drawled.

Ron couldn't blame her for doubting him; after all, he'd let her down so many times before. Lily had been a diamond for putting up with him, but for some reason, and Ron didn't know what had brought about the change, he felt as though the scales had been lifted from his eyes. He'd been a bastard, a mug who had made the bookies rich while his wife and child had gone without. No more! From now on he wanted a decent future, for all of them, and by God he'd work like a dog to see that they got it. 'Lily, I don't deserve you, but I swear I'm going to make it up to you.'

'That'd be nice, but was that another pig I just saw flying past the window?' was her sarcastic reply.

'You'll see, but for now, can we talk about Mavis? I won't be here when she leaves school, but I think she could do something better than cleaning.'

'Like what? She can't read or write, so working in a shop is out. Forget a job in a factory too. She wouldn't be safe around machinery. What does that leave?'

'I dunno, but there must be something.'

'Ron, like me, you've got to face it. Mavis is slow and when she leaves school she won't be able to find a job. I know cleaning ain't much, but it's better than nothing.'

Ron drank his tea and then stood up, pulling Lily from her chair and into his arms. 'Yeah, I suppose you're right. Christ, love, I'm gonna miss you something rotten.'

Lily was stiff for a moment, but then as always she melted. 'I'm gonna miss you too. But, Ron, please, don't let me down. Not this time. I don't think I can take any more broken promises.'

'I won't. In fact, now that I'm going to send you money every week, you could look for another house. Somewhere with an inside lav and even a bathroom.'

'We'll see,' was Lily's cryptic reply. 'I'd best get Mavis up.'

Ron tightened his arms momentarily before releasing her, his expression grave as he watched Lily walk to the bottom of the stairs, her shout loud as she called to Mavis. He wouldn't let her down, but only time would convince Lily of that. In the meantime he was leaving her with nothing. He cursed the race track, the money he'd lost on Friday and vowed never to set foot near the dogs again.

'Mavis, come on, your dad's leaving soon,' Lily yelled.

Ron heard a thump, a door opening and then Mavis was running downstairs. She hesitated for a moment when she saw him, but then ran into his arms.

'Oh, Dad, please don't go.'

'I've got to, but don't worry, the time will fly

and I'll soon be back,' Ron said. Mavis felt thin and fragile as he hugged her and Ron realised that it had been a long time since he'd held his daughter. As a little girl she had clambered onto his lap, but those occasions became rare as she grew up. He'd shown her so little attention – too little affection – and though the words felt thick in his throat he forced them out, 'I love you, darling.'

Mavis pulled back, her lovely blue eyes wide as she looked up at him. 'I . . . I love you too, Daddy.'

Oh, God, Ron thought, he didn't deserve her love, or Lily's. All he had cared about for so many years was his next wage packet, the chance to get down to the dog track, followed by the pub, and by the time he showed his face at home, nine times out of ten Mavis had been in bed. He'd shown no interest in her school work, had accepted it when Lily said that their daughter was backward. In fact, in all honesty, he had dreamed of a son.

Ron looked at Lily over Mavis's head. They had tried so hard, but surely it wasn't too late? There was still time, and once he got himself sorted out, maybe they could find out why she hadn't fallen pregnant again. It would be different this time, he'd be a decent father, a good provider, and when he and Pete made a success of their business, he'd have something to pass on to his son. With money coming in, there'd be no need to worry about Mavis's future. He'd look after her, see she was provided for, Lily too, his wife able to take it easy at last.

Lily went to answer a knock on the front door, leading Pete into the room. 'Are you ready, mate?' he asked.

'Yeah, I'm ready,' Ron said, gently moving away from Mavis. He stepped across the room, facing Lily. 'Right, I'm off, and don't worry, I'll get some money to you soon.'

'Here, Ron,' Pete said, holding out a crisp white note. 'Sorry it's late, but I forgot about that fiver you lent me last week.'

For a moment Ron hesitated. He knew that Pete didn't owe him any money, but this wasn't the time to show stubborn pride. If he accepted it, he could leave Lily with something, and once they were earning he'd be able to pay it back. He grinned now. 'Yeah, well, I didn't like to remind you, but give it to Lily.'

She frowned, but her fingers closed around it as Pete stuffed the note into her hand. 'He lent you a fiver?'

'Yeah, that's right,' Pete said offhandedly before turning to Ron. 'Now then, come on, let's go or we'll miss our train.'

Ron swiftly crushed Lily in his arms. 'Bye, darling.'

'Bye,' she whispered, then kissed him fiercely.

He gave Mavis a hug, and then picked up his case, unable to look at his wife and daughter again as he walked out, leaving Mavis with tears streaming down her cheeks.

When Lily heard the door close behind her husband, she stared down at the five-pound note in her hand. She didn't believe for one minute that Ron had loaned it to Pete. How many times had he bailed Ron out? She'd lost count, but nevertheless she was thankful for his consideration. Oh, why couldn't Ron be more like Pete? A man who was so steady and reliable that it was a wonder he hadn't been snapped up years ago. It was his looks, of course, women unable to get past his pugnacious face and baldness; yet if they got to know him, they'd realise that he had a heart of gold. Pete was thirty-eight now, but still a bachelor, and what a shame because he'd make someone a perfect husband. Unlike Ron, she thought, ruefully. Yet from the first time she'd seen him, he'd been the only man for her. Of course, she hadn't known that he'd turn out to be an addicted gambler, and was mad to stay with him, but when all was said and done, she still loved him.

Lily's thoughts were interrupted by a loud sob. Mavis was still crying, and though in truth she felt like crying too, Lily had long since learned to hide her feelings; had refused to let people see how their pity affected her. Not only that, when it came to selling, if people thought she was soft, they'd take advantage of her.

'Oh, for goodness sake, Mavis, stop blubbing. All right, your dad's working away, but it ain't the end of the world. He'll be back before you know it. Now shut your noise and get ready for school.'

Mavis fled upstairs and, thankful for the peace, Lily sank onto a kitchen chair. It was great to have a fiver but, with no guarantee that Ron would keep his word, she'd have to make it last. Still, with some decent stuff to sell, especially the biscuit barrel, it wouldn't hurt to have a little treat. She'd start by cooking the egg and a couple of pieces of toast. Mavis could have that, but once the girl was at school, she'd buy a couple more eggs along with a bit of bacon. Bacon, Lily thought, smiling blissfully.

It was ten minutes before Mavis showed her face again, wan looking, but dressed. At least she wasn't crying now, so Lily placed the breakfast in front of her, saying, 'Go on, eat it up.'

'Me! But what about you?'

'I'll have something later.'

Despite being upset about her father leaving, Mavis tucked in, bolting the food down as though frightened her mother would change her mind.

'Come on, Mavis, wash your face and then get a move on. Don't forget to go to Mrs Pugh's after school.'

'Can I go to Gran's first? I was supposed to get her some jellied eels yesterday, but I forgot.'

'Leave it out, you idiot. What sort of impression will it make if you're late on your first day? I'm popping round to your gran's later so I'll get them. Keep the money your gran gave you and you can have a school dinner. Now as I said, get a move on.'

Mavis at last moved, but when she reappeared with her coat on, Lily saw the tell-tale bulge underneath it and her eyes narrowed. 'Hold it, my girl. What are you hiding?'

'N . . . nothing.'

'Don't give me that. Hand it over.'

'Mum . . . please, let me take it back. Dad left you some money, and he's going to send more.'

'Take what back?' Lily asked, but then the penny dropped and she looked at the sideboard to see that the biscuit barrel was missing. 'You . . . you . . .' she ground out through clenched teeth and, marching up to Mavis, she pulled back her coat to snatch the barrel. 'I've a good mind to give you a bloody good hiding.'

Mavis cringed as Lily raised her hand, but begged, 'Please, Mum, that old lady was really poor.'

'Poor! Don't make me laugh. She probably owns the big house you said she lived in. She could sell it – buy something smaller and be stinking rich – whereas all I've got to flog is this biscuit barrel.'

'You . . . you've got five pounds.'

'Yes, but it's got to last us until God knows when, or are you daft enough to believe that your precious father is going to send me more?'

'He . . . he might.'

'Yes, you said it, he might. Now get out of my sight, you silly soft sod, and think yourself lucky you ain't felt my hand across your face.'

Mavis fled and, after placing the barrel back onto the sideboard, Lily slumped onto a chair again. Mavis trying to sneak the bloody thing out was the last thing she needed. It was bad enough that Ron had left and she dreaded the time they'd be apart, her head thumping as she ran both hands across her face. Mavis had been upset when Ron left too, but despite this the old woman had obviously played on her daughter's mind. Mavis didn't have an ounce of sense – that was the trouble.

Lily gulped down her cup of insipid tea. She would go round to see her mother, but wondered what she'd say when she heard that Ron would be working away. There'd be no point in telling her that he was going to turn over a new leaf, especially as her mother had heard it so many times before. She had no time for Ron, and Lily couldn't blame her. Yet maybe, just maybe, he did really mean it this time.

CHAPTER SIX

Mavis was fighting tears. She'd upset her mother again, said the wrong things as usual, but she'd decided to take the biscuit barrel back as soon as she saw her father leaving the five-pound note. She hadn't thought about the old lady owning that great big house, and had only seen the poverty she lived in. Her mum was right; the woman could sell her house, whereas they had no guarantee that her dad would send more money. Mavis blinked rapidly, wishing she hadn't upset her mum, especially as she'd given her an egg on toast for breakfast. At any other time she'd have relished it but, worried about getting the biscuit barrel out of the house, she had hardly tasted it.

Nervous of bumping into Tommy and Larry again, her eyes darted along the road, but at least they went to Battersea County School, which was in the opposite direction from hers. If she could just get out of Cullen Street without them spotting her, she'd be safe. Thankfully there was no sign of them, but Sandra Truman from next door was just leaving, and, though she too went to a different school, Battersea Grammar, after exchanging greetings, they fell into step.

'You're quiet. What's up, Mavis?'

'My dad's working away and it'll be ages before he comes back.'

'Working away? Why?'

'He'll be earning more money. When he comes back, he's gonna start up his own business.'

Sandra looked sceptical, which didn't surprise Mavis. Everyone knew her dad was a gambler and, living next door, the Trumans must have heard the rows. She and Sandra had been friends when they were younger, but after taking their eleven plus exams things had changed. Sandra was clever, had passed, and had gone on to grammar school. She'd made new friends, all as clever as her, and though they'd tried to include her, Mavis felt inadequate alongside them and had drifted away. It was the same at her secondary school. Unable to keep up, she hadn't formed any real friendships, knowing that few girls would want to hang around with an idiot like her.

'I know you'll miss your dad,' Sandra said kindly, 'but it sounds like it'll be worth it.'

Tommy Wilson came bounding around the corner, clutching a loaf of bread. Mavis froze.

She'd avoided him for ages and now in the space of two days had come face to face with him twice. He shot them both a glance, but said nothing as he ran past, leaving Mavis unaware that she had stopped walking until Sandra touched her arm.

'Mavis, you're shaking. What's wrong?'

'Noth . . . nothing,' she managed to answer, her feet moving again.

'Come on, Mavis. It was Tommy Wilson, wasn't it? Has he been giving you a hard time?'

Unable to tell Sandra the truth, Mavis just shook her head.

'Listen, I know he calls you Dumbo, but just ignore him. There's worse than name calling. Him and Larry are a right nasty pair and they tried it on with me.'

Once again Mavis halted. 'Tried it on. Do you mean they tried to touch you?'

'Yes, they cornered me on my way home from school.'

'Did you tell your mum or your dad?'

'Not my dad, he'd have killed the buggers, and, anyway, a swift kick in the right place was enough to chase them off. My mum said all boys try to get fresh, that they're ruled by what's in their trousers. She's always going on at my brother to behave himself.' Sandra paused and, as though realising something, she said, 'Here, hold on. Have they done the same to you? Is that why you're so frightened?'

Mavis felt as though a dam had burst as she blurted it all out, but then saw that Sandra's mouth was curled in disgust. Sandra must blame her — must think that she'd led them on. With a small cry of anguish she ran off.

'No! Wait,' Sandra called.

Mavis ignored the shout, running and running until she was through the school gates. Bending over, she fought to get her breath, and then seeing a group of girls staring at her she slunk off behind the toilet block until the bell rang.

Head down, Mavis walked to her class, worried sick that Sandra would pass on what she'd told her. Her mother would kill her if it reached her ears. And what about her dad? At least he was working away, but what about when he came back?

The lesson began, but as usual Mavis couldn't make head nor tail of the writing chalked on the board. It was all right when the English teacher read to them, sometimes from a novel, which she enjoyed, but unlike the other girls she couldn't write an essay on the subject. Sometimes there was so much in her mind, stories she would make up, yet no matter how many times she tried, it was impossible to put the words onto paper. Oh, it must be wonderful to read a book, something the other girls in her class could do so easily. She envied them so much. They were lucky. Unlike her, they weren't idiots.

*　*　*

Lily had been to the shops and now sat back, replete, having had fresh tea and an egg along with a couple of slices of bacon. She also had a little treat in store for dinner, and simmering on the stove was a vegetable stew, thick with pearl barley. Most women could afford to buy meat and were constantly moaning that it was still on ration. Lily, though, was nervous of spending too much money so had settled on only vegetables. At least the stew would be nourishing, and as her mother had lost so much weight she'd take a bowl round to her later.

In no mood to talk, Lily sighed when someone rapped on her letterbox. It was Kate Truman, the woman saying, 'Lily, my Sandra left for school, but then came back to tell me something. I think you need to hear it.'

'You'd better come in. Do you fancy a cup of tea?'

'Yes, if you can spare one.'

Unwilling to throw away tea leaves that had only been used once, Lily just lit the gas and, when the water boiled, topped up the pot. Kate was obviously itching to tell her something, so once they had a cup each in front of them, she said, 'Right, Kate. Spit it out.'

'You won't like it, Lily, but it's like this. My Sandra bumped into Mavis on her way to school. Mavis was upset and told Sandra something, but then she ran off.'

'She's upset because Ron's left this morning to work out of London. It was all a bit quick so I haven't had the chance to tell you about it.'

'No, it wasn't that. She's upset about Tommy Wilson and Larry Barnet.'

'Why? What's happened to them?'

'Nothing, but they tried it on with your Mavis.'

'Tried it on! You . . . you don't mean . . .'

'Yes,' Kate interrupted. 'They got her on the common.'

'Oh, my God,' Lily cried, jumping to her feet. 'She didn't tell me. Did they . . . did they . . .'

'No, no, calm down,' Kate urged as she interrupted again. 'They didn't get far, but if someone hadn't come along, they might have.'

'My Ron will wring their bloody necks—' Lily shouted, but then slumped onto her chair again, rubbing both hands over her face. 'Fat chance. He ain't here and won't be for months. Mind you, those two buggers ain't getting away with this. I'll sort them out, *and* have a word with their mothers.'

'Yes, do that, but Mavis is a very pretty girl and now that she's growing up there's bound to be others sniffing around. I've already spoken to my Sandra, but what about Mavis? Does she know about the birds and the bees?'

'No, I don't think so.'

'Lily, she may not be so lucky next time. You need

to talk to her; warn her about blokes and how to handle them if they try it on.'

'Gawd, Kate. I doubt she'd understand.'

'I know she can't read and write, but when my Sandra was at school with her, she insisted that Mavis isn't daft. In fact, in art class she was brilliant.'

'Art? What good is art? The only rich painters are dead ones.'

'I dunno, Lily, but if she can paint and draw, surely that shows intelligence?'

'It's just copying, that's all. Anyone can do that.'

'Well, I can't. I'm useless at drawing, always was and always will be.'

'Yes, but it hasn't held you back, has it? You can do other things, whereas Mavis can't.'

Kate pursed her lips. 'You have a point. But I still don't think Mavis is as bad as you think – I've been telling you that for years.'

'You were just being kind.'

'No, Lily. Unlike backward kids, Mavis doesn't sound daft when she talks. In fact, she sounds very sensible.'

'Sensible! Leave it out. She can't even wash up without breaking something.'

'All right, Lily, have it your own way, but you still need to try talking to her. If you don't, she could end up in trouble.'

'Oh, Kate, don't say that.'

'I'm sorry, I didn't mean to upset you. I know it's none of my business, but I just felt you needed to know.'

'Kate, there's no need to apologise. We've been friends for years and there ain't much about me and mine that you don't know.'

'How do you feel about Ron working away?'

'To be honest, I'll miss him. Though God knows why. Oh, sod it, me stew's boiling over.'

They rose to their feet at the same time, Kate saying, 'I'll leave you to it.'

'Yeah, all right,' Lily agreed as she hurried over to the stove. Kate called a quick goodbye as she showed herself out, and after turning the gas down under the pot, Lily once again slumped at the table. Recalling the conversation, her face darkened with anger. Why hadn't Mavis told her about those two little sods? Instead she'd told Sandra, who had passed it on to her mother. She liked Kate, but knew she was a bit of a gossip. Now the whole bloody street would know. Wait till Mavis came home. She'd have a few words to say to the girl. Not only that, she had to talk to her daughter about blokes, and the dangers. Yet what if she couldn't get it through her thick head?

The thought of her daughter getting pregnant, of the shame it would bring, made Lily feel sick. It was bad enough that everyone in Cullen Street knew Mavis was backward, but if she became an unmarried mother Lily knew the gossip would be unbearable.

Why me? Why couldn't I have a normal child? It wasn't fair – it really wasn't.

At last the English lesson was over, and though Mavis had missed her favourite art class yesterday where they used oils, the next class focused on charcoal drawings and sketching. Though she preferred painting, Mavis enjoyed this class too. Her mother refused to buy not only paints, but pencils and paper too, telling her that it was a waste of time and that she had more important things to buy, food being top of the list. There had been a time when she used to grab any scrap of paper she could find to draw on, but that had annoyed her mother too. It seemed to incense her that she could draw but not write, and she would snatch the paper to tear it up. Learn to write, not draw, Lily used to scream, but always finding it impossible, and afraid of her mother's anger, Mavis had stopped drawing at home.

Today, Mavis was unable to concentrate and her mind churned as she sketched. Why had she done it? Why had she blabbed to Sandra? Terror of her mother finding out made her hand shake and she was unaware of Miss Harwood coming up behind her. It was only when the teacher spoke that Mavis realised all she had drawn was little more than a frenzied doodle.

'Mavis, what's the matter with you today?' she asked. 'It's unlike you to do such sloppy work.'

'Sorry, miss.'

'You have talent, Mavis, and you're usually wonderful with perspective, but this isn't good enough. Start again.'

'Yes, miss.'

Miss Harwood had moved away out of earshot when the girl beside her hissed, 'She's right, Mavis. You're usually good at art.'

Mavis smiled at Maureen, who, unlike some of the other girls, was kind to her. 'I was miles away and wasn't concentrating.'

'Mavis was in cloud cuckoo land as usual,' Patricia Fenwick hissed.

'Leave her alone, Pat. You're just jealous because your artwork is rubbish.'

'Jealous of her! You must be joking.'

'Quiet,' Miss Harwood shouted.

Pat shot Mavis a look of disdain, but obeyed the teacher, her eyes going back to her work. Silence descended again, only broken by the sound of Miss Harwood walking along the rows between desks, commenting now and then on one of the girls' work.

Mavis started a new sketch, but it was little better than the first one, and for the first time she was relieved when the class came to an end. She knew that Miss Harwood was disappointed in her work from her curt dismissal and, head down, Mavis left the room.

After the lunch break it would be arithmetic, another subject that was almost incomprehensible to Mavis. She had tried and tried to write the numbers down, but was told that most were backwards and in the wrong order. Mental arithmetic wasn't too bad, but since junior school the lessons had become different, harder, with algebra, among other things, becoming impossible to learn.

'You weren't teacher's pet today, Mavis,' Pat called as she walked arm in arm with her best friend to the canteen.

Other girls were doing the same, but Maureen who lived close to school and went home for lunch, paused to say, 'Take no notice of her, Mavis.'

'It's all right. I'm used to it,' Mavis said bravely.

'Well, I think they're mean. See you later,' she waved as she hurried to the gate.

Alone as usual, Mavis joined the queue in the canteen, thinking the other girls were mad to moan about the food. She didn't always have the money for school dinners and was sometimes left hungry, so as she held out her plate Mavis looked at the ladleful of stew with relish. Next to it was placed a dollop of lumpy mash and, finding a seat as far away from Pat as possible, she sat down.

The first few mouthfuls of food tasted fine, but as her thoughts returned to Sandra, Mavis lost her appetite. She had to get to Sandra, beg her to keep her mouth shut – but what if she was too late?

CHAPTER SEVEN

'Mum, come on, you've got to eat,' Lily ordered.

'I ain't hungry now. I'll heat it up later.'

'What about the jellied eels? Do you fancy them?'

'Nah, not really. Anyway, girl, how's things?'

'Mum, don't try to change the subject. I'm worried about you.'

'Gawd, give it a rest. I'm fine. Is Mavis at school today or have you sent her out with the pram again?'

'She's in school.'

'Not for much longer. I can't believe she's nearly fifteen – I'll have to think about something for her birthday. What are you getting her?'

'I dunno. It depends on whether Ron sends me any money.'

'Sends it. What do you mean?'

'He's gone to work out of London and reckons he'll be away for at least six months.'

'Good riddance to bad rubbish. I should think you're glad to see the back of him.'

'I suppose it'll be easier with one less mouth to feed. Ron reckons that while he's away, he and Pete are going to save up enough to start up on their own.'

'If you believe that, you'll believe anything.'

'I don't, but you never know, he might mean it this time. In the meantime things are looking up. Mavis found me a biscuit barrel that should be worth a bit, and not only that, she's got a little cleaning job. An hour after school and two at weekends.'

'Blimey, fancy that. See, if she's got herself a job she ain't as daft as you think.'

Lily ignored the comment. Mavis hadn't found the job herself but Lily couldn't be bothered with explanations. She still had to sort the two boys out, and talk to their mothers. Oh, if only Ron was here to deal with it, and once again Lily knew that despite everything she was going to miss him. She also had to talk to Mavis about the birds and bees, but had no idea how to broach the subject. Sex was something her own mother had never spoken about and she'd grown up in ignorance. All right, it was a bit of a shock the first time, but it hadn't done her any harm. Maybe a stern warning to keep away from blokes would be enough to put the frighteners up Mavis, without a long-winded explanation.

'Mum, I'd best go. Promise me you'll eat that stew later.'

'Yeah, I promise.'

'I still think you should see the doctor.'

'Look, I've told you, I'm fine.'

'Why do you have to be so stubborn?'

'Me! It ain't me who's stubborn, it's you. You're just like your father.'

Lily had no memories of her father, a man who had been killed close to the end of the First World War in the year she'd been born. Lily knew it had been hard for her mother, could remember being looked after by her grandparents when she'd been forced to take on full-time work. 'How come you always compare me to him?'

''Cos you really are like him, and not only in looks.'

'Yeah, well, I'll have to take your word for that.'

'It must have been rotten for you, growing up without a dad.'

'No, not really. I had Nan and Granddad, and I still miss them.'

'Yeah, me too. I hate war, Lily. First I lost your dad, and then during the last conflict a bomb flattened me parents' house, with them inside.'

'I know, Mum,' Lily said sadly.

'I've upset us both now, and wish I hadn't brought it up.'

'Never mind, Mum, but I really have got to go.

I'll pop round again in the morning, and,' she warned, 'I want to see that you ate that stew.'

'Don't worry, I will. See you tomorrow, pet.'

Leaving her mother sitting by the fire, Lily left the house. She really was too thin, and Lily knew she had to get her mother to the doctor's somehow. For now though, she had to sort those boys out, and knowing they'd be likely to be home from school now, she hurried back to Cullen Street.

Lily went to see Tommy Wilson's mother first, pounding on the door, her head high with righteous indignation. When it was opened, she spat, 'I want a word with you about your son.'

'Oh, Gawd, what's he been up to now?' Olive Wilson asked.

'Him and his friend Larry got hold of my daughter on the common. The dirty little buggers showed her their willies, and pulled up her skirt.'

'They what!' she screeched. 'Bloody hell, you'd better come in.'

Lily stepped inside, but when they walked into the kitchen she was puzzled by Tommy's reaction. Instead of fear, Tommy just smiled when he saw her. He was a nice-looking lad with dark hair and green eyes, but at only fourteen, coming up fifteen, his build was tall and lanky. Lily fixed her eyes on his face, waiting to see his guilt when his mother spoke to him angrily.

'Mrs Jackson says you got hold of her daughter. Is that right?'

'Got hold of her. What do you mean?'

'Did you and Larry show Mavis your thingies?'

A light seemed to dawn in Tommy's eyes. 'Oh, yeah, but that was about a month ago and we only did it 'cos she asked us to.'

'She asked you to?'

'Yeah, Mum. She's a bit funny, a weirdo, and every chance she gets the daft cow latches on to us. She's always trying to get us to show her our willies and, just to shut her up, we did.'

'You're lying,' Lily snapped. 'It wasn't like that and you know it.'

'Ask Larry if you don't believe me,' Tommy said.

'Oh, I will, you can be sure of that.'

'Tommy, swear to me that you're telling the truth,' Olive ordered.

'Mum, I swear,' Tommy said earnestly. 'On my life, we didn't touch her.'

Olive turned to fix her eyes on Lily. 'I know my son and he's telling the truth. If you ask me, it's your daughter who needs sorting out. It sounds like she's acting like a little tart.'

Shocked and floundering, Lily said, 'I'll see what Larry has to say.' She spun around and without another word marched out of the house.

*   *   *

When Mavis left school she ran almost all the way to the route Sandra would take on her way home. She had to find her, to talk to her, her face pinched with anxiety as she scanned the street.

At last Mavis saw Sandra walking along, thankfully alone, and, quickening her pace, she caught up with her. 'Sandra, please, you know what I told you this morning? Please, please, don't tell anyone.'

'Mavis, it's all right. I only told my mum.'

'Oh, no! No! She'll pass it on to my mum. Oh, God, she'll kill me!' Hand over her mouth, Mavis fled.

'Wait, you didn't do anything wro . . .'

Blood pounding in her ears, Mavis didn't hear Sandra. She ran blindly at first, but then unable to carry on she at last stopped, her chest heaving as she drew in great gulps of air. How could she go home now? How could she face her mother?

Feet dragging, Mavis made her way to Mrs Pugh's house, and when the woman opened the door, she felt she had found sanctuary.

'Hello, Mavis, come on in,' the woman said. 'You look upset. Are you all right?'

It was a quarter to five, but Mrs Pugh hadn't said anything about her tardiness and, fighting for composure, Mavis said, 'Ye . . . yes, I'm fine.'

'I expect you're a little nervous, but there's no need. I'm not an ogre, though I am rather fussy when it comes to cleaning. We'll concentrate on the sitting room today,' Mrs Pugh said, indicating with a crook of her finger that Mavis should follow her.

Despite feeling sick with fear at the thought of going home, Mavis found her eyes widening. The room was immaculate. There was a cream and brown brocade three piece suite, the sofa facing the fireplace and a chair each side. The curtains were also cream, sumptuous, and under the window there was a mahogany sideboard with a crystal rose bowl on top. In one corner she saw a glass-fronted cabinet, full of porcelain figurines, and now another fear made her heart pound. *Oh, please*, she inwardly begged, *don't let me break anything.*

'Now, Mavis, as your mother told me you can be a bit clumsy, I've already dusted the ornaments. I'd like you to vacuum the carpet, and then under the cushions on my three piece suite. Is that all right, my dear?'

Mrs Pugh was smiling, her voice kind. Mavis found herself relaxing a little. 'Ye . . . yes.'

'Right then, take off your coat and hang it in the hall. I don't want any marks on my furniture, so before you start please wash your hands. You'll then find my vacuum cleaner in the cupboard under the stairs.'

'Wh . . . where do I go to wash my hands?'

'Come with me,' Edith Pugh said, leading Mavis

back into the hall. She then opened a door that revealed a small cloakroom with a lavatory and sink.

Mavis walked inside, and though still flustered, she couldn't help marvelling at the luxury of an inside lav. She ran water into the sink and washed her hands, but seeing a beautiful white, fluffy towel hanging on a small rail, she looked at it worriedly. What if she marked it? Deciding not to risk it, she wiped her hands on her skirt and then stepped outside to see Edith Pugh waiting.

'May I see your hands, Mavis?'

Surprised, Mavis held them out.

'Yes, that's better, but you haven't scrubbed under your nails. I'm sorry, my dear, I know I'm fussy but, as I said, I don't want my furniture marked. Do them again and use the nail brush this time.'

Mavis did as she was told, but even with the small nail brush it took her a long time to remove all the grime. Oh, if only she could stay here. If only she didn't have to go home and face her mother. At last, her fingers feeling sore, she faced Mrs Pugh again, thankful that this time her hands passed inspection.

'Right, Mavis, I'll leave you to it,' the woman said and after showing her the understairs cupboard, she at last went down the hall and into the kitchen.

Mavis started work, and though her mind was raging, she made sure to cover every inch of carpet around the furniture. Gran! She could go there. No, no, Gran would be just as disgusted when she found out and wouldn't want to take her in. Yet surely going to Gran's was better than going home.

'Mavis, have you vacuumed under the suite?'

Startled, Mavis spun round. 'Er . . . no.'

'Well, I'm sorry, but that isn't good enough. I told you yesterday that we'd give one room a day a thorough clean, so please don't cut corners. Now do under the suite.'

'Yes, Mrs Pugh,' Mavis said meekly.

This time the woman didn't leave, but stood watching as Mavis heaved one of the chairs to one side. It was worse when it came to the sofa, but somehow she managed to move it, thankful to see a look of approval on Mrs Pugh's face when she'd finished.

'Well done, Mavis, and now that just leaves under the cushions. When you've done that, come through to the kitchen.'

Mavis had felt uncomfortable with Mrs Pugh watching her and was glad when she left. She still wasn't sure what to make of the woman. One minute she seemed kind, the next strict and stern – but even being here with Mrs Pugh was preferable to facing her mother.

*   *   *

Edith's body was aching and she hobbled with pain to sit by the kitchen fire. Mavis had seemed nervous and upset when she arrived, but other than that, so far so good, she decided.

Mavis had meekly followed her orders and it boded well, but there was a long way to go yet. To forward her plans Edith knew she had to strike the right note. There had to be a measure of firmness, together with kindness, and somehow she had to ensure that Mavis was more presentable.

Edith laid her head back, finding that the distant hum of the vacuum cleaner was soothing. She closed her eyes, drifting, unaware that she had fallen asleep until the sound of Mavis's voice started her awake.

'Are you all right, Mrs Pugh?'

Edith looked up to find Mavis bending over her, the girl's startlingly blue eyes wide with concern.

'Yes, yes, I was just having a little nap. Have you finished in the sitting room?'

'Yes, and I've put the cleaner away.'

'Good girl,' Edith said as she glanced at the clock. 'You still have fifteen minutes to go, so do you think you could manage to make a cup of tea and then peel some potatoes?'

'Er . . . yes.'

'I won't get up, but you'll find everything you need easily enough.'

As Mavis moved away, Edith watched her every

move and at first she looked competent enough. However, when it came to handling the teapot, Edith could see that the girl's hands were trembling. She'd prepared for this, making sure that her old Brown Betty was in use, along with a couple of odd cups and saucers. Yes, Mavis was nervous, but Edith was sure that she wasn't as bad as Lily Jackson had indicated. In fact, she was sure that a lot of the girl's problems were due to lack of confidence, probably a result of the constant criticism she received, and not just from her mother.

Edith had seen a lot when she'd been school secretary – had taken an interest and observed many children she was sure just needed extra help. Of course, class sizes, along with lack of time, made it impossible for the teachers to concentrate on just a few children and though some were more prepared than others to put in the extra mile, Edith was sure that what these children needed was specialised schools.

Eyes closing with sadness, Edith wished she had been able to fulfil her dream of becoming a teacher. The war and then having Alec had put paid to that. Now, of course, with multiple sclerosis, it would remain just a dream, yet perhaps, just perhaps, she could put her theories to the test with Mavis.

When the tea was made, Mavis carefully covered

the pot with the cosy, and then looked at the tray that Edith had already set with two cups and saucers, a sugar bowl and small jug of milk. 'Pour one for both of us,' Edith said, 'but no sugar for me.'

Mavis looked worried, but Edith made sure she looked unconcerned. Hesitantly the girl poured two cups of tea, her hands shaking so much that tea slopped into the saucers.

'Thank you, my dear.'

'I . . . I'm sorry I spilt some.'

'Oh, it's only a little,' Edith said, hiding her fastidiousness as she poured the tea from the saucer, back into her cup. 'Do drink yours and then get on with the potatoes. Four medium-sized ones cut in half should be enough. It's too early to put them on yet, so just leave them in a saucepan of cold water.'

'Yes, Mrs Pugh.'

When Mavis was finished, Edith again looked at the clock. She had worked for just over an hour, but the first ten minutes had been wasted just getting the girl to wash her hands properly. However, she now needed her out of the house and struggled to her feet. 'Thank you, Mavis. You've done really well and I'll see you tomorrow.'

'I . . . I'm not in any hurry, Mrs Pugh. In fact, I'd be happy to stay longer.'

'No, my dear, you get off home. I told your mother an hour and she must be expecting you.'

The colour seemed to drain from Mavis's face. 'She . . . she won't mind.'

Edith was puzzled. Mavis seemed reluctant to go home, in fact, almost afraid. 'Is there something wrong, Mavis? Are you in some sort of trouble with your mother?'

'No, but . . . but what about the cups? I could wash them up.'

Edith didn't want the girl here when Alec came home and he was due in about fifteen minutes. Until she had sorted Mavis out, she wanted to keep them apart as much as possible, and it would be difficult enough at weekends. 'Thank you, Mavis, but I'll see to the cups. Off you go now.'

With reluctance, Mavis walked with Edith to the door. 'Goodbye, Mrs Pugh.'

'Goodbye, Mavis,' Edith said, pleased when she closed the door behind the girl that her instincts had been right. Mavis wasn't happy at home. And judging from the way she had worked, with more coaching, she was indeed the perfect choice.

CHAPTER EIGHT

Larry Barnet and his mother had been out and Lily had been forced to go back an hour later. This time they were home and without preamble she confronted Larry, told him what Kate Truman had said; but, like Tommy, he looked horrified, his large, brown eyes wide with innocence.

'It wasn't us! It was her,' he protested, going on to tell a story that matched Tommy's.

'Now look,' Jill Barnet said. 'I know they shouldn't have done it, but your daughter asked them to get their willies out. Boys will be boys and at this age they're curious. With Mavis asking for it, you should thank your lucky stars that it didn't go any further.'

'But it did. They threw her on the ground, lifted her skirt, and if someone hadn't come along I dread to think what would have happened. Mavis was able to run off, but she was frightened out of her wits and, if you ask me, she had a lucky escape.'

'We didn't do that, Mum, we didn't,' Larry cried. 'It was her. She pulled up her skirt, wanted us to see that she was different to us.'

'That isn't true! You're telling lies.'

Jill Barnet bristled. 'Hold your horses, lady. You said earlier you heard about this from Kate Truman. If your daughter is so innocent, *and* was scared out of her wits when she ran off, how come she didn't tell you about it herself?'

Lily floundered. Yes, why hadn't Mavis told her? It had happened a month ago, but she had no memories of her running home frightened.

Jill spoke again, and Lily saw the pity in her eyes. 'I think you need to talk to Mavis. If she keeps up this sort of behaviour, she could end up in trouble.'

With a gasp, Lily turned on her heel. She marched out, hurried home and slammed the door behind her. In the kitchen she began to pace, going over and over what she had heard.

Dark clouds gathered in Lily's mind, a storm building, and when she came to a conclusion, it broke with ferocity. When she got her hands on Mavis, she'd kill her! It was bad enough that her daughter was backward, but to find out that she was a little slut was like a slap in the face.

Lily craved respectability. She wanted to be like the other women in the street, ones whose husbands provided for them, and had prayed that Ron meant all his promises this time. Yes, he was a known gambler, but if he really did change and start up his own business, she would at last be able to hold her head high. Lily fumed with anger. It was never going to happen, and now this! Mavis was acting like a tramp and the gossips would have a field day. She'd never live it down. Never! Lily's eyes flew to the clock. Where was Mavis? It was after six, and though she was doing an hour's cleaning for Edith Pugh, the girl should have been home by now.

By seven, Lily was almost at the end of her tether, her mind still dark with fury. She flung her coat on and stormed out of the house, determined to find Mavis.

It was a good walk to Edith Pugh's house, yet it didn't calm Lily. She banged loudly on the woman's door, tapping her foot with impatience until it was opened, and saying bluntly, 'Is my daughter still here?'

The young man frowned as he peered out at her. 'Your daughter?'

'Yes, Mavis – Mavis Jackson.'

'Oh, Mavis. No, she isn't here.'

'Do you know where she is?'

'No, I'm afraid she left before I arrived home.'

'What about your mother? Does she know?'

'Look, I don't know what all this is about, but you'd better come in.'

Lily followed Alec Pugh to the large, spacious

kitchen at the back of the house to see his mother sitting in a fireside chair. 'Mavis hasn't come home yet. What time did she leave here?' she asked abruptly.

'Oh, she left a long time ago, at around ten to six.'

'Did she say where she was going?'

'No, but I presumed home. What is it, Mrs Jackson? Is Mavis in some sort of trouble?'

Lily wasn't about to wash her dirty laundry in front of this stuck-up, uppity woman, or her son who was looking at her as if she was something that the cat had dragged in. She floundered for a lie. 'No, of course she isn't in trouble. It's just that it's not like Mavis to stay out this late. I know she's worried about my mother so I'll try there.'

'I must say she seemed upset about something when she arrived. Is your mother unwell?'

'She ain't been herself lately. Anyway, sorry to trouble you,' Lily said.

'It's no problem, Mrs Jackson. Oh, and I must tell you that I'm pleased with Mavis. She worked really well today.'

Lily had to fight to hold back a scowl. Edith Pugh might be pleased with Mavis, but she certainly wasn't. As she was shown out, another thought struck Lily, her anger returning in force. If Edith Pugh found out what Mavis had been up to, she'd get rid of the girl like a shot. Mavis would lose the job, any earnings, and worse, she doubted anyone locally would ever employ her. Wait till I get my hands on her, Lily thought, so incensed that she hardly noticed Alec Pugh's curt goodbye before he closed the door firmly behind her.

'Mavis, you'll have to go home. Your mum will be worried sick.'

'I can't, Gran. I just can't.'

'Don't be silly. It can't be that bad. Come on, tell me why you're too frightened to face your mother.'

'No, no, I can't.'

Doris sighed. Since Mavis had turned up she'd tried and tried to get to the bottom of things, but had failed. The poor girl looked so desolate, so unhappy that she'd even refused to eat the stew that Lily had brought round earlier. There must be something seriously wrong for Mavis to turn down food, but Doris was at a loss to know what to do. If she forced Mavis to leave, there was no guarantee that she'd go home, and, now that it was dark outside, the last thing she wanted was for Mavis to be walking the streets. 'Mavis, please, talk to me. If you're in some kind of trouble maybe I can help.'

'You'll be disgusted. You'll hate me too.'

Doris felt a jolt of horror, her heart beginning to race. Oh, no! No! Surely the girl wasn't in *that* kind of trouble? She fought to hide her feelings, to ask as gently as she could, 'Mavis, love, have you, well, been with a boy? Is that it?'

Mavis jumped to her feet, eyes wild, but just as she was about to dash from the room there was the sound of the front door opening. The only other person who had a key was Lily, and Mavis knew that. The girl froze, rooted to the spot as her mother walked in.

'So, there you are, you little slut!' Lily spat. She stormed up to Mavis, swung her arm and slapped the girl hard around the face.

It didn't stop there. Her face livid with anger, Lily slapped Mavis again and again while Doris struggled to her feet. Oh, the pain was awful, but she had to stop this. 'Lily, Lily, calm down,' she begged, trying to grab her daughter's arm.

'Calm down!' Lily screamed. 'Do you know what she's been up to?'

'I can guess, but this isn't going to change anything. We need to sort something out.'

Lily's head shot round. 'Sort something out! Oh, I'll sort something out all right. I'll have her put away, that's what I'll do!'

'Put away? What are you talking about? If she's pregnant I'm sure it isn't her fault. Someone must have taken advantage of her, and it's him who needs putting away.'

Lily seemed to deflate before Doris's eyes as

she staggered to a chair, her voice a wail now. 'Pregnant? Oh, no . . . no . . . I can't stand it.'

Lost, unable to understand what was going on, Doris knew she had to sit down before she fell down. At least Lily had stopped laying into Mavis, but the poor girl looked dreadful: her cheeks scarlet from the continual slaps and tears streaming down her cheeks. Doris wanted to hug her, to comfort her, but that might make Lily flare up again. Instead she could only smile encouragingly at Mavis before sitting down and saying, 'Lily, I thought that was why you're doing your nut. Please, love, perhaps I've got the wrong end of the stick. I only said that Mavis *might* be pregnant, and I only mentioned that 'cos I can't make sense of what's going on.'

'Gawd, Mum, you scared the life out of me. No, Mavis isn't pregnant, but after what I've been hearing, it's just a matter of time. The girl's nothing but a tart!'

'Oh, Lily, don't say that.'

'Why not? It's true,' Lily spat, going on to recount what had happened.

Doris struggled to hide her pain, but she was due for a dose of painkillers and it wasn't easy. Thankfully the story didn't take long and, as her daughter stopped speaking, Doris quickly said, 'I don't believe it. Not for a minute. Mavis is a good girl, an innocent girl – it's those boys who are telling lies. Have you asked Mavis what happened?'

'No, I haven't had the chance, but they both gave the same story.'

'What does that prove? Nothing. Only that they knew they might be in trouble and worked out their stories between them. My God, Lily, you know what lads are like.' Doris turned to Mavis. 'Come here, love. Let's hear what you've got to say about this.'

Mavis looked terrified, but at least she did as Doris urged, moving to stand beside her. Doris took her hand and, after giving it a gentle squeeze, she said, 'Don't be frightened. Just tell us the truth.'

'It . . . it wasn't like that,' Mavis said, hesitant at first, but her voice slowly growing in strength.

As she listened, Doris knew that she was hearing the truth and, from the look on Lily's face, she could tell that she was seeing the light too. She just couldn't believe that Lily had been so quick to believe the boys over her own daughter – but then again, she was always hard on the girl. 'See, Lily, you should have spoken to Mavis first.'

'Yeah, maybe, but she was still on the common with boys.'

'All right, I'll give you that, but have you spoken to her about the dangers?' Doris asked while gently squeezing Mavis's hand again.

'Don't you start. I had enough from her next

door this morning. Mavis ain't a kid now and she must know,' Lily snapped.

'Unless you've warned her, I don't see how.'

'Don't go all high and mighty, Mum. You didn't tell me anything.'

'You've got a short memory, my girl. I may not have told you what to expect when you got married, but I told you enough to warn you about men,' Doris protested, but then, unable to hold it back, she groaned in pain.

'Gran, what's wrong?' Mavis asked worriedly.

'It . . . it's nothing, just a bit of indigestion. It must be those jellied eels I ate earlier.'

'Mum, you look awful,' Lily said. 'Oh, Gawd, you don't think they were off?'

'They tasted all right. No, it's just that I stuffed them down too quickly and it serves me right that I'm suffering for it now.' Doris rose slowly to her feet. 'I'll take a couple of Beecham's pills, that'll do the trick.'

'I'll get them, Gran.'

'No, it's all right. You stay here. Your mum's gonna talk to you, tell you a few facts.'

'What's the point?' Lily snapped. 'She won't understand.'

'Please, give Mavis a bit of credit for once,' Doris appealed.

'Oh, all right. I'll give it a go.'

Doris left the room, relieved that under the

cover of needing indigestion pills, she could actually take her painkillers. Blimey, talk about having to lie quickly, but with Lily so distracted by Mavis it had worked well. After glancing over her shoulder, she quickly swallowed them down, praying it wouldn't be too long before she felt the effects. For a few minutes Doris remained where she was, but fighting to gather her strength she returned to the living room.

Lily was talking to Mavis and the girl looked pink-cheeked. 'I hope I haven't wasted my time, Mavis. Do you understand what I've told you?'

'I . . . I think so.'

'You think so,' Lily echoed with disgust. 'That isn't good enough. You're too bloody thick, that's the problem.'

'Lily, don't talk to her like that.'

'Why not? It's the truth.'

'You're too hard on her,' Doris insisted as she took a seat by the fire. She then smiled gently at Mavis before saying, 'What did your mother tell you?'

Flushing pink again, Mavis mumbled, 'That boys are dirty buggers and that I mustn't let them touch me. And . . . and that I mustn't let them show me their . . . their thingies.'

'Good girl. See, Lily, she does understand.'

'Yeah, if you say so, Mum, but in future, if Mavis doesn't stay away from them, I'll skin her alive.'

'I will, Mum. I will stay away,' Mavis cried.

'You'd better, my girl,' Lily warned.

The pain had eased a little and Doris slumped back in her chair. She was tired, so tired, and knew that once the medication really kicked in, sleep would follow.

'Mum, do you feel any better?'

'Yes, I'm fine.'

'Are you sure?'

'For goodness sake, Lily! I said I'm all right and I meant it.'

'Yeah, well, I wanted to make sure before I go. Come on, Mavis. Get your coat on and we'll be off.'

Mavis did as she was told, and Doris managed to smile at her granddaughter when she leaned over to kiss her goodbye. 'See you soon, darlin'.'

'Bye, Gran,' Mavis whispered.

'I'll be round in the morning, Mum,' Lily said.

'Yeah, all right,' Doris managed, barely able to keep her eyes open as they left. She heard the front door closing, and then shifted a little in her chair, her weary eyes on the one opposite.

Walter was wagging his finger at her, but in her defence she said, 'All right, don't start. I know I lied to her, told her that I'm fine, but she'll find out soon enough. Just not yet.'

Doris knew her time was limited; her one wish now to see her daughter and Mavis living in a bit more comfort before she left. Huh, there was little chance of that. 'Walter, if only Lily hadn't married that good-for-nothing. If only she'd married a decent bloke . . .'

Walter's voice seemed to fill her head. 'Will she, Walter? Will she really be all right?'

He faded and Doris felt tears gathering in her eyes. If anyone knew that she talked to her dead husband they'd have her committed, but since the day he'd died thirty-six years ago, she had never been able to let him go.

'Well, love, it won't be long now,' she said. 'We'll be together again soon,' and though it hurt her to leave Lily and Mavis the pain was getting so bad that Doris would welcome the end.

CHAPTER NINE

Mavis walked silently home beside her mother, expecting her to rant and rave again, but instead she didn't say a word. She had sort of understood what her mother had told her, but didn't know why boys shouldn't touch her. There had been mention of dire consequences, of them making her pregnant, but her mother hadn't told her exactly *how* it happened.

They were home and in the kitchen before her mother opened her mouth, but only to say gruffly, 'I expect you're hungry. I'll bank up the fire first and then heat up some stew.'

Mavis wanted to ask questions, to understand how babies were made, but was too scared to bring up the subject again. She took off her coat, hung it up on the hook behind the back door, and then she sat at the table, still looking warily at her mother.

'Mrs Pugh said you did well today.'

'You . . . you've seen her?'

'Yeah. I went round there looking for you. Don't you ever do that again, my girl. When you've done your hour for Mrs Pugh, I want you to come straight home.'

Mavis nodded, unable to ignore the growl of hunger coming from her stomach. She'd been too scared and upset to eat the stew her grandmother had offered, but now watched avidly as her mother brought the fire to life before going to light the gas under a saucepan. On the few occasions she'd eaten school dinner, she got just a bit of bread and jam or dripping for her tea, but now she'd have two hot meals in a day.

Of course, it was down to the five pounds her dad had left, and Mavis prayed he'd keep his promise. If he did, she wouldn't have to take the pram out any more, and with less time on the streets it would be easier to keep out of Larry's and Tommy's way. But what about Larry's threats? One hadn't worked. Thanks to Gran, her mother didn't believe him, but there was the other one looming over her head, making her stomach clench with fear. He said he'd make it worse for her if she opened her mouth and she'd done just that. Mavis felt a wave of nausea. What would Larry do now?

'Here, get that down you,' Lily said as she put bowls of stew on the table.

Mavis picked up her spoon, but her hand was

shaking and as she took her first mouthful she found it difficult to swallow. Should she tell her mother? 'Mum, I'm scared.'

'Scared of what?'

'Larry said that if I told anyone, he'd make it worse for me.'

'He said that, did he? Well, don't you worry about him, my girl. I'll sort him out in the morning, and his friend Tommy. I'll also have another few choice words to say to their mothers.'

On hearing this Mavis slumped with relief. But, just to be on the safe side, she'd be extra vigilant when she went out. She tucked into her stew again, looking up when her mother spoke.

'After I've had a word in their ears, I doubt those boys will have the nerve to come near you again, but if they do, make sure you tell me. You should have come to me in the first place, and from now on, no more secrets, Mavis. Do you understand?'

'Yes, Mum,' Mavis agreed.

There was silence for a while as they both continued to eat, but then Lily said, 'I must say, from what I saw of it, Edith Pugh has got a nice place.'

Mavis found her eyes widening. Her mother was talking again, but this time making conversation. She never did that! 'Yes, but she's really fussy,' Mavis said eagerly. 'She's got cream furniture in her living room and I had to wash my hands before I started work.'

'Did you now? And what cleaning did you do?'

'Mostly hoovering, but then I made a cup of tea and peeled some potatoes before I left.'

'Gawd, Mavis. Did you break anything?'

'No. I was really careful.'

'Thank Gawd for that, but you know what a clumsy cow you are. If you start smashing her china the job won't last five minutes.'

Mavis again found her throat constricting again. Yes, she was clumsy, useless, and how would Mrs Pugh react if she broke one of her precious ornaments? Would she go mad like her mother? Would she sack her on the spot? Yes, probably, and then her mother would be furious.

Lily was so full of guilt that she was glad when Mavis went to bed at nine o'clock. Without bothering to hear her side of the story, she'd thought the worst of her daughter. She'd believed those two little sods! What sort of mother was she? Lily didn't like the way she was feeling and fought to find excuses. With a daughter like Mavis, was it any wonder? No, of course it wasn't. The girl should've had enough sense to know it was dangerous to be alone on the common with boys, but unlike other girls of her age she was as daft as a brush.

There was a knock on the door and, sighing heavily, Lily went to answer it. 'Kate, come on in.'

'I know it's a bit late, but Sandra's still upset about Mavis. I said I'd come round to see how things are going.'

Lily didn't want to paint herself in a bad light, so instead of telling Kate the whole story she said shortly, 'It's all right. She's fine.'

'Did you sort those boys out?'

'Yeah, but the little sods have convinced their mothers that Mavis led them on.'

'Huh, well, I'll put them straight. According to Sandra they tried it on with her too. If my Bill finds out he'll kill the pair of them.'

Lily stared at Kate, her mind in turmoil. Sandra was a sensible girl, a clever girl, but it hadn't stopped those two little buggers. Any lingering doubts that Mavis had led them on were now swept aside in another wave of guilt.

'What is it, love?' Kate asked. 'You've gone as white as a sheet.'

Unable to hold it back, Lily said, 'I . . . I believed them. I went for her, Kate. I gave Mavis a good hiding.'

'Oh, the poor kid.'

Once again Lily didn't like the way she was feeling, and said in defence, 'Yeah, well, she shouldn't have been on the common with them. Maybe a good hiding is the only way to make her see sense.'

For a moment Kate looked annoyed, but she

only bit on her bottom lip momentarily before saying, 'Have you spoken to her about the dangers now?'

'Yeah, and I just hope she took it in.'

'I'm sure she did.'

Lily lowered her eyes. Kate was always saying that she didn't give Mavis enough credit, but at least she could say something in her favour now. 'I must admit that Edith Pugh was pleased with her work today.'

'Work! Mavis is working for Edith Pugh? Since when?'

'She's just started and is doing an hour's cleaning for her after school.'

'Blimey, how did that come about?'

Lily told her, and then said, 'You never know. It might lead to something when she leaves school.'

'I think Mavis can do better than cleaning, especially for an uppity cow like Edith Pugh.'

'Now you sound like Ron and, as I told him, there isn't much Mavis *can* do. At least the woman thinks she can train her, and if she can do that, it could lead to other work.'

'Yeah, I suppose so,' Kate said doubtfully, but then she stood up. 'Sandra will be waiting to hear so I'd best get back.'

Lily stayed where she was, just calling goodbye as Kate left. God, what a day. She felt worn out and decided on an early night. Her mind shied away from Mavis and the unjust punishment she'd meted out, instead turning to her mother. Indigestion my arse, Lily thought. There was more to it than that and, like it or not, she was going to make sure that her mother saw the doctor.

It wasn't until Lily walked into the bedroom that it hit her. Alone! She'd be sleeping alone. With all the nights down the race track or the pub, she was used to going to bed before Ron, but this was different. There wouldn't be the feel of his body climbing into bed when he came home, his arms wrapping around her as he snuggled up for warmth. 'Oh, Ron,' she whispered. 'I miss you already, but, please, let it be worth it. Don't let me down.'

Ron sat propped up, a pillow behind him as he rolled a cigarette, his eyes scanning the hut with disgust. God, it was like being back in the army training camp with a row of beds on each side of the room. Even the orphanage he'd grown up in had more comfort. 'Blimey, Pete, when you said the contractor would arrange lodgings, I wasn't expecting this.'

'I know it ain't much, but it's been done up, and if that dinner was anything to go by, we're bound to get a decent breakfast.'

'Yeah, it was all right, but what about this dump? What was it? The cow shed?'

'I dunno, mate, but it's dry, cheap and warm. Anyway, what does it matter? With the hours we'll be working, it's just a place to crash at night.'

Four other men were sitting at a table close to the stove, one letting out a loud fart as he shuffled a deck of playing cards. He laughed, but then turned his head to call, 'Sorry, boys. It's that bloody cabbage the old girl gave us for dinner.'

'Yeah, Gerry, I know what you mean,' Pete called back.

'Fancy a few hands of poker?'

'No, thanks,' Pete replied. 'Maybe some other time.'

Ron stood up and ignoring the warning shake of Pete's head he strolled down to that end of the room. He'd met the four blokes when they'd returned to the farm after work, all of them sitting round a large, wooden, well-scrubbed table in the farmhouse kitchen. They didn't seem a bad bunch and he and Pete would be joining them on site in the morning. Gerry was another bricklayer, Eric his hod carrier, Martin was a plasterer and his younger brother, Andy, was there to learn the trade and knock up.

'What about you, mate?' Gerry asked. 'Do you fancy a game?'

Ron eyed the money on the table. He could only see small coins and was tempted. It would give him a chance to see how they played, and, if they weren't up to much, on payday he could up the stakes. He was about to answer, but then Pete called from the other end of the room.

'Ron, can I have a word?'

'Maybe later, Gerry,' he said, annoyed at the interruption as he walked away.

'What the fuck are you playing at?' Pete hissed as soon as Ron reached his side.

'Playing at? What are you on about?'

'Poker! Gambling!'

'Leave it out! They're only playing for pennies.'

'Yeah, now maybe, but I know you and it'll soon turn to pounds. You're supposed to be giving it up, or have you forgotten that already?'

'It's only cards, Pete. It ain't the dogs.'

'It's still gambling and if you lose your money as usual, don't expect me to pick up the pieces.'

'That won't happen. I'm good at poker and I can take them.'

'Yeah, like you're good at picking out winners down the dog track.'

'Bloody hell, Pete, it sounds like you're gonna turn out to be a bigger nag than Lily.'

Pete's eyes narrowed with anger. 'That's it, Ron. I've had enough. You'll never change and our first night here has proved that.'

'Look, if it upsets you that much, I won't play poker.'

With a shake of his head, Pete said, 'Please

yourself, Ron. I ain't here to be your keeper and if you want to gamble your wages away every week, that's up to you. I'm here to work, to earn enough to set up a decent future. I need a partner who'll be reliable, one with a bit of ambition, and that obviously ain't you. I'll find someone else.'

Bewildered, Ron slumped onto the side of his bed. All this bloody fuss about a penny card game! Yet even as this thought crossed his mind, Ron knew that Pete was right. As soon as he had a few bob, he'd planned to up the stakes, so sure that he could win. With a wry smile he looked up. 'I don't blame you, mate. I know I'm a lost cause, but I really do want to change.'

'Yeah, so you've said, and so many times that I've lost count.'

'Don't give up on me, Pete. Give me one more chance.'

Pete gazed back at him, about to answer when Gerry called out again. 'Ron, do you want in on this game or not?'

'Nah, sorry, mate, leave me out. Gambling's a mug's game.'

There was a choking sound and then Pete began to laugh, doubling over with mirth as he gasped between guffaws. 'A mug's game. *You* said it's a mug's game. Blimey, Ron, you're priceless.'

Ron joined in his laughter, but as they sobered he appealed, 'Don't start up a business with someone else, Pete. We're partners, you and me. Come on. Give me one more chance.'

Their eyes met, Pete's hardening as he said, 'Yeah, all right, but it's your last one.'

He meant it, Ron could see that. This really was his last chance – he'd have to make sure he didn't blow it.

CHAPTER TEN

Mavis wasn't sure what was wrong with her mother. Last week, when she'd told her that Miss Harwood wanted to talk to her at the parents' meeting, she'd been snappy, saying that she didn't have time to go. Mavis had been crushed. Miss Harwood still insisted that she could go on to art college and if her mother had spoken to her it could have made all the difference.

Dad had been true to his word, sending a fiver every week, and with money coming in the rent was paid, with food on the table too. On her fifteenth birthday he'd sent her a present, and Mavis had been thrilled with the watercolour paints and thick paper. Gran had given her a lovely new pink hat and scarf and, for just that one week, her mother had let her keep two shillings of the money she earned at Mrs Pugh's.

Mavis knew that her mum didn't have any money worries now, but she still wasn't happy.

She was quiet most of the time, distant, and when Mavis looked back it seemed that her mother had been acting strangely almost since Dad had left. Mavis had thought she must be missing him, just as she herself was, but her gran had laughed at that idea.

Her mother's unhappiness couldn't have anything to do with Gran. Yes, she was in hospital now, but it wasn't anything serious. It had been an ulcer that prevented her from eating – no wonder she'd become so thin. She had been admitted to hospital four days ago, and now that she'd had the small operation, surely her mother would take her to see Gran that evening.

Mavis clutched the small, precious canvas as she made her way home, holding it against her chest to shield it from the rain. Today had been the end of term, mid April, and her last day at school. This was it! She was so proud of her painting and when her mother saw it surely it would change everything. She couldn't wait to see her face and decided that she would show it to her now; she'd quickly pop in before she went to Mrs Pugh's.

She passed an alley, yelping when hands came out to yank the canvas from her grasp. Mavis spun around, finding herself face to face with Tommy Wilson.

'What have we got here then?' he sneered.

'Give it back! Oh, please, give it back!'

Mavis had carefully wrapped brown paper around the canvas, but Tommy ripped it away, laughing as he held up the picture. 'Bloody hell. Look at that face. In fact, no thanks,' and with that he lifted his leg to boot the canvas down the alley.

'Oh, no . . . No!' Mavis cried, pushing past Tommy to rush after it.

It had landed face down in a puddle, but, as Mavis bent down to retrieve it, Tommy was at her side, shoving her out of the way as his foot came out to stamp on the canvas.

'Oh, don't . . . don't,' she begged.

Still not satisfied, Tommy picked up the canvas again, this time slamming it down face up and, with one boot holding it in place, he used the heel of the other to gouge into the painting.

Mavis saw all her work destroyed, her dream disintegrating before her eyes. She sank down onto the wet ground, sobbing, hardly aware of Tommy's hand when it touched her shoulder.

'What's all the fuss about? It's only a daft painting.'

The contrition in his voice surprised Mavis, but she could only look up at him mutely, tears streaming down her cheeks.

'Look, it's your own fault,' he said defensively. 'Larry told you not to blab, but you didn't listen and then that bitch, Sandra, opened her mouth too.

113

Me and Larry were in right trouble and all for a bit of fun, that's all.'

Still Mavis couldn't talk. She could only shake her head, her eyes resting on the painting again. It was ruined, beyond repair, and once again she sobbed.

'I only mucked up your picture, that's all. You should think yourself lucky I didn't take it out on you.' And with that Tommy abruptly walked away.

Mavis didn't know how long she sat on the ground, rain falling heavily and soaking her coat. At last she got up, and with one last look at the ruined canvas she desolately made her way home.

'My God, Mavis. What happened to you?'

'Oh, Mum . . .'

'Get that coat off. You look wet through. Now tell me what happened.'

Mavis found her hands shaking so badly that she could barely undo the buttons. 'I . . . I was on my way home, but then Tom . . . Tommy . . .'

'Tommy Wilson! What did he do?' she cried. 'Did he touch you?'

'He . . . he grabbed my painting. He . . . he ruined it.'

'You wouldn't be in this state over a flaming picture. Tell the truth, Mavis. What did he do to you?'

'I am telling the truth. He didn't touch me, but

he . . . he destroyed my canvas. Oh, Mum, it was a good painting. Really good.'

'For Christ's sake, I don't believe this. You're supposed to be at Edith Pugh's, but instead you turn up here like a drowned rat, crying about nothing.'

'It . . . it isn't nothing. When you saw my painting I thought you might let me go to art college.'

'Art college! Are you out of your mind, girl?'

'Mum, please,' Mavis begged. 'It's the only thing I'm any good at. If you'd seen the portrait of Gran . . .'

'Shut up! Your gran's dying and you come grizzling to me about a silly painting.' Lily threw a hand over her mouth. 'Now look what you've done! She didn't want me to tell you.'

Mavis stiffened in shock, hardly aware that her mother had collapsed onto a chair. Her gran was dying? No! No! It couldn't be true. 'Oh . . . Mum . . . she can't be. You said she had an ulcer. That she was in hospital for a small operation.'

There was no answer, and then Mavis saw her mother lay her arms on the table, bending over to rest her head on them as sobs began to rack her body. She hurried forward, a hand hovering uncertainly until it came to rest on her mum's head.

Lily reared up, eyes wild. 'Don't touch me! Get out! Go on, get out of my sight!'

Mavis grabbed her still sodden coat, crying too as she dashed out of the house. She began to run, faster and faster as though trying to escape the terrible news. Gran couldn't be dying! She just couldn't!

Lily heard the front door slam, but didn't care. All she cared about was her mother. The past couple of months had been hell and almost more than she could bear. If it hadn't been for the money that Ron sent and Mavis's scant earnings, it would have been impossible. At least she hadn't had to worry about finding stock and selling it. Instead she'd been able to spend every possible hour with her mother, looking after her, making sure her pain relief was increased, until four days ago when it had become impossible for her to remain at home.

Before she'd gone into hospital, how her mother had been able to put on such a front when Mavis called round was beyond Lily, but rally she did. And how her daughter could be so naïve was beyond Lily too. She must have seen her grandmother fading away before her eyes, but the stupid girl had believed their story of an ulcer. An ulcer! God, if only it was that! *Oh, Mum, why did you leave it so long before you saw a doctor? Why did you wait until it was too late? And when you found out – why didn't you tell me?*

Lily knew the answer. As usual her mother had

been trying to protect her. Misguided love, that's what it was. If only her mother had told her when she'd been diagnosed. Lily groaned. She could have spent more time with her mother, but all she'd done was to pop round every day, too busy to make it a long visit. Yes, and if she hadn't been so busy, so trapped in trying to make enough to pay the rent every week, maybe she would've seen what was right in front of her eyes. Why! Why hadn't she taken more notice of her mother's weight loss?

When she'd found out the truth, Lily had begged her mother to move in with her, but she'd stubbornly refused. It would have made things so much easier and she could have nursed her mother at night too, but she wouldn't even allow that, nor her suggestion that she and Mavis move in with her. Instead her close friend and fellow widow next door had taken on that role, until, finally, she became so racked with pain that the doctor had insisted she be admitted to hospital.

Lily dashed a hand across her eyes. There was little time left, she knew that, and as soon as Mavis came home she'd go to the hospital again. Mavis, yes, she'd sent her daughter off with a flea in her ear, and now Lily felt a surge of guilt. She shouldn't have taken it out on Mavis. It wasn't her fault, but all that fuss about a silly painting had been the last straw.

Had Mavis gone to Mrs Pugh's? Lily didn't know, but seeing how devastated her daughter had been, she doubted it. Mavis knew the truth now, so maybe she should think about taking her to the hospital, but how would her mother react?

'Mavis, what is it?' Edith asked as the girl staggered over the doorstep. Her coat was wet, filthy with mud, and her hair hung around her face like rats' tails.

'Oh, Mrs Pugh. My . . . my gran's dying.'

Edith placed an arm around Mavis's shoulder, gently leading her through to the kitchen as she murmured, 'How awful for you. I'm so sorry, my dear. Sit there and tell me all about it.'

Mavis slumped onto a fireside chair, and, though the spring days were warmer than the preceding harsh winter, Edith had a small fire burning. The cold was no friend to her pain and it would be a long time yet before her hearth was left empty of the comforting flames.

At first Mavis could barely speak, but gradually the story emerged. 'I . . . I thought she was just in hospital for a small operation. Oh, Mrs Pugh, I can't believe she's dying.'

Edith made sure that her tone was sympathetic. 'How awful for you, but what happened, Mavis? Did you fall over on your way here? Is that why your coat is covered in mud?'

'No . . . no . . .' she said, going on to tell Edith about Tommy Wilson, the ruined painting, and her dream of art college.

Edith didn't want Mavis to go to art college; it would ruin her plans and she was secretly pleased that Lily Jackson had refused to entertain the idea. 'I know you're disappointed, Mavis, but it isn't as simple as you think to get into college. There are so many talented students who attend grammar school, and they have exam results to show for the limited places. Your teacher shouldn't have raised your hopes.'

Mavis shook her head, saying sadly, 'I don't care about college now. All I care about is my gran.'

'Have you been to see her, my dear?'

'Not yet. Mum said that Gran doesn't want me to know. What if she won't take me to see her?'

'You know now, so I'm sure she will, but maybe not in that state,' Edith said as she looked at Mavis's filthy coat. 'You can't go to the hospital looking like that so we'd better get you spruced up. Go upstairs and run a bath. Wash your hair too, and when you're ready I'm sure I can find a dry coat for you to wear.'

'Oh, thank you,' Mavis cried, tears once again filling her eyes.

'Now then, you'll need to be brave when you see your grandmother, so come on, no more crying.'

Mavis drew in a gulp of air and then standing up she once more murmured a thank you before leaving the room. Edith smiled happily. Mavis was beginning to trust her, to like her, and that was just what she wanted.

Mavis had often wondered what it must be like to have a bath, to immerse your whole body in hot water, but as she ran one and climbed in she was too distraught about her gran to appreciate how wonderful it felt. Desolately she washed, and then seeing a bottle of shampoo she knelt in the bath, dipping her head into the water. As quickly as possible Mavis washed her hair, using the bath water to wash out the suds before climbing out. There were fluffy white towels hanging on a rack, and when dry, her hair vigorously rubbed, Mavis put her damp clothes back on. She left the bathroom to hear Mrs Pugh's voice.

'Mavis, come here, my dear.'

When Mavis walked into the woman's bedroom, a room she knew well, having cleaned it every week, Edith Pugh was brandishing her pink, plastic hairdryer. Mavis was nervous as she stepped forward. She had never used a hairdryer before and didn't know where to start, but after being given a brush to run through her hair she was shown how to use it, amazed at how nice her hair looked when it was finally dry. The curls that she usually hated looked soft and shiny as they framed her face. 'Is . . . is that all right?'

'It looks lovely, Mavis, and, my goodness, you're even prettier than I realised.'

'My ears stick out.'

'With those curls you can't see them. Now try this on. I'm afraid it's a few years out of date, but I've hardly worn it,' Edith said as she held up a brown, wool coat that was fitted at the waist before gently flaring to what looked to be below calf-length.

Mavis put it on but, though lovely, it was a little big for her slim frame. She didn't care. It smelled of mothballs, but it was clean and surely she looked tidy enough to go to the hospital. 'I'll be really careful with it and make sure to return it unmarked.'

'I don't want it back, Mavis, but it will need a little altering to fit you properly.'

'I can keep it? Oh, thank you. Thank you so much,' Mavis cried as she took the coat off. 'What would you like me to do today?'

'Do! Oh, no, Mavis, the cleaning can wait. You get off home and when your mother sees how nice you look, I'm sure she'll take you to visit your grandmother.'

'I . . . I'll do an extra hour tomorrow.'

'Mavis, in the circumstances, just come when-ever you can. For the time being, now that you've

121

left school, I'm happy to fit in with your hours. Now put that coat back on and off you go.'

The woman's kindness almost made Mavis break down again. She managed a croaky thank you, and then left, praying all the way home that Edith Pugh was right. That she would be allowed to visit her beloved grandmother.

CHAPTER ELEVEN

Ron hated being away from home. He didn't like the barrack-like accommodation, or the extra hours of back-breaking work they were putting in. Yes, he and Pete were coining it in, their savings mounting, but when they returned to the hut every evening he'd become bored with just sitting around until it was time to turn in. It was all right for Pete, the man happy to have his nose in a book, but Ron craved a few beers, a chance to unwind.

'Ron, are you joining us?' Gerry called.

Pete looked up from his book, his annoyance plain. 'Don't you think you should knock it on the head?'

Ron knew Pete wasn't happy that he now joined Gerry and the others in a game of cards almost every evening, but he didn't know what all the fuss was about. He'd proved his point, shown Pete that he was making money, not losing it, and he'd do the same tonight too. 'Why should I knock it on the head? I'm quids in.'

'Yeah, but your luck could change.'

'There's no chance of that. That lot haven't got a clue and I've sussed them out. Take Martin for instance. When he's got a good hand he repeatedly looks at his cards, but with a bad one he can't help pulling his ear. Taking money off of them is a piece of cake.'

'So much for knocking gambling on the head,' Pete snapped.

'Leave it out. It's only a game of cards,' Ron retorted before walking off and joining the others.

'Was your old woman nagging you again?' Gerry quipped.

'Huh, he's worse than Lily,' Ron said as he took his usual seat, 'but sod him. Deal them out, Gerry.'

They'd upped the stakes from playing for pennies, and that suited Ron just fine. Why play for pennies when you could play for pounds – and as the last few weeks had proved, he had no reason to fear losing his hard-earned wages.

The game commenced, and though Gerry won a few hands, Ron wasn't bothered, and he remained that way even when Eric took the next. The next game went to him, but as the others had folded quickly, the pot was small.

'Not doing so well tonight, are you, Ron?' Gerry commented.

'No, but there's plenty of time,' he said, picking up his newly dealt cards. Not bad, Ron thought, discarding two, but then had to fight to keep a poker face as he looked at the replacements. Bloody hell, now he could do some damage. Careful to keep his expression neutral he surreptitiously looked at the others and was satisfied that he could read them.

The betting commenced, becoming heavy, but with four of a kind, and tens at that, Ron wasn't worried.

'This is too hot for me. I'm out,' Martin the plasterer said, folding his cards and looking worriedly at Andy, his younger brother.

Andy continued to bet, even upped the stakes, but when both Ron and Gerry remained in, he too eventually threw his cards down in disgust. 'That's it, I'm cleaned out.'

With a smile, Gerry said, 'Better luck tomorrow, mate.'

That just left Gerry and him in the game and Ron hid a smile. As usual, Gerry was giving himself away, pretending bravado, but Ron had noted over the weeks that Gerry always drummed his fingers on the table when he was bluffing. Picking up on this had served him well over the weeks, and Ron knew it would do so again. He raised the stakes again and was pleased when Gerry did the same, five-pound notes piling up in the middle of the table.

'Not had enough yet, Ron?' Gerry asked as he stuck his hand in his pocket to pull out a wad of notes and, peeling off a tenner, he increased the bet again.

Ron was surprised, but still certain that Gerry was bluffing, he shrugged. 'If you want to make it more interesting, that's fine with me,' he said, 'I just need to get a few more quid.'

'What the fuck are you doing?' Pete asked as Ron walked down the room to hastily dip into their savings.

'It's all right, I'm only taking my share, but I'll double it,' Ron whispered. 'I've got Gerry just where I want him and if he keeps on betting, I might even treble it.'

Ignoring Pete's protests, Ron walked back to the table and brandishing an equally large wad of notes he casually chucked another ten-pound note onto the growing pile.

'Are you sure you don't want to fold?' Gerry asked as he threw in another bet.

'It's you who should fold, mate, not me,' Pete said.

As the pot grew the tension in the room became palpable. Ron began to sweat, barely aware of the others watching, or that Pete was standing behind him.

'Ron,' Pete warned.

Ron licked his lips in anticipation of taking the

huge pot, and, at last, with only just enough money left to call, he threw it onto the centre of the table before flourishing his cards. 'Right, Gerry. Let's see what you've got.'

Hands stretched out, Ron was about to rake the notes towards him, but his hands were stayed when Gerry spoke.

'Not so fast, mate,' he said, turning over his cards.

'No . . . no,' Ron choked, unable to believe his eyes. Four queens! The bastard had four queens!

It was Gerry who now leaned forward to rake in the money; and, throwing his chair back, hardly aware that it crashed onto the floor behind him, Ron almost ran out of the hut, bending over to draw in great gulps of air. Bloody hell, he'd blown it, lost all of his savings, but how? He was so sure that Gerry had been bluffing, was sure he hadn't misread the signs.

'I hope you're satisfied now,' Pete said in disgust as he too walked outside. 'You've done it again, gambled away your money, our money.'

'I didn't touch your share.'

'Maybe not, and I expect you think that makes it all right. Well, it doesn't. We were supposed to be pooling the cash to go into business, but there's no chance of that now. You're hopeless, Ron, and I'm finished. Forget the partnership. I'm going it alone.'

Still unable to believe that he'd misread Gerry and angry at the thought that he might have been set up, Ron was in no mood to listen. 'Please yourself,' he snapped before marching back into the hut.

'You bastard, Gerry. You set me up.'

'I can't stand a sore loser, and that's what you are, Ron. A loser. You were so sure of yourself, so sure that you had me and the others sussed, but I bet you don't feel so clever now.'

'I'll fucking kill you!' Ron yelled as he advanced towards Gerry, but his cronies quickly jumped off their beds to stand next to him.

'I wouldn't if I was you,' Martin threatened.

Ron glanced over his shoulder, expecting to see Pete behind him, but instead he was standing by the door at the other end of the room.

'You're on your own, Ron,' he called. 'I warned you, but you wouldn't listen.'

Ron couldn't believe his ears. When there was trouble, he and Pete had always backed each other up. He hated turning away, but four against one weren't odds he was prepared to take a chance on. 'Ain't you got the nerve to face me on your own?' he said, scowling at Gerry.

'Why should I? It's you who wants a fight not me.'

With no other choice, Ron angrily marched back to his locker and, grabbing his cardboard suitcase, he began to stuff his gear haphazardly into it.

'So you're leaving,' Pete said.

'Yeah, I'm off. I've had enough of this dump, that lot, *and* you,' Ron snapped. Some friend Pete had turned out to be, but sod him, Ron thought, he'd do fine on his own. Without sparing him or the others a glance, or saying another word, Ron stormed out of the building.

CHAPTER TWELVE

Mavis found her prayer answered when she had gone home in her new coat. Her mother had taken her to the hospital, and from then on they had spent many hours beside her gran's bed. Gran hadn't been pleased at first and had tried to rally, but it was too much for her. During the next four weeks it was awful to see her deteriorating until she just lay weakly, clutching one of their hands.

For Mavis the initial shock had worn off, replaced now with a deep sadness, and for the past few days she'd had a hidden longing for her gran to just slip away. She was almost un-recognisable now: her body skeletal, her face so sunken and gaunt that it looked as if only skin covered the bone. On Monday she had slipped into a coma and if anything it was a relief. Gran seemed pain-free now, almost at peace, but she was still hanging on to life by a thread.

Mavis looked across the bed to see her mother

with her eyes closed, lips moving as though in silent prayer. There had been no money from Bracknell for weeks now and for the first time in her life Mavis was furious with her father. How could he? How could he let Mum down at a time like this? Gran was dying and the last thing her mother needed was money worries.

When the bell sounded to signal the end of visiting time, Mavis leaned forward to gently kiss her grandmother. There was no response, but she whispered, 'Bye, Gran. See you tomorrow.'

She stood up and then her mother did the same before they silently left the ward. 'I hate seeing Gran like that,' Mavis said as the doors swung shut behind them.

'Yeah, I know. Me too, but . . . but I don't think she's gonna last much longer.'

'Oh, Mum . . .'

'Don't start blubbing again or you'll set me off,' she said brusquely. 'Come on, get a move on. You need to get yourself round to Mrs Pugh's, but we'll come back this evening.'

Mavis picked up her pace. Mrs Pugh had been wonderful, happy to let her fit in the two hours she now did every day around visiting her gran. Most of the extra hour was spent learning to cook, and under Mrs Pugh's tutelage Mavis found that her confidence had grown. As she was unable to read, Mavis had to commit many recipes to memory, but Mrs Pugh had come up with a wonderful idea. She had given Mavis a notebook in which to draw pictures of the ingredients; a cow for beef, the cut, for instance, shoulder, marked with a dotted line. The same for other meats, and vegetables were easy to draw. Mavis found that making her unique recipe book was absorbing, enough to take her mind off her grandmother, if only for a short while. She'd been shy and embarrassed when Mrs Pugh had taken her appearance in hand too, but now she loved the feel of being clean from top to toe, her hair shiny from regular shampoos.

As usual, Mavis found her mother silent as they walked along, only calling a clipped goodbye when they parted at the crossroads. Mavis was used to this. Her mother still rarely made conversation, but Mrs Pugh was different. Despite her unhappiness over Gran, Mavis now liked working for her, the two hours spent in Ellington Avenue being an escape from the misery at home.

When she turned into the avenue, Mavis barely noticed the beauty of the May blossom that dripped from the trees. She was thinking about her gran again, and though it would be a kind release she dreaded losing her.

Lily was deep in her own thoughts, she too dreading her mother's end. She hated the way her mind skipped ahead to her mother's funeral, but with no money to pay for it she was almost out of her mind with worry.

Frantic, she had written to Ron, but instead of sending more money, she hadn't received a penny for over three weeks. She'd written again, but to no avail, and when the postman had passed the house again she seethed with anger as it sunk in that Ron wasn't going to send her anything. Her mother was dying, she was desperate, but he obviously didn't give a toss. She'd never forgive him for this. Never! As far as she was concerned, their marriage was over.

Lily was barely inside the door when Kate came round, her face as always showing sympathy as she asked, 'How's your mum doing?'

'She's still in a coma and . . . and I think it won't be long now.'

'Oh, Lily, I'm so sorry.'

Sympathy was always Lily's downfall and she fought tears, saying quickly, 'Are you staying for a cuppa?'

'Yeah, I won't say no.'

Lily busied herself, but when the tea was made she said, 'It's a bit weak and I ain't got any sugar.'

'Oh, blimey, don't tell me that Ron hasn't sent you any money.'

'Of course he has,' Lily lied. 'It's just that I haven't had time to do any shopping.'

Kate looked doubtful, but Lily wasn't about to

133

tell her the truth. She didn't want pity, didn't want Kate to spread the news that, as usual, Ron had let her down.

'Well, if you want anything from the shops, you know you only have to ask.'

'Yes, and thanks, Kate.'

'Where's Mavis?'

'She's at Edith Pugh's and, Kate, if you hear of anyone else looking for a cleaner, will you let me know?'

'Yeah, but it ain't likely. Nobody around here can afford a cleaner, and to be honest, I'm surprised that Edith Pugh can find the money. After all, she's a widow and I can't believe that her son earns that much.'

'Maybe she was left comfortably off when her husband died.'

'Yeah, maybe,' Kate mused. 'Here, did I tell you about Jill Barnet?'

'No,' Lily said tiredly, wishing Kate gone. She wasn't in the mood for gossip, but once Kate got into full flow there was no stopping her.

'Her old man's been nicked. He was pinching stuff from the factory where he works and got caught red-handed. Of course, it doesn't surprise me. He always looked a shifty sod and, as you can imagine, it's brought Jill down a peg or two.'

Kate's words washed over Lily and seeing that the woman's cup was now empty she laid the hint by picking it up and taking it over to the sink. Thankfully the ploy worked and Kate rose to her feet.

'Well, thanks for the tea, Lily, and don't forget, if you need anything, let me know.'

Lily managed a smile. Despite being a gossip, Kate was kind and a good friend – as long as you kept your private life just that. Not that it was easy living in houses with walls so thin between them. 'Thanks, love,' she called as the woman left, but as the door closed, Lily broke down. *Oh, Mum, Mum, what am I gonna do without you? You've always been there for me. Always helped me out when I've been in dire straits, and now . . . now I can't even afford to give you a decent funeral.*

Pete Culling didn't know what to do when he finished work that Wednesday evening. He hadn't expected any letters to arrive for Ron, but two had been delivered so far, and he now knew his assumption that Ron had gone home was wrong.

Sod it, this wasn't his problem. He'd helped Ron out time and time again, but no more. He'd been mad to think Ron would change, that the two of them could make a go of their own business, and now, deep down, he was relieved that their friendship was well and truly over. Yes, Ron had saved his skin during the war and he would always be grateful to him for that, but years and years of picking up the pieces when the man blew his wages every week on gambling had finally taken its toll.

At first he'd been able to talk Ron out of playing poker and everything had been going well. They'd worked long hours, weekends too, and their pooled money was building up nicely. Then, despite his warnings, only about six weeks after they arrived, Ron had joined a game. He'd soon become hooked – too stupid to realise that his early winnings had been a set-up to draw him in.

Pete slumped onto the side of his bed, his thoughts now on Lily. Despite deciding that this wasn't his problem, he knew he had to tell her. She didn't deserve this, to be left up in the air, her letters to Ron unopened and unanswered. He'd have a word with the gaffer in the morning, tell the man that he was taking the day off. With the hours he'd been working, Pete doubted there'd be any complaint, but if there was, well, bugger the job. He'd soon find another. In truth, Pete wouldn't mind packing this one in. He hated the accommodation, along with some of the men who shared it. Most of all he hated Gerry, the bastard who had sucked Ron in.

As if he'd conjured up the man in his mind, Gerry walked into the hut. Pete ignored him, deciding to read for a while before getting his head down for some well-earned kip. It was ironic really, here he was, reading an Ian Fleming book called

Casino Royale, with playing cards featured on the front cover – but it was a good read and he'd become absorbed with the main character.

It wasn't long before Gerry and his cronies gathered around the table and Pete stiffened when the man called out. 'Here, Pete, now that your mate's out, we're a man short. How about joining us in a game?'

'Fuck off!'

There was laughter, and Pete stood up, grinding his teeth. He'd had enough. Working quickly, he shoved all his belongings into a rucksack, leaving it on top of his bed while he marched down the room. 'Here, Gerry,' he said.

'What?' the man said as he looked up at him.

Pete grinned as his fist connected with Gerry's chin, the force sending the man backwards, both he and his chair crashing onto the floor.

'A parting gift,' he spat, before turning on his heel to stride back down the room. He picked up his rucksack, flung it over his shoulder and then walked out, still smiling as he headed for the railway station.

Pete only sobered as he sat waiting for the train. He'd walked out on the job, and would lose a few days' pay, but what did it matter? He had plenty to tide him over. Though maybe he shouldn't have decked Gerry. Mind you, he'd enjoyed wiping the smile off the bastard's face. Yes, Gerry had sucked

Ron in, but in truth Ron wasn't green and should've seen it coming. Pete wasn't a gambler, but even he had spotted what the man was up to. Ron had ignored his warnings, so sure that he was in control, until that last game when he'd taken his money from their joint savings and lost the lot.

At last a train pulled in, but it would mean a few changes before Pete finally reached his destination. He wasn't looking forward to telling Lily that Ron had buggered off. She'd either fall to pieces, or go bloody mad. Knowing Lily it would be the latter, and in truth he wouldn't blame her.

Maybe he was wrong, Pete thought as he climbed into a carriage. Maybe the letters Lily had sent had been held up in the post, that was all, and Ron would be back home in Cullen Street. But somehow he doubted it.

CHAPTER THIRTEEN

Lily and Mavis walked home on leaden feet. Lily had at first been frozen with shock. Between visiting that afternoon and then again in the evening, her mother had died; slipped quietly away they'd been told.

Mavis had been inconsolable, but as she was so wrapped up in her own misery, Lily had done little to comfort her daughter. At last, exhausted from crying, Mavis had gone to bed, but Lily was still awake. She had cried a little, but anger held back most of her grief until it sat like a hard knot in her chest. Her mother was dead, but thanks to Ron she had no money to bury her. No money to give her a decent send-off.

Lily sat wringing her hands until at ten o'clock there was a knock on the door. At that hour, Lily suspected it was Kate, but she couldn't face anyone yet. *Oh, Mum,* her mind screamed, the same thought plaguing her again and again. *What am I gonna do without you?*

She ignored the thumping on the door, but then the letterbox was lifted, a voice calling, 'Lily, Lily, are you there? It's me, Pete.'

Pete! What was he doing here? Oh, no . . . no! She ran across the room, flinging the door open. 'What is it? Has something happened to Ron?'

'No, Lily,' Pete said quickly, 'he's fine. At least he was the last time I saw him. I was hoping he was here.'

'Here! No, I thought he was with you in Bracknell.'

'Can I come in, Lily?'

Her head buzzing with confusion, Lily stepped to one side. 'Sorry, yes, of course.'

Pete crossed the threshold and Lily closed the door behind him before asking, 'What's going on, Pete?'

'Ron buggered off, Lily. About three weeks ago.'

'What! But why?'

'He got into gambling, played poker and lost all the money he'd put into our savings.'

'Where did he go?'

'I dunno. That's why I'm here.'

Her face draining of colour, Lily felt a wave of dizziness. She swayed and Pete's voice became distant as his arms came out to support her.

'Gawd, Lily. You'd better sit down.'

She clung to Pete, tight in his embrace as he

murmured, 'Bloody hell, Lily, I didn't think you'd take it like this. Don't worry, he'll turn up.'

Still Lily clutched Pete, but as her mind cleared everything hit her again. The dam burst, tears spurting. 'I don't care about Ron. It's my mum, Pete. She . . . she's dead.'

'What? Blimey, Lily, no wonder you're in a state. I'm sorry, love.'

The sympathy was too much and tears ran unchecked, down Lily's cheeks. She stayed in Pete's arms, unable to stop sobbing, until at last he pulled away.

'Come on, girl,' he urged. 'Stop crying now or you'll make yourself ill.'

Lily took a great juddering gulp of air, allowing Pete to gently lead her across the room where she sat down, at last able to stem her tears.

'Gawd, I thought you was gonna pass out. Are you all right now?'

'Yeah, thanks, Pete. It's me own fault. I've been too upset to eat and felt a bit giddy.'

Pete's face darkened with anger. 'You shouldn't be on your own. Ron should be here.'

'Huh, what good would that do? When he stopped sending me money, I wrote to him, told him what was happening, but he just ignored my letters.'

'He didn't get them, Lily. He'd gone by the time they arrived.'

Mavis appeared at the door, her expression bewildered. 'Mum . . . ? What's going on?'

'Go back to bed.'

'Why is Pete here? Where's Dad?'

'How the hell do I know? Your precious father has buggered off. He's left us in the shit . . . and I . . . I ain't even got the money to bury your gran.' And on those words Lily broke down again, tears flooding her eyes. Mavis ran forward, but Lily pushed her away, once again burying her face in her hands.

'Mavis, your mum's in a state. Why don't you go back to bed?' Pete urged. 'I'll look after her.'

'But . . . but, where's my dad?'

'I dunno, pet, but don't worry, I'm sure he'll turn up soon.'

Lily was so wrapped up in her own grief that their words washed over her, yet she was dimly aware that Mavis was crying as Pete cajoled her back to bed. He was over by the sink now, filling the kettle before putting it on the gas ring to boil. She dashed the tears from her face, finding her voice croaky as she said, 'There . . . there's only a bit of tea left. I . . . I was saving it for the morning.'

'You need a cuppa now.'

Lily didn't argue. In truth her throat was parched, but when she saw Pete about to empty the pot, she sat bolt upright in her chair. 'No, no, don't do that. Just pour boiling water over the old tea and it'll be fine.'

Pete came over to crouch in front of her. 'It's all right, Lily. Don't worry. I'll buy more tea in the morning, and you can stop worrying about your mother's funeral too. I'll pay for it, love.'

'No, Pete, it's good of you to offer, but I can't let you do that.'

'Don't be daft, of course you can. Look, if it makes you feel better, we'll call it a loan.'

Lily shook her head. 'Pete, it would be years before I could pay you back . . . if ever.'

'So what, I ain't going anywhere. One stint out of London was enough and from now on any work I take on will be local. Now no more arguments,' he said, holding up a hand as though to cut off any further protest. 'I'm paying for the funeral and that's that.'

'Oh, Pete,' Lily cried, her gratitude at his kindness overwhelming her as she leaned forward to hug him.

'Steady on, Lily. You'll have me over,' he protested, but then his arms enfolded her too.

Lily clung to Pete as if he were a life raft, but then the kettle whistled and he gently pushed her away. 'Right, girl, let's make that tea.'

Lily managed a wan smile, but her eyes were still watery with gratitude. Somehow she'd find a way to pay him back, but for now at least she knew that her mother would be able to have a decent funeral.

Mavis lay in bed, able only to hear the murmur of voices from below. *Oh, Dad, where are you? What happened to you? Please come back! Please don't leave me! Gran's gone, now you've gone too. Oh . . . Dad.* Tossing and turning, Mavis tried to cling on to Pete's words. He said her dad was sure to turn up soon, and surely he was right? Her father wouldn't just go off. He wouldn't disappear without a word. Something must have happened to him – an accident, or maybe he was ill! Perhaps that was why he hadn't sent any money. She wanted to run downstairs again, to ask more questions, to find out what had really happened.

The drone of voices had stopped. She hadn't heard the front door closing, but maybe Pete had left now. Mavis flung back the blankets and stealthily crept downstairs. If her mother was alone now, surely she would talk to her?

Mavis reached the threshold of the kitchen, her eyes widening and a hand involuntarily covering her mouth in horror. Her mother and Pete were standing in the middle of the room, wrapped in each other's arms, oblivious to Mavis as their lips met. 'Oh, no . . . no,' she gasped.

They jumped apart like scalded cats, but Mavis had already turned to flee back upstairs. 'Mavis . . .

wait . . . it's not what you think,' she heard her mother shout, but ignored the words as she dived into her bedroom, slamming the door behind her.

Her mother and Pete! So that was it! That was why her father had gone off without a word. Oh, to think she had hated him – hated that he hadn't sent her mother any money. *I'm sorry, Dad,* she inwardly cried, *but come back for me. Please come back for me!*

'Don't worry, Lily. Once you've explained things to Mavis, I'm sure she'll understand,' Pete said as Lily showed him out.

'I'm sorry, Pete. I don't know what came over me.'

'You were upset, looking for a bit of comfort, that's all.'

'Yeah, I suppose so.'

'Why don't you leave it for now – let Mavis sleep. I'll come round again in the morning and if she won't listen to you, maybe she'll listen to me.'

'Thanks, Pete, but you know what Mavis is like. Getting through to her may not be easy. Anyway, thanks for being so understanding. Another man might have, well, you know, taken advantage.'

'I wouldn't do that, Lily. Goodnight, love, and try to get some sleep too.'

Lily nodded, and as she closed the door behind Pete, a wave of exhaustion had her reeling. Yes, she'd go to bed. Talk to Mavis in the morning, but if the daft cow thought there was anything between her and Pete, she must be out of her tiny mind. She had just turned to him for comfort – that was all.

As Pete walked along the road, his thoughts were on Lily and how it felt to hold her in his arms. He had never seen her cry before, her outer demeanour usually hard, but on this occasion Lily had looked so vulnerable that he'd been unable to resist when she'd lifted her lips to kiss him. He'd said that he wouldn't have taken advantage of her in that fragile state, but if Mavis hadn't appeared he doubted that he could have held himself in check. Lily Jackson was enough to tempt any man, and in truth he'd fancied her for years, envying Ron his gorgeous wife.

Of course, Lily had just clung to him – any port in a storm, as the saying went. She wouldn't be interested in an ugly bugger like him, and he didn't blame her, but he'd treasure the memory of that one, wonderful kiss.

Where the hell was Ron? Why wasn't he there when Lily needed him? Yet in reality the man didn't know that Lily's mother had died. If he did, surely he'd come home?

Pete walked on, knowing that all he could do was to put the word out and hope that Ron got to hear it. In the meantime he'd keep an eye on Lily, make sure she didn't go short, and try to be there if she needed him.

The man that Pete was thinking about was working on a building site in Southampton. His initial anger had soon worn off, but he'd been too ashamed to go back to the hut, or to go home, unable to bear the thought of facing Pete, or Lily. He'd let them down again, but after thumbing a lift with a lorry driver heading for Hampshire, he'd decided that the only chance he had was to show them – show both of them that he wasn't a lost cause. He'd find a job, save up, and when his pockets were full of money he'd go home loaded. If he did that, Lily was sure to welcome him back.

It had been easy enough to find work on a building site, though he was only labouring, and the foreman had taken pity on him, agreeing to let him kip in the hut until he sorted out a room.

Ron felt a wave of desolation. All his big ideas had been blown with his first wage packet. He'd lost the money, gambled it away, and, sure that his luck was about to change, he'd continued to do so for the next couple of weeks. He'd borrowed from the other blokes on site, but they'd got wise to him and now wouldn't even loan him the price of a meal.

The foreman was approaching and Ron quickly

set to work, his head down as he shovelled cement into the mixer. God, he was hungry, weak, and it took all his effort to lift the shovel.

'Jackson, I want a word.'

'Yeah, what about?'

'You've been dossing in the hut for three weeks now, time enough to sort yourself out. Make tonight the last one.'

'Have a heart, mate,' Ron appealed. 'Give me a bit more time.'

'I can't do that.'

'Can't, or won't?' Ron snapped.

'Don't push me, Jackson,' the foreman retorted.

All the anger he felt at himself, all his self-disgust, was now transferred to the foreman. 'Fuck you. Stick your job,' Ron yelled as he threw down the shovel and stormed off.

Boots caked in mud, Ron swiftly left the site, but as his temper cooled, and with nowhere to go, he began to walk aimlessly, his mind twisting and turning. He'd blown the job now, blown everything, and as he continued to ramble with no sense of direction, at last Ron faced the truth. He was an addicted gambler, unable to get it out of his system, and doubted he ever could.

When he passed a café, hunger drove Ron down the side alley to the dustbins, and after rummaging inside one he found a pie. It tasted like nectar as he stuffed it down, but then he felt a wave of disgust.

He had sunk to this, digging in dustbins like a tramp to find food.

Ron eventually found himself at the harbour, and finding a wall he sat down, absently watching the bustling activity as his thoughts turned to his wife. Lily was a diamond, had given him chance after chance, but all he did was let her down. The urge to go home was strong, pulling at him, but as he pictured the recriminations, Ron knew he couldn't face her.

Cargo was being loaded onto a freighter and Ron's eyes raised to follow its course. He continued to sit there, swamped with depression, until finally he came to a decision. Lily deserved better. He was no good to her and never would be. There was only one thing he could do. He'd make enquiries about signing up on a merchant vessel. He'd leave these shores and maybe never return.

CHAPTER FOURTEEN

On her sixteenth birthday, Saturday, 26th of March, 1955, Mavis anxiously looked out for the postman; but when he passed the door without stopping, she wondered if she would ever see her father again. Sadly she turned away from the window to find her mother's eyes on her and said, 'He . . . he didn't even send me a card.'

'Yeah, well, after all this time without a word, I ain't surprised.'

Mavis voiced her fears, ones that continued to plague her. 'Mum, you don't think that he . . . he's dead?'

'Now look, I've told you before. If anything had happened to him we'd have heard about it.'

'But it's been over nine months now.'

'He'll turn up one day. Bad pennies always do.' There was a rap on the letterbox, her mother then saying, 'That'll be Pete. Let him in, Mavis.'

Tight-lipped, Mavis did as she was told and

opened the door to find a parcel shoved into her hands as she did so.

'Happy birthday,' Pete said as he stepped inside.

'Say thank you,' Lily snapped.

Mavis ground out her thanks. A couple of evenings a week, and every weekend, Pete turned up, and though her mother continued to insist that they were just friends, Mavis still had her doubts. Since that first time, she hadn't seen them kissing again but she hated the way Pete made himself at home, sitting by the fire in her father's chair, shoes off and his feet on the fender. She couldn't make sense of her dad's disappearance and still felt that Pete had something to do with it. When her dad came home he'd sort Pete out, but in the meantime Mavis avoided talking to him, and though it made her mother angry, Mavis was determined not to give in.

'Well, open your present,' Lily demanded.

Reluctantly Mavis unwrapped the parcel, fighting to hide her pleasure when she pulled out a lovely, blue cardigan. It was so soft, fluffy and, despite her feelings, Mavis was unable to resist trying it on.

'My, my, just look at you,' Pete enthused. 'You've blossomed, Mavis, and look so grown up now.'

'Yeah, it looks nice,' Lily agreed, 'but it must have cost you a good few bob. You shouldn't have spent so much, Pete.'

'Leave it out, Lily. I had to get my girl something special for her sixteenth birthday.'

Mavis stiffened. His girl! No, no, her dad called her that. She was *his* girl, not Pete's. Unthinkingly she grabbed her coat, managing to splutter before dashing out, 'I . . . I'd best get round to Mrs Pugh's.'

It was early for Mavis to go to work, but Lily didn't have a chance to protest as the door slammed shut behind her daughter.

'Blimey, what was that all about?' Pete asked. 'She ran out like a scalded cat. Was it something I said?'

Lily shook her head, unwilling to upset this man who had become her friend and companion for all these months. 'No, don't worry. I think she was just a bit overwhelmed with her present, that's all. Mind you, I still think you spent too much.'

'Mavis deserves it, Lily. With the hours she works, it's nice to give her a little treat. After all, she doesn't get much.'

'Is that a dig at me?'

'Of course not. I know you have to take her wages, but maybe it's a bit hard on her.'

'Why? I feed her, clothe her, so what else does she need?'

'Yeah, I suppose you're right, but as you can only afford second-hand gear I thought she'd love something new for a change.'

'You *are* having a dig at me!'

'I'm not, Lily. I just wish you'd let me help out a little bit more.'

'No, Pete. I've told you time and time again that it wouldn't be fair. We ain't your responsibility.'

'I wish you were,' he blurted out, colour then flooding his cheeks. 'Oh, shit, Lily. I didn't mean to say that.'

Lily found herself pink-cheeked too. Pete was nothing like Ron in looks, but she'd grown used to his face, no longer finding it so ugly. He had a lovely smile, and nice eyes, but it was his person-ality that had slowly begun to attract her. She wasn't a fool, knew that he fancied her, and as her frustration grew he'd become more and more of a temptation.

Lily kept her head down, too embarrassed to look at Pete. At first she'd only felt anger towards Ron and every day had expected him to turn up. When he didn't, she'd reported him missing to the police, her anger replaced by worry as she tossed and turned every night, praying he was safe. Now though, as she'd told Mavis, she had come to realise that if anything bad had happened to Ron, they'd have been informed.

'Lily, I can see I've upset you. Please, forget I said anything.'

Slowly Lily lifted her head again to meet his eyes. 'You haven't upset me. I . . . I like you too.'

Pete's eyes widened with amazement. 'You . . . you do?'

'Yes, but I feel like my life is on hold. I can't move forward, I'm stuck, waiting for Ron to show his face.'

'Lily, you've done all you can to find him. I understand that you feel your life is on hold, but he may never turn up. How long are you prepared to wait?'

'I dunno, Pete. I wish I did. Mind you, if he does come home I don't think I'll ever be able to forgive him for putting me through this.'

'Yeah, he's my mate – at least he was – but I could kill him for doing this to you, and to Mavis.'

Lily smiled. 'I wouldn't want you to go that far.'

Once again, Pete's face reddened as shyly he said, 'Lily, if I've got a chance with you, I'm prepared to wait, for as long as it takes.'

'Oh, Pete,' Lily said as she looked at this man, one who had been so good to her since Ron had disappeared. He'd not only paid for her mother's funeral, but since then, despite her protesting, he'd never failed to turn up without something for the cupboard, along with a joint for Sundays, which she'd insisted that he share. She knew the neighbours were talking and hated it, making sure that at least Kate knew that she and Pete were just friends. When he left she made a great show of calling goodbye before loudly closing the door, but despite that she suspected the gossips were still at it. With her conscience clear, she could still look them in the eye, and would continue to do so. No matter what she felt for Pete, no matter how frustrated, she was still a married woman. 'I can't expect you to wait. It wouldn't be fair.'

'I don't mind.'

'You may not be saying that if another eight months passes.'

'Lily, you're worth waiting for, and I'd happily take on Mavis too.'

'You're right about her. She is blossoming and hardly a child now,' Lily said, smiling fondly at Pete. Mavis had been working for Mrs Pugh for a year now, and, as the woman had predicted, she had taught the girl a lot. The coat she had once given Mavis had been too big for her at first, but now she was filling it out, and since working for the woman her daughter had become almost fastidious with cleanliness. She washed from top to toe almost every day, and how she had managed that in the outhouse during the cold winter months was beyond Lily. Still, with the house cleaning experience she'd gained, another job had come in, then another, both in Chelsea. Mavis now worked six hours a day, and at weekends she still did another two for Mrs Pugh. Mavis was earning a fair bit of money, and Lily didn't know what she'd do without it.

'Lily, I know I said I'd wait,' Pete said, snapping Lily out of her thoughts, 'but surely there's no harm in a cuddle?'

No, there isn't, she decided, and rising to her feet Lily stepped into Pete's arms. It felt wonderful to be held, to feel his muscular body against hers. She pressed against him, aroused by the touch of a man after so long, but then gasping she pulled away. 'No, no, we mustn't.'

'It's all right, Lily, I just want to hold you. I won't let it go any further.'

She sank back into his arms again. She was still married to Ron, yet the temptation was so strong, her need so great that Lily wondered how much longer she could hold out before she allowed Pete to give her the comfort she craved.

'Mavis, you're early,' Alec Pugh said as he stood aside to let her in.

'I'm sorry. I hope your mother won't mind,' she said, taking off her coat.

Alec's eyes widened. Mavis looked lovely, the blue of her cardigan deepening the blue of her eyes, and dark, shiny hair framing her face. She no longer looked like the scruffy and dirty waif who had first come to work for his mother, but when had she changed? Why hadn't he noticed?

'Er . . . er, I'm sure Mother won't mind,' he said, feeling suddenly tongue-tied. 'She's in the living room. Go on through.'

Alec followed Mavis, to hear his mother say, 'Mavis, how pretty you look. Happy birthday, my dear, and here, I've got something for you.'

'Oh, you shouldn't have.'

Alec couldn't take his eyes off of Mavis. It was as though he was seeing her for the first time; the gentle curve of her cheek, full lips, and her pretty white teeth when she smiled.

'Go on, Mavis, open it,' he heard his mother urge. 'It's from both Alec and I.'

This was news to Alec. He'd had no idea it was Mavis's birthday, but he watched as she unwrapped the gift.

There was a small gasp of pleasure as Mavis held up the necklace. Alec frowned. Surely it was one of his mother's? The aquamarine stone in the small pendant looked familiar, and wasn't the chain gold?

'Mrs Pugh, I can't take this,' Mavis protested.

'Nonsense, of course you can. You've come a long way, Mavis, and it's no more than you deserve. Now come on, put it on and let's see how it looks.'

Mavis's fingers trembled as she unfastened the tiny clasp, and when she put the chain around her neck, fumbling, Alec found his eyes widening again, astounded at his mother's words.

'Alec, don't just stand there. Give Mavis a hand.'

Shyly he moved forward and as Mavis lifted the back of her hair, he found himself transfixed by the sight of her long, white neck. His hands shook, but at last he managed to fasten the chain, hoping that Mavis had been unaware of his nerves.

'It looks lovely on you, Mavis. Don't you think so, Alec?'

'Er . . . yes, very nice.'

Mavis spun round, her eyes sparkling. 'Oh, thank you, thank you both so much.'

'You're welcome, my dear. I have another surprise too. I managed to ice the fruit cake you made yesterday, and after you've finished work I'd like to ask you to join us for a birthday lunch.'

'Me . . . you're asking me to lunch!'

'Yes, that's if you haven't got to rush off?'

'No, no, I haven't.'

'Good, and now we've sorted that out, I think I'd like a nice cup of coffee. Mavis, would you mind making it, and Alec, you can give her a hand.'

'It's all right, I can manage,' Mavis protested.

'I know you can, but Alec can carry the tray through.'

Mavis left the room without further protest and Alec followed. His mother usually advised him to avoid girls like the plague, so what the hell was she up to? Perhaps she still saw Mavis as a child, had been blind to the gentle swell of her breasts, but Alec certainly wasn't. Mavis was sixteen now, old enough, but if his mother saw that he was interested in her, she'd get rid of her like a shot.

Mavis was pink-cheeked as Alec stood watching while she made the coffee. When she came to Mrs Pugh's during the week, he wasn't there, and even at weekends she saw little of him. In fact, until now he'd hardly spared her a glance, and, feeling uncomfortable under his scrutiny, she wished it had stayed that way. She would never forget her first encounter with Alec. It had been over a year ago and she'd still been at school. He had made her feel like dirt, but recalling how dreadful she must have looked maybe it wasn't surprising. Mavis loved working for Mrs Pugh and had been taught so much, not only about cleaning, but personal hygiene too. She wondered if Alec knew that his mother allowed her to take a bath every week. When it came to housework, at first she'd thought that Mrs Pugh's standards were excessive, but her lessons had served to make sure that the other women she worked for had no room for complaint.

'It . . . it's ready if you'd like to take it through,' she stammered.

'Aren't you having one?'

'Me? No, I've got cleaning to do and had better make a start.'

'Surely as you're early, there's no rush?'

'Well, no, I suppose not, but I'd rather get on with it.'

'Please yourself,' he said rather curtly as he picked up the tray to take through to his mother.

When Alec left the kitchen, Mavis breathed a sigh of relief. Yes, he had made her feel uncomfortable, even more so when his eyes had continuously strayed to her breasts.

She had just begun to relax when Alec came back in again, saying, 'Mavis, my mother insists that you join her for coffee.'

'Oh . . . oh, right,' she said. 'I'll just get another cup.'

When they returned to the living room, Edith Pugh said, 'There you are, Mavis. Do sit down, my dear, and, Alec, pour the coffee.'

He did as he was asked, and Mavis was surprised to see how his hands shook as he handed her a cup. 'Thank you.'

'Alec has just been promoted, Mavis. Isn't that wonderful?'

'Er . . . yes.'

'Of course, I'm not surprised. He works in the accounts department at Tate & Lyle and is very well thought of.'

Surprised, Mavis looked at Alec. 'You're . . . you're an accountant?'

'No, I'm just a wages clerk.'

'Yes, but it's a very important position,' his mother insisted.

Alec drank the last of his coffee and then stood up. 'Right, Mum, I'll go and get your prescription now.'

'Thank you, darling.'

Mavis too stood up. 'I'll get on with the bedrooms.'

'No, sit down, Mavis. There's no hurry and we may as well finish this pot of coffee.'

'See you later,' Alec called as he left the room.

'Do pour us both another cup,' Edith Pugh urged, 'and then you can tell me why you looked so upset when you first arrived. Don't look so surprised. I know you tried to hide it, but I'm not blind, you know.'

'It . . . it's just that my father didn't send me a birthday card.'

'Oh, dear, no wonder you're upset.'

When her father had first gone missing and her mother had been so angry that she refused to talk about it, Mavis found herself confiding in Mrs Pugh. She had been so kind, and until now Mavis had clung to her assurances that eventually he'd come home. 'I don't think my father will ever come back.'

'Don't give up, Mavis. Now come on, cheer up

and tell me, did your mother buy you that pretty cardigan?'

'No, it was Pete, my dad's friend. He's always round our place now.' And unable to stop, Mavis blurted, 'He . . . he sits in my dad's chair, and today he called me his girl. I ain't his girl, Mrs Pugh. I ain't.'

'Mavis, I know you're upset and it's understandable, but don't forget your diction. Ain't sounds so common.'

'Yes, yes, sorry,' Mavis mumbled. She knew Mrs Pugh found her diction grating and did her best to speak nicely in front of her.

'Oh, Mavis, I can see I've upset you. And on your birthday too.'

'No, no, it isn't you. It . . . it's just that Pete seems to be taking my dad's place.'

'He could never do that, my dear. But tell me, you said he's always at your house. Does he sleep there too?'

'Oh, no. He comes round a couple of evenings a week, and every weekend, but he doesn't stay.'

'And it upsets you to see him?'

Mavis had seen the way her mother sometimes looked at Pete, and he at her, but was unable to articulate her fears, just mumbling, 'Yes.'

'Well, then, when he's at your house, why don't you come round here? You'd be very welcome.'

'Really?'

'Yes, really,' Edith Pugh said. 'Come again this evening. Alec is usually busy with his hobbies and it would be nice to have your company. There is so much I'd still like to teach you and it would be the ideal opportunity.'

Mavis was thrilled. She enjoyed being with Mrs Pugh, loved her house, and once again it felt as though she'd found a refuge. 'I . . . I'd love that.'

'Right, that's settled then. Time to get on with some work, and, after you've done the bedrooms, you can help me to make the sandwiches for lunch.'

Smiling now, Mavis went upstairs to the already immaculate bedrooms. She took clean linen from the landing closet, and then stripped off Alec's bed. They had clean linen every week, and to Mavis this was sheer luxury. How lucky Alec was. He lived in this house with its inside lavatory and bathroom, but most of all, he had a wonderful mother.

Edith was smiling. It was as though the gods were on her side. She had been in dread of Alec bringing a girl home, one who might be strong-minded and, if they married, would want a home of her own. Or one who, even if she agreed to live here, would want to take over and do things her own way. No, no, Edith didn't want that. After all, she told herself, Alec was fastidious, used to her standards, and he'd be dreadfully unhappy if he married a slovenly girl.

Edith had long decided that, unbeknownst to Alec, she would find him a suitable wife, but had been on tenterhooks, worrying that in the meantime he would find someone that she didn't approve of.

Edith smiled again. Her worries were over now. In Mavis, as hoped, she had found the ideal candidate. Mavis was lonely, shy, with no friends of her own age and that was just what Edith wanted. Not only that, Mavis was pretty presentable now, and as planned, from the look on Alec's face today, he had at last noticed her. Yes, she was still only sixteen, but that suited Edith just fine. Mavis was still so innocent, so unspoiled and malleable, the perfect choice.

When Mavis and Alec married, there'd be no question of them finding a home of their own. No, they would continue to live here, and Edith would remain in control, ensuring that as her multiple sclerosis worsened she'd have someone to look after her, and her son would have a perfectly biddable wife.

Of course, Edith knew that she daren't rush things. After all, she didn't want to frighten Mavis off, but with the girl calling round more often, surely things would move along nicely.

CHAPTER FIFTEEN

'Where the bloody hell have you been?' Lily snapped as her daughter walked in the door.

'Mrs Pugh invited me to stay on for a birthday lunch. She even iced a cake for me with candles on it too.'

'So you just decided to stay.'

'Well . . . yes.'

'How many times have I told you to come straight home after work? You should have been back by midday, but instead stroll in here at four. Didn't it occur to you that I might be worried about you?'

'I'm sorry, Mum. I didn't think.'

'If you had half a brain you'd have more sense.'

'Lily, she's home now,' Pete placated.

'I should give her a bloody good hiding.'

'There's no need for that. There's no harm done and I'm sure Mavis won't do it again.' And as his

165

eyes flicked to Mavis he added gently, 'Ain't that right, love?'

Mavis didn't answer him and Lily bristled with anger. She was fed up with the way her daughter behaved around Pete, maintaining a surly attitude towards the man who showed her nothing but kindness. She'd spoken to Mavis time and time again, told her it had to stop, but nothing worked. She had always been obedient, doing as she was told without argument, but when it came to Pete her daughter continually defied her and Lily had had enough. 'Pete asked you a question! Answer it.'

Mavis hung her head, saying nothing, and Lily surged to her feet. She marched up to her daughter and, as Mavis looked up, Lily swung her hand to slap her full across the face. 'Get out of my sight!' she spat. 'Go to your room and don't come down until you're ready to apologise.'

Holding her cheek, Mavis fled, running upstairs and out of sight as Pete said, 'Lily, you shouldn't have done that. It'll only make things worse.'

'She deserved it.'

'She's still pining for her dad, and probably thinks I'm trying to take his place. Maybe it would help if I didn't come round so often.'

'No, Pete, I'm not going to let Mavis drive you out. It's up to me who comes to my house, not her.'

'All right, but let me talk to her. It might help.'

'Go ahead, but she ain't coming down here unless you get an apology.'

Mavis heard a soft knock on her door, and when it opened Pete stuck his head inside. She turned her back towards him, curling into a ball.

'Mavis, can I come in?'

She didn't answer him.

'Mavis, listen. I know you miss your dad, but, honestly, I'm not trying to step into his shoes. I know I couldn't do that, but I care about your mum, and you. I'm just trying to look after the pair of you, that's all.'

Mavis still said nothing and heard his heavy sigh, but when he began to talk again, she just wanted to drown out the sound of his voice.

'Come on, Mavis, this can't go on. It's making your mum unhappy and she's got enough on her plate as it is. I told her I'd come round less often, but she doesn't want that. She's lonely, Mavis, and misses your dad too. For her sake, can't we at least call a truce?'

When Pete's hand came out to touch her shoulder, Mavis shrugged it off. 'Le . . . leave me alone.'

Pete's voice hardened. 'All right, please your-self, but this is your mother's house and, as she said, it's up to her who comes into it. She wants me here, so I won't be staying away. It's up to you, Mavis. You can make an effort to at least be civil to me, or you can carry on like this and be sent to your room every time I show my face.'

Or she could go round to Mrs Pugh's, Mavis thought, but then realised that Pete was right. If she wasn't nice to him, instead of being allowed to go out, she'd be made to stay up here.

'Well, Mavis, what's it to be? Can I tell your mother you've apologised?'

With no other choice, Mavis nodded her head. 'Yes.'

'Good girl, now come on, come downstairs.'

When they walked into the kitchen, Pete said, 'It's all right, Lily. Me and Mavis had a little talk and everything's all right now.'

'It better be, my girl,' Lily warned.

'I . . . I'm sorry, Mum,' Mavis said, forcing a contrite expression.

'I should think so too.'

'I tell you what,' Pete suggested. 'After all this upset, I think we could do with a little treat. It's still Mavis's birthday, so how about I pop out to get fish and chips for our dinner?'

'You don't have to do that. I can cook something.'

'No, I insist. What do you fancy, Lily, a bit of cod or maybe haddock?'

'All right then. Cod please, and a pickled onion.'

'What about you, Mavis?' Pete asked.

She forced a smile. 'The same, please.'

'Right, cod and chips all round. I won't be long,' he said, throwing his overcoat on before hurrying outside.

'Right, Mavis. Now that Pete's gone you can tell me what he said to bring about this sudden change.'

'He . . . he said that he isn't trying to take dad's place.'

'That's right, he ain't. He's just being a good friend and I ain't having you being rude to him again. Is that understood?'

'Yes, Mum,' Mavis said, hating that she had to do this. If she was nice to Pete, it would feel like she was being disloyal to her dad, but once again she knew there was no other choice.

'Good, now get the plates out and lay the table for when Pete comes back.'

This was something her mother would never have allowed a year ago, but thanks to Mrs Pugh Mavis was confident now when it came to handling china. She'd been told to do things slowly, to make sure that everything was gripped firmly and it had made such a difference. Of course, unlike Mrs Pugh, her mother didn't have fine porcelain, but she still carried the thick white plates carefully to the table.

It wasn't long before Pete returned, smiling as he put the newspaper-wrapped packages on the table.

'There you go, fish and chips for my two lovely girls.'

'Girl . . . me? No, I don't think so, Pete.'

'Leave it out, Lily. You're still a spring chicken.'

Mavis was fighting to hide her feelings. She wasn't his girl, would never be his girl, and hated the silly little smile on her mother's face when she looked at Pete. Somehow she sat at the table to eat the food that tasted like sawdust in her mouth, and when Pete asked her if she was enjoying it she managed to say, 'Yes, it's lovely, thanks.'

'Shame we didn't think about a cake, Lily.'

'She did all right with your cardigan and I let her keep a few bob out of her wages.'

'Mum, when I've finished my dinner, can I go out again?'

'Out! Where?'

'To see Mrs Pugh.'

'What on earth for?'

'She . . . she invited me, said there's more she'd like to teach me.'

'Oh, yeah, like what?'

'I dunno, but can I go, Mum?'

'I don't suppose it would do any harm, but I want you home by ten and not a minute later.'

'Yeah,' Pete agreed, 'we don't want you out on the streets any later than that.'

Mavis pushed her plate to one side. 'Can I go now, Mum?'

'You ain't finished your dinner.'

'I can't eat any more. It was a large portion and I'm full up.'

'All right, but don't be late, or else.'

She grabbed her coat, called goodbye, and dashed out, thinking about Pete's last words: *we* don't want her on the streets – not *your mother* doesn't want you on the streets. To Mavis it proved that, no matter what he said, he *was* trying to step into her father's shoes.

Tommy Wilson turned the corner and saw Mavis Jackson walking towards him, but with her head down she hadn't yet seen him. It had been over a year since they had both left school and in that time Tommy had seen the transformation. In fact, Mavis now looked flipping gorgeous. She had turned from a gangly schoolgirl into a right looker, but since that last encounter when he'd smashed up her painting he'd kept out of her way. She might be a bit dumb but he'd never forgotten the look on her face, the anguish, and he was still racked with guilt. Yes, he'd been angry that she'd blabbed, but he wasn't a silly kid now and knew that he and Larry had deserved the rollicking they got.

Mavis looked up, saw him, paled and stopped in her tracks.

'It's all right, Mavis, I ain't gonna hurt you.'

Her eyes flicked to the other side of the road

and Tommy guessed she was going to bolt, so said quickly, 'I've kept out of your way, you must have seen that, but, well, it's about time I said I'm sorry.'

'S . . . sorry?'

'Yes, for smashing up your painting. I know it was a long time ago, but I shouldn't have done it.'

'It . . . it was a portrait of my gran, but . . . but she's dead now.'

'I know, I heard, and I'm sorry. Have you done another one?'

'No, I don't paint any more.'

'That's a shame. I know I took the mick out of it, but it was good.'

'Th . . . thanks.'

Now that he was this close, Tommy couldn't take his eyes off Mavis and wanted to prolong the encounter. 'I'm an apprentice signwriter and, as it needs a bit of an artistic eye, we have something in common. Well, maybe not the writing, but the artistic bit.'

Mavis moved to step around him, saying curtly, 'I've got to go, but thanks for the apology.'

Tommy could have kicked himself. Signwriting, what an idiot! It must have sounded like he was having a dig, but he hadn't meant it like that. It was odd really, Mavis didn't sound daft, or look daft, but he hadn't really noticed that before. She'd just been Dumbo, and that was all he'd seen, a girl to make fun of; but somehow he suspected there was more to Mavis Jackson than met the eye. Not that he was interested in her, of course. Mavis might be a bit tasty, but his mates would take the piss out of him if he took out a girl who was known to be loopy. Not only that, his mother would have a fit. At the moment he had his eyes on a girl who worked on the make-up counter in Woolworths. Next week he was determined to ask her out.

Mavis was thinking about Tommy too. She hadn't had to worry about Larry Barnet for some time now, not since he and his family had moved away, and she had to admit that it was true – Tommy had kept out of her way. Until now. She had still been scared when she saw him, but it had been unfounded. It was nice of Tommy to apologise, but then he had spoiled it with that dig about signwriting.

She picked up her pace, looking forward to going to Ellington Avenue. Mrs Pugh was the only one who didn't treat her like an idiot, and when she was with her Mavis felt her confidence growing – but then, as always, her mother, and now Tommy Wilson, shot it down again. Oh, if only she could show them. Show them that she wasn't daft – but on that thought, Mavis saddened. She couldn't read or write, so she must be.

When she arrived at Mrs Pugh's, it was Alec

who opened the door, his smile warm. 'Mavis, come on in. My mother said you might call in to see her again.'

She took off her coat, hung it in the hall closet, and then followed Alec into the sitting room. 'Hello, Mrs Pugh.'

'Mavis, how lovely to see you. I was hoping you'd accept my invitation. Sit down, my dear. As my son is busy with his stamp collection I can hardly get a word out of him, so you're a welcome sight. Alec, if I can drag you away from your albums for five minutes, why don't you make us all a drink?'

'I'll do it,' Mavis offered.

'No, sit down, Mavis. While Alec is making the drinks, there's something I want to talk to you about. I had intended to wait until I had gathered all the facts I can, but I think you need something to cheer you up.'

Mavis sat on the sofa, and echoed Mrs Pugh's words, 'Cheer me up?'

'As I've mentioned before, I can always tell when you're unhappy, and as you accepted my invitation to come here, it must be because that man is still in your home. Am I right?'

'Yes, he's still there.'

'I thought so, but listen, Mavis. I've been looking into the problems that a minority of school children have with reading and writing. It's amazing what you can find in the library, and I think I've discovered something. For instance, in 1896, a Dr Pringle Morgan wrote a paper about congenital word blindness.'

'Word blindness. What's that?'

'It's a medical condition. I think it may be the root of your problem and why you can't read and write.'

Excited, Mavis asked, 'If . . . if it's medical, can it be cured?'

'Not that I know of, but I'm sure further research is being done. I did find reference to an American man, Samuel Orton, who wrote a text in 1937 about what he called a specific reading disability. He advocates certain teaching methods, so you see, my dear, perhaps with a lot of patience and hard work, I'll be able to teach you to read.'

Mavis gasped, unable to believe her ears. 'Me! Read!'

'Yes, but as I said, it may take some time. You'll probably have to spend at least two evenings a week with me, as well as a few extra hours each weekend.'

'I don't mind, in fact, I'd love it. Oh, Mrs Pugh, this is like a dream come true! I've always been called stupid, or slow. If I can learn to read it'll show that I'm not. I . . . I don't know how to thank you.'

'There's no need, Mavis. I'll enjoy the challenge.'

'What challenge?' Alec said as he walked in carrying a tray.

'Your mother's going to teach me to read,' Mavis blurted out, so happy that she wanted to share this wonderful news with the world.

'I'm going to try,' Edith corrected.

Alec frowned. 'But I thought . . .'

'Yes, I know what you thought, but I've always suspected that Mavis is bright, more so since she's been working for me. I've been looking into the subject and, though it will take some time, hopefully we'll get there.'

'This is all very commendable, Mother, but are you sure you're up to it? You need to rest and I don't want you wearing yourself out.'

'Alec, I'm not braindead, and don't want to be. It's my body that's letting me down. I need a challenge, something other than this illness to focus on.'

'Very well,' Alec said as he at last put the tray down. 'If this is what you want to do, that's fine. Anyway, when you get an idea into your head, there's no arguing with you.'

'Mavis, there's just one thing,' Edith then said. 'I'd rather that the three of us kept this to ourselves for the time being. I wouldn't want to raise your mother's hopes, only to dash them down again if these methods don't work.'

'Oh . . . but . . .'

Mavis found her words cut off as Edith Pugh interrupted her to say, 'Mavis, I insist. Think what a wonderful surprise it would be if one day you pick up a book or newspaper and begin to read out loud to your mother. Surely that would be better than the disappointment she'd face if this doesn't work?'

'Yes . . . yes, I suppose so.'

'Good girl, and also, if your mother knows what I'm trying to do, she's bound to want progress reports. I don't want that, because as I said it may take some time and the last thing you need is to feel under any pressure.'

Mavis took in Mrs Pugh's words, and had to agree that she was right. Oh, please let it work, she thought, anticipating the look on her mother's face if she could read. She'd see pride at last and, maybe, even love.

CHAPTER SIXTEEN

On Saturday Ron woke up bathed in sweat, but at least the delirium had passed. He smiled gratefully at Pat Higgins, the woman who all those months ago had come to his rescue, tending him then as she was now.

All his big ideas about boarding a ship and leaving these shores forever had come to nothing, just as everything he tried to do came to nothing. Mind you, on that occasion it hadn't been down to him. It had been down to a rotten pie, the one he'd found in a dustbin. He'd been fine at first, but by that night he'd been in agony, sweaty, shivering, sick, and chucking his guts out in an alley. Things were a bit foggy after that, but according to Pat she had found him lying in his own vomit, and with the help of another tom she had got him back to her flat.

'How are you feeling, love?' she asked now.

'A bit better, but I could do with a drink.'

'I don't think that's a good idea.'

'Come on, Pat, just one. Look at me hands, they're shaking and you know a drink will see me right.'

'Yeah, but just a small one for now.'

Ron watched eagerly as Pat crossed the room, immune now to the way she dressed and the make-up she plastered on her face. Yes, Pat was a tom, but one with a heart of gold and one who plied her trade every night to provide the alcohol they both craved. The only thing she wouldn't do was to give him money for gambling, but nowadays all Ron cared about was his next drink, and when Pat shoved a glass of whisky in his hand he downed it in one go. 'Thanks, love, but what happened last night? I can't remember a thing.'

'You had a go at one of me punters, that's what.'

'Did I? Bloody hell. Why did I do it? Was he being a bit rough?'

'No, he wasn't. Shit, Ron, how many times have I got to tell you this? Unless I call you, stay out of the way when I bring a punter back. In the state you were in you'd have been useless anyway and you're lucky he didn't deck you.'

'I'm sorry, Pat.'

'Not as sorry as me. He didn't pay.'

Ron knew how to placate Pat. He wasn't any good to her in bed, found an erection impossible these days, but that seemed to suit her just fine.

All she craved was a bit of affection, a cuddle without any strings attached. 'Come here, love.'

'Bugger off. You're not going to soft-soap me this time.'

'Come on, just a little cuddle.'

She scowled, but then, with a small shake of her head, climbed beside him on the bed. Ron wrapped his arms around her, his feelings of distaste long gone now, and stroking her hair he murmured, 'I'm a useless bastard, Pat, and I don't know what I'd do without you.'

'Nor do I, you daft bugger.'

Ron held her for a while, and like a child she snuggled into him. A wave of depression swamped him. Unlike his daughter, Pat wasn't a child. She was a woman in her forties. Yet Mavis wasn't a child now either. She was sixteen, and on her birthday he'd persuaded Pat to buy a card, which she then posted. It had assuaged his guilt, and thanks to Pat the rest of his daughter's birthday passed in a haze of alcohol. And it was whisky he craved again now. It drowned out his memories, helped him to forget his past, one that, unless he stopped drinking and pulled himself together, he could never return to. 'Pat, any chance of another drink?'

'Yeah, all right,' she said.

Pat climbed off the bed and once again Ron watched eagerly as she went across the room, this time returning with the bottle of whisky and two glasses. The measure she poured was large and Ron took the glass with a shaking hand, gulping the liquid gratefully.

He felt better shortly afterwards, mellow, and as Pat snuggled up to him again, he held her for a while, until she was ready to pour them both another drink.

Pat Higgins was smiling inwardly. She had come to love this tall, good-looking man who, unlike all the others, didn't want to use her body. At first, as Ron recovered from food poisoning, all he had talked about was his wife and kid, along with his dreams of making it big so he could go back to them. Pat didn't want that. Ron was different and she never wanted to let him go. All her life she had been abused by men. First by her father, and then, when she was taken into care, by a man in the children's home. Even in foster care she'd been abused, until finally she had run away, surviving on the streets by telling herself that this time it was her choice that the bastards were using her body, and that at least she was getting paid.

She'd done all right over the years, made enough money to rent this place, but had always felt that there was something missing in her life. It certainly wasn't sex. She'd had her fill of men, and when she'd found Ron in that alley, another tom had told her she was mad to take him back to her flat.

Pat knew she was right, but there was something about Ron's helplessness that drew her to take the chance.

Pat snuggled closer to Ron. At first she knew that he hated what she did for a living, but then she had opened up, told him about her past and had seen the horror on his face. She knew it had been an impulse, that he had been driven by pity when he had drawn her into his arms, and had expected the inevitable to happen. But it hadn't! He had just held her, comforted her, and for the first time in her life Pat had felt affection without any strings attached – felt that someone actually cared.

When Ron had fully recovered, she hadn't wanted him to leave, and as he had nowhere else to go, she'd persuaded him to stay. Pat knew he was depressed and it hadn't taken Ron long to become hooked on alcohol, in no fit state to find work, and dependent on her for his next drink.

Her face saddened. She wasn't a fool and knew that Ron didn't love her. It was just the alcohol that held him here, yet in truth she encouraged his need. She couldn't let him go, wouldn't go back to the loneliness she now knew had gripped her all her life.

'Pat, I can't stop thinking about my daughter. I hope she got my card.'

'Of course she did. Why wouldn't she?' Pat said,

knowing that the birthday card had never been posted.

'Maybe I should write to Lily again, you know, just to let her know that I'm all right.'

'Yeah, all right, I'll post it for you when I go out,' Pat said as she sat up to pour Ron another glass of whisky. A couple more and he'd forget about his wife and daughter as usual. If he did write a letter, it would go in the bin like previous ones. Ron was hers now and, as far as she was concerned, she'd make sure that his wife never heard from him again.

'Mavis, surely you're not going to Edith Pugh's again?' Lily asked. 'You were there cleaning this morning, so why go back now?'

'She's teaching me things.'

'Like what?'

Mavis bit her lip as though searching for an answer before saying, 'I can cook a complete dinner now, and do a pudding.'

'Oh, yeah,' Lily said doubtfully, 'well, I'd like to see that. You can cook ours today.'

'I can't. My cookery book is at her house.'

'Book! Since when could you read a book?'

'I can't,' Mavis said sharply. 'It's all done with drawings.'

Lily's eyebrows shot up. 'Oh, yeah, and where did you get this book?'

'I made it. It was Mrs Pugh's idea, and I've got lots of recipes now, cakes too.'

'I don't see how you can draw a recipe for making a cake.'

'It's easy. For instance, I draw cups for measurements. Two cups means two cups of flour, and for margarine I draw a block, with dotted lines on it to show me how much to use.'

'It sounds like a bloody good idea,' Pete said. 'That Edith Pugh must be a clever woman to have thought that up.'

'I'm off, Mum,' Mavis said. 'I'll be back in time for dinner.'

'Yeah, and don't be late,' Pete called.

With a curt nod, Mavis hurried out, and Lily sighed. Mavis had been a bit better with Pete for the past month, yet she still went out almost as soon as he arrived. There was a change in Mavis too, something Lily couldn't put her finger on. 'Pete, do you think Mavis is up to something?'

'Like what?'

'Oh, I dunno, but she ain't the same lately.'

'She's just growing up, love, and wants a bit more independence. You can't expect a sixteen-year-old to be stuck in here with us. She's just spreading her wings a bit, that's all.'

'Leave it out, Pete. She only goes round to see Edith Pugh and the woman's older than us.'

'Yeah, but don't forget that she's teaching her

things, and, if you don't mind me saying, I think Mavis is more intelligent than you give her credit for.'

'Why? Just because she can cook from drawings! Kids learn to read and write at infant or junior school, but not Mavis. Unlike the other pupils, she was too daft to pick it up.'

'Maybe it's her eyesight. Have you had it tested?'

'Pete, that was one of the first things they suggested at infant school, and yes, we had her eyes tested. They're fine. Now can we change the subject?'

'All right, but have you thought about Edith Pugh's son? Maybe that's who Mavis really goes to see.'

'Alec Pugh. You must be joking. Mavis doesn't like him, and from what I saw I don't blame her. He's a right stuck-up sod and he ain't much to look at either.'

'Nor am I, Lily. Let's face it – I can never compete with Ron.'

'You don't have to. You're a good man, kind and reliable, and that's what matters.'

'Yeah, if you say so, but women have never fancied me.'

'I do,' Lily said, and it was true. Pete may not be much to look at, but he had a wonderful muscular body and after so long she craved a man's touch.

'Don't say that, Lily. It makes it even harder. I know I said I'd wait, for however long it takes, but to be honest it's hell. If I saw less of you it might help.'

'Oh, no, Pete, don't stop coming round.'

'Until Ron shows his face, it's for the best, love. When he turns up and you tell him that it's over between you, I'll still be around, waiting.'

At that moment, Lily came to a decision. Ron might never turn up and she too was finding it harder and harder. Behind closed doors, the neighbours would never know, and she could still put on a front that Pete was just a friend.

She stood up, walked over to his chair to take his hand, saying softly, 'You don't have to wait any longer, Pete. Come on, let's go upstairs.'

CHAPTER SEVENTEEN

Mavis found her mind wandering as she made her way to Ellington Avenue. She wasn't sure when the dream had started, but it kept returning, and last night had been the same. There was a young man, reaching out for her, but she couldn't see his face. She wanted him to get to her, felt a deep yearning, but there was always a barrier, something or someone in his way. Who was he? Why couldn't she see his face? And why did he haunt her dreams?

Mavis shook off the image as she knocked on the door of Mrs Pugh's house. Alec opened it and smiled his usual welcome as he invited her in. She found him more relaxed now, less formal, and after her lesson he would often join them for an update on how things were going. Not that there was much to tell him. So far, despite all Mrs Pugh's patient efforts, Mavis found that she was still unable to make sense of the words that seemed to swirl on the page. She was beginning to despair, but Mrs Pugh always managed to pick her up, saying it was early days yet.

'Look,' Alec said, waving his newspaper as Mavis took off her coat. 'It's been nearly a month, but the Fleet Street maintenance workers have gone back to work.'

Mavis knew that both he and Mrs Pugh had missed their daily newspapers and smiled as she said, 'I bet your mother's pleased.'

'Yes, but let's hope they don't go on strike again. They still haven't come to an agreement about the two pounds a week wage increase they're demanding.'

'What does your mother say about it?'

'Oh, you know her. She's all for the unions, the rights of workers – there's no arguing with her.'

'Alec, I heard that,' a voice called.

They grinned at each other, then both walked into the living room. 'Well, Mother, there's nothing wrong with your ears,' Alec said, still smiling.

'No, there isn't. Now run along and leave us in peace.'

'Yes, Mother. After all, far be it from me to interfere with your protégée's lesson.'

'Don't sulk, Alec. It's only for an hour and then you can join us.'

Mavis frowned, wondering about Alec's curt remark, but as he left the room, Mrs Pugh spoke again.

'Don't take any notice of Alec. He seems to like your company nowadays and resents being chased out.'

'Likes my company?' Mavis squeaked.

'Alec knows now that he misjudged you at first. He's too much in my company and it makes a pleasant change for him when you're here. He likes you, my dear, very much, but as a pretty and intelligent girl, I'm not surprised. Now come on, it's time we got on with your lesson.'

Mavis was thrilled that Mrs Pugh had said she was intelligent, but wasn't sure what to make of her comments about Alec. It was nice to hear that he enjoyed her company, that he liked her, but was Mrs Pugh implying that there was something more to it than that? No, no, surely not? She liked Alec too, but not in *that* way. And surely he wasn't the young man who haunted her dreams?

Kate Truman was tight-lipped. It was early afternoon, but she'd lived next door to Lily Jackson for years and in that time, when she was upstairs, she'd come to recognise certain noises through the thin walls. Lily was always a bit loud, a passionate woman, something Kate envied. Her husband had never managed to raise the same passion in her, and their sex life was disappointing to say the least. Still, Bill was a good husband in other ways, and unlike Lily's old man he was hard-working and reliable.

Kate didn't consider herself a prude but, when all was said and done, Lily was a married woman. Huh, so much for Pete just being a friend. Of course, she'd had her suspicions, but Lily had been adamant that nothing was going on, and like a mug she'd believed her, even jumping to her defence when others in the street made sly comments.

With an angry huff, Kate stuffed the rest of the freshly ironed sheets into the cupboard and then marched downstairs, all her previous doubts about Lily that she'd shoved to one side coming to the fore as she stormed into the kitchen.

'Bill, you're never going to believe this, but Lily and her so-called friend have been at it like rabbits.'

Bill just shrugged, his eyes going back to his newspaper.

'Lily's a married woman and should be ashamed of herself.'

'As her old man did a runner about ten months ago, you can hardly blame her.'

'It's still adultery and not only that, what about Mavis?'

'What about her?'

'How's she going to feel about the way her mother's carrying on? It's hardly a lesson in morals, is it?'

'For Gawd's sake, Kate, get off your high horse.'

Kate ignored Bill's comment. 'Poor Mavis. Lily has used her like a workhorse for years, treating her like she's an imbecile and it ain't right.'

'She's backward, ain't she?'

'No, I don't think so, and I've been telling Lily so ever since Mavis was little.'

'She must know her own daughter.'

'Lily has never had any time for Mavis. Honestly, Bill, it's as if she's ashamed of the girl.'

'Kate, it's none of our business, now if you don't mind, I'm trying to read me newspaper.'

Her anger still raging, Kate snapped, 'You've been reading the bloody thing all day and must have read it back to front by now. Oh, sod you, I'm going across the road to see Olive Wilson.'

'Keep out of it,' Bill called, but once again Kate chose to ignore her husband as, fuelled by right-eous indignation, she hurried to Olive's house.

Lily had lied to her and there'd be no more jumping to her defence this time – instead she'd tell Olive just what her neighbour was up to.

By the time the weekend had passed, the gossip in Cullen Street had spread like wildfire. Lily wasn't aware of it until she went out on Monday morning, puzzled by the filthy look she got from Olive Wilson and the woman she was talking to on her doorstep.

Since her run-in with Olive and her son, Lily had ignored the woman, and did so now as she passed her. It had surprised her when Kate and Olive became friendly, especially as Tommy had tried it on with her daughter too, but that was Kate. When Jill Barnet's husband had been nicked for thieving, Kate had gone to offer her sympathies, and, of course, it got her first-hand news of what was going on that she could pass on to the rest of her cronies. The gossip had been so bad in the street that finally Jill and her family moved away, and it wasn't long after that that the friendship between Olive Wilson and Kate had blossomed.

Dismissing them from her mind, Lily's thoughts turned to Pete and the blissful weekend they had spent together. As soon as Mavis went out of the door they fell into each other's arms, both so starved of sex that they couldn't get enough of each other. Of course, she made sure there were no shows of affection in front of Mavis, and insisted that Pete went home at a reasonable hour.

'Morning, Mrs Davidson,' Lily said absently to the old woman in the end house who was polishing her letterbox.

'Slut,' the woman spat before walking inside and slamming her door.

Lily blanched as the penny dropped. Oh, God! Oh, God, no! Olive Wilson had given her a filthy look, and now she'd been called a slut. They must know about her and Pete, but how?

With her heart thumping in her chest, Lily shot round the corner, hurrying away from Cullen Street. How was she going to face her neighbours now? How was she going to live this down? *Oh, Pete, Pete, what am I gonna do?* She'd have to stop seeing him, keep him away, but dreaded the thought of life without him. She had to talk to him, somehow prevent him from turning up at the house. There was only one thing to do, she'd have to go to see him at the building site, and, as it was only about a fifteen-minute walk away, she headed in that direction.

At last Lily reached the gates, her eyes scanning the site; seeing Pete, she shouted and waved to get his attention. At last he turned around, his face anxious as he hurried towards her.

'What is it, Lily? What's wrong?'

Pete had become her rock, her lover, but Lily knew she had to let him go. 'I'm sorry, Pete. I don't want to see you any more.'

His eyes widened, the questions coming fast. 'What? But why? Has Ron turned up? Is that it?'

'No, he hasn't. It . . . it's just that you've got to stay away. All the neighbours know about us, and one has already called me a slut.'

'That's no reason to keep me away. Sod the bloody neighbours.'

'It's easy for you to say that, but I have to live in Cullen Street. Every time I go out of the door I'm gonna have to face them and their nasty remarks. If I keep flaunting you under their noses it'll just get worse, but it's bound to die down eventually if I stop seeing you.'

'Lily, I don't understand. What does it matter what people think, or say? How you run your life is your business, not theirs.'

'I can't face being called a slut, or worse. I just can't.'

'Well, then, there's only one thing to do. I've got the perfect solution,' Pete said and, as he continued, Lily at last began to smile.

Yes, he was right, it was the answer to their problems. 'Oh, yes, Pete, I'd love that.'

'Right, leave it with me and I'll sort things out. Now how about a kiss before I go back to work?'

Lily kissed him, her heart lighter as she got in a few things from the shop before making her way back to Cullen Street. She'd tell Mavis when the girl came home from work. If her daughter didn't like it, that was just too bad. Like it or not, as always, she'd do as she was told.

Mavis walked home, her day's work over. She always started with Mrs Pugh and then went over the bridge to Chelsea. Both of the houses she cleaned in that area were key jobs, ones where the owners were at work by the time she arrived. It was nice to be trusted with house keys, and though her employers were absent ones, Mavis never stinted on the cleaning and always made sure everything was immaculate, just as Mrs Pugh had taught her. Once she had found money lying on the floor and had left it on the sideboard where her employer would see it. When she had told her mother, she had laughed, saying that it was obviously a test to see if she was honest. In each house there had been occasions when her employers had turned up when she was working, and Mavis suspected that they were checking up on her. They had never found anything to complain about, had in fact praised her work, and nowadays she rarely saw them.

Mavis turned into Cullen Street and almost collided with Sandra Truman. 'Oh . . . sorry,' she said.

'Listen, Mavis, I'm glad I bumped into you. I know it's going to be rotten, but don't take any notice of the gossips.'

'Gossips? What do you mean?'

'Oh, God, you haven't heard.'

'Heard what?'

'Sorry, I've got to go,' Sandra said hastily as she hurried away.

'Wait!' Mavis called, but it was too late. Sandra had turned the corner and was out of sight.

Puzzled, Mavis walked to her door, and letting herself in, she went through to the kitchen. 'Mum, do you know what's going on? I just bumped into Sandra and she was on about some kind of gossip.'

'Yeah, but don't worry about it. We're moving anyway.'

'What? Where are we going?'

'I dunno yet, Pete's sorting it out, but a long way from this bloody area and soon I hope.'

'But why?'

'Look, you ain't a kid and old enough to hear the truth. Me and Pete are moving in together.'

'But . . . but you can't. What about Dad? When he comes back, he won't know where we are.'

'I've waited long enough without a word from your precious father. What do you expect me to do? Hang around forever, while my life passes me by? Well, no thanks. Pete's a good man, he'll take care of me, and he's willing to take you on. He'll be a proper father too.'

'No, no! He's not my dad,' Mavis cried and turning she fled the house, running and running, unaware until she was almost there that she was at Ellington Avenue. Her refuge.

CHAPTER EIGHTEEN

Edith heard the doorbell and frowned as she glanced at the clock. Alec wasn't due home for nearly an hour, and, anyway, he had a key.

She struggled to her feet, groaning in pain. When Mavis had left after cleaning that morning, the house had felt so empty, and, feeling that the walls were closing in on her, Edith had ventured out to the library, trying to find more information on word blindness. So far she hadn't had any success in helping Mavis to read and was hoping to find out what methods Samuel Orton used. She had scoured the reference section without success, but, unwilling to return home to the deserted house, she had ventured to the shops. Of course, she had overdone it, and, though she had since rested, had listened to *Mrs Dale's Diary* and *The Archers* on the wireless, Edith's body still screamed in protest as she slowly made her way to the front door.

One thing Edith knew for sure, it wouldn't be a friend calling round to see her. She had none. Friends would gossip, would want to pry into her past, and that was something she could never allow. To that end Edith had kept herself remote, and it had been fine while she was working, her days full and busy with the school activities, but nowadays, though she hated to admit it, she was sometimes swamped by loneliness.

At last, Edith reached the door, and opening it her eyes widened as Mavis staggered inside. 'Mavis, what is it, my dear?'

'Oh, Mrs Pugh . . . Mrs Pugh . . .' she cried, gasping and unable to carry on.

It was obvious that Mavis was in deep distress so, gently urging, Edith said, 'Come through to the kitchen.'

Mavis followed her, and taking a chair Edith gestured Mavis to sit down too. She took a breath, tried to ignore her pain as she asked, 'Now, my dear, tell me why you're so upset.'

Mavis ran both hands over her face, and then stammered, 'It . . . it's my mum. She . . . she said we're moving, and . . . and away from this area.'

'What?' Edith cried, shocked and bewildered by this turn of events. No, no, this was the last thing she wanted. 'When, Mavis? Did your mother say when? Or, come to that, why?'

'She . . . she said we're moving in with Pete, and

I think as soon as possible. I don't understand, Mrs Pugh. I don't like him, but why can't he just move in with us?'

'I should think that's obvious.'

'What do you mean?'

'Mavis, how do you think your father would feel, or react, if he came home to find your mother living with another man?'

'But . . . but Pete would only be a lodger.'

'I doubt that,' Edith said, struggling to think. The girl was so naïve, so innocent, and obviously had no idea what was going on. 'I must admit I'm shocked by your mother's behaviour. She must be the talk of the street.'

Mavis looked puzzled, but then said, 'I bumped into Sandra, the girl who lives next door to us, and she said something about gossip.'

'There you are then. Your neighbours have obviously found out and no doubt your mother will be ostracised. No wonder she wants to move.'

'Found out what?'

'What your mother and this Pete are up to.'

'Up to? But they aren't up to anything and I don't know what ostracised means.'

'It means cut out, shunned.'

'But why would they do that? All right, I know my mum once kissed Pete, and though she should only do that with my dad, surely it isn't that bad?'

'I think there's a little more to it than that.'

'My mum hasn't done anything wrong, and I don't want to leave Battersea. My dad might come back, and if he does he won't know where we are.'

'In the circumstances, I should think that's for the best.'

'For the best? Why?'

Edith sighed. This was harder than she'd anticipated, but somehow she had to make Mavis understand. If she could turn the girl against her mother, there still might be a chance to bring her plans to fruition. 'Mavis, hasn't your mother told you about the facts of life?'

'Er . . . er . . . she told me to keep away from boys, said that I mustn't let them touch me, but that's all.'

Edith dreaded this, but it had to be done. She closed her eyes for a moment, gathering her thoughts, and then began to explain the facts of life.

Mavis listened without interruption, gulping at points, and she was red-faced with embarrassment when Edith finally stopped. 'But that's awful,' she gasped. 'Disgusting . . . and . . . and my mum's doing that with Pete!'

'Yes, I'm afraid so, but between a man and wife it isn't awful, Mavis. It's a part of marriage, of love, and, as I explained, it's what brought you into the world. However, between your mother and Pete, it's called adultery, and no wonder the neighbours are gossiping. If they leave this area, Pete and your mother can live as man and wife. They can pretend to be married, but to keep up this pretence you will probably have to tell anyone who asks that Pete is your father.'

'Oh, God, I remember now,' Mavis cried, 'and it all makes sense. My mum said something about Pete taking care of us, of taking me on too. I won't go. I'll find somewhere else to live, that's what I'll do.'

'Yes, I suppose you could, but it won't be easy, my dear. You'd have to pay rent, your bills, buy food, and tell me, do you earn enough to do that?'

'I'm not sure. My mother takes all my wages and . . . and I don't know how much it costs to rent somewhere to live.'

'It isn't cheap, and as you're so young you may not find anyone willing to rent you a flat, or even a room.'

'Oh, Mrs Pugh. What am I going to do?'

'I don't know, my dear, but let me think and maybe I can come up with something. In the meantime, why don't you make us both a cup of tea?'

Mavis nodded; then dashed the tears from her cheeks as she went to fill the kettle. Edith closed her eyes. Why had this happened now? Things were just starting to go her way, but now she would have to move her plans forward. It was too soon, with neither Mavis or Alec ready – yet what choice did she have?

'Here you are,' Mavis said, breaking Edith out of her reveries as she held out a cup and saucer.

'Lovely,' Edith murmured as Mavis sat down again, and after taking a sip of the tea, she asked, 'Mavis, do you like Alec?'

'Er . . . yes, he's nice.'

'He likes you too. Very much, but I think I've already told you that.'

'Yes, you did.'

'When you think about it, Mavis, my son is a good catch and would make some lucky girl a fine husband.'

'Yes, I'm sure he would,' Mavis said.

Edith sighed. Mavis hadn't taken the hint, and with time of the essence she would have to be more forthright. 'If, for instance, *you* married my son, you could live here with us.'

'What? Me! Marry Alec?' Mavis spluttered.

'Yes, and wouldn't it be wonderful? I'm so fond of you, Mavis, and you'd be able to give up work, all those cleaning jobs. It would give us more time for your reading lessons, and I know we'd get along so well together.'

'But . . . but . . .'

'All I'm asking is that you think about it,' Edith interrupted as she glanced at the clock. 'I know this is all a bit sudden, but I'm sure you'll come to realise that it's the ideal solution. You won't have to live with your mother and Pete, or pretend that he's your father. Instead you'll be able to stay here, in comfort, with people who care about you.'

'Yes . . . but . . .'

'Mavis, my son will be home soon, and until you've come to a decision, I'd rather we kept this little conversation to ourselves. I don't want to raise his hopes only for them to be dashed.'

Mavis jumped to her feet, eyes wild as she said, 'I . . . I'd better go, Mrs Pugh. I . . . I'll see you in the morning.'

'All right, and after you've given it some thought, perhaps you'll have an answer for me.'

Mavis barely nodded, and then as she called a quick goodbye she ran from the room. Edith heard the front door close, sighed, and then sank back in her chair. She had planted the seed, but would it be enough? Mavis hadn't looked very keen on the idea, but surely the girl would realise that it was the best choice. That it was, in fact, her only choice.

Mavis was walking rapidly, heading for home. Marry Alec! No, no, she didn't want to marry him. So much had happened – so much had been said in such a short time that her head was reeling.

Thanks to Mrs Pugh, she now knew how babies were made, how an egg from her mother and father had brought her into the world, but the rest of it sounded awful. Mrs Pugh had said it was a part of marriage, that it was nice between a husband and wife; but the thought of doing *that* with Alec made her stomach crawl. Surely he wasn't the man who kept appearing in her dreams? No, he couldn't be. Alec didn't arouse that curious yearning, the need for the man to overcome all to reach her.

As she neared Cullen Street, Mavis slowed her pace. When she thought about her mother and Pete, what they were doing, she felt sick inside. She didn't want to go home, didn't want to look at her mother, but there was no other choice.

If only her dad would come home, he'd sort them out, and on that thought Mavis almost stopped walking. Her dream! The man in her dream could be her dad! Was he trying to come home, but something was stopping him? Oh, if only she could find him, help him, but how?

Wait! Thinking back, it all stemmed from Pete turning up, and on that same night she'd seen her mother in his arms. Bile rose. Friends! She'd believed her mother when she said that she and Pete were just friends. God, what an idiot she'd been. They must have been carrying on before Pete turned up, and somehow her father had found out. No wonder he hadn't come back. It was her mother's fault, Pete's fault. They were the barrier

204

that kept her away from her father. Livid now, Mavis found her pace picking up as she almost marched the rest of the way home.

Lily glared at her daughter. 'Now you listen to me, my girl. I'm fed up with you running off without telling me where you're going and it's got to stop. When we move I ain't having you carrying on like this, and I doubt Pete will stand for it either.'

'I don't care. He ain't me dad, and you . . . you're disgusting, that's what you are!'

Lily paled. This wasn't her daughter – this girl who stood in front of her, the innocence gone from her eyes. 'What did you say?' she yelled.

'You heard! I know about you and Pete, what you've been up to. Dad must have found out and no wonder he left you.'

'What are you talking about?'

'I'm talking about you carrying on with Pete behind Dad's back.'

'I did not! I don't know what's put this daft idea into your head, but it ain't true.'

'Yes, it is. As soon as Pete turned up I saw you kissing him.'

'It wasn't like that and I explained it all to you at the time.'

'Yeah, but now I don't believe you. Dad won't come back because of you, but when you're gone, he'll turn up again, I know he will. He'll take me to live with him.'

'You're out of your tiny mind. Your father buggered off without a word and it had nothing to do with me and Pete. Turn up again! Don't make me laugh.'

'He will! He will, and I'm gonna wait right here for him.'

'Don't be stupid. I'm giving up this place, and I don't doubt that someone else will soon move in. Now get this into your thick head. We're moving, and you, my girl, are coming with us.'

'I won't. I won't go and you can't make me!'

Lily puffed with exasperation. This was more like it, Mavis acting like a child again, one who was having a tantrum. Not that Mavis had ever been prone to tantrums, the girl too docile for that, but at least Lily felt in control again. 'You'll do as you're told.'

'No, I don't want to live with you and Pete!'

Lily's temper rose again. 'You ain't got any choice, you daft cow!'

'Yes, I have.'

'Oh, yeah. Like what?'

Mavis went mute then, staring at her stubbornly, and Lily had had enough. 'I said you're coming with us and that's that. Now get out of my sight! Go to your room and bloody well stay there until I say you can come down!'

With a final glare, Mavis turned on her heels to run upstairs while Lily angrily slumped in a chair. Pete said that when they moved in together, there'd be no need for her to work, but she still wanted a bit of independence. Pete was a good man, and Lily doubted he'd go the same way as Ron, but there were no guarantees in this life. She'd relied on a man before and look where that had got her. She'd make sure Mavis found work in Peckham, other cleaning jobs, and hand over her wages as usual. Lily intended to save as much of this money as she could, build up a nice little nest egg, and if things didn't work out with Pete, she'd have this money to fall back on.

Of course, without Mavis it wouldn't be possible, but Lily wasn't worried. There was no way she was going to let her daughter scupper her plans. Mavis would go with them because, despite her act of bravado, the girl had no choice – like it or not.

Kate took her ear from the glass she had placed against the wall. It had gone quiet next door now, but she'd heard enough and her face was livid with anger. So, Lily was moving, no doubt hoping to sneak off without a word.

'Sandra, you're not going to believe this,' she said, placing the glass down.

'Mum, if Dad saw you doing that, he'd go mad.'

'If I want to find out what's going on next door, I ain't got any choice. Lily has always been close-mouthed, but she was my friend and I put up with it 'cos I liked her. Not now though, not after what she's been up to. She lied to me, Sandra, told me that bloke was only a friend, and like a mug I believed her.'

'She could hardly tell you the truth.'

'I don't see why not. I wouldn't have said anything.'

Sandra's brows rose, her tone sceptical. 'Really?'

'Yes, really, but listen, I just heard Lily rowing with Mavis. Like I said, you ain't gonna believe this and I couldn't catch it all, but they're moving.'

'Moving! When?'

'I dunno, but Mavis doesn't want to go. I've always felt sorry for the girl, and I've lost count of the times I've tried to tell Lily that she ain't as daft as she makes her out to be.'

'I don't think she is either,' Sandra agreed, 'but she had a rotten time of it when we were at junior school. The kids used to take the mickey out of her all the time and I saw the way Mavis reacted. She used to try to hide away, keep herself to herself, but I stuck up for her when I could.'

'I know you did, love, but you hardly see her now.'

'That isn't my fault, Mum. I know we used to be good friends, but when I went to grammar school, Mavis sort of drifted away. I don't think she's backward, but she is sort of, oh, I don't know, unworldly, I suppose.'

'She's too much on her own, that's the trouble. All right, she drifted away from you, but why hasn't she got other friends?'

'Maybe she had a hard time of it at secondary school too, and she might have been made to feel the odd one out again. If that's the case I think Mavis would have put up a defensive wall, pretended she doesn't care, and cut herself off from the other girls.'

'Gawd, the poor cow. She hasn't had much of a life, and Lily just uses her as a workhorse.'

'Mum, you're making me feel so guilty. Maybe I should have tried harder to keep up our friendship.'

'Oh, love, I'm not having a go at you. You've got your own life to lead and Mavis isn't your responsibility. It's Lily who's got my back up. Like I said, she's moving and I reckon she was hoping to sneak off without telling me. Yeah, and wait till Olive Wilson hears about this too.'

'Mum, maybe you should keep out of it.'

'That's what your dad said,' Kate mused as she looked at the clock, 'but no way, and I'm popping over to Olive's. Your dad won't be home for about fifteen minutes, but keep an eye on those spuds for me.'

'Mum, wait,' Sandra called, to no avail. Her mother was already hurrying out of the door.

Tommy Wilson opened the front door and sighed. He hadn't been home from work for long, but now Kate flaming Truman was at the door. She and his mother were as thick as thieves, a right pair of gossips, and he'd already heard all the talk about Lily Jackson. No doubt Kate was here to spread a bit more and, trying not to scowl, Tommy did his best to put her off. 'Mum's busy cooking our dinner.'

'It's all right, I only want a quick word,' Kate said as she pushed past him to walk inside.

Shaking his head, Tommy walked behind Kate into the kitchen, the woman saying as soon as she saw his mother, 'Olive, you're not going to believe this.'

'Go on, tell me,' Olive said, her expression avid.

'Lily's moving.'

'What? Blimey, did she say when?'

'Oh, I haven't spoken to her, but you know how thin our walls are. She was yelling her head off at Mavis and I couldn't fail to hear. Apparently she's moving in with that bloke, but from what I heard Mavis doesn't want to go with them.'

'You can't blame the girl for that. Her mother will be living in sin, and it's bloody disgusting. Still, I won't be sorry to see the back of Lily, or her daft daughter.'

'Mavis isn't daft, Olive.'

'Yeah, so you've said before, but if she isn't, how come she's only fit for cleaning jobs? Oh, bugger, me spuds are boiling over,' Olive said as she hurried over to the stove.

'I'd better go. Our dinner's cooking too.'

'Righto, but if you hear any more, like when Lily's moving, let me know.'

'Of course I will,' Kate said, 'but, like I said to my Sandra, I reckon she's gonna try to sneak off without a word. We've been friends for years and I ain't too happy about it.'

'Huh, who needs friends like that! Lily Jackson is nothing but a strumpet. It's good riddance to bad rubbish, as far as I'm concerned. We don't need tarts like her in Cullen Street.'

'Yeah, I suppose you're right. Bye for now, Olive, and don't worry, I'll see myself out.'

'Yeah, see you, Kate.'

Tommy had listened to this exchange, and once again it had emphasised how much his mother had changed. Yes, she had always liked a bit of gossip, but it had once been harmless chatter and not judgemental. All right, Lily Jackson was going to shack up with another bloke, but as her old man had left her what did his mother expect – that the woman would live like a nun for the rest of her life? Yes, probably, and it gave his mother an excuse to become all high and mighty, something she probably loved. She spoke, her voice softer now.

'Are you off out again tonight, Tommy?'

'Yeah, I've got a date with Connie.'

'You've been seeing her for a while now and it's about time you brought her home.'

'Leave it out, Mum. I've only been going out with her for about a month and it ain't as if I'm gonna marry the girl.'

'I should think not. You're far too young to think about marriage, but I'd still like to meet her.'

'No way, Mum. If I bring her home it might give her ideas. I don't want her thinking that it's anything serious. We just date, that's all.'

'You see her at least three times a week, so it must be more than casual. Where did you say she works? Woolworths, wasn't it?'

'Yeah, that's right.'

'What counter is she on?'

Tommy hid a smile. His mother wanted to take a look at Connie. She was a wily old bird, but he was wise to her. He hated being an only child – hated that his mother wanted to know his every move. 'She hasn't got a set counter. They move her about.'

'Oh, yeah?' she said sceptically, but then began to carve the cold meat left over from the Sunday joint.

With his mother intent on her task, Tommy was finally left in peace while his thoughts went back to when his mother had become so bitter. It had started after Lily Jackson, followed by Kate Truman, had accused him and Larry of trying it on with their girls. He'd thought it had been nothing really, just a bit of fun, but it wasn't how his mother saw it. She hated it when the gossip in the street had turned on him and, by extension, on her too. When it finally died down, as though frightened to become the focus of talk again, she went out of her way to find other people to pull apart. Larry's father had been the first of her witch hunts when he had nicked a few bits from his employer, so much so that Tommy still felt his mother had been instrumental in the family leaving the street, taking his mate Larry with them.

Now the Jacksons were going too, and maybe it was for the best. He knew it didn't help that his mother saw Mavis all the time, and it might make a difference now that she was leaving, but, unlike his mother, Tommy found that he wasn't pleased. It was daft really, he knew that, but somehow Mavis had got under his skin. He would never forget her anguished face when he destroyed her painting, and perhaps his attraction to her now was tied up with feelings of guilt. Yet somehow he felt there was more to it than that. He fought it, of course. His mother was right. If Mavis had half a brain, she'd find a decent job. With the way she was, there could never be anything between them, yet even so he couldn't help wondering where Mavis was going. Or if he'd ever see her again.

CHAPTER NINETEEN

Mavis had lain awake for hours, stomach rumbling with hunger until sure that her mother had gone to bed, she had sneaked downstairs to grab a couple of slices of bread. Yet still she hadn't been able to sleep, her mind twisting and turning. She didn't want to move away. She wanted to stay close by where she could wait for her father to come home. Yet would he? Her mother's words had played over and over until she couldn't think straight. Was she telling the truth? Either way, no matter what, she didn't want to move in with her and Pete.

When she awoke on Tuesday morning Mavis had no memory of falling asleep. Yawning, she got up, but almost immediately her mind returned to her problem. Mrs Pugh had given her a way out, a chance to remain in this area, but she just couldn't face the thought of marrying Alec. When Mavis went downstairs she ignored her mother as she walked through to the outhouse, but shortly afterwards she heard someone knocking on the door, followed by Pete's voice. For once her wash was perfunctory, and, ears pricked, Mavis stood just behind the door, listening.

'You shouldn't have come round, Pete. There's enough gossip as it is.'

'Sod the gossip. What does it matter anyway? I've found us a place, Lily, and we can move in on Saturday.'

'What? How did you find it so quickly? And where is it?'

'It was a bit of a fluke, word of mouth really, through a bloke on the site. It's in Peckham Rye, well away from here, and I reckon you'll love it, Lily.'

'What's it like?'

'There's two bedrooms and a bit of a garden, but best of all it's got a bathroom. No more going to an outside lavvy for you, Lily.'

'A bathroom. Oh . . . oh, Pete.'

'I've got to go, Lily. I'll be late for work but I had to pop round to tell you. Start packing, girl, and don't worry about furniture. It comes fully furnished and it's decent stuff too.'

'Pete, come round again this evening and you can tell me more about it.'

'Are you sure?'

'Yes, it's as you said. Sod the neighbours.'

'What about Mavis? Have you told her about us and that we're moving?'

'Yeah, I told her.'

'How did she take it?'

'Not very well, but don't worry, she'll come round. After all, she ain't got any choice. Now come on, give me a cuddle and then bugger off. I've got a lot to do before Saturday and loads of stuff to get rid of.'

There was a pause, one in which Mavis could picture her mother in Pete's arms, and then his voice called out, 'See you later, love,' followed by the sound of the front door closing.

For a moment Mavis remained where she was. Her mother had told Pete that she'd go with them, that she had no choice. It wasn't true, there was an alternative, one her mother knew nothing about, but could she take it?

'I suppose you heard all that, Mavis?' her mother said as she walked into the outhouse.

Lips tight, Mavis nodded.

'Yeah, well, this means you'll have to tell Mrs Pugh that Friday will be your last day. I'll give you notes to leave for the jobs in Chelsea. I know it's short notice, but they should still pay you for the hours you put in until then.'

Mavis didn't care about the jobs in Chelsea, but found that she dreaded the thought of leaving Mrs Pugh. Not only had her house become a sanctuary, Mrs Pugh was the only person who made her feel of any worth. The thought of never seeing her again, of giving up the reading lessons, her one chance to prove that she wasn't stupid, was too much. 'Please, Mum, can't we stay here?' she begged.

'No, and don't start whinging again. I'll make you a bit of toast and while you're eating it I'll get on with writing those notes.'

'But . . .'

'Mavis, I'm warning you, I've just about had enough. Now I don't want to hear another word about it. We're going. You're coming with us. And that's that!'

Mavis ate the toast that was put in front of her automatically, her thoughts still all over the place. When the notes were ready she put on her coat and then stuffed them into her pocket, saying not a word to her mother as she walked out. She was going to Mrs Pugh's, was supposed to tell her that she was leaving, but the thought was almost too much to bear. There was another way. She could marry Alec – but could she take it?

Undecided, Mavis found that for once, she wasn't hurrying to Ellington Avenue.

Kate saw Mavis as she passed her window, and, satisfied that Lily was now alone, her back rigid, she walked next door. Lifting a hand she thumped on Lily's door, and when it was opened she stomped inside. 'I saw that bloke leaving this morning. I suppose he stayed the night.'

'No, he didn't. Not that it's anything to do with you.'

'You told me that he was just a friend, but you've forgotten how thin these walls are. It's bloody disgusting what the pair of you have been up to. It's no wonder you're the talk of the street.'

Lily flushed, but then she seemed to grow in stature as she shouted, 'Yeah, and now I know who spread the gossip. Get out of my house, you two-faced bitch. Go on, get out!'

'Me! You've got the cheek to call me two-faced. You're the one who lied to me, *and* the one who was gonna sneak off without a word.'

'My, my, you have been busy,' Lily said, her voice ringing with disgust. 'To know that I'm moving, you must have spent hours with your ear pressed to the wall.'

'I didn't need to. You were shouting so loud the whole bloody street must have heard.'

'And just in case they didn't, you'll make sure they find out. Huh, some friend you turned out to be.'

'I'm no friend of yours, not now I know you're nothing but a tart.'

Lily's face darkened with fury and before Kate had time to react, Lily slapped her hard across her cheek, screeching, 'Get out!'

'Why . . . you . . . you . . .' Kate ground out, but then Lily shoved her over the threshold, slamming the door so loud that the windows rattled.

For a moment Kate just stood on the pavement, but then stomped across the road to Olive's house, stiff with indignation, and still in shock that Lily had actually slapped her.

In Southampton, Pat Higgins was worried. Ron's skin looked yellow, and even the whites of his eyes were tinged with the same hue. 'Ron, you look funny. I think you should see a doctor.'

'There's nothing wrong with me that a whisky won't put right.'

'You haven't been right for weeks and you hardly get out of bed.'

'I'm tired, that's all.'

'What about those pains in your tummy?'

'It's nothing. I'm fine.'

Pat grabbed the mirror from her dressing table set and held it up in front of Ron's face. 'Do you call that fine?'

'Blimey, I'm a bit yellow.'

'I think it's jaundice, Ron. You've *got* to see a doctor.'

'Yeah, yeah, all right, but can I have a drink first? Please, love.'

'Just the one,' Pat said, 'but then I want you up and dressed.'

Ron gulped whisky and then with a bit more urging he got up, staggering a little as he went through to the tiny kitchen to wash at the sink. When he returned to get dressed, Pat saw his bloated stomach and swollen legs. She had to help him with his shoes, but finally he was ready for the short walk to the surgery.

They sat in the waiting room, thankfully with only a couple of people ahead of them, but when Pat looked at Ron she saw that his eyes were closed. 'Don't go to sleep,' she hissed, 'it'll be your turn soon.'

'Yeah, yeah, don't nag.'

When Ron's name was called, Pat urged him to his feet, the doctor's eyebrows shooting up as they walked in. 'Sit down,' he ordered.

After only a few questions, it was established neither were registered with the doctor. They gave their details, and, once the doctor knew they were unrelated, Pat was ordered to wait outside. She was fuming as she walked out, leaving Ron to be examined by the doctor.

As the door closed behind Pat, the questions began, but Ron was evasive. 'No,' he said, 'I'm not a heavy drinker.'

'Mr Jackson, it's obvious that you are jaundiced,' the doctor said, then taking Ron's blood pressure. 'The readings are high, and I'd like to take a look at you now. Get undressed, please.'

With reluctance Ron did as he was told, and when lying on the bed the doctor came around the tattered curtain to look at him. It was obvious that he wasn't happy with the examination, his lips pursed as he asked yet more questions.

'Yes, I've been a bit tired,' Ron answered, flushing when the doctor finally asked if he was impotent.

'Right, you can get dressed, Mr Jackson.'

Ron sat facing the man across his desk again, watching as he scribbled a letter before he looked up, his expression grim as he said, 'You have an enlarged liver, I suspect cirrhosis, and it needs further investigation immediately. I want you to take this letter along to the Southampton Infirmary, and don't be surprised if you're admitted.'

'Leave it out. I just need a bit of something for this jaundice.'

'Mr Jackson, if it were only a mild case of jaundice I would advise you best rest and to avoid any fatty foods. However, your symptoms indicate that you may have chronic liver disease and for that you need to be hospitalised.'

Ron avoided the man's eyes and, as he was handed the letter, he stuffed it into his pocket, murmuring his thanks as he walked out.

'Well, what did he say?' Pat asked anxiously as she hurried to his side.

'It's nothing,' Ron lied, 'just a bit of jaundice. I've just got to rest and keep off fatty food.'

'Gawd, that's a relief,' Pat said, tucking her hand through his arm as they walked home.

All Ron wanted was to get back into bed. The pain over his liver was excruciating and it was a bit of a job to hide it from Pat, but once he'd had a few more drinks he'd be all right.

Hospital. There was no way he was going into hospital. Unlike Pat, the nurses wouldn't keep him supplied with whisky.

CHAPTER TWENTY

Edith was wondering what to do. Should she raise the subject? Yet if Mavis wasn't ready to give her an answer, pushing her might be the worst thing to do. She waited until Mavis had been there for almost two hours, but then, unable to bear the apprehension any longer, she called the girl into the kitchen.

'Mavis, is there any news? Has your mother said when you'll be moving away?'

'Yes, we're moving to Peckham on Saturday. Mum said to tell you that Friday will be my last day here and I've got letters for my other jobs too.'

'Three days,' Edith gasped, 'that soon! Mavis, I'm going to miss you so much.'

'I'm . . . I'm gonna miss you too.'

Edith closed her eyes against the jolt in her chest. Mavis had said she was going to miss her, and that must mean that she'd decided to go. Edith knew she'd failed, that the future was once again uncertain, and she cursed Lily Jackson. If she'd had more time her plan could have worked. Her eyes snapped open when Mavis spoke again.

'I've been thinking about what you said, but I still don't know what to do. I hardly know Alec, and . . . and though like I said, I like him, I . . . I don't love him.'

Edith waved a dismissive hand. 'Liking someone is more important and it's a good foundation for a happy marriage. If you like someone, love can grow, and usually does, especially with intimacy.'

Mavis was pink-cheeked. 'Really?'

'Yes, my dear. In fact, in some cultures it's the parents who choose their daughter's husband. The couple hardly meet, if at all, before the ceremony, and, let me tell you, in most cases these marriages are very successful.'

'They . . . they are?'

'Mavis, I can guess what is worrying you, but how can I put this delicately? Perhaps to say that my son is a very kind young man and if you're nervous, apprehensive, about a certain aspect of married life, I'm sure he won't rush you.'

'He . . . he won't?'

'Of course not.'

Mavis was quiet for a moment, but then said, 'I'm only sixteen and would need my mum's permission.'

'Yes, you would, but talk to her and I'm sure she'll agree.'

'But, Mrs Pugh, Alec hasn't asked me to marry him yet.'

'Mavis, if you come back this evening I'm sure that Alec will go down on one knee.'

Her eyes widening, Mavis said, 'Really? Did he tell you that?'

'He certainly did,' Edith insisted, her lie ready. She had wanted to wait for Mavis's answer before she spoke to Alec, but the girl didn't need to know that. In fact, she didn't want either of them to know that they were being manipulated and would have to tread carefully. 'When Alec came home from work yesterday and I told him you were leaving, he was devastated. He said he couldn't bear to lose you, that he'd do anything to keep you here. My son thinks the world of you, Mavis.'

'He . . . he does?'

'Yes, and if you agree to marry him I know you'll be happy living here with us. Can you say the same about living with your mother and that man in Peckham?'

'No . . . no . . . I suppose not,' Mavis said. She hung her head, quiet for a while, but at last raised her eyes. 'All right. I'll marry Alec.'

'Mavis, that's wonderful. I can't tell you how happy this has made me. Though there's just one thing.

I think it might be best if you don't mention this conversation to Alec. As I said, he's rather shy, and might be embarrassed that I've spoken to you about his feelings.'

'I won't say anything,' Mavis said, but then glanced at the clock. 'I'd better go or I'll be late for my next job.'

'Considering that you're leaving, that's very commendable, Mavis. Yes, go along, my dear, and I'll look forward to seeing you later.'

'Bye, Mrs Pugh.'

'Goodbye, Mavis,' Edith called happily. All she had to do now was to talk to Alec, and she'd do that as soon as he came home. Of course, she wasn't worried. She'd seen the way her son looked at Mavis lately, and knew that with a bit of gentle persuasion he'd see the sense of marrying her.

It would be such a relief when it all came to fruition, but then Edith frowned as she realised there'd be another problem. There was no way the marriage could be arranged before Saturday and, until it could, Lily Jackson might insist that her daughter went with her. Edith didn't want that. With Mavis so far away she'd be out of her control – and with a distance between them, the girl might change her mind.

Edith narrowed her eyes in thought. Under the circumstances, what she now had in mind might not be appropriate, but it was the only way to ensure that Mavis remained close by.

For the rest of the day, Mavis found it hard to concentrate on her work. She'd agreed to marry Alec, and it had been lovely to see how delighted Mrs Pugh was, but deep down Mavis felt a sense of dread. Surely she shouldn't be feeling like this? Mrs Pugh had said that Alec wouldn't rush her and that had gone a long way in alleviating her fears, but Mavis couldn't shake off the thought that she'd made the wrong decision. Yet what choice had she had? Oh, if only her mother wasn't moving, if only she hadn't been backed into a corner, with marriage to Alec the only way out.

Her work done, Mavis made her way home, still undecided and wondering if she should change her mind. Should she marry Alec? Or should she tell Mrs Pugh that she'd made a dreadful mistake?

It wasn't until Mavis was nearly home that her mind suddenly quietened. Battersea was her home and she would never move away while there was a chance that her father would return. Yes, she would marry Alec, remain close to Cullen Street, and one day she might even come to love him.

Mavis walked in to find chaos. Her mother had stuff piled all over the place: odd bits of china, saucepans and frying pans, clothes that let off a pungent aroma of mildew.

'Thank God you're home,' Lily said. 'This lot wasn't fit to sell and we need to get rid of it. I want you to load the pram and dump it. You'll probably have to make a couple of trips.'

'Dump it! But where?'

'I dunno, but maybe on that bombsite a few streets away.'

'Why dump it? Why not just leave it here?'

'What, and have the new tenants talking about me? They'll be telling everyone that I'm a mucky cow who left them to clear a load of tatty stuff from the house.'

Bewildered, Mavis shook her head. 'What difference does it make? You won't be around to hear about it, and, anyway, the landlord will probably clear it.'

'I doubt that. The landlord had done nothing when we moved in and this place was in a right state. Now don't argue, Mavis, just do as I say and get rid of it.'

Mavis knew that she couldn't win, and so began to pick up as much as she could carry to the yard, throwing it haphazardly into the pram. It had been a while since she'd been made to take it out, and it certainly wasn't something she'd missed.

Mavis suddenly paused. She'd never have to do this again. She was going to be married, would stay at home with Mrs Pugh, and on that thought she brightened. It was going to be lovely, but she wouldn't tell her mother yet. She'd wait until Alec had proposed, something he'd be doing later. He might not be the man in her dreams, but Mrs Pugh was right, he was kind, caring, and she had seen that in his concern for his mother.

Edith waited impatiently for Alec to come home, and when he did she said, 'At last. Sit down, Alec, I want to talk to you.'

'What is it, Mother? You look agitated. Are you all right?'

'I've had a bit of bad news and I'm rather upset.'

'Bad news?' Alec repeated as he took a seat opposite.

'Mavis is leaving us, moving out of the area.'

'What! When?'

'On Saturday, and, oh, Alec, I'm going to miss her so much. I know Mavis is young, but she's become so much more than our cleaner and I'm so fond of her.'

'I know you are. This is all a bit sudden. Do you know why she's moving?'

'Yes, it's because of her mother. Lily Jackson has been having an affair with another man, and she's going to live with him. Of course, her name is now mud around here so she's moving to Peckham. Mavis is dreadfully upset about it. She had to give me notice this morning and the poor girl was in tears. I'm going to be lost without her, Alec.

Mavis has become like a part of the family and I'll never be able to replace her.'

'Of course you will.'

'No, and I don't think I'll even bother to try.'

'Mother, you'll have to. You know you can't manage on your own.'

Edith decided that now was the time to move things forward and asked, 'Alec, do you like Mavis?'

'Yes, of course I do.'

'She likes you too and I wouldn't have to find someone else if you marry her.'

'Marry her! Mother, don't be silly. I hardly know the girl.'

'Alec, I've seen the way you look at her.'

'All right, I'll admit Mavis is pretty, but she's only sixteen.'

'You're only eight years older and a young wife would be perfect. Mavis is innocent, untouched and, unlike a lot of other girls nowadays, she isn't flighty.'

'Maybe, but without getting to know her better, I can hardly ask her to marry me.'

'Darling, I know it's very quick, but as she's moving away on Saturday, there's hardly time for courting.'

Alec abruptly stood up and shaking his head he said, 'No, this is ridiculous. I'm going to change for dinner,' but then he paused. 'Anyway, Mother, what makes you think that Mavis would agree to marry me?'

Once again, as with Mavis, Edith had the lie ready. 'Because I've seen the way she looks at you too. Trust me, Mavis more than likes you and if you don't do something about it now, you'll lose her.'

'I think it's you who's more worried about losing her,' he said, about to leave the room.

'Alec, wait,' Edith appealed. 'All right, I'll admit I dread Mavis leaving, but can't you see how ideal the marriage would be? You said I can no longer cope on my own, and I know you're right, that my condition will only get worse. If you marry Mavis, I'll have someone here to look after me permanently, and, though I hate to say it, someone who can take over the burden of looking after you too.'

Alec looked shocked and bewildered as he sat down again. 'You see me as a burden?'

'Darling, don't look at me like that. No, burden was the wrong word. You could never be that, but I worry so much. I know the time will come when I won't be able to cook for you, to do anything for you, and when that time comes, what will happen? I hate the thought that it is I who would be the burden, that unless you put me into some sort of care home, you'd have to give up work to look after me.'

'Oh, Mother.'

'Alec, I know this has all come as a bit of a shock, but surely you can see that my suggestion is the perfect answer for all of us?'

Alec didn't answer straightaway, but then he nodded slowly. 'Yes, I suppose it makes sense, but I can't do it, Mother.'

'Why not?'

'For all the reasons I've already mentioned, and not only that, despite what you say, I don't think Mavis will want to marry me. If I ask her I'll just make a complete fool of myself.'

'No, you won't, darling. Mavis will say yes, I'm sure of it.'

'How can you be so sure?'

'Oh, dear, this is rather difficult and Mavis would be shattered if she found out I'd told you . . .' Edith left the sentence unfinished.

'Told me what?'

'Alec, I can't tell you unless you promise that you'll never mention this conversation to Mavis.'

'All right, I promise. Now what did she tell you?'

'It feels awful breaking her confidence, but I have your promise so Mavis need never know. I told you that Mavis was in tears when she gave notice this morning, but what I didn't tell you was that she was crying at the thought of never seeing you again.'

'What! No, Mother, I can't believe that. Mavis

has never given any indication that she cares a fig about me.'

'Mavis is dreadfully shy, and she's been made to feel worthless. As she said to me, someone like you would never be interested in her.'

'She said that!'

'Yes, my dear, she thinks the world of you, but, as I said, all this was told to me in confidence. Mavis has been hiding her feelings from you, and even from me, but I had my suspicions.'

'I can hardly believe this. You really do think she wants to marry me?'

'Yes, my dear, and think what a lovely wife she'd be.'

Alec was quiet then, deep in thought, but at last he said, 'Yes, she would, and as you say, it would be nice to know that you have someone here all day to look after you.'

'Does this mean you're going to ask her to marry you?'

'Yes, I think I will.'

'Alec, that's wonderful,' Edith enthused. 'Now then, dear, go and get changed while I see to our dinner. Mavis is coming round later and it will be the perfect opportunity to propose.'

'What! But I've hardly got my head around this yet.'

'I know, but as Mavis is moving on Saturday she must have a lot to do. This may be the last time she'll call round in the evenings, and unless you propose now you'll never see her again.'

'Never see her again,' Alec echoed, now looking less than pleased at the idea. 'I hadn't thought of that. All right, Mother, I'll speak to her this evening.'

When Alec left the room, Edith struggled to her feet. She was ecstatic. Her plans had come to fruition, and though it was earlier than she'd antici-pated, the timing was in fact ideal. It was getting to be more and more of a struggle to cope, but with Mavis there to care for her full time, she no longer had to worry. Of course, Mavis would still have to tell her mother, but Edith wasn't worried about that. Lily Jackson was moving in with another man and no doubt she'd be glad to get rid of the girl.

CHAPTER TWENTY-ONE

Alec found that he had little appetite and as he washed up the dishes his nerves were jangling. Mavis was so young, so beautiful, and he could hardly believe that she was interested in him. He knew he wasn't much to look at, especially after his one encounter with a girl who'd cheated on him. She had denied it, of course, but then she'd mocked him, saying he was a boring, stuffy, mummy's boy.

In the office he often heard the girls giggling about their latest antics or boyfriends. One minute they were in love, the next minute it was over, usually because someone with better prospects came along. They were all so empty-headed, only interested in fashions, make-up and the latest music trends. They swooned over Dickie Valentine, Jimmy Young, and now someone called Tennessee Ernie Ford who'd had a hit record in March. Of course, once someone with another big hit came along, the country singer was out – their taste in music, along with men, fickle.

At least Mavis was different, Alec mused. She wasn't out gallivanting at night, but instead she came round here to see his mother for reading lessons and to him that was commendable. He now knew that he'd been wrong in his original assessment of Mavis. Even though there hadn't yet been any progress in her lessons, she wasn't backward, but it had taken his mother's research on word blindness to bring that to light.

When there was a knock on the door at eight o'clock it felt to Alec that his stomach turned a somersault, and nervously he said, 'Mother, I don't think I can do this. I'm sure you misunderstood. Mavis may like me, but I doubt she'll want to marry me.'

'Alec, she will, I promise you. Now then, the two of you need to be alone. Let Mavis in and take her to the living room.'

'Oh, Mother.'

'For goodness sake, Alec, you can't leave Mavis standing on the step. Do get a move on.'

With reluctance, Alec went to answer the door, finding as he let Mavis in that he couldn't speak without stammering. 'Er . . . er, come in, Mavis. Let . . . let me take your coat and then you can go on through to the living room.'

'Th . . . thanks.'

Alec found his eyebrows rising. Mavis looked pink-cheeked and sounded equally nervous, but, as she had no idea that he was going to propose, he didn't know why. 'Are you all right?'

'Yes . . . yes, I'm fine.'

'That's good,' Alec said as he took her coat to hang up in the downstairs closet. 'As I said, go on through.'

Mavis was perched on the edge of the sofa when Alec walked in, her eyes avoiding his as she said, 'Where . . . where's your mother?'

'In the kitchen, but I want to speak to you alone, Mavis.'

'You do?'

'My mother tells me that you're moving out of the area.'

'Yes, that's right.'

'She's going to miss you, and . . . and I will too.'

At last Mavis's eyes briefly met his, her cheeks still pink as she asked, 'You . . . you will?'

Mavis looked so nervous, so vulnerable, that it suddenly infused Alec with courage. 'Yes, very much, and I don't want you to go.'

'I don't want to go either, but I haven't any choice.'

Her words opened the opportunity that Alec needed and he moved swiftly to kneel in front of her. 'But you have, Mavis. You could stay here . . . marry me.'

Mavis's answer was equally swift. 'Yes, all right.'

Alec had expected surprise, shock – certainly not an immediate answer. He sat back on his heels, stunned. 'You . . . you'll marry me?'

'Yes, Alec.'

Her beautiful, large blue eyes suddenly filled with moisture and Alec scrambled to sit beside her on the sofa. He hadn't expected tears of happiness, and he wonderingly pulled Mavis into his arms. 'Oh, Mavis, I can't believe you said yes.'

She was stiff, rigid in his embrace, and Alec was at first puzzled, but then remembering how innocent she was, how untouched, he gently said, 'It's wonderful to hold you. May . . . may I kiss you too?'

Mavis seemed to relax a little and as she drew back Alec saw that her eyes were closed, her lips comically pursed. He smiled, feeling a surge of happiness and satisfaction. It was obvious that Mavis had never been kissed; he would be the first to do even that, and briefly he laid his lips on hers. Yes, he'd kissed a girl before, held one, but that was all. He too was a virgin, but now that Mavis had agreed to be his wife that was going to change. Alec felt a stirring in his loins.

For a moment Alec was tempted to drag her into his arms again, but somehow held back. Mavis was so young, so skittish, and he didn't want to frighten her off. Until she was officially his wife, he would have to be gentle, but God, he could hardly wait for their wedding night.

'Come on,' he said. 'Let's go and tell Mother.'

Mavis nodded, her face still pink as they went into the kitchen where Alec saw his mother smiling with anticipation. 'We have something to tell you,' he said as though she'd been unaware he had just proposed. 'It might come as a bit of a surprise, but Mavis has just agreed to marry me.'

'How lovely!' she cried. 'Have you decided on a date?'

Perplexed, Alec shook his head. 'Well, no, not yet, but soon I hope.'

'Mavis is moving on Saturday, and it can't be arranged before then, even at a registry office.'

'Oh, no, that means I'll still have to go to Peckham.'

'I know my dear, and with you so far away, I doubt you'll be able to see much of each other. Perhaps just weekends.'

'Mother, there must be something we can do.'

'The only thing I can think of is that Mavis stays here with us until the wedding can be arranged. However, it isn't really appropriate and her mother might not agree.'

'God, her mother! She might not even agree to the marriage.'

'Of course she will, Alec, why wouldn't she? In fact, why don't you take Mavis home now and you can officially ask for her daughter's hand in marriage? You can also tell Mrs Jackson that Mavis can remain with us until the service is arranged, but assure her that nothing untoward will happen and that I will personally see to that.'

'Yes, yes, all right,' Alec said. His mother seemed to have a ready answer for everything and he wondered now if she had worked just about everything out in advance. It wouldn't surprise him, and maybe he should feel annoyed at her interference, yet when he glanced at Mavis he couldn't feel anything but happiness. He hadn't planned on marriage yet, but now this lovely girl was going to be his wife, and along with that he wouldn't have to worry about his mother's illness any more. Mavis would look after his mother, and she would no longer have to worry about being a burden as her illness progressed.

'Come on, Alec, run along now, and, Mavis, I can't tell you how happy this has made me.'

Mavis looked reluctant to leave, her voice hesitant as she said, 'Maybe it would be better if I spoke to my mother first.'

'No, my dear, it's only proper that Alec speaks to her, and, anyway, I'm sure there's nothing to worry about. Your mother will be as pleased as I am.'

Alec hoped she was right, but then she usually was about most things. They both said goodbye, but Alec found himself increasingly nervous as they walked to Cullen Street.

He reached out to take Mavis's hand, clutching it tightly, finding his equally gripped in return. She was nervous too, but surely they had nothing to worry about?

Mavis was feeling sick inside as she walked home with Alec. She had agreed to marry him, but deep down there were still doubts. She should be happy, but instead felt lost and alone. Alec had reached out to take her hand and she had found herself clutching his as though her life depended on it. She had smiled at him and he had smiled back as he held her hand a little tighter. It was then that it hit Mavis. She would be dependent on this man. He would be her husband; she would be living with him, sleeping in the same bed as him, and the thought made her blush. What would it be like? She shivered as they turned into Cullen Street. But the thought of sleeping with Alec evaporated when she saw Tommy Wilson walking towards them.

Tommy frowned as he drew closer, his eyes on their clutched hands. 'Hello, Mavis.'

'Hello, Tommy. Th . . . this is Alec,' and then she found herself blurting out, 'We're getting married.'

'What! Married! Bloody hell, the grapevine missed out on that one. I didn't even hear that you were courting. What is it? A shotgun wedding?'

Alec stiffened, answering for her. 'It most certainly isn't,' he snapped. 'Come on, Mavis, let's go.'

'Yes, run along, Mavis,' Tommy mocked, his voice a copy of Alec's haughty tone.

'Tommy, don't be nasty,' Mavis appealed.

He had the grace to look shamefaced. 'Yeah, sorry, it's just that it's come as a bit of a shock, that's all.'

Mavis didn't get the chance to answer as Alec urged her swiftly along the street, muttering, 'Damn cheek. I don't know who he thinks he is, but it's obviously sour grapes.'

'Sour grapes?'

'Yes, he's jealous that you're going to marry me.'

'No, no, you're wrong,' Mavis protested. 'Tommy isn't interested in me.'

'If you say so,' was Alec's terse reply.

They had reached the front door, Mavis saying nothing more as they walked inside. Alec was wrong, of course, the idea of Tommy being jealous was ridiculous. Unlike Alec, Tommy saw her as an idiot; he used to call her Dumbo, and probably thought that Alec must be out of his mind to marry her.

Alec stood in front of her mother now, tense about asking permission to marry her daughter but, as he spoke, Mavis found that she was still thinking about Tommy Wilson.

It was only when her mother yelled that Mavis came to her senses, shocked by the expression on her face.

Lily stared at Alec in horror. 'Marry my daughter! Are you out of your mind? No, I won't allow it.'

'But, Mum, why not?' Mavis asked.

''Cos you're only sixteen, you silly cow. That's far too young to get married.'

'Hold on, Lily, let's hear them out,' Pete urged. 'Alec didn't say right now and he's probably talking about getting engaged. Is that right, lad?'

'No, I'm afraid not. We want to get married as soon as it can be arranged.'

'What! My God, don't tell me you've got my daughter up the spout!'

'No, of course not,' he spluttered.

'Well, that's something,' Lily said, but then her eyes flared with anger again. 'You've been lying to me, Mavis. I thought you were going round to Ellington Avenue to see Mrs Pugh, but all this time you must have been sneaking out to see him.'

'That isn't true. I was going to see Mrs Pugh, but . . . but Alec was there too and . . . and well . . .' Mavis trailed off.

'All right, you don't have to paint a picture. Anyway, it doesn't make any difference. You ain't marrying him and that's that. You're coming to Peckham with us.'

'No, no, I won't.'

'Yes, you bloody well will!'

'Lily, Lily, calm down,' Pete cajoled. 'Sit down, love, all of you sit down, and let's talk about this calmly.'

'Calm! You expect me to be calm?'

'Lily, I know you're upset, but getting out of your pram isn't solving anything.'

Lily ignored him, and also turned her back on Alec as she spat, 'Mavis, what does Edith Pugh say about this? Don't tell me she's agreed to her precious son marrying an idiot like you.'

'She has. Mrs Pugh doesn't think I'm daft. She likes me.'

Alec drew Lily's attention again and she turned to face him as he spoke.

'Mrs Jackson, Mavis is telling the truth. My mother is very fond of her and delighted that she agreed to marry me.'

'Who asked you, you pompous git?' she spat.

'Lily, stop it, there's no need for that,' Pete snapped. 'I can't believe you're acting like this. This young man has come round to tell you that he wants to marry Mavis, and surely it ain't the end of the world?'

'Shut up, Pete. Mavis is my daughter and this has nothing to do with you!'

Though it was unlike him, Pete's eyes darkened with anger as he reared up out of his chair. 'Right then, if that's how you feel, I'll bugger off and leave you to it.'

'No, don't go,' Lily cried as she rushed to clasp his arm. Pete had no idea why she was desperate for Mavis to go with them to Peckham, and she could hardly tell him the truth. Pete had said he would take Mavis on and was trying to act the role of a father figure, but she'd shut him out.

'I can see where I ain't wanted, Lily.'

'I'm sorry, really I am. It's just that I'm upset and spoke without thinking. Please stay.'

'If I can't offer an opinion, what's the point?'

'Pete, please, I can't handle this on my own,' Lily lied. 'Please stay.'

He nodded, but said nothing as he sat down again.

'Thanks, love,' Lily said before turning to Alec again. 'Right, you say you want to marry my daughter, but why the all-fired hurry?'

'Because you're moving out of the area and it will make it very difficult for us to see each other.'

'There's weekends and it ain't as if we're leaving the country. We're only moving to Peckham.'

'Yes, but as we want to get married, I can't see the point in waiting.'

'Can't see the point! She's only sixteen.'

'I know, but I promise I'll look after her. I . . . I have a good job, and Mavis won't want financially. In fact, she'll stay at home with my mother.'

'Live with your mother! You won't have a place of your own? Blimey, Mavis, how do you feel about that?' Lily asked.

'I don't mind, Mum. I like Mrs Pugh.'

'You're still too young to think about marriage. I don't see why you can't wait, get engaged first, and in the meantime you'll come with us.'

'No, I've told you, I don't want to go,' Mavis cried. 'You're . . . you're going to live with him, pretend to be married and . . . and that ain't right.'

'Don't you dare shout at me!'

Pete had been sitting quietly, but now said, 'I know you want me to keep my mouth shut, Lily, but if Mavis feels that strongly about it, you can't force her to live with us.'

'She's my daughter and she'll do as she's told.'

'If you make me come with you I won't pretend that Pete's my dad,' Mavis said defiantly. 'I'll tell anyone who asks the truth . . . tell them that you ain't married.'

'You wouldn't dare!' Lily threatened. 'I'd knock your bloody block off!'

Pete suddenly reared to his feet again to grab Lily's arm. 'Come with me. I want to talk to you in private for a minute. You two wait there,' he ordered.

Lily found herself urged upstairs, and when they were in her bedroom she shrugged off his grip. 'What do you think you're doing?'

'I'm trying to make you see sense. If you insist that Mavis comes with us, she'll be sulky, miserable, and what sort of life will we have?'

'What is this, Pete? Do you want rid of Mavis? Is that it?'

'No, I said I'd take Mavis on and I meant it, but I don't think she's bluffing. She's growing up, standing on her own two feet, and what if your threats don't stop her? If she tells our new neighbours that we ain't married, where will that leave you? Back to how it is now with everyone giving you the cold shoulder.'

'She wouldn't dare.'

'All right, I've never been one to care about gossip. If you want to risk it, that's fine with me.'

Lily didn't want to admit it, but Pete was right. If Mavis opened her mouth the gossip would start again, and any chance of respectability would be gone. Yet still she balked at the thought of leaving Mavis behind, of losing the wages her daughter would bring in.

'Well, Lily, have you made up your mind?'

Still thinking, Lily lowered her eyes. Mavis *had* to come with them, and as her mother she'd see to it that her daughter kept her mouth shut. Yet Lily knew she was losing control of her daughter, and doubts crept in.

'Lily . . .' Pete urged.

It was the thought of being back to square one,

of losing any chance of holding her head high in the new neighbourhood that finally swayed Lily, and anyway, if Pete didn't stint on the house-keeping, she'd still be able to salt a few bob away.

At last she looked Pete in the eyes. 'All right, maybe I *should* let Mavis marry that stuck-up git.'

'She could do worse, love.'

'Come on then. Let's put them out of their misery.'

Both Mavis and Alec looked delighted, and when Alec said that his mother had suggested that Mavis live with them until the wedding could be arranged, with all the fight gone out of her, Lily didn't argue.

Who'd have thought it, Lily mused, her eyes on her daughter. The girl was as thick as two planks but had landed on her feet. Unlike her, Mavis wouldn't be forced to sell junk to make ends meet, but then Pete grinned at her and Lily smiled back. Pete wasn't like Ron, he wasn't a gambler, but as always on the few occasions she dared to think about her husband, Lily's heart jolted.

Once again Lily found her eyes on Mavis, and she gulped. The resemblance to Ron was so marked and she wondered how he'd feel if he knew his daughter was getting married, and that he wouldn't be there to give her away. This thought sparked off another and she said brusquely, 'Are you having a church wedding?'

'My mother suggested the registry office.'

'Did she now? Well, it ain't up to your mother. How do you feel about it, Mavis?'

'I . . . I don't mind.'

'What about family and friends? Will you be having a bit of a do afterwards?'

'I'm afraid we haven't really discussed it,' Alec said. 'We haven't any family and, well . . . there aren't friends, just acquaintances.'

'Yeah, same here,' Lily said, thinking that there'd only been her mother. As for friends, she *had* classed Kate as a friend, but the woman had turned out to be a viper. 'So,' she mused, 'there's just gonna be us there. Blimey, some wedding this is gonna be.'

'I tell you what,' Pete said. 'How about we go for a meal afterwards, my treat?'

'That's very kind of you, Mr . . . Mr . . . er . . .'

'Culling,' Pete offered, 'but there's no need for formality. Call me Pete.'

'Thank you, and as I said, it's very kind of you.'

'Right then, that just leaves you to sort out the date and then let us know,' Pete said.

'Yes, of course. I'll go to the registry office tomorrow.'

Lily looked at her daughter to find that she was miles away, showing no interest in her own wedding plans. Mavis had always been a bit gorm-less, but this was something else. Did she really want to marry Alec, or was she just using it as a way out? Oh, what did it matter? Now that she'd accepted it, Lily had realised that it was probably for the best. Mavis would be all right with Alec and his mother, while she and Pete could make a fresh start. There'd be just the two of them, and maybe this time, just maybe, she'd find the happiness and respectability she craved.

CHAPTER TWENTY-TWO

PART TWO
1962

Sometimes Mavis found it hard to believe that nearly seven years had passed since her marriage to Alec, nearly all of them unhappy ones. She blamed Edith Pugh, her mother-in-law, a woman who had turned out to be nothing but a manipulating harridan. Mavis had longed for a place of their own; she had begged Alec, but she was helpless against her mother-in-law's guile. Nowadays she had given up, despising her husband, a man who let his mother rule the house, her, and their children with a rod of iron.

How long had it taken her to find out that Edith Pugh was nothing like the woman she'd portrayed before her marriage to Alec? It had been all right at first – well, other than Alec's incessant demands in bed – but she had thought herself happy. The reading lessons had continued for some time, but when Mavis still found it impossible, her mother-in-law had eventually lost patience, her scorn making Mavis feel worthless again.

'Mummy, Mummy, can I come down now?'

'Don't you dare let that boy come downstairs. He needs to learn that he can't talk to me like that and he's to remain in his room until his father comes home.'

Mavis nodded, too browbeaten to argue with her mother-in-law. At least James had only been sent to his room, but if Alec had been there the boy would have faced a thrashing. She had always thought that Alec was too hard on their son, but both he and his mother insisted that when James was naughty the discipline was necessary. Spare the rod, spoil the child was their adage, and though Mavis had tried to intervene, it only made things worse and her five-year-old son's punishment even harder. Thankfully James was a good little boy and thrashings were rare these days.

'Mummy, please, can I come down now?' James shouted again.

'No, James, not yet,' she called, unable to miss her mother-in-law's smile of satisfaction.

'Make me a cup of tea and then get the dinner on,' Edith ordered. 'Alec will be home in an hour and when I tell him what that boy's been up to he'll get the hiding he deserves. An old witch! How dare he call me an old witch?'

'He's already being punished, Mother,' Mavis said before she left the living room. Of course, it could hardly be called that now, not since it had been turned into a bedroom for her mother-in-law, who these days found the stairs impossible.

Mavis walked to the kitchen, hating herself, this house, her marriage, but most of all hating Edith Pugh, the woman she now had to call 'Mother'.

Grace, her nearly three-year-old daughter, was sitting on the floor, showing no interest in her colouring books and her expression mutinous. 'Want James,' she demanded.

'I know, darling, but he can't come downstairs yet.'

'Why not?'

'You know why. He was rude to Granny.'

'Don't care. Want James.'

Mavis tensed. She knew her daughter wouldn't be easy to placate. Since James had started school, Grace had lost her playmate and she missed him. The antithesis of her brother, who'd been an easy baby, gentle and amenable even as a toddler, Grace had come into the world fighting, squalling, demanding attention from the start. Now she was doing it again and if the screaming started Edith would take great delight in telling Alec what a useless wife and mother she was, one who couldn't even control her own children. 'Listen, darling, James will be able to play with you soon, but until then why don't you colour in one of your pictures?'

'No, don't want to.'

'How about a biscuit?'

'Yes, bickie.'

Mavis felt her knees weaken with relief. Grace was a greedy child, chubby from too many bribes of biscuits and cakes to shut her up, but Mavis was pleased that at least she'd managed to divert another temper tantrum. She gave her daughter a digestive, the child stuffing it into her mouth, while Mavis put the kettle on to make Edith a cup of tea. That done, she'd have to get dinner ready, and with any luck her mother-in-law would leave her in peace until it was ready.

'More, Mummy,' Grace demanded, holding out her hand.

Oh, God, Edith was right, Mavis thought as she gave her daughter another biscuit. She *was* a useless mother. If only she could be more like Jenny Bonner, a woman only a few years older than her, who had moved in next door two years ago. Jenny had become a light in her life, a friend and confidante, and Mavis would slip next door to see her whenever she got the chance.

'Mummy, please, I want to come down now.'

'Not yet, James, but soon,' she called, too afraid to abandon the punishment dished out by the boy's grandmother, rules that had been set down the moment Mavis had brought her newborn son home from the hospital. If James had cried between feeds, her mother-in-law insisted he shouldn't be picked up and, as a nervous new mother, Mavis had taken her advice – even though it had broken her heart to hear her baby's sobs.

Mavis heard the handbell, a small brass one that Alec had given his mother when she'd become confined to bed. She was being summoned again – nowadays nothing more than a servant in a kingdom ruled by her mother-in-law.

Alec was on his way home, the early February evening cold after the warmth of his office. He quickened his pace, walking upright, well satisfied with his job and his life. He'd gained a promotion, and then another, until he was now head of his department.

Of course, Alec knew he wasn't liked by many people, especially the girls he supervised, but that didn't worry him. Unlike his predecessor, Alec had been determined when he took over the department that it was to be run professionally. He had instigated changes, stopped the girls' incessant chatter, and among other things, had insisted on a dress code. None of his many changes had been popular, but Alec knew that the now calm efficiency of his department hadn't gone unnoticed by the management.

'Hello, Mother,' he said as he walked straight into what was once the living room. 'How are you?'

'In agony as usual,' she complained, 'and it doesn't help that since I've been confined to this room your son has become out of control.'

'What has James done now?'

'He called me a witch!'

'Did he now? Well, don't worry, Mother. I'll have a word with the boy.'

'James needs more than a word. He deserves a thrashing.'

'Do you really think that's necessary?'

'Alec, you have no idea what I have to put up with. I misjudged Mavis from the start, thought the girl had hidden intelligence and that I could teach her to read. As you know, that proved impossible. She's useless, an idiot who isn't fit to look after me, or the children.'

'Don't you think that's a bit harsh?'

'No, I don't. I'm in so much pain, and need peace and quiet, but Mavis does nothing to stop the children's unruly behaviour. They were chasing each other all over the house, running in here and then out again, slamming doors until I couldn't stand it any more. All I did was to ask them both to stop, to stay out of this room, and I had to give Grace a little smack before she'd obey me. That was when James shouted at me. He said he hated me, that I'm an old witch. Not only that, Alec, I'm in agony and need my pills – but as usual Mavis seems to have forgotten them.'

Alec's lips tightened. Every day when he came home from work it was to find the same: his mother upset and, since her continual relapses, in great pain. 'Leave it to me, Mother,' he said, walking out of the room and along to the kitchen.

Mavis was at the stove, stirring something in a pan, and there was no smile of welcome on her face when she said, 'Hello, Alec.'

'Daddy, Daddy,' Grace said excitedly as she jumped up and ran towards him.

'Not now, Grace,' he said crossly.

Her face crumbled, then went red before she flopped onto the floor again, kicking her legs and thumping the lino with little fists as she began to scream.

'That's enough!' Alec yelled. 'Stop that right now!'

Grace was instantly quiet and Alec glared at Mavis. 'See, that's all it takes, a little discipline, yet from what my mother tells me you've been allowing the children to run riot. Not only that, how dare you allow James to call my mother a witch?'

'He didn't mean it. He was upset that your mother smacked Grace.'

'That's no excuse. If the children were upsetting my mother, they deserve to be punished. You know how much pain she's in, how she suffers, and you should see that the children leave her in peace.'

'Alec, I do my best,' Mavis appealed.

'Well, your best isn't good enough. Show me your list. I want to see that everything has been done.'

Mavis handed it to him and Alec saw that his mother had drawn a double bed, a vacuum cleaner, windows and an iron. 'Our bedroom,' he said. 'I'll check it when I go upstairs, but what about the ironing? Have you finished it?'

'Yes, it's all done.'

'Good, but my mother's in pain. She said you've forgotten her medication again.'

'No, Alec. I'm sure I gave her painkillers less than an hour ago.'

'You couldn't have. One look at her is enough to prove that. Now see to her pills while I sort James out.'

'Please don't smack him. He's already been sent to his room. Isn't that enough?'

'On this occasion, no, it isn't. I won't have my mother upset and James has to learn that.'

Mavis looked distressed as she left the room, but Alec didn't care. She should care for his mother properly instead of leaving her to suffer. He went upstairs, taking his temper out on his son as he gave the boy the thrashing he deserved.

In Peckham, Lily had her feet up on the fender, skirt up over her knees as she toasted her legs in front of the fire. Life was good to her now and she was happy, or so she told herself. Pete was a good man, a good provider, but there was none of the passion in her love life that she'd enjoyed with Ron. There'd been no news of him for over eight years now, yet from time to time Lily still found her mind straying to her absent husband. He'd been a bugger, there was no getting away from that, but Ron had been the only man she had ever really loved and lately Pete had been pushing her to see a solicitor about a divorce. He wanted marriage, but up until now she'd resisted. Oh, she was fond of Pete, yet her feelings for him hadn't deepened, in spite of all the years they'd been together.

The back door opened, a frizz of brown hair above a round face appearing. 'Can I come in? I'm all in a tizzy.'

'Yeah, of course you can,' she said, pulling her skirt down as Marilyn Foster walked in. 'What are you in a tizzy about?'

'It's my Rhona, and you're not going to believe it, Lily.'

Lily doubted that. Marilyn's daughter was a handful, boy mad, and had been since she was fourteen. 'What's she been up to now?'

'I found these in her handbag.'

'What are they?'

'The birth control pill, that's what.'

'Blimey, she's only sixteen. How did she get hold of them?'

'According to Rhona she got them from the clinic, but of course she's lying. When Enoch Powell announced that they were going to be issued on the National Health last year, he said they were only for married women.'

'Somebody must have flogged them to her, but surely it's better for Rhona to take the pill than risk getting pregnant?'

'Lily, she's only sixteen and shouldn't be going with boys yet.'

'My daughter was married at sixteen.'

'Yeah, you told me,' Marilyn said, 'but I still think that's too young. All right, don't look at me like that. You know I ain't one to keep my opinions to myself and it ain't something I haven't said before.'

Lily had to agree. Marilyn had never been slow in speaking her mind, and at first she'd been wary of her neighbour. Gradually though, she'd learned that though Marilyn might be a bit opinionated, she wasn't a gossip. In fact, Lily had never heard her say a bad word against anyone, even old Mrs Biggs on the other side who was the bane of their lives. 'Yeah, I know Mavis was young, but she's doing all right, at least she was the last time I saw her. James must be five now, and Grace nearly three.'

'You don't look old enough to have a couple of grandchildren, Lily. Wouldn't you like to see more of them?'

'Thanks, but my mirror tells a different story,' Lily said, hiding a secret that she had yet to reveal. At the moment she was keeping it to herself, but when she was ready to let it out, Marilyn would be the first to know. Shrugging now, she continued, 'Yeah, of course I'd like to see more of my grandchildren, but I've told you what it's like. Mavis rarely has time to visit me, and with the reception I get from my daughter's hubby and his equally stuck-up mother, I hate going there. Anyway, back to your Rhona. What are you going to do about those birth control pills?'

'I dunno, but I'll have to make sure her father doesn't find out that she's got them. You know Ian. He'd go bloody potty.'

Yes, Lily thought, he probably would. Ian Foster was all right, and he and Pete had become friends, but where his daughter was concerned the man was blind. When Rhona wanted something she could wrap him round her finger and the daft bloke still saw her as his innocent little girl. Lily was sure that one day he was in for a rude awakening, but so far he was in ignorance of what his daughter got up to. 'You're right, but if she got herself in the family way, it'd be even worse. To be on the safe side, maybe you should just let her take them.'

'It doesn't seem right, Lily. We were scared shitless of getting pregnant and it kept us in line. These pills take away that fear and God knows what it'll lead to. Blimey, a girl could sleep with any number of men before she settles down and gets married.'

And Rhona probably would, Lily thought, but kept this opinion to herself. Marilyn was worried enough about her daughter without adding fuel to the fire.

'I'd best get back,' Marilyn now said. 'Ian will be home soon.'

'Pete too,' Lily said, feeling sorry for Marilyn as the woman left. To think she had once been worried about Mavis, about boys taking advantage of her, but there was no need for concern now. In fact, on the rare occasions she saw her daughter, she'd been impressed by how good a mother she was, and, thanks to Mavis, Edith Pugh's house was always immaculate. Yes, Mavis had done well for herself and was well and truly off her hands now.

Mavis undressed slowly, worn out after seeing to dinner, clearing up, and then getting the children to bed. She'd been upset to see the red marks on James, the tell-tale signs that he'd been more than just smacked. For a while she had lain beside her son, cuddling him, loving him fiercely. It was her fault that James had been punished so harshly, and though doing everything she could to keep her mother-in-law happy, sometimes it just seemed impossible and Edith would go out of her way to complain, to antagonise Alec. Mavis knew that to protect James, she had to try harder to placate her mother-in-law, but it was so difficult to keep the children quiet all the time.

When the children were both asleep she had gone back downstairs, Alec insisting as always that they sat in his mother's room to watch television until ten o'clock. It was then Mavis's task to sort her mother-in-law out for the night. It wasn't easy, the woman virtually bedridden now, and her constant chiding didn't help.

Mavis did the best she could, washed her, helped her onto the commode, but she dreaded what would happen when Edith could no longer manage even this small task. At six in the morning she would have to be up, Edith waiting to use the commode again, but there had been times lately when she had gone downstairs to find that it was too late and the sheets were wet.

Alec was already in bed, waiting as usual, his eyes avid as she climbed in beside him. There was rarely a night when he didn't demand her body, but nowadays, knowing as always she'd be left unsatisfied, reaching out for something that was never there, she was just thankful when it was over quickly.

'Did you get my mother settled?'

'Yes, she's fine.'

'Good,' he said.

'Did you have to punish James so harshly?'

'I was angry, and that was your fault. In future, I don't want to find my mother in pain.'

She felt the sting of tears again. James was rarely naughty these days and didn't deserve to suffer because of her. Thankfully it had been a long time since Alec had punished the boy so harshly, but once again Mavis knew she'd have to try harder, work harder to keep her mother-in-law happy and James safe.

As Alec's hands moved across her body, Mavis closed her eyes, trying to lose herself in the memory of her dream. Despite the passing of time it still came to haunt her and was always the same. Someone, a man, reaching out for her, yet she still couldn't see his face.

'Who are you?' she asked inwardly, yearning to find out and wishing that, instead of just a dream, there really was someone to take her away from her wretched life.

CHAPTER TWENTY-THREE

After Jenny Bonner had dropped her seven-year-old son, Greg, at school, and Mavis her son James, the two women walked home together, Grace in her pushchair. 'Are you coming in for a cup of tea?' Jenny asked.

'Yes, but I'll have to see if my mother-in-law is all right first. If she is, I'll tell her I've got to get a few things in from the shops.'

'Why don't you just tell her the truth?'

'If I do that she'll just find one excuse after another to keep me busy and I'll never get away.'

'Out, Mummy!'

'Not now, darling. We're nearly home.'

'Want out,' Grace demanded as she struggled against her reins.

Mavis gave in and, taking her mother's place, Grace began to push the pram haphazardly along Ellington Avenue. It made conversation difficult as Mavis constantly had to assist with the steering, and though she knew that Mavis gave in too easily to her daughter's demands, Jenny kept her own counsel. Mavis had a rotten life, and she was too soft for her own good, but she had to put up with enough criticism from her mother-in-law. 'See you soon,' Jenny said as they parted outside her house.

'Yes, hopefully in about fifteen minutes or so,' Mavis called.

Jenny went inside, thanking her lucky stars that her life was nothing like her neighbour's. She had a good marriage, her own home, freedom to come and go as she liked, whereas Mavis was living under her mother-in-law's roof and tied to acting as her nursemaid. Though she had lived in Ellington Avenue for two years, Jenny had never met Edith Pugh and, from the sound of her, she didn't want to.

Jenny made a pot of tea, but then her eyes strayed to the letter she had tucked behind the clock. It saddened her that her cousin's marriage hadn't worked out, but she had never thought much of his choice for a wife. Of course, she'd have to talk to her husband before she could give Willy an answer, but surely Stan wouldn't mind? They had a spare room and it was only until her cousin could sort himself out.

Less than fifteen minutes later, there was a knock on the door and, opening it, Jenny smiled at Mavis. 'You managed to get away then?'

'Yes, but I daren't stay for more than half an hour,' Mavis said, urging Grace inside.

Jenny found a few of her son's toy cars to keep Grace amused, and with the child now pushing them around the floor she poured two cups of tea, saying, 'I don't know how you put up with that old witch.'

'That's funny. James called her a witch yesterday and she was none too pleased.'

'Good for him. At least he's got the bottle to stand up to her. Oh, sorry, Mavis. I shouldn't have said that.'

'It's all right. I wish I had my son's courage too, but I just can't seem to stand up to my mother-in-law.'

'I don't know why. She's confined to her bed now, and would be lost without you. You should try taking the upper hand. When she rings that flaming bell, make her wait until *you're* ready, and let her know that if she's nasty she'll have an even longer wait next time.'

'I couldn't do that. She'd tell Alec and he'd go mad.' Mavis shook her head sadly. 'You may not believe this, but when I first married Alec my mother-in-law was really nice.'

'Really?' Jenny said, her brows rising sceptically.

'Oh, yes, and she welcomed me into her home with open arms.'

'So what changed?'

'I'm not sure, but I know she hated it when Alec showed me any affection in front of her.'

'Jealousy. I bet that was it.'

Mavis looked startled, but then said, 'You could be right. When I think about it now I can see that slowly but surely she began to belittle me, telling Alec how useless I was. Nowadays of course, Alec believes everything she tells him and he always takes her side.'

Jenny had heard some of this before from Mavis, and though she could understand what had led her to marry Alec Pugh, she couldn't comprehend why she allowed her husband to treat her like dirt. Mavis was beautiful, with a figure to turn any man's eye. She could have done so much better, but instead was stuck with a man who was not only nothing to look at, but also dull, without a shred of humour.

Mavis looked so downcast, and deciding that she needed cheering up, Jenny said, 'Never mind. You'll come into your own one of these days, I'm sure of it, and I'll tell you what,' she added, taking the letter from behind the clock, 'have a read of that and you'll see that you aren't the only one who's having a hard time of it.'

Mavis paled as Jenny held out the envelope. 'No, I can't read your letter.'

'Go on, I don't mind.'

Mavis shook her head vigorously. 'You read it to me.'

Jenny was puzzled by Mavis's reaction and continued to flourish the letter. 'Don't be silly. Read it for yourself.'

'I wish I could, but I . . . I can't read.'

'What? Why not? Didn't they teach you in school?'

'They tried, but I just couldn't pick it up. I was considered backward, stupid, and the other kids used to call me Dumbo.'

'Mavis, I've known you for two years, and one thing I'm sure of is that you aren't backward.'

'As a child I always thought I was stupid, but my mother-in-law said I have something called word blindness. I was hoping she'd be able to teach me, but it was hopeless. You see, when I look at words they appear to jump all over the page. I also see them back to front and in a jumbled mess. I tried so hard, really I did, despite getting terrible headaches. My mother-in-law would spend hours just trying to teach me one word, but the next time we went back to it I'd find it unrecognisable. In the end she gave up and, to be honest, I don't blame her.'

Jenny didn't know what to say, so instead she took the letter from the envelope. 'Well, love, I'm happy to read this to you, but suffice to say that it's from my cousin. He moved out of the area when he got married and was doing well, buying a house in one of those new towns.'

'That's funny. My father worked in a new town just before he disappeared.'

'Yes, you told me, and it's awful that you've never heard from him. I know it doesn't sound as bad, but my cousin says here that he found out his wife was carrying on behind his back, and not with just one bloke either. Now Willy doesn't even know if their kid is his or not.'

'How awful for him.'

'Yes, and to make matters worse, when they filed for divorce his wife got nearly everything. The house can't be sold until the boy's an adult, and so he needs somewhere to stay until he can sort himself out.'

'Oh, dear,' Mavis murmured, 'the poor man.'

'He's asked if we can put him up, but I can't understand his mother. My aunt has always been a nasty piece of work, but would you believe she blames him, says he's a failure and that she won't take him in.'

'Does she live in London?'

'Yes, she's local, but I keep well out of her way.'

Grace was becoming fractious, obviously tired of the cars now, and apologetically Mavis said, 'I think I'll have to take her home. Sorry to rush off, but thanks for the tea.'

'You're welcome and I'll see you later when we collect the boys from school.'

Grace ran ahead of her to the door and with a rueful smile, Mavis said, 'Back to the witch.'

'Witch, witch,' Grace echoed.

'Now look what I've done! She heard me,' Mavis cried worriedly as she crouched down in front of her daughter. 'Grace, you mustn't say that, darling, and definitely not in front of your grandmother.'

It would serve the old woman right, Jenny decided as Mavis stood up again, but kept these thoughts to herself.

'Bye, Jenny,' Mavis now said.

'See you later,' Jenny called, and after closing the door decided that, as Stan was sure to agree, she'd reply to her cousin's letter and then get his room sorted out.

In Cullen Street, Kate Truman was at her window again, staring at the house opposite, sure that she'd seen the old bit of filthy curtain moving again. The place had been empty for over a year now, with no sign of new tenants moving in, and to her this reinforced the rumour that Cullen Street was going to be demolished. The area was changing, with streets being torn down and replaced by high-rise flats. The demolition gangs were slowly encroaching, but so far this street and others around them remained untouched.

Yes, the curtain had definitely moved, and after seeing a brief flicker of light in there last night this now confirmed her suspicions. Someone was in there, and as they were obviously hiding it was someone who didn't want it known. Was it a criminal? Kate shivered, frightened by the thought. She wanted to tell someone, but from day one she hadn't got on with the family who now lived next door, taking over Lily Jackson's house. There was still Olive Wilson, of course, and throwing on her coat Kate left the house, staying on her own side of the road until she crossed to number eighteen.

'Hello, Kate, come in,' Olive said. 'I was just talking to Tommy's wife on the telephone.'

'That's nice, and how is she?' Kate asked as she managed a thin smile. Olive had been one of the first people in Cullen Street to have a telephone installed and loved the fact that she was one up on her neighbours. She was still one of the few and took every opportunity to rub it in.

'She's fine,' Olive said as they both walked through to her kitchen.

'I just popped over to tell you that someone's in number ten.'

'It's about time. That house was going to rack and ruin.'

'I don't mean officially,' Kate said. 'I reckon someone's hiding out in there, and it might be a criminal on the run.'

'Who in their right mind would hide out in

Cullen Street? With the nosy parkers around here they wouldn't last five minutes – you've proved that. It's probably a squatter.'

'I'm not a nosy parker,' Kate said indignantly, 'but I could hardly miss the curtain moving.'

'Did you spot anyone?'

'No, but I'll get my Bill to check it out when he comes home.'

'Fine, and if he needs a hand to get rid of anyone he can give my old man a shout.'

'Thanks, Olive,' Kate said, relieved that if things turned nasty Bill wouldn't have to handle it on his own.

Edith hated her dependency, the indignity of having to ask her daughter-in-law for help. She rang her handbell, saying curtly as Mavis walked into the room, 'I need my commode.'

'Yes, all right,' Mavis said.

Edith also hated being confined to this room, unable to see what was going on in the rest of the house. Alec said that Mavis was keeping everything up to scratch, but without her supervision Edith doubted it. Not only that, she had lost control of the children, something she abhorred, and she dreaded to think what they got up to now that they were mostly out of sight. For a little while she had been able to use a wheelchair, but even that was beyond her now, her bed the only place that offered any comfort. 'You were long enough at the shops,' she snapped.

'I'm sorry, Mother, but I was out for less than half an hour.'

'I don't see why you have to shop three or four times a week,' Edith said as Mavis helped her out of bed. 'Why don't you get everything we need in one go?'

Mavis hesitated, but then said, 'It would take too long. Doing it this way I'm only out for a short while.'

'Yes, yes, I suppose you're right,' Edith said impatiently as she was helped onto the commode. Grace was shouting for her mother now, the child making a racket as usual. 'Go and see what Grace is up to, and keep her out of my room. Her incessant whining drives me mad.'

'I'm sorry. I'll try to keep her quiet. Ring your bell when you've finished,' Mavis said meekly as she hurried from the room.

When it was time to summon Mavis again, Edith did just that, grimacing in pain as Mavis helped her back into bed. When alone again she picked up her book, deciding to read for a while, but after only a few pages her vision blurred, a symptom of her illness that was almost impossible to bear.

Impatiently, Edith put the book down. She'd hoped to teach Mavis to read, something that had proved impossible, but giving up the lessons turned out to be a blessing. When they married, Edith hadn't foreseen that Alec would become besotted with his new wife. He had fawned over Mavis all the time, so much so that he seemed to resent his own mother's presence. She'd been unable to hide her annoyance and the kind façade she had presented to Mavis dropped. It had been a mistake. It had played into her daughter-in-law's hands, the girl then nagging Alec for a place of their own.

Of course, Edith wasn't going to stand for that, and so she had begun to undermine Mavis in everything she did. The fact that Mavis hadn't been able to learn to read had served her well, and she had also complained of being neglected, something that appalled her son.

Slowly, Alec's rose-tinted vision had dimmed, and now Edith smiled with satisfaction. Mavis had had the audacity to try to take her son away from her, something she would never forgive, but the girl would never win. Edith knew that Alec was hers again now; her role of the poor, suffering mother, neglected by his useless wife, simple to play.

CHAPTER TWENTY-FOUR

'That smells like my favourite,' Pete said, sniffing the air as he walked in after a day's work.

'Yeah, sausages, onions and mash,' Lily told him.

'Smashing,' he said, walking over to kiss her cheek. 'I'll get myself cleaned up.'

Lily smiled. Pete's routine was always the same. He'd come in, kiss her and then say the same thing before going upstairs to the bathroom. Yes, the indoor bathroom, a luxury she now took for granted. There was something else she had taken for granted too, but she'd been proved wrong, and now she didn't know how Pete was going to take the news. After all this time it would come as a shock, just as it had to her.

Lily could time Pete like a clock and knew he'd be down soon so, mixing the Bisto, she made the gravy, and as expected he appeared just as she put their dinner on the table. He'd say the same thing at this point too, and smiling, Lily waited.

'I timed that just right, love.'

'Yes, you did,' she said, deciding to keep the news to herself until he'd finished eating. It didn't take long, the food disappearing rapidly off his plate.

'That was great,' he said, laying down his knife and fork.

'Marilyn's in a bit of a state.'

'Is she? Why's that?'

'If I tell you, you'll have to keep it to yourself. If Ian finds out, he'd go mad.'

'Well, we can't have that. Don't worry, I won't say anything – but mad about what?'

'Marilyn has found out that Rhona is taking the birth control pill.'

'Is she? Blimey, you're right. Ian would go potty.'

'Maybe I should have been on it too.'

Pete's brows creased as he looked at her. 'You, but why?'

'Ain't it obvious, you soppy sod?' Lily said, nerves making her sound snappy.

He shook his head. 'Not to me it ain't.'

'If I'd been on the pill, I wouldn't have gone and got myself pregnant.'

'Surely the pill wasn't around when you had Mavis?'

'I'm not talking about Mavis. I'm talking about the baby I'm carrying now.'

The penny dropped at last, and Pete's face

stretched with astonishment. 'A baby! You're having a baby! Oh, Lily, Lily,' he cried, jumping to his feet to pull her into his arms. 'I can't believe it.'

'I couldn't either. I mean, I'm forty-four, and thought it was the early change when my monthlies stopped.'

'How far along are you?'

'Just over four months.'

Pete pulled back, his hand now stroking her tummy. 'Yeah, I can feel a bit of a bulge but you ain't showing much.'

'I doubt that'll last much longer.'

'Sit down,' he now urged. 'You need to take it easy.'

'I'm not ill, Pete, I'm pregnant, though I must admit I tire easily. To be honest, I wasn't sure how you'd take it, but you look pleased.'

'Pleased! Blimey, love, that's an understatement. I'm over the moon!'

Lily wasn't. From the moment the doctor told her she was pregnant, all she'd felt was a feeling of dread. Mavis was backward. What if this baby was the same? Surely it wouldn't happen again? Surely this time she'd have a perfect son or daughter?

Kate Truman had kept watch on the house opposite on and off all day, at one time sure that she had glimpsed a face looking back at her. It had frightened her, so much so that when her husband came home, she pounced as soon as he walked in the door. 'Bill, there's someone in number ten, and I reckon it's a nutter.'

'A nutter! Where's Ellie?'

'She's upstairs getting ready.'

'Ready for what?'

'She's got a date with Jack, you know, that lad who lives a couple of streets away.'

'She can forget it. I ain't having her going out if there's a maniac on the prowl.'

Kate sighed. Ellie was seventeen now, but unlike Sandra and their son, both of whom had left home a few years ago, Bill still treated her like a child. If he tried to keep her in all hell would break loose and, cursing her thoughtlessness, Kate placated, 'I could be wrong and, as Olive said, it might just be squatters. Before you keep Ellie in, why don't you go over and check it out?'

'Bloody hell, woman, I've only just walked in the door and I'm starving.'

'It won't take a minute, Bill, and anyway, the potatoes aren't ready yet.'

'All right, all right,' he said, turning on his heel to march across the street. Kate stood on the doorstep, shivering in the cold as she watched nervously, but though Bill thumped repeatedly on the door, nothing stirred.

'Try going round the back,' she called.

Bill threw her a look of annoyance, but did as she

suggested. When he'd been gone for several minutes, Kate began to worry. What if she'd been right? What if there was someone dangerous in there? She'd sent Bill over to face him alone; but just as she was about to run for help, the front door was flung open.

Bill appeared, beckoning frantically. 'Kate, quick. Get over here.'

Kate ran across the road, and after following her husband into a room at the front of the house, she looked to where his finger was pointing. At first Kate thought she was looking at a pile of rags, but then she saw it was someone hunched over, their face hidden.

'He needs our help,' Bill said quietly.

It was then that the man looked up and Kate saw a filthy face with a long, scraggly, matted beard. The man coughed, and then, with a voice that was little more than a croak, he managed to speak. 'Hello, Kate.'

She stepped back in shock, puzzled. The man was a tramp, a filthy, dirty tramp. How did he know her name?

Bill moved to crouch in front of him, and then, turning to look over his shoulder at Kate, he said, 'Come on, love. Give me a hand. We need to get him over to our place.'

'Our place! Are you mad?'

'Kate, don't you recognise him? It's Ron – Ron Jackson.'

'Ron! Oh, my God,' Kate cried, but as she went to Bill's side she reeled back again. It couldn't be Ron, it just couldn't. This filthy, emaciated man stank, an eye-stinging mixture of stale urine, dirt and booze.

'Can you stand up, Ron?' Bill asked.

'No, Bill,' Kate cried. 'We can't take him in. He's not only dirty, he's probably flea-ridden as well.'

'We ain't leaving him here!'

The man raised his head again, and with great effort he gasped, 'I'll be all right, Bill. Just tell me where she is. Where's Lily?'

There was an awful groan, and before Bill got a chance to answer his question, Ron sank backwards.

'Kate, for God's sake, give me a hand,' Bill cried.

At last she moved, holding her breath as she crouched beside her husband. 'He ain't dead, is he?' she asked nervously.

Bill looked worried as he felt for a pulse, but then said, 'He's alive, but from the look of him he's in a bad way. Give me a hand and we'll see if we can carry him.'

'No, I ain't touching him,' she insisted. 'Anyway, he ain't our responsibility, there's someone else who should take him in. Leave him here and I'll send Ellie round to fetch her.'

'Do that, but in the meantime I ain't leaving him here to freeze to bloody death,' Bill snapped as he lifted Ron into his arms. 'Bloody hell, he's so light he must be all skin and bone.'

Tight-lipped, Kate said, 'He's gonna stink the place out. If you insist on taking him home I want him stripped and washed straightaway. And you'll have to do it, Bill, 'cos I ain't.'

'Huh, you're all heart, Kate.'

As they walked outside, Olive Wilson came running towards them, saying breathlessly, 'I saw you going over to number ten,' but then her face paled. 'Bill, who is that?'

'It's Ron Jackson and he's in a bad way,' Bill called without stopping as he carried the man across the road.

'Ron Jackson,' Olive gasped. 'For a minute I thought . . .'

'Thought what?' questioned Kate.

Olive waved a hand dismissively. 'Oh, it was nothing, but I can't believe that's Ron Jackson. He looks like a tramp!'

'He is, and sorry, Olive, but Bill's daft enough to lay him on our sofa without covering it first,' Kate said as she too hurried away.

Olive followed behind, walking in without an invitation as Kate shouted, 'Wait, Bill, don't put him down yet.'

'He stinks,' Olive said, as Kate threw an old blanket on the sofa, only then allowing Bill to lay Ron down.

'You're telling me,' she agreed, staring pointedly at her husband.

'All right, all right, I'll clean him up. Get me a bowl of water and he'll need a change of clothes.'

Kate marched from the room, returning with the water, a rag and an old towel. She also had a few of Bill's old clothes over her arm. 'Right, Bill, get on with it.'

'Kate,' said Olive. 'I think he needs to see a doctor. Would you like me to ring the surgery?'

Here we go again, Kate thought, Olive taking yet another opportunity to let it be known that she had a telephone. 'It's hardly worth it. He ain't staying here for long.'

'I don't think we should wait,' Bill urged.

'Oh, all right,' she huffed, and as Olive hurried out Kate called her daughter. The sooner she got Ron Jackson out of her house, the better.

CHAPTER TWENTY-FIVE

Mavis was clearing up the dinner things and at the same time doing her best to keep an eye on the children. Other than seeing Jenny for a cup of tea that morning, the day had been like any other. She was only twenty-three but, married with two children, she felt so much older. Oh, to be free of this house for a while. If only Alec could take her out in the evenings, if just to the pictures, but he had always been so staid, happy to stay at home with his books or stamp collection. Of course, nowadays, even if they wanted to, his mother's illness meant it was impossible to go out. She would never allow it – would refuse to let anyone else in to look after her, or the children.

Careful not to drop anything, Mavis put the dishes away, thankful that the children were still quietly absorbed with their drawing books. The doorbell rang, startling Mavis, but as she wondered who it was, a strange feeling washed over her.

The doorbell rang again, but Mavis just stood, unmoving, dread clutching her stomach into a knot. Alec must have left his mother's room to answer it and she could hear a murmur of voices, yet still Mavis remained frozen to the spot until her husband's voice summoned her.

'Mavis, come here. There's someone to see you.'

On leaden feet she walked to the door. What was the matter with her? Why did she feel like this? Alec hadn't invited the caller in, and just hissed in her ear as he moved to one side, 'It's someone called Ellie Truman.'

Mavis didn't recognise the young woman, but Truman? 'Hello,' she said. 'You . . . you wanted to see me?'

'Yeah, my mum sent me round. She said you've got to come straightaway.'

'Come? Come where?'

'To our house in Cullen Street.'

'Cullen Street,' Mavis repeated, but then it hit her. Ellie Truman, Sandra's younger sister. 'Why does your mother want to see me?'

'She said to tell you that your dad's turned up and that he's in a bad way.'

'My father!' Mavis gasped, reeling in shock.

'Are you coming or not?'

'Yes, yes, of course,' she said, and turning she rushed to the hall cupboard to grab her coat.

'Mavis, what on earth do you think you're doing?'

Alec asked as he watched her in disbelief. 'What about my mother? The children? You can't just dash off.'

Something swelled inside Mavis. Her father was back and from what Ellie said he was ill. Nothing was going to keep her away from him – nothing!

'You see to them for once,' she yelled, ignoring Alec's indignant expression as she flew out of the house.

Alec couldn't believe it. 'Mavis, come back at once,' he shouted.

'No, Alec, I won't,' she yelled, running hell for leather down the avenue.

Fuming, he called to her again, but to no avail. James, followed by Grace, ran along the hall, both looking close to tears.

'Where's Mummy gone?' Grace wailed.

Alec took in great gulps of air, fighting to hold his temper. 'She had to go out, but she'll be back soon,' he said, closing the street door. 'Now come and say goodnight to Grandma and then it's time for bed.'

'Don't want to,' Grace said petulantly.

'You'll do as I say. Now come along,' Alec insisted as he bent down to grab his daughter's hand, dragging her into his mother's room.

'Alec, what's going on? Who was that at the door?'

'I'll tell you after I've got these two to bed. Say goodnight, James, you too, Grace.'

'Goodnight, Grandma,' James said dutifully.

Grace just scowled, but his mother said impatiently, 'Leave it for once. Just get them out of here.'

Alec nodded and, grim-faced, he took the children upstairs. Mavis wasn't there to bathe them, and as though sensing his mood both children obeyed him when he told them to wash their hands and faces. That done, he left James to get into his pyjamas and into bed while he saw to Grace.

'Go straight to sleep,' Alec ordered his daughter, and then marching into James's room he said the same, unconcerned that both of them looked close to tears.

'Alec, tell me what's going on, and where is Mavis?' his mother asked as soon as he walked back into her room.

'She's gone to see her father.'

'What! He's back?'

'Yes, it seems so, but from what I could gather, he's ill.'

'How long is she going to be?'

'I've no idea.'

'As usual, Mavis hasn't given a thought to me, or my needs. The least she could have done was to make sure I didn't need my commode before she left.'

'I know, Mother. I tried to stop her, but she wouldn't listen.'

'It isn't good enough, Alec.'

'I doubt she'll be long.'

'I hope you're right, but this can't happen again. I can't be left on my own while she goes off to see her father.'

'Don't worry, Mother. Your needs must come first and I won't have you neglected. I'll talk to Mavis and make sure she understands that.'

Mavis flew to the sofa, unable to believe that this was her father until his blue eyes opened, the only thing recognisable in a face so thin it looked almost skeletal. The whites of his eyes looked yellow, his skin too, and breaking down she fell to her knees beside him. 'Oh, Dad . . . Dad.'

'Mavis? Is that you, Mavis?'

'Yes, Dad, it's me.'

'Where's your mother?'

'She moved away, Dad, years ago.'

'I want to see her – have to see her,' he said weakly, his eyes then closing again.

'Dad,' Mavis cried.

'He keeps drifting in and out of consciousness,' Kate Truman said. 'If you ask me, he should be in hospital.'

'Has anyone called a doctor?'

'Yeah, and hopefully he's on his way.'

'What happened to him, Kate?'

'Search me. We found him in number ten and brought him here. Bill cleaned him up a bit, but he's hardly said a word, well, except to ask for your mother.'

'Have . . . have you told him?'

'No, we thought we'd leave that to you. Now listen, Mavis, I ain't being funny, but if the doctor doesn't have your dad admitted to hospital, he can't stay here. He ain't my responsibility and you'll have to take him to your place.'

'No . . . hospital . . . too . . . too late,' he gasped.

'Oh, Dad,' Mavis cried again, but then there was a knock on the door and Kate answered it to let in the doctor.

'No . . . need,' Ron groaned, but the doctor ignored him, insisting the others leave the room while he examined his patient.

Mavis hovered close by, Kate too, but it was some time before the doctor came out of the living room. 'Are you his daughter?'

'Yes.'

'I'm afraid your father is a very sick man. He won't go into hospital and, as there's little they can do for him, I've agreed that he can remain at home. He'll need round-the-clock care – and get him this,' he said, scribbling a prescription. 'It might ease his pain.'

It was Kate who asked bluntly, 'Is he going to get better?'

'I'm afraid not, and he knows that.'

'But there must be something you can do!' Mavis cried.

The doctor shook his head sadly, the sympathy in his eyes too much for Mavis. Sobbing, she fled into Kate's living room to kneel by her father's side again, an arm across his frail body and her head on his chest. He couldn't be dying, he just couldn't.

'Don't cry, love,' he said weakly.

Without thought, Mavis blurted out, 'Oh, Dad, why did you leave me?'

'I'm no good to you . . . or . . . or anyone.'

Mavis lifted her head, about to protest, only to find that her father had closed his eyes again.

Kate came into the room. 'Mavis, I'm sorry, love, really I am, but you'll have to take him home.'

'How?' she appealed. 'Look at him, Mrs Truman. I doubt he could walk.'

'Don't worry about that. I'll send Bill over to have a word with Olive Wilson's husband. He's got a van and we can put a mattress in the back for your dad to lie on.'

Mavis nodded. Yes, she'd take him home, and, no matter what the doctor said, surely if her father had decent care and good food to put flesh back onto his bones, he'd get better.

Over an hour after Mavis ran off, Alec heard a vehicle pull up and went to the window to see her climbing from the back of a van. Two men got out of the front, and Alec rushed to the street door, flinging it open, just in time to see them carrying a man from the van.

'Be careful,' he heard Mavis say, and then in a procession they moved towards the street door.

Alec refused to stand aside when they tried to walk in, demanding, 'What's going on?'

'Please move out of the way, Alec,' Mavis appealed. 'My father's very ill and we need to get him inside.'

'You can't bring him in here!'

'What!' Mavis spluttered. 'But . . .'

'From the look of him he should be in hospital and that's where you can take him.'

Mavis seemed to grow in stature before Alec's eyes and, eyes blazing, she pushed her way in. 'No, Alec, I'll do no such thing.'

Alec found himself forced to one side as Mavis held the door wide, saying to the two men, 'Take no notice of my husband. Please, would you mind carrying him upstairs?'

Both men gave Alec a filthy look, one saying, 'Of course not. Just lead the way.'

Alec was pushed aside again as they followed Mavis and angrily he hurried behind them, ignoring his mother's calls as he shouted, 'No, Mavis. You can't do this.'

'Just try and stop me,' she cried as she dashed

to the landing cupboard to grab linen and blankets. 'I'll need to make up the spare bed. Would you mind holding him for a while longer?'

'It's no trouble, love,' one of the men said. 'The poor sod's as light as a feather.'

Alec could hear his mother ringing her bell incessantly now, and impatiently he turned to hurry back downstairs again. 'Mother, not now!'

'Alec, don't you dare shout at me. Now tell me, what's going on?'

'It's Mavis. Her father *is* ill and she's brought him here. She's upstairs now, putting him to bed.'

'What! Without permission, she's dared to bring him into *my* house. I won't have it, Alec. Tell her he's got to go – and now!'

'Mother, from what I saw, the man can't even walk. He had to be carried upstairs.'

'Then he can be carried down again. Now get him out of here.'

'I don't think Mavis will stand for it, Mother,' Alec said, bewildered by the change in his wife. 'She's like a different person and I've never seen her like this before.'

'Mavis will do as she's told. Tell her I want to speak to her.'

'Very well,' Alec said, leaving his mother's room to find the men coming downstairs. 'Wait,' he ordered. 'He can't stay here. Wherever the man came from, you'll have to take him back again.'

'No way, mate. It ain't my old woman's place to look after him and she'd have my guts for garters if I took him back. What's the matter with you anyway? I can't believe you'd turn away a dying man and Mavis's father at that.'

'Dying? He's dying?'

'Yeah, that's right, and from the look of him the poor sod ain't got long.'

Alec's jaw dropped, and though the men called a grudging goodbye he didn't answer as he closed the door behind them. Still unable to take it in, he slowly went upstairs to find Mavis sitting by her father's side. The man had his eyes closed, either asleep or unconscious, and now that Alec could see him properly, he was shocked to see that Ron Jackson did indeed look to be at death's door. 'Those men just told me. I'm sorry, Mavis.'

'Told you what?'

Keeping his voice low, Alec said, 'That your father's dying.'

'Don't. Don't say that.'

'He should be in hospital.'

'He won't go.'

'My mother said he can't stay here.'

Mavis reared to her feet. 'Oh, she said that, did she? Well, in that case you can tell her that if he has to go, I'm leaving too.'

'Mavis, don't be ridiculous.'

'No, Alec, I'm not being ridiculous. I've looked

after your mother for years and this is the thanks I get. My father is desperately ill yet she wants to throw him out and, let me tell you, I mean it. If you allow this to happen, I'll go with him. You can find someone else to look after your mother, *and* her precious house.'

'You're forgetting the children, Mavis.'

'No, I haven't. I'll take them with me.'

His temper rising, Alec said, 'No, Mavis. I won't allow it.'

'I won't leave James here for you to take your anger out on him. When I go, my children will come with me.'

'They are my children too and you are *not* taking them out of this house.'

Mavis lunged forward, her fingers like talons. 'I hate you! I hate you *and* your mother,' she screamed, trying to rake his face with her nails.

Alec reared back, unable to believe that this screaming banshee was his wife. Mavis was like a mad woman and, unsure how to handle her now, he grabbed her arms. 'Stop this, Mavis. Stop it at once.'

'Look at him! Look at my father! Your mother can't throw him out. She can't!'

'All right, Mavis. If you calm down I'll talk to my mother again. I can see how ill he is, and perhaps when I tell her she'll allow him to stay.'

There was a groan and Mavis yanked herself

free to run back to her father's side. 'It's all right, Dad. It's all right.'

'Where's Lily? Get Lily.'

'I will, Dad. I will . . .'

Ron closed his eyes again, and though Mavis's voice was quiet it was venomous. 'I mean it, Alec. If my father has to go, I'll go with him, and there's nothing you can do to stop me.'

Alec left the room abruptly, hoping as he went downstairs that he could persuade his mother to let the man stay. He was seeing a new Mavis, one out of his control, and for the time being it looked as if he would have to tread carefully. Alec had a horrible feeling that if he didn't, Mavis would carry out her threat.

Mavis stroked her father's head as he drifted away again, her fingers trembling. She had gone for Alec, stood up to him, and she was still seething with fury. She had told Alec that she hated him, his mother too, and as the words had left her mouth, Mavis knew they were true. It had taken this to wake her up, to see that this house had never been her home. She just lived here, a slave to the demands of her mother-in-law and husband, her only solace being her children.

Slowly Mavis calmed, her anger replaced by worry. Alec was talking to his mother now, but if Edith still insisted that her father left Mavis didn't know what she'd do. She had threatened to leave, and, no matter what Alec said, she'd take the children. But where could they go?

Mavis had no idea how long she had sat there before Alec returned, her eyes lifting to meet his as he walked into the room. 'Well, what did she say?'

'It's all right, your father can stay, but you'll have to go downstairs to see to my mother now. She needs the commode.'

Mavis saw that her father was still asleep and rose to her feet. It wasn't going to be easy with both her father and mother-in-law to look after, but she was too relieved to worry about it now.

'Thank you, Alec,' she said coldly, and after one last look at her father she quietly left the room.

She had more to ask of her husband yet, and it would probably mean another argument, but her father had asked something of her and there was no way she was going to let him down.

CHAPTER TWENTY-SIX

The next morning, Edith was still fuming. She felt she'd been blackmailed, that unless she allowed Mavis's father to stay, her daughter-in-law would leave. Of course, she couldn't manage without Mavis, the girl for once having the upper hand. The only thing that made it bearable was the fact that Ron Jackson was dying and would soon be out of her house.

Edith rang her bell, already feeling neglected, and when Mavis at last appeared she snapped, 'It's about time.'

'I came as soon as I could.'

There was no apology for keeping her waiting, and Edith could sense a change in Mavis. She no longer appeared obsequious; had barely thanked Edith for allowing her father to stay, and, not only that, she had somehow persuaded Alec to take the morning off work, something he had never done before unless forced by severe illness. 'You've forgotten my pills again.'

'No, Mother, I haven't. I gave them to you half an hour ago, and I know that because I had to give my father his medication at the same time.'

'I have *not* had my pills,' Edith insisted. 'Now go and get them, and to prevent this happening again, I want them left in here.'

'Very well,' Mavis said, 'but, remember, you're only supposed to take two every four hours.'

'I know that, you silly girl.'

Mavis left the room, returning shortly afterwards to shake two pills out of the container. She held them out, and then poured a glass of water, saying as Edith swallowed them, 'There, and if you don't need me for anything else, I've got a lot to do.'

'Yes, yes, go,' Edith waved, 'but you can leave the rest of my pills here. I'm sick of you forgetting to give them to me on time.'

Mavis handed them over and marched out of the room without a word. With an angry huff, Edith lay back on her pillow. She wasn't going to stand for her daughter-in-law's attitude. Now that she'd had time to think about it, she was sure that Mavis's threat to leave had just been bluff. After all, she had nowhere to go.

Edith felt her pain easing. What did it matter if she took a couple of extra pills? They relieved her symptoms, and that's what mattered. She found herself drifting, her mind on the plans she had to make. As soon as Alec returned there'd be more disruption in the house, something that she was determined to put an end to.

'Alec, what are you doing here?' Lily asked as she ushered him inside.

'You aren't on the telephone so I couldn't ring you. Mavis asked me to come here. Her father has turned up and he's asking for you.'

'Ron! Ron's back,' Lily gasped, her knees caving in shock.

'Yes, but I must warn you. He's very ill.'

Lily found that she had to support herself and gripped the edge of the table as her thoughts spun. 'Where is he?'

'He's staying with us. Mavis is looking after him, but he's in a very bad way.'

'What's wrong with him?'

'I'm not sure, but I'm afraid he's dying.'

Lily's knees went entirely then and she was hardly aware of Alec pulling out a chair, supporting her until she was able to sit down. She fought to pull herself together. Despite all that had happened, all he had put her through, Lily found that she wanted to run to Ron, to be by his side. 'Give me a minute and I'll get me coat,' she said.

'Are you all right?' Alec asked.

'I'm fine. It was just a bit of a shock, that's all,' Lily told him, taking in a few deep breaths to calm her churning stomach before she stood up again. She should be back before Pete came home, but, just in case, Lily scribbled a quick note to say she'd gone to see Mavis, leaving out any mention of Ron. There'd be time enough to tell him face to face, but for now she just wanted to get to Battersea.

Lily picked up her handbag, fighting tears as they left the house. Despite trying to make a new life she had never been able to get Ron out of her mind. *Ron, Ron,* she cried inwardly, *you've only just come back. Don't leave me again.*

Mavis was sitting by her father's side, Grace playing with toys on the floor beside them. It was odd really. Her daughter was usually such a difficult and demanding child, but since the moment she'd met her grandfather Grace had been strangely quiet.

Alec hadn't been happy when she'd gone to ask for Jenny's help earlier, but her neighbour had been wonderful. She'd agreed to take James to school and bring him home again. Jenny had also offered to look after Grace, but her daughter would have none of it, only calming down when she was allowed to be with her grandfather. He had hardly been able to speak when Mavis had led the children into his room that morning. James had been nervous, hanging back, but Grace had gone straight to him, taking his hand as though an instant bond had formed. But now, hearing her mother's voice, Mavis rose to her feet. It had taken another argument to get Alec to go to Peckham that morning, but at last her mother was here.

'Oh, Ron,' her mother cried when she saw him, blind to Mavis and Grace as she rushed to his side.

Though she had thought him asleep, Mavis saw her father's eyes open, a weak hand reaching out as he croaked, 'Lily, Lily.'

'Ron, where have you been? What happened to you?'

'Doesn't matter. Had to see you. Had to say I'm sorry,' he gasped, every short sentence an effort, but then Mavis saw that his eyes had closed again.

'Mavis, has he seen a doctor?'

'Yes, Mum, he saw one last night, and I rang our doctor this morning. He'll be round after his morning surgery.'

'He looks terrible.'

'Mavis, can I have a word?' Alec asked as he poked his head into the room.

'Yes, all right,' she said, lifting Grace into her arms to walk outside.

'I've got to go to work now,' Alec said urgently, 'though I'm a bit worried about my mother. I just looked in and found her sound asleep. She doesn't look right, Mavis.'

'She tires easily and I'm sure she's fine, but when the doctor calls round to see my father, I'll ask him to look at her too.'

'Good idea, but until then keep an eye on her, Mavis.'

'Of course,' she said, relieved when Alec then left for work. It had surprised her that he'd gone to Peckham, but his manner since she had threatened to leave him had been subdued.

Mavis walked back into the room, still holding Grace, to find her mother clutching her father's hand. 'I'll make you a cup of tea, Mum.'

'Thanks, love. I must admit I could do with one. I thought that bus was never going to get here.'

'Stay here, Mummy,' Grace said.

'Yeah, leave her, love. I ain't seen the kid for ages.'

Mavis lowered Grace down, amazed when she ran to stand quietly beside her grandmother. She hardly ever came to visit them and, too busy looking after Edith, they couldn't go to Peckham, yet even so there seemed to be an instant rapport. Shaking her head in bewilderment, Mavis went down to the kitchen, and after making a pot of tea she first carried one into her mother-in-law's room. Alec was right, she was asleep, but that suited Mavis fine and, hoping she'd stay that way for a while longer, she crept out again.

It was late afternoon and Lily was still sitting with Ron. The doctor had been and gone, James was back from school, but thankfully the woman next door had insisted on taking both children home with her. She seemed a nice sort, and though Grace had kicked up a bit, the woman had made it seem an adventure that they'd be sleeping in her house that night.

'Stop worrying, Mavis. Your fault or not, Edith is gonna be fine. I just wish I could say the same thing about your father.'

'Don't, Mum. I can't face it,' Mavis begged.

'We've got to,' Lily said, fighting tears as she turned to look at Ron. The doctor had been kind and sympathetic when after examining Ron he'd warned that he might not even last the night. Worse was when the doctor said that Ron knew he was dying, knew that years of alcohol abuse had finally taken its toll. Lily looked at Ron's face, unable to believe how old he looked, his hair and beard streaked with grey. He'd been drifting in and out of consciousness since she arrived, hardly able to talk, yet when awake he had enough strength to cling on to her hand.

His eyes opened again now, seeking hers, the

appeal in them almost breaking her heart as he fought to speak. 'Forgive me, Lily.'

Lily had never expected to be able to say these words, but now she blurted out, 'Ron, Ron, of course I do.'

'Don't . . . don't deserve it, but . . . but had to come. Where . . . where's my girl?'

'I'm here, Dad,' Mavis cried, rushing forward.

Ron looked at Mavis, managing the ghost of a smile. 'My lovely girl,' he gasped, his breathing ragged, tortured, as his eyes closed again.

'Oh, Mum, Mum.'

'I know, love, I know,' Lily said.

'Mum, you . . . you won't leave, will you?' Mavis sobbed.

'Of course I won't,' Lily assured.

Mavis drew in juddering breaths, dashing tears from her cheeks, and saying as she left the room, 'Th . . . thanks, Mum. I . . . I'd better see to dinner. Alec will be home soon.'

Lily felt a surge of guilt. Mavis had sounded so grateful, but in truth she knew that wild horses wouldn't have been able to drag her away from Ron's side. The room was quiet now, with just the sound of Ron's shallow, tortured breathing, and Lily found herself breathing in time with him – fighting with him.

Lily was so wrapped up in looking at Ron that it was some time before she became aware that downstairs, Alec was home and shouting. Lily felt sorry for Mavis. When the doctor had looked in on Edith, he said it appeared that she'd been given too many pills, though Mavis had denied it. All right, maybe she had made a silly mistake with Edith's medication, but with her father dying and the state she was in, surely it was understandable.

At least no harm had been done, Lily thought, but then, instead of Alec yelling, it was Edith Pugh. Lily stood up and crept onto the landing to listen. She had never liked Edith, but felt sorry for her now that she'd been confined to bed – though with her voice bordering on a screech, she certainly didn't sound weak.

What was that she said? Lily's eyes widened in shock. Mavis was crying out now, begging, but Lily was enraged. Over my dead body, she decided, ready for a fight as she stormed downstairs.

'Please, please, you can't make him leave. He can't be moved again. He's dying! My father's dying,' Mavis was pleading.

'He ain't going anywhere!'

Mavis spun around to see her mother on the threshold of the room, and, though small in stature, she looked like an Amazon, blazing with temper.

'Yes he is,' Edith spat. 'Thanks to your daughter I nearly died and I won't be neglected again.'

'Died! Leave it out. You took a couple of pills too many, that's all, and from what Mavis told me, it wasn't her fault.'

'I can assure you it was, and this has proved that she's incapable of looking after both her father and me. I've hardly seen her today, despite repeatedly ringing my bell.'

'You lying cow! You're forgetting I've been here to see how you've run her ragged.'

'I did no such thing,' Edith blustered. 'And, anyway, *you* seem to be forgetting that thanks to Mavis's negligence, I've been really ill.'

'Ill my foot! If you want to see ill, go up and take a look at my husband.'

'Yes, your husband, and as such he's your responsibility. Now I suggest you either take him home with you, or make arrangements to have him admitted to hospital.'

'You bitch. The doctor said he might not even last the night, yet you'd see a dying man disturbed. My God, I don't know how my daughter puts up with you.' But then, as though struck by a thought, Lily's eyes narrowed into slits. 'But she doesn't have to. When I go, Mavis can come with me. She can live with me, and in future you can find someone else to wipe your shitty arse. Ain't that right, Mavis?'

Mavis stared at her mother in amazement. 'Er . . . er, yes.'

'Right then, girl. I'll see about getting your father taken into hospital, and in the meantime get some stuff packed for yourself and the kids.'

Alec stepped forward. 'No, you can't go, Mavis. I won't allow it.'

Mavis didn't have to answer. Her mother did that for her. 'You little shit. How do you think you're gonna stop her?'

'She's my wife! James and Grace are my children!'

'Wife! Don't give me that. Mavis is nothing but a bloody slave to your mother. How my daughter puts up with the way she's treated is beyond me, but this is an end to it. She's coming with me and I'll see that she files for divorce *and* custody of the kids.'

'Mother!' Alec cried, his eyes wide in appeal.

'Mavis, perhaps taking too many pills *was* my mistake,' Edith said quickly. 'It frightened me and I'm afraid I overreacted by insisting that your father leaves. I'm sorry, and of course he can stay.'

'I should think so too,' Lily snapped. 'Right, that's sorted and, if you don't mind, I'll get back to Ron.'

Still reeling, Mavis watched her mother march from the room. She couldn't believe that she'd stood up for her like that, offered her a way out – a home.

Alec suddenly ran towards his mother, asking anxiously, 'What is it? Mother, are you all right?'

'Oh, dear, I'm afraid this has all been a bit too much for me. I just need a little peace, a chance to rest.'

'Of course you do,' he said, 'and we haven't eaten yet. Mavis will see to our dinner and then you can settle down for the evening.'

Alec turned to look at her and Mavis nodded. Yes, she'd see to dinner and then leave Alec to sit with his mother. She wanted to be upstairs with her father, and, not only that, she needed to talk to her mother.

Though over an hour had passed, Edith was still angry. She'd had to give in and hated it, but when Lily Jackson had offered Mavis a home, Edith knew that she had gone too far – that if she continued to alienate Mavis, the girl might actually leave.

'Do you feel a little better now, Mother?'

'Yes, a little, though I can't believe the way Lily Jackson spoke to me. The woman is so coarse and her language appalling. Not only that, the dinner that Mavis just cooked was barely digestible.'

'I know, but with so much on her mind, I'm sure Mavis did her best.'

'The housework is probably being neglected, just as I am.'

'Mother, you know her father's dying and she's dreadfully upset. If you hadn't changed your mind, I think she really would have left.'

'I could have died too, Alec, and you seem to have forgotten that,' Edith snapped, annoyed to hear her son standing up for Mavis and determined to nip it in the bud.

'I'm just glad you're all right,' Alec said, but then his eyes moved to the bedside table. 'Why are your pills in here? You know I like them kept in the cupboard and out of the children's reach.'

With so much on her mind, Edith didn't think before she lied, 'Because Mavis forgot to give me any this morning and I didn't want it to happen again. All she cares about is her father and I've been dreadfully neglected.'

'Mother, you became ill because you overdosed on painkillers and said that Mavis was to blame for giving you too many. Now you're saying that she forgot to give you any pills. This doesn't make sense.'

Edith cursed her woolly mind, and knew that somehow she would have to respond carefully. 'Oh, dear, I'm so tired, confused, and don't know if I'm coming or going. Maybe it really was my fault, but I just can't seem to remember,' she said, forcing a sob of distress.

'Please, don't upset yourself,' Alec soothed. 'You're all right, and that's all that matters. Now try to rest and I'll put these away.'

Edith could do nothing to stop Alec as he walked out of the room with the bottle of pills. Her mind was getting worse, her thoughts more confused, yet Edith was aware that this time she had gone too far – pushed her daughter-in-law too far.

With a snort of annoyance, Edith knew she had to ensure that Mavis stayed, and to achieve that it would mean she would have to be kinder, perhaps show a little appreciation. It wouldn't be easy. It still rankled that Mavis had tried to take her son away from her, but she had no fear of that happening in the future. She had seen to it that Alec had no respect for Mavis, that he thought his wife a fool.

Yes, Edith thought with satisfaction, her son was hers again now, and she, his mother, the most important woman in his life. Yet Edith also knew that to make sure she didn't become a burden to Alec, her daughter-in-law had to remain.

Mavis ignored Alec as he walked into the kitchen, but turned her head when he spoke.

'My mother's pills were in her room. I'll put them away before she does the same thing again.'

'Oh, so you believe me now?' Mavis said, unable to keep the sarcasm from her tone.

'Yes, and I'm sorry for doubting you.'

'Well, that's something,' she said, turning back to the washing up and hoping that Alec would just go away.

'Mavis . . . we need to talk.'

'Not now, I'm busy,' she snapped.

'All right, but maybe later,' he said, saying no more as he left the kitchen.

Mavis washed the dishes and then put them away before going to her mother-in-law's room. 'I'd like to sit with my father. Is there anything else you need before I go?'

'No, my dear, don't worry about me. You have enough to do and as Alec is here now, he can fetch me anything I need.'

'Yes, I'll see to her,' Alec agreed.

'Oh, Mavis, I might have to call you if I need the commode. Is that all right?'

'Yes, of course,' Mavis said, surprised by Edith's kindly tone, but dismissing it from her mind as she went upstairs to her father's room. 'Mum, how is he?'

'The same, but I don't think his breathing is any worse.'

'Did you manage to get him to eat any of that soup?'

'No, he wouldn't touch it.'

Mavis pulled up another chair, still speaking softly as she said, 'Did you mean what you said?'

'Mean what?'

'That I can come to live with you? The children too?'

'Of course not, you daft cow. I ain't got room

313

for you lot and was only bluffing. Of course, Alec and his flaming mother don't know that, but it certainly did the trick.'

Mavis felt tears filling her eyes. Yes, she was daft, stupid enough to think that her mother would take her in. For a while she had dared to hope but the bubble had burst now. With nowhere to go she'd have to stay here, but as her father moaned softly Mavis leaned forward. He was all that mattered for now, and she closed her eyes in prayer, begging God to let him live.

CHAPTER TWENTY-SEVEN

Pete looked anxiously at the clock. It was after eight but where was Lily? She had left a note to say she'd gone to see Mavis, but should have been back by now. He paced up and down, and then grabbed his coat, deciding to tell Marilyn where he was going in case he and Lily crossed paths.

Marilyn said she'd keep an eye out for Lily, and now Pete was frantically looking for a taxi. A bus would take too long and though a cab would cost a fortune Pete was too worried to care. Something must have happened. But what?

At last he arrived and was thumping on the door, his face creased with anxiety as Alec Pugh answered it. 'I'm looking for Lily. Is she still here?'

'Yes, she's upstairs,' Alec said as he stood back to let him in.

'Is she all right?'

'Er . . . yes, she's fine.'

'What is it then? Is it one of your kids?'

'No,' Alec said. 'I'm afraid it's Mavis's father. He's very ill and they're both sitting with him.'

'Ron! He's here?'

'Yes, but as I said he's very ill. If you'd like to wait I'll go and get Mavis.'

Wait! No, he wasn't going to wait, and though Alec protested, Pete followed him upstairs. My God, after all these years Ron had turned up – but why hadn't Lily put that in her note?

'Pete,' Lily cried, jumping to her feet as he walked into the room.

'What's going on, Lily?'

She moved towards him, urging quietly, 'Come outside.'

He ignored her, instead walking over to the bed, shocked at what he saw. This couldn't be Ron, this skeletal form, barely breathing. 'Bloody hell, Lily.'

'He's dying, Pete,' she said, her voice barely above a whisper. 'I had to stay. I . . . I couldn't come home.'

'No, of course you couldn't,' Pete murmured. He looked down at Ron, unable to work out his feelings. This man had been his friend, one who had saved his life during the war, and there was a part of him that felt a deep sadness. Yet sickeningly there was another side that felt relief. He knew that Lily had loved Ron, had feared his return, knowing that, despite what she said, when that happened he'd lose her. He had nothing to fear now. Ron was dying, and Lily would be free to marry him, eliminating the worry that their child would be born a bastard.

Pete shook his head in disgust at his own thoughts, and then moving to stand by Lily again, he said, 'I'm sorry, love. Are you all right?'

'It's just so awful to see him like this.'

'Yeah, it is, but how did he get in that state?'

'We don't know. Kate Truman and her husband found him in an empty house in Cullen Street. Apparently he was looking for me,' she said, before breaking down in tears.

Pete pulled her into his arms, aware immediately of her resistance. He knew why. It was Ron she wanted. It was Ron that she had always wanted, but somehow he had to hold on. Pete knew that Lily had never really loved him, and maybe she never would, but he couldn't face life without her.

Lily was glad when Pete finally left. It had been awkward while he was there, and she had felt that she could no longer hold Ron's hand. Mavis had gone downstairs to get Edith sorted out for the night, the girl looking as exhausted as Lily felt.

She had seen little of her daughter since Mavis had married Alec, and maybe that was why, but Lily was surprised to hear how sensible Mavis sounded, how capable she was. She could see now why some people didn't think that Mavis was backward, but, of course, as her mother, Lily knew better.

Ron opened his eyes, and Lily leaned forward. 'I'm here,' she whispered.

He struggled to speak, but it was too much for him and it was all Lily could do to stem her tears. She threw an arm over his frail body. 'Oh, Ron, I love you. I'll always love you.'

She saw a ghost of a smile on his lips, but then he closed his eyes again. For a moment Lily thought he'd gone and her stomach jerked, but then slumped with relief when she saw that he was still breathing.

The thought of losing him was more than she could bear, and clutching his hand Lily willed him to live. 'Don't let go, Ron. Please, don't let go.'

It was fifteen minutes later when Mavis came into the room carrying two cups. 'How is he, Mum?'

'He's still with us, but we've got to face it, love, he's getting worse.'

Lily could see that Mavis was fighting tears as she said, 'I've made us both a cup of coffee.'

'Thanks, love,' Lily said, taking it gratefully and feeling a twinge of guilt. Mavis had been up and down stairs all day, but she'd done little to help. 'Has Alec gone to bed?'

'Yes, ten minutes ago.'

He hadn't bothered to say goodnight to her,

but Lily wasn't surprised. Alec had always been uppity, looking down his nose at her – his mother too. Still, she'd sorted Edith Pugh out, the woman's dependence on Mavis giving Lily her ammunition. Mavis should take a leaf out of her book, Lily thought, but the girl had always been too soft for her own good. 'Is Edith settled for the night too?'

'Yes, and I'm just glad that Jenny offered to have the children. They've never spent the night away from home before, I hope they're all right.'

'Blimey, Mavis, they're only next door. Jenny seems a nice sort and I'm sure they're fine.'

With a sigh, Mavis sat down, the two of them gazing at Ron as they sipped their coffee until Lily said, 'Mavis, you don't really want to leave Alec, do you?'

'I can't so there's no point in talking about it.'

'I thought you were happy. What changed?'

'My mother-in-law.'

'What do you mean?'

'She was fine at first, teaching me to read, but then . . .'

'Teaching you to read?' Lily interrupted. 'But you can't read, you never could.'

'Yes, but it isn't because I'm backward. Edith did some research and found out that I have something called word blindness.'

'What's that? I've never heard of it.'

319

'Neither had I, but apparently it's a medical condition. In some cases learning to read is possible, but mine is very severe and, though she tried to teach me, I found it impossible.'

'But why didn't you tell me?'

'At first it was because I wanted to surprise you, to see your face when I read to you. For once I wanted you to be proud of me; but when Edith finally gave up, I couldn't see the point in telling you.'

'Why ever not?'

'Mum, without proof, I knew you'd never believe me.'

Lily felt sick inside. Edith Pugh, Kate Truman and Pete, among others, had been right. Mavis wasn't backward. It was a medical condition that prevented her from reading, nothing else. Guilt almost overwhelmed her. She'd been ashamed of her daughter, found it hard to love her, and had treated her like a moron. 'Oh, Mavis, if you'd explained this word blindness thing I would have believed you, really I would.'

'Well, you know now and so far there's no sign that either James or Grace has inherited the same problem. I was worried sick at first and, unable to help James when he started school, I had to rely on Alec. He and Edith are keen to see that both children have a good education and are equally relieved to see that they show no signs of it.'

320

Lily's hands moved to cup her stomach. She'd been worried sick about the baby – worried that it would be born backward like Mavis. But her daughter was fine, and her new child would be too. She had nothing to fear now.

'Mum, why are you holding your tummy? Are you all right?'

'I'm just upset about your dad and feel a little bit sick, that's all,' Lily said. Mavis didn't know that she was pregnant, and this was hardly the time to tell her. With two children of her own it might come as a bit of a shock to hear that she was going to have a half brother or sister, and that the baby would be an aunt or uncle to James and Grace.

Alec could hear the soft murmur of voices drifting from the spare room as he lay in bed, deep in thought. He'd been shocked to find that his mother had overdosed on painkillers and furious at first at what he'd thought was his wife's negligence.

Alec shifted uncomfortably. Yet it hadn't been Mavis at fault, it was his mother, and he now feared that her illness had affected her mind. She seemed so confused and complained of neglect, had in fact been complaining about Mavis's lack of care for some time. Lily Jackson had disputed it, said that his mother had run Mavis ragged and, in light of the fiasco with the pills, Alec believed her.

He turned onto his side, plumped up his

pillow, yet still couldn't sleep. He knew his mother hated disruption and, if Ron Jackson had just been ill, wanting him to leave would have been understandable. Yet he wasn't just ill, the man was dying, and it had shocked him that despite knowing that fact, his mother had still wanted him thrown out. It seemed overly harsh, cruel, another reason to think that his mother's mind was going.

If her father had been made to leave, would Mavis really have gone with him? Alec didn't know, but there was no denying the threat had seemed real enough. Mavis had said she hated him, but surely that wasn't true? No, he assured himself. Of course Mavis loved him, though in all honesty he couldn't say he felt the same about her.

Alec knew that he'd been besotted with Mavis at first, but of course it had just been lust, and though he knew his mother was right, that Mavis lacked intelligence, their sex life was something he still enjoyed. Other than that, Mavis was pretty much useless and though his mother may have been wrong on this occasion, there was no denying the fact that Mavis was incapable of doing anything else without instruction.

Despite his wife's failings, Alec was sure that he'd been a good husband. He worked hard to ensure that Mavis and the children were well provided for, and though she had the burden of looking after his mother, her life now was far superior to the one she had left.

Frowning, Alec again plumped up his pillow. Mavis had stood up to him, argued with him, and he still wasn't sure how long he should put up with that sort of behaviour. At last Alec felt himself drifting off to sleep, his last thought that he'd give Mavis a little leeway, try to show a bit of understanding, but once things got back to normal she had better not raise her voice to him again.

It was two in the morning and Lily was struggling to stay awake. Mavis was bent over, her head on the bed as she dozed fitfully. It was a cold February and Lily was glad that there was a small electric fire to heat the room, yet even so she shivered.

Since that last time, Ron hadn't opened his eyes, and Lily knew by his breathing that he was now clinging on to life by a thread. She leaned forward again, her mouth close to his ear as she whispered, 'I'm still here, love, still with you and . . . and wherever you go, you'll take a piece of my heart with you.'

Mavis lifted her head, her eyes glazed, unfocused, and in the dim light that glowed from the bedside lamp, for a split second, Lily found that looking at her daughter was like looking at Ron, the young, handsome and vigorous man she had married.

'Mum, he hasn't gone, has he?'

'No, he's still with us, but . . . but he's worse. Here, change places with me. Talk to your dad. He still might be able to hear you.'

They exchanged chairs and, taking her father's hand, Mavis said, 'Dad, it's me, Mavis. Don't go, don't leave me again. Please, Dad, other than Gran you're the only one who ever stood up for me, who cared. You . . . you can't die. You can't.'

As she listened to her daughter, Lily felt as though her heart would break. She'd been a rotten mother who hadn't shown Mavis an ounce of love or affection. She wasn't fit to have another baby, didn't deserve another baby, but then Lily heard an awful sound and cried out in anguish. It was the death rattle, the last breath that left Ron's body as he slipped from this world.

'No, Ron! No!' Lily cried, rearing to her feet, but then Lily felt a stirring in her stomach. She shivered, covered in goosebumps, and it felt as though every hair on her body was standing up on end.

'Dad, Dad,' Mavis sobbed, throwing herself across his body.

Lily fought to stop the thought that flew into her mind. It was madness, of course it was madness, but she couldn't let it go. At the moment of Ron's death her baby had stirred to life, almost as though the two had become entwined. Stop it, stop it, she told herself. It was impossible, of course it was impossible.

Mavis was still sobbing, and Lily knew that somehow she had to find the strength to comfort her. She'd been a useless mother, but perhaps now she could start to put it right. She pulled her daughter away from Ron's body, gently cajoling, 'Come on, sweetheart. He's gone now, he's at peace.'

'Oh, Mum, Mum . . .'

'I know, darling, I know,' Lily murmured, and urging Mavis to her feet she pulled the girl into her arms. Mavis clung to her, both of them in tears, both grieving. Mavis for her father, and Lily for the only man she had ever really loved.

CHAPTER TWENTY-EIGHT

Mavis was still in a dreadful state and Jenny wasn't sure what to do. She'd looked after James and Grace for five days now, glad to have been able to help, but her cousin was arriving tomorrow and would need the spare room. Grace was sleeping in there at the moment, while James was in with her son, Greg, the two boys getting on well together. Grace, however, was a different matter and even if she wanted to, Jenny knew she couldn't squeeze the child in with them.

'I want to go home,' Grace appealed.

'Soon, darling,' Jenny placated, 'and anyway, it's nearly time to fetch James and Greg from school.'

This seemed to satisfy the child and Jenny sighed with relief. Grace became fractious when James was in school and Jenny had done the best she could to keep her amused. Though the weather was cold they went to the common every day, the child happy to play on the swings or go to the pond to feed the ducks.

Yet it wasn't a fractious child that worried Jenny. It was James, and the bruises she had seen on his body the first night he'd come to stay. She had no problem with a child being given the occasional smack if they were very naughty, but this was far worse and looked more like a beating.

Jenny bit on her lower lip. She couldn't just leave it, allow this to continue, and somehow had to raise the subject with Mavis. She would have to wait as Mavis wasn't up to it right now, but Jenny loathed the thought of James going home to face more abuse.

A knock on the door startled Jenny out of her thoughts and, seeing that Grace was intent on dressing her doll, she left her there while she went to answer it.

'Mavis, come in,' she invited. 'How are you?'

'I felt like the walls were closing in on me and had to get out of the house, if only for a little while. Not only that, it's time I took James and Grace off your hands.'

'Are you sure?' Jenny asked. 'What about ... well ... the ...'

'Funeral,' Mavis finished for her, eyes dark with pain. 'For once, Alec has been marvellous. With my mother in Peckham it's difficult, but when

Alec suggested it she agreed to leave all the arrangements to him.'

'Mummy!' Grace shouted as she ran along the hall.

'Hello, darling,' Mavis said as she swept the child up into her arms.

'Can I come home now?'

'Yes, pet,' Mavis said, hugging the child to her.

'Would you still like me to collect James from school?' Jenny asked.

'Yes, if you wouldn't mind. I know I have to pull myself together for the children's sake, to get back into some routine, but somehow I'm finding it impossible.'

'Mavis, it's early days and though you're taking Grace home now, why don't you leave James with me? He's no trouble and I know Greg loves having him here.'

'Thanks, Jenny, you've been wonderful. I don't know what I'd have done without you, but Grace wouldn't settle without James.'

With her cousin coming, Jenny knew that she no longer had room for Grace, and with no other choice she murmured, 'Yes, I suppose you're right. Why don't you come through to the kitchen, though I'm afraid I haven't time to make a cup of tea.'

Mavis put Grace down, but the child still clung to her hand as they walked along the hall. 'I know, and as I told my mother-in-law I wouldn't be long, I'll have to get back in a few minutes.'

'How is she?'

'Not too well and in a lot of pain, but she's kinder these days so that's something.'

'Can we go now?' Grace asked. 'I want to see the sad man.'

'Oh . . . oh . . .' Mavis gasped.

Jenny could see that Mavis was close to breaking down and took over. She crouched down in front of Grace, saying softly, 'I'm afraid the man has gone, darling. He had to go to a place called heaven, but now that he's there he won't be sad any more.'

'Can I go too?'

'One day I'm sure you will, but not yet,' Jenny said, hugging Grace to her as the child's eyes filled with tears. 'Anyway, what about James? He'd miss you if you went away. Mummy would too, and Daddy.'

'What about Granny? Can I go to see Granny?' Grace said, pulling away from Jenny's arms.

Mavis had somehow managed to pull herself together and, sweeping Grace up again, she said, 'I don't suppose you mean Granny Pugh, but your other grandma will be coming to see you again on Saturday.'

'That . . . that's not the day of the . . . ?' Jenny asked, again failing to utter the word 'funeral'.

'No, it's just a visit and a chance to talk over what arrangements Alec has made.'

Jenny glanced at the clock. 'I'm sorry, Mavis. I'll have to go. It's time to pick the children up from school. I'll drop James off with you and then sort out their things to bring round later.'

'Thanks, Jenny,' Mavis said as Jenny put on her coat.

Together they walked to the front door, Grace clinging on to her mother like a limpet as they went outside.

Jenny called a quick goodbye as she hurried off, regretting the fact that she hadn't been able to talk to Mavis about the bruising she'd seen on James's body. She feared for the boy, dreaded him returning home, and knew she would have to talk to Mavis as soon as the funeral was over.

When Pete arrived home from work he found Lily sitting by the fire, her hands resting on her stomach. 'Hello, love.'

Her eyes looked glazed as she turned her head. 'Pete, I didn't hear you come in.'

'You were miles away,' he said. Lily had been the same since Ron's death, distant, remote, as though a part of her had died with him. Pete was sure that it would pass, that if he was patient, caring, Lily would turn to him again.

When Lily did talk, she avoided mentioning

Ron and instead it was always her daughter. Pete had always suspected that Mavis was bright, and now that Lily knew that too she was racked with guilt, saying what a rotten mother she'd been. He knew she wanted to make amends, to see more of Mavis, and hoped she'd be over the moon with his purchase.

Lily stood up now, avoiding his eyes as she said in a dull tone, 'Dinner's nearly ready.'

'Leave it for a minute. I've got something to show you. Come with me.'

Her brow creased, but she followed him to the front door, and throwing it open Pete said, 'What do you think of that then?'

Lily looked at the small, white van parked outside, and then at last met his eyes. 'Is it yours?'

'Not mine. It's ours. I thought it was time for a bit of transport and it'll fill two roles. I can use it for work, and it'll come in handy to run you back and forth to see Mavis.'

'Oh, Pete,' she gasped, fighting tears as she stumbled back to the kitchen.

'Lily, what's the matter? I thought you'd be pleased.'

'I am, Pete, honestly I am.'

'Why the tears then?'

''Cos I know I don't deserve you, that's why.'

'Don't be soppy and, anyway, the van isn't the only

surprise. I've arranged for us to have a telephone installed.'

'A telephone? But why?'

'It'll be another way to keep in touch with Mavis.'

Lily surged to her feet, throwing herself into his arms. 'Oh . . . Pete . . . Pete.'

He held her, letting her cry, feeling her vulnerability. Lily still showed a hard front and rarely broke down, but it had cracked now. It didn't matter. He'd be there for Lily and would shore her up for as long as she needed him.

Mavis heard Alec come in, his routine different now. Instead of going straight in to see his mother, he now came to the kitchen first and she braced herself for his kiss. He was trying, she knew that, his manner kinder, but for Mavis it was too late. Her father's death had acted as the catalyst that opened her eyes. If he hadn't disappeared she would never have married Alec. She had used him as a means of escape, had allowed herself to be led into it by her mother-in-law, but really there was nobody to blame but herself. She had been stupid, naïve, had felt so worthless that she'd let both Alec and his mother dominate her and the children.

'Hello, my dear, how are you feeling?' Alec asked as he strode over to kiss her cheek.

'I'm all right,' she said, trying to avoid flinching at his touch. Yes, she might only have herself to blame, but if Alec and his mother had acted differently, she may have found some happiness. Oh, they were trying now, both of them, but it didn't fool Mavis. It was fear, that was all – fear that she would leave. If only she could do just that, release the bonds, but with no income of her own, and nowhere to go, Mavis knew she was trapped.

'Hello, James. Hello, Grace,' Alec said.

'Hello, Daddy,' they chorused as Grace leaped to her feet to throw her arms around her father's legs.

'Drawing again, I see,' he said. 'I think we have an artist in the family.'

James had remained sitting, and it didn't surprise Mavis. Alec had always favoured Grace, and she was rarely smacked; her daughter was shown far more affection than her son.

'Look at mine, Daddy,' James appealed.

'Not now, James. I must pop along to see your grandmother. I hope you've been good and haven't disturbed her.'

'He hasn't,' Mavis insisted through clenched teeth. Never again would she allow James to suffer at his father's hands. She might have to stay with Alec, but he and his mother would find that if they reverted back to normal, she would no longer stand for it.

She'd been a meek and biddable idiot, but no more. If not for her own sake, then for James's, she had to change, and in doing so maybe, just maybe, life in this house would be bearable.

CHAPTER TWENTY-NINE

The funeral was sparsely attended, with just Mavis, Lily and Pete along with a couple of old neighbours from Cullen Street.

Lily ignored Kate Truman and Olive Wilson as she clutched Pete's hand on one side and her daughter's on the other. Alec wasn't there. He'd had to stay at home to look after his mother and the children, but Lily had to admit that her son-in-law had come up trumps with the arrangements. The coffin was nice, and the beautiful spray of white lilies on the top looked lovely, but she'd felt awful that Pete had been the one to bear most of the costs.

The service ended and Lily dreaded going to the graveside. When they got there it was as much as she could do to stay on her feet, barely aware that Pete was holding her up.

'Ashes to ashes and dust to dust,' the minister intoned as Ron's coffin was lowered.

Lily drew in great gulps of air, but at last it was over and somehow she managed to steady her shaking legs. She saw Olive Wilson looking at her, disdain in her eyes, but quickly averting her face Lily reached out to touch her daughter's arm. 'Come on, let's go.'

They turned to walk away, but Kate Truman moved to stand in front of them, saying softly, 'Hello, Lily. I'm sorry for your loss.'

'Yeah, well, Mavis told me that you found Ron and took him in for a while so I'll thank you for that. Now if you'll excuse me,' she said, almost dragging Mavis away, but not before Olive Wilson's words reached her ears.

'I don't know how she's got the cheek to play the grieving widow.'

'Olive, shut up,' Kate hissed. 'Now's not the time.'

Lily's jaw was clenched, determined not to give Olive Wilson the pleasure of a reaction. Back straight, she walked away from the graveside and to the car.

Edith endeavoured to sit upright, but it was proving impossible, the pain across her shoulder blades excruciating.

Alec came in and seeing that she was struggling he moved quickly to help her. 'Mother, why didn't you call me?'

'I was about to,' she said as Alec placed pillows

behind her back. 'Thank you, that's much better. The children are quiet for a change.'

'They know better than to misbehave when I'm around.'

'I should think Mavis will be back soon and, now that the funeral is over, things can get back to normal.'

'Mavis is finding it hard to cope with her father's death. I doubt she'll be back to normal for some time yet.'

'I meant the routine of the house, Alec.'

He moved to the window. 'There's the car now.'

Edith pursed her lips. No doubt Mavis would invite her mother in again. She just hoped the awful woman wouldn't stay for long. She heard their voices but, instead of going along to the kitchen, Lily Jackson poked her head in the door.

'We're back,' she said.

'Yes, I can see that,' Edith said abruptly, annoyed when Lily then walked fully into the room.

'Mavis is making us a cup of tea,' she said, taking a seat without invitation, 'but then we'll be off home. Now that we've got a van we'll be able to drive over to see Mavis and the kids every week. On top of that, we're getting a telephone so I'll be able to ring her every day to see how she's doing.'

Edith heard the implied threat and her jaw

clenched. It was the last thing she wanted, but somehow Ron Jackson's death had brought Mavis and her mother closer.

The door was pushed wider and Grace came running into the room. 'Gran,' she cried, scrambling onto Lily's lap.

'Hello, sweetheart,' Lily said, wrapping her arms around Grace.

Alec appeared, his expression one of annoyance. 'Grace, I told you not to disturb your grandmother. Now come back to the kitchen.'

'I dunno which grandmother you're talking about, but she's fine with me,' Lily said. 'What about you, Edith, is she disturbing you?'

'I do have a bit of a headache.'

'Come on, Grace,' Alec insisted.

The child looked sulky, but did as she was told and Edith heaved a sigh of relief that there wasn't a tantrum. Not that Alec would stand for it, of course, but she couldn't say the same for Mavis.

'It's funny,' Lily mused. 'I ain't great with kids, but Grace seems to have taken to me.'

'She's wilful and needs discipline.'

Lily's eyebrows shot up. 'She doesn't seem wilful to me.'

'How would you know? You've hardly seen the child.'

'Yeah, but that's gonna change.'

'I do *not* like disruption in my house. If you

want to visit, please make sure that you give us advance notice.'

Lily's face reddened, but then Mavis came in carrying a tray with the tea things on, Pete behind her with a plate of sandwiches.

'Thanks, Mavis, but I'll have mine in the kitchen,' Lily said. 'I'm finding it hard to breathe the sour air in here.'

'Yes, do that,' Edith snapped. 'It'll be nice to be left in peace.'

Mavis looked bewildered, but as her mother marched from the room she followed her, asking, 'Mum, what's the matter?'

Edith didn't hear Lily's reply and, anyway, she didn't care what the woman had to say. This was *her* house – and she intended to keep Lily Jackson out of it as much as possible.

Pat Higgins had stood well back from the mourners, but as soon as the coast was clear she went to Ron's grave. When he went missing she'd been frantic, but though she'd searched the area there'd been no sign of him. She'd tried the hospitals, and had even ventured into the police station, but as a well-known tom a fat lot of good that had done her.

It had taken her three days to remember Ron's letter, one he'd given her to post some time ago. Ron knew he was ill, had wanted to contact his wife again, but Pat hadn't posted it. The last thing she wanted was his flaming wife rushing to his side, pushing her out and taking over. She would have taken Ron back to London, nursed him better, and Pat would never have seen him again.

No, Ron was hers, but even as this thought had crossed her mind Pat knew it wasn't true. She and Ron had been together for years, but he had never stopped talking about his wife and daughter, always on about how he'd get on his feet one day, save up and go back to them.

Pat looked down into the black chasm, barely aware that two men were waiting to fill the hole with soil. When Ron had given her the letter, she'd stuffed it in her handbag, intending to destroy it like the previous ones, but it had made its way to the bottom of her bag, forgotten under all the paraphernalia she always carried.

She had searched for her old handbag and found it in the bottom of her wardrobe, the letter still there. Her eyes had fixed on his wife's address, unable to believe that Ron would have had the strength to travel to London.

'I shouldn't have done it, Ron, but I couldn't help myself,' Pat said, still looking down into Ron's last resting place. 'I opened your letter, and, oh, Ron. Why didn't you tell me?'

Though hardened from her years on the game,

Pat couldn't hold back a sob of anguish. If she had posted the letter, there would have been nothing to fear. Ron hadn't begged his wife to come, and there'd been no return address. He'd just asked that she forgive him, told her that he would never be able to change, but that he had found a woman who loved him as he was. He told his wife that he wouldn't be coming back, and urged her to find love and happiness with someone else, just as he had.

Another sob escaped Pat's lips. It had been one sentence that had left her sitting on the side of the empty bed, clutching the letter, reading it over and over again. Ron had found happiness and love with someone else! With her! He had found it with her!

She had to see him, had to find him, but after a few more days of fruitless searching, Pat began to wonder if Ron had somehow made it to London. He was dying, he knew that, yet had a desperate need to see his wife somehow given him the strength to make the journey? He didn't have a penny, but with trucks leaving the docks regularly, had Ron managed to appeal to a driver with a kind heart and cadge a lift?

When there was no sign of him locally, Pat had made the journey to his wife's address, only to be told that Lily Jackson didn't live there any more. The woman who now rented the house was happy to gossip, and how Pat had remained on her feet when told that the man who used to live there had recently died, she would never know.

It hadn't been hard to find out about the funeral, taking only a few calls to local undertakers, and now, lifting her hand, Pat threw a single red rose onto Ron's coffin. 'I was too late, Ron. I wanted to hear the words, wanted you to tell me that you love me, because only then would I have believed it was true.'

Pat blinked away tears then, desolate as she walked away. Yes, she had read his letter over and over again, finally understanding why Ron had written it. He knew he could never change, that he would never be any good to his wife, his love so deep that for her sake, he wanted to set her free.

'Oh, Ron, yet you were never free of her, were you?' Pat whispered. The final proof lay in the journey. Only a deep and abiding love could have kept him going long enough to get to London to see his wife, and somehow Pat was glad that he'd made it.

CHAPTER THIRTY

'No, Mum, I'm sorry,' Mavis said, 'but you won't be able to come over on Sunday. Edith is still too ill and she won't allow any visitors.'

Lily fumed. Over four weeks had passed since the funeral, but every Sunday since then when she'd wanted to see her daughter, Edith Pugh had found an excuse to keep her away. 'There's nothing wrong with that woman that a good kick up the backside wouldn't cure,' she snapped.

'Mum, honestly, she really has got a bad dose of bronchitis.'

'It's only Friday. She might be a bit better by Sunday,' Lily said, impatient to see her daughter.

'I doubt it and if anything she seems to be getting worse. When I looked in on her just now she looked dreadful. In fact, I was about to call the surgery when you rang.'

Lily had wanted to tell Mavis face to face, but now, because of Edith Pugh, there was no hiding her swelling stomach. 'Mavis, I didn't want to tell you this over the telephone, but I ain't got much choice . . .' Lily paused as she tried to find the right words.

'Are you still there, Mum?'

'Yeah, I'm here, but this ain't easy, Mavis. You see, love, I . . . I'm pregnant.'

When there was only silence from the other end of the phone, Lily had no idea how her daughter was taking the news. When she had thought Mavis backward, Lily knew that she'd never considered her daughter's feelings, but now guilt kept her awake at night. She'd thought Mavis was fit for nothing, had sent her out to do other people's cleaning and used her as nothing but a workhorse. All that had changed with Ron's death. When she looked at Mavis now, she saw Ron, her daughter all she had left of the man she loved.

'Mavis, say something,' she appealed.

'I . . . I don't know what to say, Mum. This has come as a bit of a shock.'

'I know, love, I was shocked too.'

'When . . . when is it due?'

'It'll be a summer baby, born in July.'

'That soon! But how long have you known?'

'I didn't find out until I was four months gone and I'm five now.'

'How . . . how does Pete feel about it?'

'Oh, he's over the moon.'

There was silence again, but then Mavis spoke, her tone brittle. 'He must think it's a stroke of luck that Dad's gone. There's nothing to stop him from marrying you now.'

'Mavis, don't be like that. Yes, we're going to get married, but only because I don't want this baby to be born a . . . a . . .'

'Bastard,' Mavis interrupted, but then almost immediately she blurted out, 'Oh sorry, Mum, I shouldn't have said that. It's just that I feel a bit all over the place.'

'It's all right,' Lily said quickly. 'I know it ain't like you to swear. You've had a bit of a shock so it's understandable.'

'I can't take it in really. Can . . . can we talk later?'

'Yes, all right, and you can ring me anytime, you know that.'

'Bye, Mum.'

Lily didn't get a chance to answer and found that she was listening to the dialling tone. Slowly she replaced the receiver. Mavis knew that she was pregnant now, and surely, once she'd got over the shock, her daughter would come round to the idea?

The handbell was ringing, something that Edith had taken to doing every time she heard the telephone. It made talking to her mother difficult, but on this occasion Mavis had been happy to hang up. On leaden feet she walked along the hall and into her mother-in-law's room to find her struggling for breath as she tried to sit up higher in the bed.

'Mavis,' Edith gasped, 'you look as white as a sheet. Who was that on the telephone?'

'It was my mother.'

'Is there a problem?'

Mavis placed more pillows behind Edith. 'I suppose I might as well tell you, after all, there'll be no hiding it. My mother's having a baby.'

'What!' Edith exclaimed, but then, hit by a fit of coughing, she was unable to continue.

'You sound awful and I really must ring the surgery now.'

'Mavis, wait,' she wheezed. 'Did you say that your mother's having a baby?'

'Yes.'

Though Edith's voice was weak, her tone was derisive. 'She's a grandmother twice over, and if you ask me having a baby at her age is disgusting.'

'My mum is only forty-four,' Mavis snapped, surprised to find that she was jumping to her mother's defence.

Once again there was a dreadful fit of coughing, and Mavis was seriously worried. Edith felt so hot and was left exhausted when the coughing fit passed.

'I won't be a minute,' she said, hurrying to make the call.

Until the doctor arrived, Mavis didn't feel she could leave her mother-in-law on her own, but she still had to keep an eye on Grace. She found the child absorbed with her toys and, squatting down in front of her, Mavis said, 'Listen, darling, we're going to your grandmother's room and I want you to be a good, quiet girl.'

'Can I have a biscuit?'

'Just this once,' Mavis said, and, after handing Grace a biscuit, she picked up a few toys before taking the child into her mother-in-law's room.

'Mavis, do you have to bring Grace in here?'

'I want to sit with you until the doctor arrives.'

'There's no need,' Edith said, her voice reedy.

'I think there is, and Grace will be good, won't you, darling?'

'Yes,' the child said as she sat on the floor to eat her biscuit.

Thankfully there was no further argument from her mother-in-law, and, as she had hoped, Grace played quietly. Mavis sat by the fire, her eyes on her daughter. Unlike Grace, she'd been an only child and had longed for a brother or sister. Her mother was pregnant now and she should be pleased, but instead felt sick inside. Why? Why was she feeling like this? Mavis closed her eyes, unwilling to acknowledge the truth.

'Mavis, I'd like some water.'

Snapped out of her thoughts, Mavis poured a

measure from the jug into a glass, and supporting her mother-in-law she held it to her lips.

Edith choked, water spilling out of her mouth. 'Oh, dear, that must have gone down the wrong way,' Mavis said as she hastily put the glass down and patted Edith's back.

'I . . . I couldn't swallow it.'

'Give it another try,' Mavis urged.

Edith took a sip, but then her arm flailed to push the glass away, water dribbling down her chin. 'Mavis, I can't. I just can't. What's wrong with me? Why can't I swallow?'

'Don't worry,' Mavis reassured, doing her best to stay calm. 'It's probably nothing, and the doctor will be here soon.'

Edith sunk back onto her pillows, eyes closing; seriously worried now, Mavis walked over to the window. When she'd rung the surgery the reception-ist had said the doctor was just about to go out on his rounds, and her mother-in-law would be placed first on his list. The surgery wasn't far away, but as yet there was no sign of his car.

'Biscuit, Mummy?'

'No, Grace, you'll spoil your lunch.'

'I want . . .'

'I said no,' she said firmly.

There was no tantrum, just a sulky expression, and thankfully Mavis saw the doctor's car pulling up outside. She hurried to let him in, saying without preamble, 'I'm sorry to call you out, but my mother-in-law isn't getting any better and now she can't seem to swallow.'

'It sounds like dysphagia; a symptom of advanced multiple sclerosis. I'll take a look at her.'

Though Grace protested, Mavis took her out of the room, doing her best to keep the child occupied while the doctor carried out his examination.

At last, after what seemed ages, he appeared in the kitchen doorway, his expression grave.

'Is she going to be all right?' Mavis asked worriedly.

'I've prescribed another dose of antibiotics for the bronchitis, but the dysphagia is my main concern. Mrs Pugh will need a change of diet. You will have to avoid giving her thin liquids, or food of a crumbly texture. There is also the danger of liquid slipping into the lungs, therefore I would advise you to ensure that she drinks and eats slowly.'

'Will it improve?'

'In some patients the condition improves: however, in others it worsens.'

'What happens if liquid goes into her lungs?' Mavis asked.

'There would be the danger of pneumonia. I'll call in again in a few days,' the doctor said, holding out a prescription.

Mavis took it, almost in a daze as she showed

him out, her mind racing. She would have to stay with her mother-in-law every time she had a drink *and* at every meal, but during the day, with Grace to look after, it wasn't going to be easy. If she fed Edith before Alec left for work, breakfast would be manageable, and he'd be there at dinner to keep an eye on the children. It would mean a change of routine, an earlier start in the mornings, but it had to be done.

'I'm hungry, Mummy,' Grace said as Mavis closed the door behind the doctor.

'All right, I'll make us some lunch.'

Mavis looked in on Edith, saw that she seemed to be resting comfortably, and then went back to the kitchen. She had to prepare something that would be easy for her to swallow, perhaps a thick soup.

Once heated, Mavis poured the soup into bowls and then picked up the tray. 'Come on, Grace. Let's take this to your grandmother, and you can eat yours in there too.'

Grace didn't protest and, going into Edith's room, Mavis said, 'Mother, I've made you some soup.'

'No, I can't swallow it.'

After settling Grace, the child soon happily dunking bread into the soup, Mavis sat next to her mother-in-law and urged, 'Come on, you've got to eat. At least give it a try.'

With her lips clamped firmly together, Edith shook her head. It reminded Mavis of trying to feed the children when they were little, the coaxing games she had used to make them open their mouths. She could hardly use the same tactics with her mother-in-law, so gently said, 'Just try one small spoonful.'

'Oh, very well.'

Mavis saw the look of relief that crossed her mother-in-law's face when she was able to swallow the soup without difficulty, and slowly, so slowly, the bowl began to empty.

'Can I have some more, Mummy?'

'In a minute, Grace.'

'No, now!'

'You'll have to wait,' Mavis called over her shoulder.

Grace began to cry and Edith implored, 'Mavis, get that child out of here. She's giving me a headache.'

'Mother, I can't leave Grace outside. In future she will have to come in here with me when I feed you.'

'Oh, this is intolerable. Just go. I'm still capable of feeding myself.'

'The doctor said that you can't be left alone when you eat.'

'Take the soup away then. I've had enough.'

With Grace screaming in the background, Mavis

was happy to do just that and, after giving her daughter another bowl of soup, she flopped onto a kitchen chair.

With this additional burden she didn't know how she was going to cope, and longed to talk to someone, to vent her feelings. For a moment she was tempted to ring her mother, but then she'd have to pretend that she was happy about the baby.

Mavis felt sick inside – hated how she was feeling. Instead of being pleased to have a brother or sister, she was jealous. She was a grown woman, twenty-four now with two children of her own, but as soon as her mother had told her that she was pregnant, Mavis had felt like a child again. A child who longed for her mother's love, a love she would now shower on the new baby.

CHAPTER THIRTY-ONE

Lily threw the documents down. 'You shouldn't have done it, Pete, not without asking me first.'

'Look at you, Lily. It's June and you're nearly eight months gone. Time's running out.'

'But Saturday? That's only three days away and I can't arrange things by then.'

'What's to arrange? You said you don't want the neighbours to find out that we're not already married and agreed to a quick trip to the registry office. No fuss, no do, just us and a couple of witnesses. The only thing you wouldn't set is the date.'

Lily lowered her eyes. It was hard to hide her feelings from Pete, but it had only been four months since Ron died and she was still grieving. She knew Pete wanted to get married before the baby arrived, and in truth she didn't want their child born out of wedlock either, yet every time he tried to set a date she fobbed him off. How could she marry

Pete when the man who filled her mind, her thoughts, was Ron? Even Pete's touch was unbearable now and she'd been using her pregnancy as an excuse. Now Pete had taken matters into his own hands, set the date for Saturday, and she'd run out of excuses to put him off.

'What's up, Lily? Don't you want to marry me?'

Slowly she lifted her eyes to meet his. 'Of course I do, and Saturday it is.'

'Thank Gawd for that.'

Lily stood up, pushing her hand into the small of her back as she walked over to the cooker. 'My back's killing me,' she complained. 'I'll get your dinner sorted out and then ring Mavis.'

'Do you think she'll come to the wedding?'

'I doubt it. With Edith Pugh going downhill, Mavis hardly has a moment to herself these days.'

'Alec could look after her for a couple of hours.'

'He can't see to his mother if she needs her commode.'

Pete pursed his lips. 'No, I suppose not.'

Lily dished up Pete's dinner and a smaller portion for herself, but when they sat down to eat she had little appetite. Though she hadn't actually said so, Lily knew that her daughter wasn't happy about the baby and, even if she was able to, she doubted that Mavis would want to come to the wedding.

If only the girl would talk to her, tell her what

the problem was. With this in mind, Lily said, 'Pete, instead of ringing Mavis, I'd rather tell her about the wedding face to face. When you've finished your dinner, would you run me over there?'

'Yeah, all right, but you'd better give her a ring to let her know we're coming.'

'No, we'll just turn up,' Lily said, sick of always being put off because of Edith Pugh's health. She wanted to sort things out with her daughter, and this time nothing was going to stop her.

Jenny looked up as her cousin walked into the room. He'd been with them since March, with no sign of him leaving. Not that Jenny minded. The money Willy handed over for his keep was coming in handy, and he was no trouble. He was building up his new business, working long hours, and other than on Sundays they didn't see much of him. He and Stan got on well, and Greg now treated him like a part of the furniture.

Now, though, Jenny could see that there was something wrong as she took in his grim face. 'Hello, Willy, I've kept your dinner hot,' she said, 'but you don't look too happy.'

He flopped onto a chair, raking a hand through his hair as he said, 'You're not going to believe my flaming mother.'

'Why? What's she done now?' Stan asked.

'She came to the yard again, marched into my office with the same demand.'

'What! She still wants you to leave?'

'When I refused last time she fobbed off her neighbours by telling them that I'm here to open a second branch of the business. That sounds very grand, doesn't it? Right up her street. However, I'm supposed to be returning to my wife and child when it's up and running.'

'She's mad to lie,' Jenny said, 'but, knowing your mum, I can see why she's doing it. For years she's bragged about how well you were doing, how you'd started up your own business. Then, of course, when you got married and were buying your own house, she had more to brag about.'

'Yeah, well, that's gone now; but worse, I'm divorced and she doesn't want anyone to find out.'

'But it wasn't your fault,' Jenny protested.

'Try telling my mother that. To her divorce is a dirty word and she wants me away from this area before anyone finds out.'

'You ain't going to let her drive you out, are you?' Stan asked.

'I'm not leaving the yard. The business is just starting to take off and I'm staying in Battersea, whether she likes it or not.'

'Good on yer, mate,' Stan said. 'Mind you, I hope she doesn't come round here shouting the odds.'

'Don't worry, I've found a flat at last so I'll be moving out.'

'Willy, honestly, you're welcome to stay here,' Jenny protested. 'I'm not worried about your mother. If she turned up here she'd get the door shut in her face.'

'Thanks, Jen, but it's time I moved on.'

'We're going to miss you.'

'You'll still see lots of me, especially for Sunday dinner. The flat's only about a fifteen-minute drive away.'

'Where is it?'

'It's near Burntwood Lane, in Wandsworth.'

'Why Wandsworth? Why not stay around here?'

Willy shrugged. 'When I went to see the flat I liked the area. I only need one bedroom, but there are two and it's furnished.'

'It'll mean a longer drive to your yard,' Stan pointed out.

'I don't mind,' Willy said as he stood up. 'Anyway, Jen, I'll just go and have a quick wash before I have me dinner.'

'All right, love,' Jenny said as she went to light the gas under the saucepan. She wasn't happy that Willy was moving out. Stan wasn't much of a talker and spent his spare time tending his precious garden, but when Willy came home, however late, she had someone to chat to.

That train of thought led her to Mavis. Other

than walking the kids to and from school, she saw little of her neighbour these days. With her mother-in-law becoming increasingly ill, Mavis had her hands full, and so far there hadn't been the right opportunity to mention the bruises she had once seen on James's body. It weighed heavily on Jenny's mind, but when they walked the children to school she had to admit that James seemed happy enough.

Jenny placed a knife, fork and condiments on the table, her mind still on her neighbour. Mavis had told her that her mother was going to have a baby, but she hadn't seemed happy about it and Jenny didn't know why. It wasn't easy to have an in-depth conversation on the short walks and Jenny missed their occasional chinwags over a cup of tea.

Poor Mavis. She'd had little freedom, and now had even less. With her mother-in-law so ill, she was virtually a full-time carer, and in the last couple of months the weight seemed to have dropped off her. It worried Jenny, but there was nothing she could do, other than to tell Mavis, as she always did, that she was there if she needed her.

Mavis was close to exhaustion. In between looking after her mother-in-law and Grace, she tried to keep up with the housework, but it was growing impossible. The laundry was a nightmare. Edith was incontinent now, and though Mavis had devised a rubber cover for the mattress, her sheet constantly needed changing.

Alec was sitting with his mother while she got the children bathed and into bed, and after that Mavis knew she would have to tackle the stack of ironing that was waiting to be done.

'Tell me a story, Mummy,' Grace appealed.

'Oh, darling, not tonight,' Mavis said tiredly, but then, seeing the look of disappointment on her daughter's face, she relented. Grace had been so good lately, playing quietly in her grandmother's room whenever Mavis had to attend to her, and it wasn't nice that the child had to be present when she changed Edith's sheet.

Mavis sighed. Other mothers could take their children to the park, push them on swings, run and play; but with the exception of the short walk to take James to and from school, her children were as much prisoners in this house as she was.

Now that it was June and warm, at least Grace could play in the garden, but when James was in school she was always alone, lacking the attention she needed. Mavis gave Grace a hug, loving her daughter dearly, and wished she had more time to be a better mother.

'Love you, Mummy.'

'I love you too, darling,' she said and softly began

to tell Grace one of the fairy tales she had made up. 'Once upon a time . . .'

Grace closed her eyes, thumb in her mouth as slowly she drifted off to sleep.

Mavis sat quietly, relishing this moment of peace, but with so much to do before bedtime, she forced herself to stand up and leave the room. She peeped in on James, saw that thankfully he was asleep too, and then went downstairs.

'Alec, I've got ironing to do,' Mavis said, but he was watching *Z Cars* on television and a brief nod was his only acknowledgement. Edith was propped up on pillows, but her eyes were closed as she dozed, something she did more and more these days.

The doorbell rang and Alec looked round briefly to say, 'Who on earth is that?'

'I don't know,' Mavis said. She went to answer it, her face stretching with surprise. 'Mum! What are you doing here?'

'I've got something to tell you.'

'You'd better come in,' Mavis said, 'but how did you get here? Where's Pete?'

'He's popped down the road for a drink. I told him to pick me up in an hour.'

As her mother stepped inside, Alec appeared, looking none too pleased when he saw her. 'Mrs Jackson. Mavis didn't tell me you were coming.'

'That's because she didn't know.'

'Mavis, my mother isn't up to seeing anyone.'

'It's all right. I'll take my mum along to the kitchen.'

'Very well,' Alec said, his feelings plain as he went back into his mother's room, closing the door firmly behind him.

'Still a pompous git, I see,' Lily observed as she followed Mavis along the hall.

Mavis didn't respond. She was stunned to see her mother and wondering why she hadn't telephoned to say she was coming. 'Why didn't you ring me?'

'Because you'd have fobbed me off as usual,' Lily said as she flopped onto a chair.

Mavis's eyes avoided her mother's stomach as she too sat down. 'It isn't that I don't want to see you. It's just that my mother-in-law is too ill for visitors.'

'Yeah, and judging by the state of you, she's running you ragged as usual. You've lost weight and look awful.'

'Thanks, Mum.'

'I ain't having a go at you, girl. I'm just annoyed to see you looking like this and I've a mind to have a word with that no good son-in-law of mine.'

It sounded like her mother really cared, but, of course, Mavis knew it was just an illusion. 'Alec has to work, Mum. When he's home he is trying to be a bit more helpful.'

'I should think so too, but you still look worn out. He shouldn't let you be a slave to his mother. It ain't right.'

'What choice is there?'

'He could get you some help, a cleaner or something.'

'Yes, maybe,' Mavis said tiredly, 'but, come on, you said you had something to tell me.'

'Yeah, well, it's just that Pete's booked the registry office. We're getting married on Saturday.'

Mavis had been expecting this and was in fact surprised that her mother had left it this long.

'Say something, Mavis.'

'What do you want me to say?'

'I dunno, maybe congratulations? I'd like you to be there.'

Mavis knew it wasn't true and the resentment she'd long held in check flared up. She was foggy with tiredness, the words leaving her mouth without thought. 'You don't want me there. You've never wanted me.'

'Mavis, how can you say that?'

She saw that her mother had flushed, cheeks red, and now that she'd started Mavis found that she didn't want to stop. 'You've always been ashamed of me and . . . and you wouldn't listen when I said I wanted to take up art. All you thought I was fit for was taking that pram out, begging for cast-offs, and then you sent me out to work as a cleaner.'

'Oh, Mavis . . . Mavis . . . don't . . .'

Mavis ignored her mother's cry as she reared to her feet, the words spewing from her mouth. 'You're having another baby now and if it's perfect you'll love it, which is more than you can say for me. You . . . you never loved me.'

Spent, Mavis slumped, tears on her cheeks that she angrily rubbed away. There was only silence for a while, but then her mother spoke.

'Mavis, listen to me, please listen. I wish I could deny everything you've said, but I know I can't. You're right, I haven't been much of a mother, but I do love you, honestly I do.'

'You . . . you love me?'

'You're my girl, ain't you?' Lily said as she stood up, pulling Mavis awkwardly into her arms.

Mavis could feel her mother's swollen stomach as it pressed against her, but she didn't move away. Her mum loved her and joy filled her heart.

CHAPTER THIRTY-TWO

Alec was surprised to hear Mavis humming as she prepared his breakfast on Friday morning. He'd expected her to be sulky, resentful that she couldn't go to her mother's wedding, but instead she seemed lighthearted, happier than he'd seen her for a long time.

'James, Grace, come on, breakfast's ready,' Mavis said, and as the two children scrambled onto chairs, she placed the plates on the table.

The morning routine was different these days, earlier, and Alec still found it trying. At six o'clock Mavis got up to see to his mother, inevitably disturbing his sleep. The children usually woke at around seven, but by then Mavis had usually changed his mother's sheets, washed her, and he didn't have to worry about the children as he shaved and got dressed for work. Breakfast, however, was a different matter. There had been a time when he could read his morning paper in peace, but nowadays he had to keep an eye on the children while Mavis fed his mother. 'Grace, eat your porridge,' he ordered.

'Don't want it.'

'I said, eat it,' Alec said forcefully, and, though sulky, at least Grace picked up her spoon. He rarely had to reprimand James, and glancing at his son Alec saw the boy's wary look. Alec felt a surge of satisfaction. It was discipline, of course, the boy knowing better than to misbehave at the breakfast table.

As soon as Mavis returned, Alec would look in on his mother before leaving for work and now, as he pushed his bowl to one side, he glanced impatiently at the clock. Lateness was something Alec wouldn't tolerate in his staff and he led by example, making sure he was always at his desk before the others arrived.

At last, he thought, as Mavis returned and, rising to his feet, he said, 'I'm off.'

'All right, see you later,' Mavis said, leaning away from him as he tried to kiss her cheek.

Alec was fed up with tiptoeing around his wife, fed up with the way she avoided his lovemaking. He'd made allowances because she'd been grieving for her father, but it was three months now and he'd had enough.

It was time to assert his authority again, to demand his marital rights. He no longer feared

Mavis's threat of leaving him. He'd seen how small her mother's house was, and now that Lily Jackson was having a baby, there'd be no room for Mavis. No, his wife couldn't go to Peckham. She had no alternative but to stay here.

Jenny left her house at a quarter to nine. Mavis was just leaving too, and they joined up to walk along Ellington Avenue together. 'Good morning, Mavis. Isn't it a lovely day?'

'Yes, it's gorgeous,' Mavis agreed, smiling happily.

'You look chirpy today. Is your mother-in-law's health improving?'

'No, she's just as bad, but my mum came to see me yesterday. She's getting married tomorrow.'

'Oh, so that's why you look so happy. You're getting out of the house for a change and going to her wedding.'

'No, I can't leave my mother-in-law for that long.'

'Alec won't be at work. Surely he can see to her?'

'I'm afraid not. She's incontinent now, and lately she's been messing the bed too.'

'Yuk, how on earth do you cope with that?'

'It isn't easy, and I must admit it makes my stomach turn, but I can't leave her lying there in that state.'

'No, I suppose not, but if you can't go to the wedding, why are you looking so cheerful?'

'I've just found out that my mother loves me,' Mavis said, her eyes bright with emotion.

'But she's your mum. Of course she loves you.'

'Yes, I know that now, but all through my childhood I thought she was ashamed of me, that she didn't want me.'

'Blimey, you should have my cousin's mother. She wants him out of the area and is making his life a misery.'

'Oh, dear. I've seen a van parked outside now and again, and though I haven't seen him, I guessed he was still staying with you. What is he going to do?'

'Willy's business is doing well and he isn't budging. I'm not surprised you haven't seen him. With the hours he works we hardly see him either, but he told us last night that he's found a flat,' Jenny said as they stopped at the school gates.

She bent down to kiss Greg goodbye, Mavis kissed James, and then the two boys dashed into the playground.

They made their way home again, but with Grace playing up there wasn't much chance to talk. As usual the child wanted to get out of the pushchair, but Mavis didn't give in until they were back in Ellington Avenue.

'She's cooped up indoors too much, that's the trouble,' Mavis said as she helped her daughter to push the pram.

'A nursery has opened just around the corner. They take three- to five-year-olds for three hours a day, and if they've got any places left I think Grace would love it.'

'Oh, Jenny, that's a marvellous idea.'

'Don't get your hopes up. They may be full,' Jenny cautioned.

'I won't, but fingers crossed,' Mavis said. 'I'll go round there as soon as I get the chance. How do I find it, and do you know if they're open in the morning or afternoon?'

'Mornings, I think, and it's in that hall at the end of the next road.'

'Yes, I know it. Thanks, Jenny, this could make such a difference,' Mavis called as they parted outside Jenny's house.

Jenny paused to watch Mavis for a moment. She had looked happier this morning, her eyes for once sparkling, and Jenny had been struck by how pretty she looked. Though Mavis had lost a lot of weight, strangely it suited her, and with a bit of make-up she'd be a stunner. How old was Mavis? Twenty-three, twenty-four maybe, still so young, but trapped in an unhappy marriage and a life of drudgery.

With no idea that Jenny was watching her, Mavis hurried inside. A nursery! Oh, please let there be a place left, she thought, and leaving the pushchair unfolded in the hall she looked in on her mother-in-law.

Edith was awake, and Mavis walked over to the bed, stacking pillows behind the woman's back. 'I've just heard that a nursery has opened close by. Will you be all right if I go out again to see if they can take Grace?'

'No, no, don't leave me,' Edith said weakly, her eyes pathetic with appeal. 'I . . . I don't feel at all well.'

Mavis closed her eyes in defeat. 'All right, I'll leave it until Monday. You might be feeling a little better then. Can I get you anything?'

Edith shook her head as her eyes closed again. Mavis left her to doze while she went to let her daughter out into the garden to play. She was tempted to ring the surgery again, but the last time Dr Hayes had been called out he had said there was nothing further he could do. His patient was over the bronchitis and able to eat, if slowly. Her main problem was the multiple sclerosis, and his only suggestion had been that she and Alec might like to consider a nursing home.

Of course, Alec wouldn't hear of it, Mavis thought as she began to wash up the breakfast things, beginning her long day of trying to fit in the housework along with keeping an eye on her mother-in-law and daughter.

The sun was shining through the window and

she could hear the twittering of birdsong. For a moment Mavis paused, wishing she could just open the window and fly; she longed to soar like the birds, free, if only for a day.

Leaving the washing up, Mavis walked out into the garden to see Grace laying out her toy tea set, her dolls arranged in a circle. She was chatting to them as she poured imaginary cups of tea and Mavis smiled at the scene.

No, even if able to fly, she would never want freedom from her children, just from her mother-in-law. Her stomach did a flip. Oh, God, it was almost as if she was wishing Edith dead and it was awful to think like that.

Mavis left Grace to her game, feeling sick with shame as she returned to finish the washing up.

CHAPTER THIRTY-THREE

The ceremony was over and Lily was now Mrs Culling. She rested a hand on her swollen stomach as they left the building, glad that her child wasn't going to be born out of wedlock with the stigma that carried.

Eddie, Pete's friend from work, and his wife were there as witnesses, and now Eddie said enthusiastically, 'Come on, you two. Stand together and I'll take a couple of photographs.'

Lily held Pete's arm, smiling into the Box Brownie, her small bunch of flowers held ineffectually in front of her distended stomach.

'Oh, shit,' Pete said. 'Look, it's Mrs Biggs and she's coming this way.'

Lily frantically looked for escape but there was none. She quickly moved away from Pete while shoving her flowers into Eddie's wife's hands.

'Don't tell me that you've just got married,' Mrs Biggs said, her voice high.

'Us! Leave it out,' Lily protested. 'We're just here as witnesses for these two. Ain't that right, Sylvia?'

'Yeah, that's right,' Sylvia said quickly.

'You must think I was born yesterday.'

'I told you, it ain't us,' Lily protested, but Mrs Biggs was already marching away.

'Who the hell was that?' Eddie asked.

'Our neighbour, and the biggest mouth in the street,' Lily wailed. 'Now everyone will know and I'll never be able to hold my head up again.'

'Don't be daft,' Pete said. 'It's her word against ours. Now come on, we're going for a meal to celebrate and sod Mrs Biggs.'

'I don't feel like celebrating.'

'Now listen to me, Lily. You're my wife now and I feel like shouting it to the world. I know I can't do that, but the restaurant is well away from here and that bitch isn't going to stop me from raising a glass to toast our marriage.'

Lily was touched by Pete's words. He was right, it *was* their word against Mrs Biggs's and they could brazen it out. She'd done it with Mavis, told her daughter that she loved her, had held her in her arms, waiting for that special feeling that never came.

She did feel a sort of bond with Mavis, all she now had left of Ron, but that special love a mother should have for her child was still missing. She'd somehow convinced Mavis that it was there, touched at least by the joy in her daughter's eyes.

Of course, for Mavis's sake, she would have to keep it up, play the role of a loving mother, but now Lily's hand moved to touch her stomach again. What if she was unnatural? What if she couldn't love this baby either?

Martha Biggs was a small, wiry woman, thin-faced with short, grey hair. Though well into her sixties, she was still vigorous and her pace brisk as she walked back to Harwood Street. She had lived in Peckham all her life. It was a respectable area, the home she moved into when she married in a nice street, but not any longer, Martha thought, her back stiff with indignation.

As she turned the corner, there was only one woman in sight. Marilyn Foster was on her knees, scrubbing her doorstep. Martha hurried to her side. 'I'm disgusted. I really am.'

'With what? I'm only cleaning me flaming step.'

'I'm not talking about you. It's our neighbour, the one who lives between us.'

'What, Lily?

'Yes, her . . . that . . . that hussy.'

Marilyn scrambled to her feet. 'Hold on, I ain't having that. Lily's a friend of mine.'

'Oh, so you knew she was getting married this morning?'

'Married! Lily? Don't be daft. She's already married to Pete.'

'No, she wasn't, but of course they are now and I saw it with my own eyes. They've been living in sin, but now that she's pregnant they sneaked off to the registry office to get married. Eight months gone and only just wed. It's disgusting, that's what it is and I don't know what this street's coming to. We don't want her type living here and I'm going to make it my business to get her out.'

'You mean-minded old bitch,' Marilyn snapped as she picked up her bucket again. 'Anyway, I don't believe you.'

Martha bristled, but didn't get a chance to say another word before Marilyn marched inside, slamming the door behind her.

With her lips puckered with annoyance, Martha looked around and, spotting the woman who lived opposite leaving her house, she hurried across the road.

'You're not going to believe this,' she said, launching into her story.

Mavis glanced at the clock. The service would be over now, her mother married to Pete, and Mavis wished she could have been there. So much had changed in such a short time, her feelings about Pete, the baby – and it was all thanks to finding out that her mother loved her.

She looked back at the past with different eyes now, thought about how awful her mother's life had been, and, though she still grieved for her father, Mavis knew that much of her mother's unhappiness and bitterness had been down to him. Because of his drinking and gambling, her mother had been forced to be the provider, her life one of hard work and drudgery. Like her, she'd had no time to be a proper mother, but at least Mavis knew she didn't suffer the grinding poverty that her mum had faced.

Mavis grimaced. God, she'd been awful to Pete and he hadn't deserved it. She had blamed him when her father disappeared, had refused to accept him in her mother's life, had even married Alec rather than live with them. If only she could turn back time – have the understanding that she now had when she was sixteen. Her life would have been so different. She wouldn't have married Alec and maybe she would have met the elusive man she still saw in her dreams.

'Mummy, Mummy, I love you. Can I have a biscuit?' Grace appealed.

'Oh, darling, I love you too,' Mavis said, sweeping Grace up and into her arms. 'And no, you can't have a biscuit.'

'See, told you,' James said.

Mavis's smile was a loving one as she looked at her son. No, she didn't want to turn the clock back.

If things had been different she wouldn't have had her beautiful children, and the thought of that was gut-wrenching. If only she could give them more of her attention, spend more time with them, but, of course, with Edith so ill, it was impossible.

'Mavis, my mother's bed needs changing again,' Alec said as he came into the room.

'Go on, you two,' Mavis said as she lowered Grace to the floor. 'It's a lovely day and you should be playing in the garden.'

The children ran off and without looking at Alec Mavis left the room. He had changed lately, had reverted back to being more demanding, and refused to accept any excuses when he wanted to make love on a nightly basis.

Love! No, it wasn't love. His attacks on her body were more like an assault. At first she'd resisted, but he had become short with James and, fearing that his anger would turn on her son, that he would start thrashing him again, Mavis had been forced to give in.

When her father had been ill, she had been determined to be strong, to assert herself, but Mavis realised that despite her resolve, she was no match for Alec. He knew he could hold the children over her, threaten them, and used her fear for them to get his own way.

Mavis hated her life. She might not know the poverty her mother had suffered, and had material comforts in her marriage, yet still a bleak future stretched ahead. Count your blessings, Mavis told herself. At least she had James and Grace, along with a new baby brother or sister soon. Cheered a little by these thoughts, she went into her mother-in-law's room.

'I . . . I'm sorry, Mavis,' Edith said forlornly.

Mavis knew from the awful stench that she had more than wet the bed, but managed a smile. Her mother-in-law was a different woman nowadays, weak and grateful for anything that was done for her. The bossy, formidable Edith Pugh had been replaced by a gentler, kinder persona, but, oh, if only the same could be said of Alec.

'Don't worry, I'll soon sort you out,' Mavis said, forcing brightness into her tone as she gently rolled Edith to one side, gathering the soiled sheet from beneath her.

By the time she and Pete arrived home, Lily knew that half the street would probably have heard Mrs Biggs's story. She had chucked her flowers away and removed the carnation that was pinned on Pete's lapel, ready to brazen it out if anyone asked questions.

Fortified with a few glasses of port and lemon, Lily held her head high as she climbed out of the van, but the only person she saw was Marilyn, running out of her door to greet her.

'Lily, where have you been?'

'To Pete's mate's wedding.'

'Oh, so that's it,' Marilyn said, smiling widely.

'That's what?' Lily said, her brows rising in mock surprise.

'Martha Biggs has been on the warpath. She's been going round telling everyone that she saw you and Pete getting married this morning.'

'Blimey, what did she do?' Lily joked. 'Go back in time? Did you hear that, Pete, it seems that you and I are newlyweds.'

'Really? Does that mean I'll get a decent honeymoon night this time?'

'You should be so lucky,' Lily quipped. 'I could murder a cup of tea. Are you coming in, Marilyn?'

'You should have stuck to tea on our wedding night,' Pete said as he walked in behind them.

'It wasn't my fault. I wasn't used to drinking and how was I to know that a few glasses of sherry would go to my head?' Lily said, keeping up the improvised story that Pete had started.

'I don't know how Mrs Biggs got it into her head that you were getting married this morning,' Marilyn said as she sat down. 'It's bloody daft and I told her that.'

'That's easy,' Lily said, this part of the story rehearsed in advance. 'She saw us at the registry office. Pete had taken some photographs of the happy couple, and I said in passing that when I married

Pete the camera went wrong so none of ours turned out.'

'Oh, what a shame,' Marilyn said.

'It was only a joke really, but when I told them that his mate insisted on taking a photo of us. Sylvia, his new wife, shoved her flowers into my hand and we were just posing when Mrs Biggs saw us. It's no wonder she got the wrong idea, but she wouldn't listen when I pointed out her mistake.'

Marilyn laughed. 'The silly cow. Mind you, with her spreading the news there might be a bit of talk.'

'If anyone is silly enough to believe her, that's up to them,' Lily said, managing a dismissive tone.

'Like me, they'll know she's talking rubbish. If you weren't married, you'd have tied the knot before your stomach swelled, just like that woman's daughter at number six. Look at you, you're eight months pregnant and can hardly hide it.'

Yes, it was true, Lily thought. If a girl got pregnant, the marriage followed quickly, so maybe waiting had inadvertently worked in their favour. 'Yeah, and can you imagine the registrar's face if someone turned up to get married with a stomach like this?'

Marilyn chuckled. 'He'd have a shock, that's for sure.'

Lily made the tea, knowing that if she looked

at Pete she wouldn't be able to stem her laughter. The registrar had indeed looked shocked when he saw her, his face blood red as he began the short service.

Relief flooded through her. They had pulled it off and, like Marilyn, Lily doubted anyone would believe Mrs Biggs. It was time to move forward, to make the most of her marriage to Pete. He was a good man, a good provider, and soon their baby would be born.

It was a second chance, and maybe this time it would be all right. Maybe this time she'd feel an instant maternal instinct when her baby was placed in her arms.

CHAPTER THIRTY-FOUR

Mavis got the call on Tuesday, 17th of July. Her mother had gone into labour in the early hours of the morning and Pete was ringing to tell her that she'd just given birth to a baby boy.

'How is she? How's the baby?' Mavis asked.

'Your mum's fine, and my boy's a right little bruiser with a face like a boxer.'

Mavis laughed. 'I bet he's gorgeous.'

'Yeah, he is and we've decided to call him Robert.'

'Robert, that's nice,' Mavis mused. 'Oh, I can't wait to see him.'

'Your mum's got to stay in hospital for another eight days, but you can visit them.'

'I wish I could, but with my mother-in-law so ill, I don't think I'll be able to make it.'

'Never mind. As soon as I get the chance I'll bring them over.'

'Thanks, Pete, and in the meantime give Mum my love and my new baby brother a kiss from me.'

'Will do, and bye for now.'

Mavis replaced the receiver. Her new baby brother, yes, she had a new baby brother, but there was no jealousy now, just joy. Oh, if only she could see him now and see her mother, but, of course, it was impossible. Edith was so weak and it had taken ages to change her sheet that morning, even longer to settle her comfortably. She had got behind with her tasks, trying without success to get Edith to eat, and it had made Alec late for work. He'd been furious, dashing out without looking in on his mother or saying goodbye. Shortly after she'd taken James to school, and as she'd managed to get Grace into nursery, she had to stop off there too. Thankfully Grace had taken to it like a duck to water, but no sooner had Mavis returned home than the telephone had rung, Pete passing on the wonderful news.

With a sigh, Mavis went to check on her mother-in-law now, her face paling. Edith had slipped off her pillows and was lying flat, her breathing dreadful and a lot worse than it had been earlier.

She ran forward to prop Edith up but it didn't help, and, frantic, Mavis was struck by a feeling of déjà vu. Her father had looked like this at the end, sounded like this, every breath strained.

In horror, Mavis ran from the room. No, it couldn't be happening again! Her mother-in-law couldn't be dying. In the hall she snatched up the telephone, quickly dialling the surgery and imploring that the doctor came as soon as possible.

Mavis started to pace, her eyes flicking again and again to Edith. Where was the doctor? Again and again she went to look out of the window, until at last she saw his car pulling up outside.

She dashed to let him in, gasping in panic, 'She . . . she's having trouble breathing.'

'I'll take a look at her,' the doctor said, walking ahead of Mavis.

The examination didn't take long, his face grim as he spoke. 'It's pneumonia and she needs to be admitted to hospital. I'll ring for an ambulance.'

'Pneumonia! Oh, no!'

'I did warn you that there would be the danger of liquid slipping into her lungs,' he said brusquely before walking into the hall again to phone for an ambulance.

Mavis stood in shock, her mind paralysed for a moment, but then as the doctor finished the call she ran to grab the receiver. She had to tell Alec, had to ring his office. When the receptionist answered, she said, 'I'd like to talk to my husband, Alec Pugh.'

'One moment, please, I'll put you through.'

It was only seconds later that she heard Alec's

voice, her own stuttering as she said, 'Alec, we're . . .
we're waiting for an ambulance. Your . . . your
mother's got to go into hospital.'

'What? Why?'

'The doctor said she has pneumonia.'

'Oh, my God. What hospital are they taking
her to?'

Mavis floundered. 'I . . . I don't know.'

'Is the doctor still there?'

'Yes.'

'Well, ask him then,' Alec snapped impatiently.

Mavis held her hand over the receiver as she
called out to Dr Hayes, and when he told her
St Thomas's she passed it on to Alec. 'I'll go with
your mother in the ambulance, and I'll see you
there.'

There was no reply as Alec hung up. Mavis stood
for a moment, but then moved into action. The
children, she had to sort out something for the
children. Calling out that she wouldn't be long,
Mavis dashed next door.

'Jenny, oh, thank God you're in!'

'Mavis, what's the matter?'

'It's my mother-in-law. She's got pneumonia.
We're waiting for an ambulance. Please, Jenny,
would you pick up Grace for me and, if I'm not
back, James too?'

'Of course I will. Now go on, just go, and don't
worry, they'll be fine with me.'

'Thank you, thank you,' Mavis cried before running home again.

The ambulance arrived ten minutes later and they were on their way to hospital. Edith was rushed to intensive care, but it was nearly an hour before Alec arrived.

'Thank God you're here,' Mavis said as he was led to his mother's bed.

Alec just threw her a look, pulled out a chair and sat down. He didn't speak at first, but then he turned, his eyes hard as they bored into hers. 'Look at her. Look at my mother. What happened?'

'When I went in to see her, she . . . she had slipped off her pillows.'

'No wonder she accused you of neglect. I can see why now.'

'Alec, I don't neglect her, it's just that when I returned home after taking the children to school, the telephone was ringing.'

'Oh, so that's why *my* mother was lying there in that state – I suppose you were chatting on the telephone to *yours*.'

'No, it was Pete ringing to tell me that my mother gave birth to a son.'

'Bully for her, but it sounds to me as if you're just making excuses. Just go, Mavis. I don't want you here.'

Mavis hesitated, but Alec looked venomous as he hissed, 'Just go.'

With one last look at her mother-in-law, and with Alec ignoring her whispered goodbye, Mavis left the ward.

She'd have to get a bus home and went to find the right stop, her heart heavy as she waited in the queue. Why hadn't she noticed how shallow Edith's breathing was when she had changed her sheet first thing that morning? Not only that, Edith had refused to eat, but, worried about the time, she'd let it pass, deciding to try again later. She'd been impatient, anxious that Alec would be late for work, and that she still had to get the children ready for school.

She would never forget her horror of finding that Edith had slid off her pillows. How long had she lain there like that? Did it happen while she was taking the children to school? She should have looked in on Edith as soon as she got back, but instead she had dashed to answer the telephone.

Yes, she had neglected Edith, and, if anything happened to his mother, Alec would never forgive her.

Jenny opened her door at twelve thirty, surprised to see Mavis. She'd only been to collect Grace half an hour earlier and had expected to have her for much longer. 'You're back from the hospital? Is your mother-in-law all right?'

'No, I'm afraid not. She's in intensive care.'

'Oh, dear, I'm sorry to hear that. Are you coming in?'

'Yes, if you don't mind,' Mavis said, following Jenny to the kitchen. 'Where's Grace?'

'She's playing in the garden and she's fine.'

'That's good,' Mavis said as she sat down.

Jenny saw how pale Mavis looked, her manner somehow distant, but said nothing until she had poured them both a cup of tea. She handed one to Mavis and then sat down opposite, asking softly, 'Are you all right?'

Mavis shook her head. 'Not really. I'm worried about my mother-in-law. If anything happens to her, I dread to think how Alec is going to react.'

'I'm sure she'll be fine, but if the worst happens, Alec will grieve, just as you grieved, and probably still are for your father. You'll be able to comfort each other.'

'I doubt that,' Mavis said. 'I neglected his mother, and if she dies, he'll blame me.'

'Mavis, that's rubbish,' Jenny said kindly. 'You've looked after his mother for years. You've been marvellous and Alec knows that. Now come on, buck up, I'm sure you're worrying about nothing and she'll be fine.'

Mavis's face was etched with guilt as she told

Jenny what had happened. 'So you see, I should have checked on Edith before answering the telephone. It was Pete, ringing to tell me that my mother has had the baby. I was so happy for her, but . . . but, Jenny, by taking the call, I *did* neglect Edith.'

'Mavis, listen to me – your mother-in-law's health has been deteriorating for ages. All right, she had slipped off her pillows and I don't suppose that helped, but she had pneumonia.'

With a heavy sigh, Mavis looked at the clock. 'It's nearly one o'clock, and I'd best get back. Alec might ring me, but then again I doubt it. Oh, Jenny, I hope she's all right.'

'Look, why don't you go back to the hospital? I don't mind having Grace and I can pick James up from school too.'

'No, he told me to leave, said he didn't want me there.'

'But why?'

'I told you, I neglected his mother, and though you say slipping off her pillows wouldn't cause pneumonia, don't you see, I should have noticed how bad she was earlier. I was up at six, changing her sheet, washing her, but I was so tired, Jenny, hardly able to keep my eyes open, and she had messed the bed. It took ages to clean her up, and I got all behind; I heard the children waking up, knew that Alec would be annoyed that I wasn't there to see to them. Oh, listen to me, it sounds like I'm making excuses. Alec said that and he's right.'

'Mavis, stop it! You don't have to explain yourself to me, or come to that, anyone. How you've coped with looking after your mother-in-law, the children, and the house single-handedly for years is beyond me. I've seen how tired you are, how the weight has dropped off you. If you ask me, you deserve a bloody medal.'

'I . . . I still should have noticed, especially when she wouldn't eat her breakfast.'

'For goodness sake, you're not a nurse with medical training and, let's face it, she's been going downhill for ages.'

'If anything happens to her, Alec won't see it that way.'

'Then sod Alec,' Jenny snapped, her hand then going to her mouth in horror. 'Oh, blimey, I shouldn't have said that.'

'What's sod Alec?' a small voice asked.

'Grace,' Mavis said as she jumped to her feet. 'Goodness, I didn't see you there.'

'Sod Alec,' Grace repeated.

'Mavis, I'm so sorry,' Jenny said, and crouching in front of Grace she fought for an explanation. 'Sod is, er . . . er . . . another word for a lump of mud, or grass.'

Grace looked puzzled, but Mavis burst into

laughter. 'Alec, a lump of mud,' she gasped, doubling over with mirth.

At first Jenny chuckled, but then her face straightened as Mavis's laughter turned first to hysteria, then sobs – sobs that racked her body. Jenny swept Grace up into her arms and hurried into the garden. 'Come on, darling,' she urged. 'Let's pick some flowers.'

'What's the matter with my mummy?'

'She's just a bit upset, but she'll be fine soon.'

'Me give her the flowers?'

'Yes, of course you can,' Jenny said, leading Grace to Stan's immaculate flower border. He wouldn't be happy to see his precious blooms cut, but she wanted to distract Grace, to give Mavis time to cry, to let it all out, and maybe, just maybe, it would help.

Alec faced the doctor, sick with worry. He had watched his mother fighting for breath, had touched her forehead to find it hot yet clammy, but this was the first time he'd been called to talk to a doctor.

A nurse stood by his desk while the doctor steepled his fingers, his expression grave. 'I'm sorry, Mr Pugh, I'm afraid your mother's prognosis isn't good. Is there anyone you'd like to call, any other relatives?'

'No, there isn't anyone else.'

'Would you like to talk to the hospital chaplain?'

'Why? No, no. Are you telling me that my mother's dying?'

'We are doing all we can, but . . .' his voice trailed off.

'Would you like to sit with your mother again, Mr Pugh?' the nurse asked as she stepped forward.

'Yes, yes,' Alec said, reeling with shock as he rose to his feet.

'I'm sorry, Mr Pugh,' the doctor said.

Alec barely heard him. His head was buzzing and he felt dizzy, but he fought it off as he was led back to his mother's side. This couldn't be happening. It was a nightmare, it wasn't real.

'I'll get you a cup of tea,' the nurse said kindly.

Alec looked at his mother, took her hand and faced the truth. This was real, his mother was dying and, unmanly or not, he allowed his tears to flow.

It was some time before Alec was able to pull himself together, before he was able to think clearly again. Perhaps he should ring Mavis, tell her what was happening, but then his lips tightened in anger.

No, he still didn't want Mavis here. He knew that his mother slipping off her pillows hadn't caused this, but Mavis should have seen earlier how ill she was. If only he'd had looked in on her before he left for work, but it was too late now, too late to save her.

Alec looked at his mother's face, pleading with her to speak to him. 'It's me, Mother. It's Alec.'

There was no response, not a flicker of movement, and in despair he laid his head on the side of her bed.

Mavis couldn't stand it any longer and rang the hospital again at eight that evening, only to be told that there was no change. What was going on? If his mother was all right, if there was no change, why was Alec still there?

The children were asleep, the house silent and, mentally exhausted, Mavis sat down, her head sinking back into the corner of the winged armchair. She closed her eyes, felt sleep overcoming her and gave in to it. Ten minutes, she'd doze for ten minutes, that was all.

'Mavis!'

She awoke with a start, blurry-eyed as she tried to focus on Alec. He was standing right in front of her, his eyes blazing with anger.

'Alec, you're back. How is your mother?'

'She's dead,' he snapped.

'What! Oh, no!' Mavis cried, stumbling stiffly to her feet.

'Yes, Mavis, she died an hour ago, and it's all thanks to you.'

Mavis looked at the clock, unable to believe that it was two in the morning, and when she spoke again, her voice was high with shock. 'Oh, Alec, please don't blame me.'

'Why not? She's dead because of your neglect,' he snapped.

Mavis didn't know what to say, what to do as she looked at her husband. He threw her a look of disgust and then marched from the room. She heard his footsteps on the stairs and, helpless, she slumped onto the chair again. As she had feared, Alec blamed her for his mother's death, and, no matter what Jenny said, he was right.

Mavis hunched forward, shivering, fearing the future, fearing living with a man who had looked at her with such hatred. Alec would probably make life intolerable for her now – but then she'd neglected his mother and it was no more than she deserved.

CHAPTER THIRTY-FIVE

By the end of August, if it hadn't been for the fact that she had more freedom now, Mavis knew that she wouldn't have been able to stand the strain. The atmosphere when Alec was at home was awful, his grief still manifest in the anger he directed towards her.

He marched into the kitchen now, his drawings of her allotted tasks for the day in his hand. 'Make sure you clean these two bedrooms thoroughly. My mother loved this house and had high standards. I want them kept up.'

'Yes, Alec,' Mavis said as she placed his breakfast on the table. She had hoped to see what had once been the living room on his list, but so far he had refused to let her touch it. Edith's bed remained where it was, the side table, and even her commode untouched.

Mavis knew grief, knew that Alec still rightfully blamed her, and tried to make allowances, but she was worried about the children. Alec barely acknowledged their presence and when he did it was just to snap at them. She shielded them as much as possible and during the school holidays took them out to the park or the common, but there was only one week left before James started his new term and Grace returned to nursery.

Both children were withdrawn when Alec was at home, unnaturally quiet, as if instinctively knowing not to disturb their father. It worried her, but at least he hadn't laid a hand on them. If he did, Mavis didn't know what she'd do. As long as he took his temper out on her, she could just about bear it, but not if he started on the children.

'Pour me another cup of tea,' Alec demanded.

She did his bidding, and then quietly leaving the kitchen Mavis went upstairs to look in on the children. They were in James's room, sitting on the floor and playing with his Meccano set. 'Has Daddy gone yet?' James asked.

'Not yet, but soon,' she said.

'Don't like Daddy,' Grace whined, her expression sulky.

This was Grace's usual refrain now and Mavis had given up trying to explain that her daddy didn't mean it when he was sharp with her, that he was just sad and missing his mother. Grace and James had no concept of death and, once told that their grandmother was in heaven now, they barely mentioned her.

The children, like Mavis, enjoyed being able to go out now, and yesterday they had ventured to Peckham again. They had now been a few times, and even though Pete's initial description that he looked like a boxer had proved to be accurate, the baby was so adorable. Her brother might only be her half brother but Mavis already loved him dearly.

As though aware of her thoughts, James said, 'Can we go to see Robert again?'

'Not today, darling, but perhaps on Friday. We'll go to the park today, and maybe Jenny will come with Greg.'

'Goody,' James clapped, but then hearing Alec calling her, Mavis swiftly left them.

'I'm going to work now,' he said, standing at the bottom of the stairs as Mavis walked down them. 'The kitchen looks a mess so you can add it to your list.'

'Yes, Alec,' she said. The kitchen wasn't in a mess, there were just his breakfast things to clear up, but she didn't argue. It was simpler that way.

At last the door closed behind him, and immediately the children came running downstairs. 'Can we go now, Mummy? Can we go to the park?' James begged.

'Not yet, darling. I'll need to do a bit of house-work first, but it won't take long,' Mavis told him.

She knew that Alec would check to see if the rooms had been properly cleaned, but she had learned how to cut corners now, which parts he'd inspect and which she could leave.

The two bedrooms could be done in under an hour and so, ushering the children into the garden, she began to wash up the breakfast things, just as anxious as they were to get out of the house.

On Saturday, Alec began going through his mother's things. After her death, the will had been easy to find, and there had been no surprises. She had left him this house, and from her annuity a yearly income, but now he had finally found the strength to sort out other old files and papers.

His mother's death still haunted him: the thought of her lying alone, fighting to raise herself up, while Mavis chatted on the bloody telephone. He would never forgive his wife, could barely look at her, and when he did his anger rose up inside him.

Forced to sleep downstairs, his mother hadn't used this bedroom for years, but her clothes still hung in the wardrobe, her other things in drawers. Alec could barely bring himself to look at them, and maybe he should instruct Mavis to clear them out; but for now he pulled out one of his mother's dresses, burying his nose in the lingering smell of lavender perfume.

At last Alec hung the garment up again, but then, as he looked at the top shelf, he thought he could see something tucked in the corner. Unable to reach it, Alec dragged a chair over, and standing on it he pulled forward an old wooden box. It was something he hadn't noticed before, and puzzled he lifted it down. It was locked, but though Alec looked in all the drawers, he couldn't find a key. What was in it? As it was locked, surely it was something of importance.

Alec ran downstairs and, Mavis being in the garden with the children, the kitchen was empty. He pulled open a drawer, found a screwdriver and then hurried back upstairs again where he impatiently worked at the lock until, at last, it opened.

Inside Alec saw what looked like an old diary, and intrigued he sat on the side of the bed to open it, instantly recognising his mother's beautiful, flowery handwriting. For a moment he had to blink back tears of emotion, but then, as he began to read, his feelings turned to anger. No! No! It couldn't be true – but there was no denying his mother's written words. Alec surged to his feet. Everything his mother had told him about his father was a lie! Her whole life had been a lie!

Fury blazed in his eyes as Alec tore the diary to shreds, but the act didn't have the power to calm him. Still livid, still burning with anger, Alec ran downstairs. 'Mavis, come here!' he yelled as he flung open the back door.

'What is it?' Mavis asked nervously, closing the door behind her as she walked into the kitchen.

'Did you know? Did my mother tell you about my father?'

'I don't know what you mean. I don't remember her ever mentioning him, except to say he died of tuberculosis.'

Alec was sure he could see a shifty look in Mavis's eyes and didn't believe her. 'Tell me the truth! What did she say?'

'Alec, she didn't say anything.'

'You're a liar! You're as bad as my mother. In fact, women are all the same – all rotten, lying bitches,' Alec shouted as he laid into Mavis, impervious to her cries of pain as, careful to avoid her face, he punched her again and again.

'Daddy! Daddy, don't . . .'

Alec spun around and seeing James standing in the kitchen doorway, Grace hovering behind him, he spat furiously, 'Get out of my sight!'

Mavis pushed past him, hurrying over to the children. 'It's all right, James. It's all right. Go back into the garden, both of you,' she urged, pushing them outside and quickly closing the door.

'I've a good mind to give the pair of them a thrashing too.'

'No, Alec! No! You can do what you want to

me, but if you touch the children, I . . . I'll leave you.'

'Huh, and go where?'

'I don't care, anywhere,' Mavis said, her voice quavering.

'Just try it, Mavis. Just try it,' Alec warned, surging forward to hit her again. 'Don't you dare threaten me! You're useless, an unfit mother, and if you try to leave with my children, I'll drag you back.'

'All right, but please, Alec, please stop,' Mavis begged as she cowered from his blows.

At last, his temper cooling, Alec slumped onto a chair, hardly aware that Mavis had fled back outside. He ran a hand through his hair, his thoughts returning to his mother's diary, hate replacing the love he had once felt for her.

CHAPTER THIRTY-SIX

On Monday, Lily was holding her son, gazing down on his face. There were none of her features – Robert was the image of his father, and Pete was already spoiling him. She stroked Robert's soft cheek, her heart swelling with love, a love that had been born with him, from the moment she'd heard his first cry.

'Are you busy, Lily?'

She glanced around to see Marilyn at the back door. 'No, come on in.'

'Gawd, Lily, are you sure you don't want me to bleach your hair? You've got inches of root showing.'

'No, I told you, I'm growing it out.'

'Yeah, but how are you gonna feel if it comes through grey?'

'Don't be daft. I'm not old enough for grey hair.'

'I'm only three years older than you, but look at that,' she said, bending over in front of Lily to part her frizzy curls. 'Oh, ain't he gorgeous.'

'He looks just like Pete,' smiled Lily.

'Yeah, but on him, it looks cute.'

'Oh, so a flat nose doesn't on Pete?'

'Gawd, that didn't come out right,' Marilyn blustered, her cheeks red.

'It's all right,' Lily chuckled. 'I know Pete's no oil painting.'

'Looks ain't everything and he's a smashing bloke.'

'Yes, I know,' Lily agreed. Along with Robert's birth had come a deep fondness for Pete, and though she didn't know if it would turn to love, she was happier now than she'd been in a long time. When Ron was alive, deep down she had always been waiting for him to come back, but he was gone now and somehow it made it easier. Mavis would always keep his memory alive, and every time Lily saw her daughter she was reminded of him, but at least since Robert's birth it was now without grief.

'It was nice to meet your daughter the other day. She's a beautiful girl, Lily, and them kids of hers are lovely too. Mind you, she doesn't look much like you, or Pete.'

Lily was about to find an excuse, to say that Mavis resembled her late mother, but then decided that it would make life less complicated if she told Marilyn a version of the truth. 'Mavis isn't Pete's. She's a child from my first marriage.'

'What? You've been married before?'

'Yes, and I married Pete after my first husband died.'

Marilyn frowned. 'So was your Mavis just a nipper at the time?'

'Yes, she was,' Lily said, and, though it was a lie, at least it was a small one. 'Here, take the baby and I'll make us a cup of tea.'

Marilyn cooed over him, and while she made the tea, Lily thought about her daughter. It was lovely to see Mavis with baby Robert. She was totally enchanted with her new half brother and her kids adored him too, but they had yet to explain that Robert was their uncle.

It was nice that Mavis had time to pay them the occasional visit now, but she still avoided inviting them to her home. Lily was sure there was something wrong, something going on, but every time she tried to talk to Mavis, the girl clammed up.

Still, at least the girl had a life of her own now, instead of being nothing but a slave to Edith Pugh. Oh, it was sad that the woman had died, and from what Mavis had said her funeral had been awful, with just the two of them there.

Alec must still be in an awful state, and Lily knew how hard it was to lose a mother, her own grief having devastated her. Yes, maybe that was it, Lily thought. Maybe Mavis felt that Alec wasn't ready for visitors yet.

* * *

Jenny sat next to Mavis on a bench, both of them watching the children as they raced from swings to roundabouts, the slide and the seesaw. 'Mavis, is Alec still blaming you for his mother's death?' Jenny asked gently.

'Yes, of course he is, and he's right.'

'No, Mavis, he isn't – I've told you that before.'

'I know you have, but I still think I should have seen earlier that she was dying.'

'All right, let's say you did. Let's say you noticed when you first got up that morning. She would've been in hospital a few hours earlier, but do you really think that would have made any difference?'

'Alec said it would, but something else seems to be on his mind now. He was sorting out his mother's things and asked me if she'd ever mentioned his father. I told him that she hadn't, but he's been in a terrible mood ever since.'

'Did you ask him why?'

'There's no talking to him nowadays.'

'So you're just going to go on allowing him to make your life a misery?' Jenny snapped. She was fed up with this. Since Edith Pugh had died, she often popped round to visit Mavis when Alec was at work. She had seen the lists Alec left every day, the drawings of housework he demanded Mavis carried out, the meals he insisted she cook. Alec even told her what shops to go to, how much to spend, and like an idiot Mavis obeyed his every command. All right, the man was still grieving, and maybe he needed someone to blame for his mother's death, but to lay it on Mavis just wasn't fair.

'I'm all right, honestly, I am,' Mavis insisted.

'Yeah, and pigs might fly,' Jenny replied, deciding that it was no good, she'd never convince Mavis that she hadn't done anything wrong and might as well give up. One day she hoped both she and Alec would come to their senses, but for now all she could do was to be a friend – there as always if Mavis needed her.

Alec knew he had let standards slip in the office, but he just couldn't bring himself to do anything about it. When his mother died he'd been unable to pull himself together. He'd been to see Dr Hayes, the man telling him that it wouldn't have made any difference to the outcome if his mother had been admitted earlier, yet still he had blamed Mavis.

Now though, he didn't care if his mother had been neglected or not. It wasn't grief that made him angry now. It was his mother's diary. Lips tight, Alec threw down his pen. He hadn't been able to believe his eyes, and had searched frantically for a wedding certificate. Of course, he hadn't found one, the proof had been in the diary, but he hadn't wanted to believe it. His mother had lied to him, said his father had died of tuberculosis when he was just a baby. All lies – and now he didn't even know if Pugh was his real name or one she had manufactured to put on his birth certificate.

The telephone rang and Alec snatched it up. 'Yes, what is it?'

He paused as he listened to the receptionist, then spat, 'No, I can't talk to him now. Tell him to ring back later.'

Alec heaved a sigh of annoyance as he sat back in his chair. He had told Dulcie not to disturb him unless it was important, but the blasted girl still tried to put calls through. There was a stack of correspondence on his desk waiting to be dealt with but he irritably pushed it to one side.

God, he had worshipped his mother, put her on a pedestal, and had deeply admired the way she had worked to bring him up without the support of his father – his father, a man he now knew was already married, one who had paid her off. The house she'd said had been left to her in an aunt's will, the money she had supposedly left that had been invested to provide an income – fabrication, it was all fabrication. Instead, according to her diary, she'd been paid off for her silence, and handsomely.

Teeth clenched in fury, Alec knew that if it wasn't for the diary he'd never have known. There was no paperwork, the transaction obviously destroyed, and no reference to his father's name either, just the initial *C*, and that could be either a Christian or surname.

Alec's lips now curled in disgust. His mother had had high moral standards, had instilled them in him, but it had all been a sham. She was nothing but a tart and he was a bastard! He stood up. It was no good. He had to get out of there, to breathe fresh air and his back was rigid as he marched out of the office.

'Mr Pugh . . . Mr Pugh, can you take a look at this please?' one of the girls called.

Alec ignored her. He hated women now, all women, and would never trust another one for as long as he lived.

CHAPTER THIRTY-SEVEN

Winter came in with force on a Friday in early December, an icy wind rattling the windows as Mavis piled more coal onto the fire. James was in school, Grace at the nursery, and though there was housework waiting to be done, Mavis couldn't yet face going upstairs to tackle the freezing bedrooms.

As time had passed, and at Jenny's urging, they had been to the reference library where her friend had looked up her mother-in-law's symptoms, finally finding conclusive evidence that Mavis wasn't to blame for Edith's death. Mavis had tried to explain that to Alec but he wouldn't listen, and, if anything, her efforts had increased his wrath.

She hated this house, and now that winter was here it was a prison again; only nowadays Mavis waited in fear for her jailer to come home. If only she were stronger, if only she could stand up to

Alec, but if she tried he would turn on James or even Grace, and she couldn't bear that.

As long as she could keep the children safe, that was all that mattered, Mavis thought as she sat by the fire, rubbing her bruised arm as she thought about what happened earlier that morning. All she had done was to break the yolk when she was frying an egg for Alec's breakfast, but it had been enough to arouse his violence – violence that had steadily increased since August. There was nothing in Alec's eyes but hate now. Hate when he took her body, inflicting yet more bruises over the old ones.

When there was a ring on the doorbell, she hurried along the hall. It would be Jenny, and Mavis forced a smile as she opened the door. 'Hello, come on in.'

'It's bitter out there,' Jenny said, leaving her coat on until she got to the kitchen where she eyed the blazing fire with appreciation. 'I've banked mine up and it'll be fine till I get back.'

'Sit down,' Mavis invited. 'I'll make us a coffee.'

'Do you know what I hate about the winter, Mavis? I hate having wet washing draped all over my kitchen. How come I never see any in yours? In fact, your kitchen always looks immaculate and you put mine to shame.'

'You know how fussy Alec is. I prefer yours. It's homely, lived-in.'

'You mean it's always in a mess,' Jenny said, chuckling as she held her hands out to the flames.

Yes, it might be a mess, Mavis thought as she made two cups of coffee, but she envied Jenny so much. Envied her happy home and marriage, and longed for such happiness too. She couldn't go on for much longer, Mavis knew that, but with no money of her own, no means of supporting or feeding her children, she was trapped in this house, her marriage not only loveless, but violent now too.

'How's your mum and the baby, Mavis?' asked Jenny.

'They're fine, though I haven't seen them for a while. When the children break up from school I'll be able to take them to Peckham again, and I can't wait to see baby Bobby.'

'Oh, it's Bobby now, is it? Not Robert?'

'Yes, and funnily enough it was Grace who started it off. She just couldn't say Robert and it came out as Wobbert. It was my mum who suggested Bobby.'

'For a baby, somehow it sounds cuter.'

Mavis had to stifle a groan as she turned too quickly, her back so sore from the punch Alec had taken pleasure in giving her last night.

Sharp-eyed Jenny missed nothing, her face showing concern as she asked, 'What's wrong, Mavis? You've gone a bit pale.'

'It's nothing, just a bit of backache,' Mavis said as she handed Jenny her drink. She had hidden Alec's violence since it started not long after Edith's death, afraid that he would take it out on the children if she opened her mouth.

Even if she did tell Jenny, or her mum, Mavis knew there was no escape. Her mother didn't have room to take her in and now only her dreams kept Mavis going. One day the children would grow up, would leave home, and when that happened she would do the same. She'd leave Alec, and if she had to spend her life cleaning for other people to raise enough money to live on, it would be heaven after this.

For now she had to endure it and, forcing another smile, she sat down opposite her friend. Jenny began to talk about Christmas and as it was only a few weeks away it remained the subject of the conversation until Jenny said that it was time for her to go.

Mavis walked with her to the door, shutting it behind her friend as the walls of the house closed in on her again. How many years stretched ahead of her before she could be free? So many, so many. Unbidden tears welled in her eyes.

She walked to the hall cupboard and took out the vacuum cleaner, her heart heavy as she began the housework.

* * *

Lily was battling the wind as she pushed the pram home. There were few people around, but as she turned into Harwood Street her eyes widened. There was a van parked outside Mrs Biggs's house, men loading furniture onto it. The old girl must be moving and that suited Lily just fine.

Since Lily had married Pete, Mrs Biggs had been on a campaign against her, but thankfully she hadn't won the battle. Few believed her story, but it hadn't stopped the old girl from doing her utmost to make Lily's life a misery. She was determined to get her out of the street, but all her efforts had backfired. Most people supported Lily and Mrs Biggs had become very unpopular.

Lily knocked on Marilyn's door, a wide smile on her face. 'Mrs Biggs is moving out.'

'Yeah, I saw the van when it arrived. She's lived here for donkey's years and I can't believe she's leaving.'

Lily turned her head as Mrs Biggs appeared, berating the removals men to be careful with her sideboard.

'Yes, you can look,' the old woman snapped when she saw Lily, 'and I hope you're satisfied. You might have fooled everyone else but you haven't fooled me and I refuse to live next door to a tart.'

'Lily isn't a tart,' Marilyn snapped as she stepped over her doorstep, clutching her cardigan around her chest as she was hit by a blast of wind.

'Yes, she is, and your daughter is going down the same road.'

'How . . . how dare you!' Marilyn blustered.

'Oh, I dare, and what do you expect? No doubt she's been tainted by the likes of *her*, and with this street going to wrack and ruin I'm glad I'm moving in with my son. Thank God he moved away before he too became tainted.'

'It's more like you drove him away,' Marilyn said. 'Blimey, I don't envy his wife if you're moving in.'

To Lily's surprise, the old woman's face crumbled.

'You've done this,' she said, looking Lily in the eye. 'I moved here on my wedding day and it's been my home for over forty years, but you . . . you've turned everyone against me.'

'No, she didn't,' Marilyn said. 'It was your own doing and you shouldn't have gone around spreading lies. Now come on, Lily, come inside. It's freezing out here.'

Lily couldn't look at Mrs Biggs as she pushed the pram over Marilyn's doorstep. She felt awful. Mrs Biggs had told the truth, but just because she'd lived with Pete it didn't make her a tart. She just thanked her lucky stars that nobody had believed Mrs Biggs – that she could continue to live in Harwood Street with her head held high.

* * *

413

Alec strode home from work, fuming. He'd been called in to see his superior, told that his work was no longer up to standard, and though the man had sympathised with his loss, he'd nevertheless warned that he'd been given enough leeway and there had to be a marked improvement in his office and management skills.

All right, Alec thought, he'd let things slide a bit, but there'd been no mention of all he'd achieved before – his successes in bringing the office up to scratch now forgotten.

Shivering after leaving his warm office, Alec thrust his hands into the pockets of his overcoat, cursing that he'd been unable to find his leather gloves when he had left for work that morning. Of course, Mavis denied moving them, but Alec was sure he'd left them on the hall table. Useless, his wife was useless.

At last Alec arrived home, still fuming with anger as he went inside. He took off his overcoat, hung it in the cupboard, and as he approached the kitchen he could hear the children giggling.

All went silent as Alec walked in, three pairs of eyes looking at him in fear. This was what Alec loved, being in control, the house ruled by a man now instead of a woman. Yes, his mother had always been in charge, of the house, of him, but not any more. Not now.

His expression was hard as he looked at James

and Grace, saying abruptly, 'Get out of my sight. Go to your rooms.'

'Alec, the bedrooms are freezing,' Mavis protested.

That was enough for Alec. How dare she undermine him! All his anger, all his shame at being hauled before his superior, was swiftly taken out on Mavis as the children fled the room in terror.

CHAPTER THIRTY-EIGHT

'Come on, you little bruiser,' Lily said as she lifted her son onto her lap. His chubby legs kicked, his hands clutched into fists, and Lily grinned. Bobby was certainly living up to his reputation. It was a new year, 1963, and he'd soon be six months old, yet still looked like a boxer. Bobby chuckled as Lily bounced him on her lap, dribble running down his chin, and Lily felt her heart would burst with love.

When the front door opened Lily looked up, surprised to see Pete coming in. 'What's this? No work?'

'It's tipping down with rain and it ain't safe to be up on the scaffolding. I told the blokes to bugger off home and I've done the same.'

'You'll still have to pay them.'

'Don't worry, we're doing fine and I can stand the loss.'

Lily smiled happily. Pete had finally started up

his own business and so far he was doing really well. He loved being his own boss, relished the challenge, and what's more he'd found a good crew to work for him.

'Hello, Bobby, my boy,' he said. 'Give your daddy a smile.'

The baby did just that and Pete grinned proudly. 'Look at the size of those legs,' he said, taking him from Lily's arms.

'Pete, I know you've only just come in, but when you've dried out and warmed up, would you take me over to see Mavis?'

'You rang her yesterday and she put you off again.'

'Yes, but on Sundays Alec's there. If we go today he'll be at work and it'll give me a chance to find out what's going on.'

'Yeah, all right. Get yourself ready and we'll go.'

It was over an hour later when they arrived in Ellington Avenue and they were just in time to see Mavis hurrying along the street, clutching Grace's hand, the child having to run to keep up with her mother.

Lily handed Bobby to Pete, and then struggled to open her umbrella as she climbed out of the van. 'Hello, Mavis.'

'Mum! What are you doing here?'

'Do I need a reason to visit my daughter?' Lily asked brusquely, before she went round to the other side of the van, taking Bobby in her arms and doing her best to shield him from the rain.

'I've just been to collect Grace from nursery and we're soaked. Let's get inside,' Mavis urged.

Lily moved quickly and with Pete behind her she shoved her umbrella at him as she followed Mavis into the house. He stood on the step, shaking it madly, while Mavis took off Grace's wet coat, and then her own.

Lily did the same and as Mavis took it from her, Lily opened the living room door, only to stop in her tracks.

'Don't go in there, Mum. It's warmer in the kitchen.'

'What's going on? Why haven't you turned this back into your living room?'

'Because Alec won't let me.'

'Won't let you? What do you mean?' Lily asked as she followed Mavis to the kitchen. A lovely fire was burning in the grate and Lily sat next to it, Bobby in her arms. 'Pete, get that wet coat off and sit down too,' she ordered as he hovered uncertainly.

'Yes, give it to me and I'll hang it up,' Mavis suggested.

As soon as her daughter returned, Lily said, 'Now then, Mavis, I asked you about Edith's room.'

'Alec just wants it left as it is.'

'That's bloody daft.'

'I dunno, Lily,' Pete said. 'Grief takes people in different ways. My old mum hung on to my dad's clothes for years. She said she could still smell him on them and refused to let us chuck them away.'

'Clothes, yeah, I can sort of understand that. But a whole room? It's like he's turned it into some sort of shrine. It ain't healthy.'

'It's been under six months, Lily. Give the bloke time.'

Grace was fascinated by Bobby, and now that he could sit up Lily placed him on the rug. Bobby was equally fascinated, his hands reaching out to grab Grace as he chuckled happily.

'I . . . I'll make you a cup of tea,' Mavis said.

Lily frowned. Her daughter looked awful, pale and thin. 'What's going on, Mavis?'

'Going on? I don't know what you mean.'

'Don't act all innocent with me, my girl. You ain't been yourself for ages.'

'I'm fine.'

'No, you're not. Now tell me what's going on,' Lily demanded again.

'Mum, please, don't bully me,' Mavis begged as she turned away. 'I can't take any more, I really can't.'

'What are you talking about? I'm not bullying you,' Lily said as stood up to walk over to Mavis. She took her daughter's arm, turning Mavis to face her, but couldn't fail to miss her wince of pain. 'Sorry, love, I didn't mean to hurt you.'

'Daddy hurts Mummy,' Grace said.

Shocked, Lily spun round. 'What do you mean, darling?'

'No, Grace. No, he doesn't,' Mavis said hurriedly.

'He smacks Mummy.'

Lily took her daughter's arm again, and though Mavis tried to resist, she pushed up the sleeve of her jumper, eyes boggling. 'My God, look at those bruises. Did Alec do that?'

'No, no, I fell over, that's all.'

'Don't take me for a mug, Mavis. Tell me the truth.'

Mavis lowered her eyes, paused, but then said, 'All right, Alec did it, but he didn't mean to bruise me. He just gripped my arms a little too tightly, that's all.'

Lily didn't believe her daughter, and shook her head impatiently. 'That isn't what Grace said.'

'Mum, she's just a child.'

'Grace has seen something, that's for sure, and it isn't Alec just gripping your arms,' Lily snapped as the awful truth gripped her mind. The doorbell rang, and impatiently she said, 'You stay where you are. I'll get it.'

Lily was soon at the front door where she yanked it open to peer at the young woman standing there, an umbrella held over her head. Though it had been a long time since she'd seen her daughter's friend and neighbour, she recognised her. 'It's Jenny, isn't it? Come in,' Lily said.

'No, it's all right, I'll go. I usually pop round for a coffee about this time, or Mavis comes to my place. I didn't realise she had visitors today.'

Lily wondered if Jenny knew what was going on, and leaning forward she said quietly, 'Grace has just told me that Alec hits Mavis. Do you know anything about it?'

Jenny's eyes rounded. 'Hits her? No, surely not? I know Alec can be difficult, but he just doesn't seem the type. What does Mavis say about it?'

'She denied it, of course, but I saw some nasty bruises on her arm.'

'Bruises? I don't like the sound of that.'

Lily's eyes narrowed in thought. 'I'd like to get to the bottom of this, but I doubt Mavis will talk about it in front of Grace. I know she's fond of you and if I bring her round to your place, between us we might be able to get her to open up. Pete's here with me and he won't mind keeping an eye on Grace.'

'You're on,' Jenny said. 'I'll shoot back home, but you'll have to think up some sort of excuse for coming round.'

'Leave it to me,' Lily said, thinking hard as she hurried back to the kitchen and was pleased when she came up with an answer. 'Pete, would you mind

421

looking after Grace and Bobby? We won't be long, but Jenny next door is in a bit of a state and needs a bit of help.'

'Jenny! What's wrong with her?' Mavis asked worriedly.

'I've just said, ain't I? She needs a bit of help. Now come on, Mavis, get a move on.' With that Lily rushed out again, leaving Pete looking bemused; but thankfully Mavis followed her.

'Mum, is Jenny all right?'

'You'll see in a minute,' Lily said and they hurried next door.

Jenny was waiting to usher them inside, saying nothing as she led them to the kitchen. Once there she said, 'Please, both of you, sit down.'

'Jenny, what's wrong?' Mavis asked anxiously.

'With me, nothing. It's you we're worried about.'

'Me! But why? I'm fine.'

'No, you're not,' Lily said firmly. 'Now, tell me the truth. How did you get those bruises on your arm?'

'I . . . I can't tell you.'

'Don't be daft. Of course you can.'

'Alec, he . . . he'd take it out on James or Grace.'

Jenny gasped. 'Oh, no! I saw bruises on James when he was staying with us and suspected that Alec was heavy-handed. He hits him too, doesn't he?'

'No, no, he used to smack James, but not any

more, not now. It . . . it's only me.' And now that she had started, something in Mavis broke. It all came out as, between sobs, she told them everything while Lily and Jenny listened in horror.

Lily was rigid with anger. How dare he? How dare Alec hit her daughter? She wasn't going to stand for this and her need to protect her daughter became all-consuming. It was then that the truth hit Lily in a rush. She loved Mavis, really loved her, but it had taken this to wake her up. Maybe it was the life she'd once been forced to lead, the need to flog her guts out to keep a roof over their heads, along with the way that Ron had always let her down. She'd been too wrapped up in herself, ashamed of her so-called backward daughter, so unhappy that she had taken her pain out on Mavis. Selfish, self-centred, that's what she'd been and now the thought sickened Lily. She had pushed Mavis away instead of loving her. Yet the love must have always been there – how else could she be feeling it now?

'Oh, Mum, what am I going to do now? If Alec finds out I've told you, he'll go mad.'

'You leave him to me. He won't touch you again, I'll see to that.'

'No, Mum, please. I have to live with him and if you say anything, it'll make things worse.'

'No, Mavis, you don't have to live with him. You ain't alone, you've got me, and I'll sort something out.'

'How, Mum? You haven't got room for me and I've nowhere else to go.'

Lily wanted to take Mavis and the children in, to keep them near to her, and even if they had to sleep on the floor, she'd find a way. Wait, though, there was a solution. Her eyes lit up. 'Mavis, the house next door to me is still empty. I'll have a word with the landlord; ask him if you can rent it.'

Mavis dashed the tears from her cheeks. 'And how am I supposed to pay the rent, or support the children? I haven't any money of my own.'

'I'll pay it. I'll support you.'

'No, Mum, I can't let you do that.'

Lily crouched down in front of her daughter. She'd been a bad mother, had taken every penny that Mavis had earned and, if wasn't for her, the girl wouldn't have felt forced to marry Alec Pugh. Unlike Mavis, Lily knew that life had been kind to her since then, and, thanks to Pete's generosity, she had a nice little nest egg tucked away.

'Listen, love,' Lily said. 'I know I wasn't much of a mother, but give me a chance to make it up to you. I'm not hard up and, anyway, once you file for divorce that bastard will be made to support you and the kids.'

'I . . . I don't know, Mum. I haven't got any furniture, and I can't ask you to buy any. Yes, I'd love to be able to leave him, to take the kids somewhere safe, but it doesn't seem right to ask you to support us.'

'You're not asking. I'm offering. As for furniture, once we know you've got the house I can soon pick up some second-hand stuff for next to nothing,' Lily said as she rose to her feet. 'In the meantime I'll put Bobby in with me and Pete, but I haven't got any spare beds. We'll have to sort something out, if only mattresses on the floor, so let's hope we can get hold of some and quickly. The room's only tiny and it'll be a bit of a squash, but it shouldn't be for long.'

'I can't believe this,' Mavis said, her expression bewildered. 'I'm leaving Alec? Really leaving him?'

'I could have you here for a while, Mavis, but I doubt you want to stay that close to Alec,' Jenny said, but then her face took on an animated expression. 'Hold on, I might have just the answer. Lily, would you mind if Pete runs me down to my cousin's yard?'

'No, but what for?'

'Willy's got a flat in Wandsworth, and I'm sure if I tell him the circumstances he won't mind letting Mavis and the kids have it for a while. He can move back in here and problem solved.'

'I dunno,' Lily said. 'I'd prefer to have them with me.'

'It's not just Mavis and the children. It's all their things too, clothes, toys.'

'We don't have to take everything now. Just a few bits would do.'

'You don't know how Alec's going to react. When he finds out that Mavis has left him I think he'll be furious, vindictive enough to chuck everything out.'

'He wouldn't dare,' Lily snapped.

'You can't be sure of that.'

With so much going on in her mind, Lily couldn't think straight. 'Mavis, what do you think?'

Mavis blinked, the bemused look at last leaving her eyes as she said, 'Mum, I'd love to come to Peckham now, but Jenny's right. Alec's cruel enough to destroy all our things and I'd rather take as much as we can now. Once we're living next door to you and Pete, he wouldn't dare to come near us, but until then, as long as Alec can't find us, the flat might be all right.'

'Don't worry,' Jenny said. 'You'll be safe there until you can move to Peckham.'

'All right, Mavis,' Lily reluctantly agreed, 'if you want to take all your stuff, it'll have to be the flat for now.'

'Right, you start packing while I go and get Willy's keys,' Jenny said.

'He hasn't agreed yet,' Lily warned.

'He will. I know my cousin and he's a smashing bloke.'

They all trooped next door where Mavis ran

upstairs to pack, while Lily took Pete to one side. She told him what happened, and, though he at first looked angry on Mavis's behalf, he quickly agreed to drive Jenny to her cousin's yard.

'Yeah, I'll do it, Lily, but Alec Pugh ain't getting away with this. I'll leave it for now, just until we get Mavis sorted out, but then I'll be back to sort the bastard out.'

'You and me both, Pete,' she said, standing on tiptoe to kiss his cheek. 'But won't it be nice to have Mavis and my grandchildren living next door?'

'Yes, love,' Pete agreed before going with Jenny to the van, leaving Lily praying that the house was still available.

Mavis had stuffed James's clothes into a suitcase, and now started on Grace's. She felt as though she was in some kind of wonderful dream, but that at any moment she'd wake up into the nightmare of reality.

Toys, she had to take as many toys as possible, but needed some large boxes. Why wouldn't her mind function? Why was she running around like a headless chicken? She was getting away from this house, from Alec, but please, if this is a dream, she prayed, don't let me wake up. Let it go on forever.

'How are you getting on, love?'

Mavis spun round. 'Oh, Mum, is this really happening?'

'Of course it is. Now I'd like to help, but I've got my hands full with Grace and Bobby.'

'Can . . . can you really afford to support us?'

'Stop worrying, love. Since I've been with Pete I've been tucking money away. Money he knows nothing about.'

'But why?'

'To be honest, I wanted a little nest egg in case things didn't work out between us. I didn't want to go back to how things were before, living hand to mouth and trying to make ends meet by flogging other people's junk.'

'But surely you're happy with Pete?'

'Yes, of course I am, but putting money aside got to be a sort of habit, I suppose. I know that me and Pete are set for life, and as he's always generous I've never had to touch me nest egg. Honestly, love, you're welcome to it.'

'Oh, Mum . . .' Mavis said, hardly aware that Grace was taking her toys out of a box she had just started to fill.

'Now don't start crying again. You need to get the rest of your stuff sorted out, and then once we've picked James up from school, we'll be off.'

'I'll never get it done in time. I haven't even started on my clothes yet.'

'Pete can always come back later to fetch the rest.'

'Alec might not let him in.'

'Huh, he won't be able to stop him. Men who hit women are nothing but cowards and, believe me, Alec won't be able to stand up to a man, especially one like Pete.'

Mavis hoped her mother was right, but what did it matter if she had to leave some of her things behind? She was going to be free of this house, free of fear, and she and the children were starting a new life. Oh, it was wonderful, wonderful, and for the first time in months she found herself smiling.

CHAPTER THIRTY-NINE

It had been a mad dash to get the van loaded while Jenny volunteered to bring James home from school. Alec wasn't due home for hours yet, but Mavis was frantic to leave as soon as possible, fearful that fate would deal her another blow and for some unknown reason, he'd come home early. She was being silly, she knew that. Pete would protect her, but she didn't want the children to witness yet another scene and her heart thumped in her chest as she urged them into the back of the van.

'I'll be over later with my cousin,' Jenny said as she handed Mavis the keys to his flat. 'Willy will need to pick up a few things.'

'All right, I'll see you then,' Mavis said as she gave Jenny a hug.

With Lily in the front, Bobby in her arms, Pete now urged, 'Right, Mavis. Are you ready?'

'Yes, let's go,' she said, climbing into the van.

Pete closed the back door, and with only two small windows, it was gloomy, claustrophobic, as Mavis sat next to the children.

Grace looked close to tears and bewildered as they set off, surrounded by cases and boxes. 'Want to get out.'

'Soon, darling.'

'Mummy, where are we going?' James asked.

Mavis put an arm round each child to support them, doing her best to make it sound like an adventure, yet worried that she was failing dismally. 'Isn't this exciting? We're moving into a nice flat for a while and it's going to be lovely.'

'Why?' James asked.

'Er . . . it's a sort of holiday.'

'Is Daddy coming?'

'No, darling, it'll be just us.'

'Good,' James said, quiet now as he cuddled closer.

'Bobby coming too?' Grace asked.

'He's in the front of the van and you'll see him soon,' she placated.

'I want sit in front. Want Granny.'

'You'll see her soon,' Mavis placated.

Every time the van turned a corner they were thrown sideways, but Mavis held on to the children, making it a game until finally they began to giggle. It was an uncomfortable journey, but Mavis didn't care. They were getting further and further away from Alec's dominance, his violence, and at last she began to relax.

Intent on keeping the children amused, Mavis had no idea how long the journey took, but then the van stopped and the back doors were thrown open.

'We're here,' Pete said.

Soon they were on the pavement and Mavis was looking at a large house. Jenny had said the flat was on the ground floor, and had warned that her cousin said it was in a bit of a mess, but she didn't care. It was a place of safety until they could move next door to her mother.

She shuddered to think she had once seen Ellington Avenue as a refuge, had loved going to Edith Pugh's house; but instead it had turned into a prison. Well, she was free now. Taking a deep breath, Mavis exhaled loudly, her shoulders losing some of the tension that had gripped her for so long. Taking out the keys, she opened the door. 'Right, come on then, let's get inside.'

'Well, this ain't bad,' Lily said as she looked into the first room.

'Yes, it's nice,' Mavis said as she scanned the spacious lounge.

'I'll start bringing your stuff in,' Pete said.

'Mum, can you keep an eye on the children while I give him a hand?'

'Of course I can. Come on, kids, let's explore.'

By the time everything was unloaded and carried into the flat, Mavis was dry-mouthed and worn out, gratified when her mother held out a mug of tea.

'Here, get that down you,' Lily said, then handed one to Pete. 'I helped myself. I hope Jenny's cousin won't mind.'

'Just in case, I'll replace anything you used.'

'You need to get yourself sorted out and there are two single beds in one room that need making up for the kids. While you get on with it, Pete can run me to the nearest shops to stock you up with groceries. Thankfully I found a guard to put round that fire,' Lily said, nodding towards the children.

Mavis felt tears of gratitude pooling in her eyes. Grace and James had Bobby between them, all sitting on a rug in front of the electric fire and giggling as they played happily.

She had once wanted to escape her mother and Pete, but now, seeing such a lovely family scene, she was glad that living in this flat was only a temporary arrangement. She couldn't wait to move close to them.

Alec arrived home just after six, frowning when he walked into the kitchen. It was empty. Where was Mavis? Why wasn't his dinner ready? The fire had gone out, the house cold, quiet, and he angrily stomped upstairs.

James wasn't in his room, and impatiently Alec went into Grace's, only to pause, a frown on his face. It looked abandoned, a few toys scattered across the floor, her dolls that were usually arranged on shelves missing.

Alec rushed into his own room where he threw open Mavis's wardrobe. There were a few clothes, but the vast majority of hangers were empty, and when he pulled open drawers, he found most of hers empty too. No, she couldn't have left him! She wouldn't dare!

Alec went back downstairs and into the cold kitchen, where it finally sank in. Mavis had gone, but where? Her mother's house? Yes, it could only be her mother's. He marched into the hall and indignantly dialled the woman's number.

'Is Mavis there?' he snapped when Lily answered.

'No, she ain't.'

'Do you know where she is?'

'Even if I did, I wouldn't tell you. In fact, if I was you I'd watch me back. You've been beating my daughter and one day you're gonna pay for it.'

'Wh . . . what?' Alec blustered.

'You heard me,' Lily snapped.

'Look, I don't know what Mavis told you, but I hardly touched her.'

'Shut your lying mouth. I saw the bruises for myself. Now bugger off – the next time you see my daughter it'll be in court when she files for divorce.'

Lily hung up, and Alec was left shaking, fear replacing anger as he gripped the receiver. Mavis had opened her mouth, told her mother, and Lily's threat played over and over in his mind. Despite Lily's denial, he was sure that Mavis was with her in Peckham, yet Alec knew he couldn't go there to drag her back. He not only feared Lily, he feared Pete, the man built like a tank with a boxer's face to match.

At last Alec moved, and going into his mother's room he stared at her empty bed. He had kept this room exactly as it was to serve as a reminder of her treachery and now he looked at the imprint on the pillow where she had once laid her head.

'You did this, Mother,' he spat. 'You talked me into marrying Mavis, manipulated me, and all for your own ends. You wanted someone to keep this house immaculate, along with looking after you. Mavis fitted the bill, didn't she, but she's gone now, Mother and, like you, good riddance to her.

'Oh, and as for this house,' Alec continued, smiling sardonically, 'it's my house now. I might just sell it. Instead of this four-bedroom mausoleum, a nice little flat would do me. Yes, I'll move out, leave you here, and then I'll never have to listen to your voice again.'

Satisfied that he'd said his piece, Alec returned to the kitchen where he slumped onto a chair and stared into the empty hearth. Lily had told him to watch his back, but how dare she threaten him? She was another tart, just like his own mother, and if she or her husband came near him he'd call the police, get them locked up, and it would serve them right.

What was all the fuss about anyway? Yes, he'd hit Mavis, but she was useless and it was no more than she deserved. The room was cold and Alec shivered. He knelt down to light the fire, watching with satisfaction as flames began to lick the chimney.

Right, Mavis had left him, but how did he really feel about it? It was an inconvenience, but that was all. He had no time for the female sex now, and in truth, all he'd really miss was the use of his wife's body. At last Alec calmed.

He went to search the cupboards and, finding a tin of beans, decided to have them on toast. Alec's mind was now made up. He'd definitely sell this house, start afresh, and he'd manage perfectly well on his own in a small flat. Yet maybe something more than a flat beckoned. He was free now, free of his mother and of Mavis. There was something he'd always wanted to do, something that with the burden of his mother, of work, of supporting his wife and children, had been impossible.

Alec's thoughts turned to James and Grace. Mavis had taken them and to get them back, as her mother had said, he'd have to have his day with his wife in court. Did he want that? Did he want to have joint custody and the bother of looking after them probably every weekend and school holiday? They'd be in the way, a hindrance, and that was the last thing he needed. No, Alec thought, he didn't want that burden. He wanted to move forward, to do what he liked, to be who he wanted and the last thing he needed was constant reminders of the past.

Mavis had had the audacity to leave him, and now she'd suffer for it. She could keep the children and would have to work to earn enough money to bring them up. His wife would be back to living in poverty again – back to the life she had come from. After the comfort he'd provided, she'd know nothing but hardship and that suited Alec just fine.

Mavis flopped onto the sofa. Grace had been murder when her mother left, but she had finally settled. The living room floor was strewn with toys that she just couldn't be bothered to pick up.

It hadn't helped that she couldn't find any sheets or blankets for the single beds, so finally Mavis had popped them both into the double. Sleeping in the same bed, and the same room, was a novelty, their giggles making Mavis smile too. Both children might be unsettled, but they were happy to be away from Ellington Avenue and, after being told a story, they finally went to sleep.

Alone now, Mavis yawned as she looked around the living room. It had been untidy when they arrived, but was worse now. Yet on the whole the flat was nice, if in need of a woman's touch. It was past nine o'clock, but so far there was no sign of Jenny and her cousin.

Mavis looked forward to meeting Willy. She wanted to thank this man, her heart full at his generosity of spirit. She was a stranger, but he had thought nothing of letting her take over his flat, even telling Jenny that she was welcome to stay for as long as she needed.

It was dark outside but Mavis saw headlights and looked out of the window to see a van pulling in. Even in the gloom she recognised Jenny as she got out of the passenger side, but, with his head down, she didn't see the driver's face until she went to open the front door.

'Hello, Mavis,' Jenny said, the first one to walk inside. 'Sorry it's so late, but as usual Willy only came home an hour ago.'

Mavis barely took in Jenny's words, her eyes fixed on the man who had followed her inside. He looked equally shocked as they locked gazes, but it was Mavis who was the first to find her voice. 'Tommy! Tommy Wilson! What are you doing here?'

'I've come to pick up a few things.'

'But . . . but surely this isn't your flat? Jenny said it's her cousin's, a chap called Willy.'

'It's just a nickname, a joke really,' Jenny said, 'but Tommy earned it when he was a kid. You see he was a naughty little bugger and got into trouble a couple of times for flashing his willie to girls. Oh, sorry, Tom, me and my big mouth. I shouldn't have told Mavis that.'

'It's all right,' he said dryly. 'Mavis was one of them.'

'No! Really? Oh, blimey, I can't believe you two know each other.'

'We lived in the same street,' Mavis said, 'and as a child I used to be terrified of him.'

'Was I that bad?' Tommy asked.

'Yes, but thankfully you changed.'

'I think the last time we saw each other was when you told me you were getting married. I left Cullen Street soon afterwards to take up a course and for a while I lived in lodgings.'

'When Tommy came to stay with me, the pair of you were in the same street again, or, should I say, avenue. It's a wonder you didn't bump into each other.'

'Other than taking James to school, I hardly left the house, Jenny.'

'Yeah, that's true.'

Tommy's face was sober as he looked at Mavis.

'When Jenny came to the yard and told me what her neighbour was going through, I still didn't twig it was you. Your husband should be shot.'

'At least I've got away from him now – I can't thank you enough for letting us stay in your flat.'

'I'm glad I could help, especially now I know it's you.' His face began to redden and he added hastily, 'I'll just grab a few of my things and then we'll leave you in peace.'

Jenny was grinning as Tommy hurried into his bedroom. 'I still can't take it in that you two know each other, and, by the look on his face, I reckon Willy, sorry, Tommy, has got a soft spot for you.'

'Don't be silly, of course he hasn't,' Mavis protested. 'We might have lived in the same street, but we were just kids and hardly knew each other.'

'You knew him well enough to have seen his willie,' Jenny chuckled.

'Don't remind me. I was so scared when he did that. He used to frighten the life out of me and I avoided him as much as possible.'

'Yeah, I've got to admit he was a right little sod, but he's turned out fine, despite having my Aunt Olive for a mother. Oh, blimey, you must know her too.'

'Yes, I remember her.'

'I'm ready, Jenny,' Tommy said as he returned to the room. 'I should have enough stuff for a while, but if I need anything else, I can always come back. That's if you don't mind, Mavis?'

'Of course I don't, but with any luck I should be out of here in about a week.'

'There's no hurry,' Tommy said. 'Right then, let's go, Jenny.'

Jenny hugged Mavis, her voice now somber. 'I know you had to leave Alec, but I'm going to miss you.'

'Jenny, thank you so much for being such a good friend. I'm going to miss you too, and though I know I'll be living in Peckham, if you get the chance, please, please come to see me.'

'Don't worry. I will,' Jenny said, giving Mavis one final squeeze.

Mavis watched them leave. Yes, she'd miss Jenny, but she was still unable to believe she was staying in Tommy Wilson's flat.

'Bloody hell, Jenny,' Tommy said as they settled in the van. 'Dumbo Jackson, I could hardly believe me eyes. When she got married, gossip was rife in Cullen Street and my mother said the bloke must be mad to take her on.'

'Mavis is very intelligent and I'd thank you not to call her Dumbo!'

'All right, I'm sorry, it just sort of slipped out, and I must admit I started to suspect that she wasn't as daft as people made out.'

'Mavis has a medical condition, something called word blindness. In all other ways she's the same as anyone else and, if you must know, she's brighter than me.'

'Well, that doesn't take much,' Tommy joked.

'You cheeky sod,' Jenny said, but then chuckled, used to his teasing.

'Yeah, but I'm nice with it.'

'Tommy, did you hear that Mavis's father died?'

'Yes, but only because my mother admitted that, when she saw a bloke, a tramp, being carried out of an empty house in Cullen Street, for a moment she thought it was me.'

'You! But why?'

'I'd left my wife, asked my mother to take me in, but she'd refused. For a while she didn't know where I was, but then of course I opened the yard. When she told me about Mavis's father, I still didn't twig that she was living next door to you. Still, it ain't surprising. I hadn't thought about Mavis in years.'

'I suppose your mother still wants you to leave the area?'

'Yes, but tough,' Tommy said, and as they reached the main road he pretended to be intent on the traffic, but really his thoughts were all over the place. When Mavis left the street, he'd gone on to complete his training and had put her from his mind. When he'd qualified he hadn't wanted to return to Cullen Street, had wanted more out of life – and he'd succeeded.

It had been hard work, but he'd done it, started up his own signwriting business and made it a success. He'd then met Belinda, thought she was the girl of his dreams and had married her, only to be taken for a mug. When he found out about Belinda's affairs, the number of men she'd slept with, he'd worked out the dates, sure that he'd been working away when Davie was conceived. Unable to prove it, he still provided for the boy and would do so until he left school. He wasn't Davie's father and, other than supporting him, Tommy had made the decision to stay out of the boy's life. With one man after another coming in and out of his life, the last thing Davie needed was another one who he would see only at weekends. Maybe one day Belinda would work it out and would be able to tell Davie who his father was – at least Tommy hoped so.

Tommy found his grip tight on the steering wheel. Now, after all these years, he'd seen Mavis again, and he was still reeling with shock at her startling resemblance to Belinda.

'Mavis has had a rotten life, a rotten marriage, and I feel so sorry for her. Are you listening to me, Willy?' Jenny was saying.

'Yes, I'm listening,' he said, though in truth he was still thinking about his own marriage and subsequent divorce. He'd been taken for a ride, but it was nothing compared to what Mavis had been through. God, he'd forgotten what a stunner she was and he'd hardly been able to take his eyes off her.

Still, stunning or not, the last thing he wanted was another woman in his life. Once bitten, twice shy, and all he was concentrating on now was his new business. Women! No thanks.

CHAPTER FORTY

Lily knew that Mavis didn't like to use the telephone in the flat so she had rung her daughter every day, but now, as Pete drove her to Wandsworth on Saturday, she wasn't happy. She'd had a word with the landlord's agent about the house, but so far he hadn't got back to her.

'You're quiet, Lily. Are you all right?' Pete asked.

'I'm just worried about the house. It's been empty for ages, but the agent hasn't been in touch. What if it's gone?'

'Lily, you only spoke to him a few days ago. Give the bloke a chance.'

'Yes, but if Mavis can't have it she'll be left in a fix. She won't be able to stay in that bloke's flat indefinitely.'

'Then we'll find her another place. Now stop worrying. Look, we're here,' he said, pulling in alongside the kerb.

Lily climbed out of the van, Bobby in her arms.

He was a chubby and contented baby, but so heavy now that she was glad Mavis was swift to open the door.

The children squealed with delight when they saw Bobby. 'Granny, Granny, put him down,' Grace begged.

'All right, love, give me a chance,' Lily said, yet she was relieved to lower Bobby onto the rug. She looked around the room to see that, other than toys scattered across the floor, it looked immaculate. 'Blimey, Mavis, you've been busy.'

'I haven't got anything else to do and it's kept me occupied. I wish I could say the same for the children. James is missing school, Grace her nursery, and it's getting them down being cooped up.'

'Cooped up. Why? There's a nice little common close by and I'm sure I saw some swings. I know it's cold, but if you wrap them up warmly, they'd be fine.'

Mavis glanced at the children and keeping her voice low she said, 'No, we can't go out.'

'Why not?'

'Alec must be looking for us, he might see us,' she hissed.

Lily looked at the children too, her voice quiet but firm. 'Mavis, you're miles away from Ellington Avenue, and Alec has no idea where you are. Anyway, despite the fact that I denied it, he probably thinks you're living with me.'

'I can't risk it, Mum. I just can't.'

'Don't be silly. You can't stay in this flat for twenty-four hours a day. It isn't fair on the children.'

'If Alec finds me, he'll take them away, I know he will.'

'All right, have it your own way and stay in, but at least it shouldn't be for much longer. I've asked about the house and hope to hear something soon. Now how about making me and Pete a nice cup of tea?'

'I . . . I haven't got any milk left.'

'So you haven't even been to the shops?'

'No, I told you. I daren't go out.'

'Oh, love, you're making your life a misery and there's no need.'

'No, Mum, I'm not miserable. I'm happier than I've been in years. Yes, we're cooped up, but we're safe and it's heaven.'

'Pete, if Mavis tells you what she needs, would you mind going to the shops?'

'Of course I will,' Pete said. 'Mind you, it might be better to write me a list.'

'I wish I could, Pete,' Mavis said wryly.

'Sorry, love, I forgot, but tell your mother what you want and she'll write it down.'

Lily followed Mavis to the kitchen, and like the living room it was tidy, every surface gleaming. 'You put me to shame, Mavis,' she said, opening the cupboards to find most nearly empty.

'I told you, it's kept me occupied and, let's face it, housework is all I'm fit for.'

'Stop it, my girl, stop putting yourself down. All right, you can't read and write, but what about art? You used to love it, and there's nothing to stop you taking it up again.'

'No, Mum, it's too late now.'

'Will you stop talking like an old woman whose life is nearly over? You'll be twenty-five in March, not seventy-five.'

'I wouldn't be any good. Alec said I'm useless at everything and he's right.'

'No, he is not!' Lily said, enunciating each word firmly. 'Mavis, I used to put you down too, but I ain't proud of myself. I know better now, and if you want to take up art again, I'll do everything I can to help you.'

'Mum, all I want right now is to get the children settled.'

Lily could sense that this wasn't the time to push it, so for now she said, 'Whatever you say, but let's get this list done.'

'Milk should be first on the list, and bread,' Mavis said.

'Yes, plus eggs, bacon, cheese, tea, sugar, more cereals, and what about meals for the week? Shall we say sausages, mince for shepherd's pie, and beef for a stew? Think of a few other meals while I write down what vegetables you'll need.'

'Mum, please, don't go mad. I . . . I've only got a couple of pounds in my purse.'

'Who said anything about you paying for it?'

Mavis ran both hands over her face, her voice agonised. 'I thought I could do this, but I can't, Mum. I can't let you keep us. Until I can stand on my own two feet, I . . . I'll have to go back to Alec.'

'You'll do no such thing,' Lily insisted. 'Mavis, let me do this for you. I not only want to, I need to do it. All I want is to see you happy, with you and the kids close to me.'

'Oh, Mum . . .'

Lily held out her arms and Mavis almost fell into them, the two of them holding each other until at last Lily said, 'Tell me you ain't going back to him, Mavis.'

'All right, I won't, but someday I'll find a way to pay back every penny that it's going to cost you to support us.'

'Yeah, all right,' Lily agreed, relief flooding through her, 'but there's no hurry.'

Blast, Tommy thought. What was the matter with him? He hadn't seen Mavis since he'd gone to collect a few things, but he couldn't put her out of his mind. Despite telling himself that he must be out of his mind, Tommy found that he desperately wanted to see her again. Mavis had only just escaped an abusive marriage, and she wouldn't want another man in her life, not for a long time – if ever. And not only that, he didn't want another woman in his.

Tommy tried again to concentrate on his account book. He liked doing them on a Saturday morning, but the figures swam before his eyes. Since moving back to Jenny's, he'd heard more about Mavis's married life, and though he'd only seen Alec Pugh once, it was enough to make him want to throttle the bastard.

An hour later, Tommy was still trying to put Mavis from his mind, but it was no good. Despite all his resolve, he picked up the telephone, searching for an excuse.

'Mavis,' he said when she answered. 'Do you mind if I pop over later to collect a few more things?'

'No, of course not, but my mother's here at the moment.'

'I didn't mean right now. I meant later.'

'That'll be fine, and is Jenny coming with you?'

'I dunno, but I could ask her if you like.'

'I'd love to see her and I'm sure my son would love to see Greg.'

'All right. Shall we say around four o'clock?'

'Yes, see you then.'

'Thanks and bye, Mavis.'

'Bye, Tommy,' she said softly.

He replaced the receiver, finding that he had an inane smile on his face. Why did Mavis have this effect on him? He tried to sort out his accounts again but found it impossible. He couldn't stop looking at the clock, his thoughts on Mavis and the fact that he'd see her again in a few hours.

Impatiently he closed his account book and throwing on his coat he left the office, locking the door behind him. He might as well go back to Jenny's, have a bath and spruce himself up. The last time Mavis had seen him, he hadn't even had a wash, had just bolted his dinner before going to the flat with Jenny.

What did it matter? Why was he bothering to spruce himself up this time? *You know why,* a small voice whispered from the back of his mind, one that Tommy couldn't ignore. Yes, he knew why, but it was madness, sheer madness.

By four o'clock, Mavis was ready. She had changed into her nicest skirt and top, and had even put on a little make-up. The compact was old, hardly used, and the lipstick she'd found at the bottom of a handbag little more than a stub, yet even so she felt a little better when she looked at her reflection in the mirror.

The last time Tommy had seen her, Mavis had

been aware that she looked a mess and had felt gauche when he looked at her, but at least this time she felt a little more confident. Yet why had she bothered? It wasn't as if she cared about what Tommy thought of her. After all, she wasn't on the rebound and looking for another man in her life. No, that was the last thing she needed.

When there was a knock on the door, Mavis found her heart thumping in her chest, but managed to open it with a smile on her face. 'Jenny, it's lovely to see you,' she said, avoiding Tommy's eyes as she turned to her son. 'Look, James, look who's come to see you. It's Greg.'

'Greg!' James said, jumping to his feet, a wide smile on his face.

It was nice to see James happy, the two boys soon sitting on the floor together, Grace pestering them as usual, unwilling to be left out. Mavis found that she still couldn't look at Tommy, but thankfully it was Jenny who held her attention.

'Mavis, there's a for sale sign outside your house.'

'What! Alec's selling it?'

'If there's a board up I should think that's obvious,' Tommy said dryly.

Mavis felt herself flushing. He'd only been there for a few minutes and already she'd made herself sound foolish. 'But . . . but I can't believe Alec's going to sell it. He loves that house.'

'I must admit I'm surprised too,' Jenny said,

'and don't take any notice of Tommy. He's always had a sarcastic sense of humour.'

'Yes, that's true, but look at this place,' Tommy said as his eyes swept the room. 'It looks amazing.'

'Yes, and Mavis does too,' Jenny said. 'Don't you think so, Tommy?'

'Stunning,' Tommy said, 'but then you always were a looker, Mavis.'

'Me!' she said, flushing again when she heard her voice come out in a high squeak.

'Yes, and no wonder you flashed your willie at her,' Jenny chuckled.

'Do you have to keep bringing that up?' Tommy admonished. 'It isn't something I'm proud of.'

'Sorry, love, but you've got to admit it's funny.'

'To you maybe, but I doubt Mavis sees it like that. I was just a stupid kid, but that's no excuse and, Mavis, I can't tell you how sorry I am, how much I regret it now.'

'It was a long time ago and all water under the bridge,' she said softly. 'Now can I get you both anything? Tea? Coffee?'

'Coffee, please,' Tommy said.

'Yeah, me too.'

Mavis was glad to escape to the kitchen. Tommy had changed so much and it was nice that he'd apologised. He'd also said she was stunning and Mavis still couldn't believe it. He was just being kind, of course, and she knew that, but it was such a nice thing to say and her heart warmed towards him.

'How are you getting on?' Jenny said as she joined her in the kitchen.

'I'm fine, but I still can't believe that Alec is selling the house.'

'Maybe he's trying to get out of giving you your share. You should see a solicitor and quickly.'

'No, I don't want anything from him.'

'Mavis, don't be silly. You might not want anything, but you've got to think about the kids.'

Mavis knew that Jenny was right, that she'd have to see a solicitor. It would be taken out of her hands then, left for the divorce court to decide on her settlement. 'Yes, all right, I'll see a solicitor.'

With drinks in hand they returned to the living room to see Tommy sitting on the floor with the children, doing his best to put James's train set together.

Jenny placed a cup beside Tommy as Mavis sat down, watching as he bantered with the children. He was good with them, and Mavis could see they liked him, Grace even inching over onto his lap. Tommy wrapped his arms around her as though it were the most natural thing in the world. Mavis wished Alec could have been like that, but he had never been a father who played with his children, instead taking the role of a dictator.

'Mavis, is there any news on the house in Peckham?' Jenny asked.

'Shh,' Mavis hissed. 'I haven't told the children yet. My mum has spoken to the agent, so hopefully I'll hear something soon.'

With the track now fitted together, Tommy stood Grace up before standing up too, but Grace clung on to his leg like a limpet. With a wry smile he sat on a chair, and immediately she climbed onto his lap again, laying her head against his chest.

'Tommy, you've got yourself a fan,' Jenny said.

'That's nice, but I don't know why.'

'Grace is like that,' Mavis explained. 'There are certain people that she takes to, my mum being one, and when my dad was ill we could hardly drag her away from his side.'

'Well, darlin', I'm sorry to disturb you,' Tommy said, smiling down at Grace, 'but it's time to grab a few more of my things, and then we can leave your mum in peace.'

'No, nice man stay.'

'Tommy, surely we don't have to go yet?' Jenny protested. 'We've only been here for about half an hour and Greg's hardly had a chance to play with James.'

'All right, if Mavis doesn't mind, perhaps another half an hour.'

'Stay as long as you like,' Mavis said.

Tommy lowered his head, whispered something in Grace's ear, and she grinned up at him.

Mavis decided she had to be mistaken. Surely Tommy hadn't whispered, *forever*? But then Tommy gave her a cheeky wink and Mavis blushed.

Embarrassed, she lowered her head. She'd once been afraid of Tommy Wilson, but it wasn't fear she felt now – it was something else, an attraction, but one Mavis refused to acknowledge. She was making a fresh start, moving next door to her mother, and her priority would be her children. They had seen too much, had witnessed their father's violence, and her only goal now was to keep them safe and happy.

CHAPTER FORTY-ONE

Nearly two weeks had passed since Mavis had left Alec, and on Friday, rent day, Lily opened her door to the agent, her book and the money held out.

'Well,' she said impatiently as he marked the rent book, 'have you spoken to Mr Pellerman again?'

'What about?'

'The house next door.'

'Oh, yeah. He's still thinking about it.'

'What's to think about? He can't be making money on an empty house.'

'Look, he isn't happy about a woman and two kids living there without a husband. I mean, what if she can't pay the rent?'

Lily thought quickly. 'Tell Pellerman she'll pay six months in advance. That should keep him happy.'

'Six months you say? All right, I'll have

another word with him, but I ain't making any promises.'

'When will you let me know?'

'I dunno, but as soon as I can. I'm a busy man and no doubt there'll be others wanting to talk to me about that house,' he said, giving Lily a pointed look as he handed back the book.

Lily's eyes narrowed. 'Wait there a minute,' she said, puffing as, with Bobby in her arms, she hurried upstairs. In her bedroom Lily placed Bobby on the floor while she pulled a tin box from the back of her wardrobe, and, after taking out a five-pound note, she swept Bobby into her arms again.

'Here,' she said, thrusting it at the young agent when she was back at the front door. 'Will that help?'

'Yes, missus, it certainly will,' he said, giving her a swift cheeky wink. 'I'm sure I can persuade Mr Pellerman to let your daughter have the house now. In fact, she can move in on Monday.'

'Thanks,' Lily ground out through clenched teeth, and as the agent walked away she almost slammed the door. Bastard, she thought. He must have been waiting for a backhander all this time – but at least she had the money to pay it.

She lifted Bobby in the air, grinning now as she looked up at his face. 'I've done it, darling, and now your big sister will be moving in next door. I'll ring her to pass on the good news.'

There was another knock on the door and, settling Bobby back in her arms, Lily went to answer it.

'What did he say?' Marilyn asked as she stepped inside. 'Can Mavis have the house?'

'Yeah, I think so, but it took a backhander.'

'When that new agent took over, I didn't like the look of him. The last one was all right, firm if you got a bit behind with the rent, but fair, and I never heard of him taking a bribe. You should report this one to Mr Pellerman.'

'No, I'm not risking it, not until Mavis has moved in. Even then it might be dodgy. It's his word against mine and I don't want him finding ways to get her out again. She needs to be settled, Marilyn, to feel secure, safe.'

'Yeah, the poor girl, and after what she's been through, she deserves a bit of happiness.' Marilyn tickled Bobby under his chin. 'And you, darling, will have James and Grace to play with. I'll be off, Lily. I've got a cake in the oven and only popped round to see if there was any news.'

Lily closed the door behind her friend and then rang Mavis. 'It's good news, love,' she said as her daughter answered. 'You can move into the house on Monday.'

'Mum, that's wonderful.'

'Get packing, girl, and first thing on Monday morning me and Pete will be over to pick you up.

Hang on, have you got enough food to get you over the weekend?'

'Yes, I'll manage.'

'That's good, and you'd better tell Tommy Wilson that he can have his flat back. I still can't get over that it's his place, and it was nice of him to let you stay there.'

'Yes, it was and I'll ring him now.'

'All right, and I've already scouted around for some furniture. It ain't much, but it'll see you through for now.'

'I don't care what it's like, anything will do.'

'It ain't that bad, but I'd best ring off. I need to shoot down there to arrange delivery for Monday.'

'Thanks, Mum.'

'There's no need to thank me. I'm just chuffed to bits that we've got the house sorted out at last,' Lily said, saying a quick goodbye before ringing off.

Lily smiled with happiness. As Marilyn said, it would be lovely for Bobby. He'd grow up with family around him, and once Mavis had settled, no matter what it took, she'd see to it that it was a happy, loving environment.

Tommy picked up the telephone, his stomach doing a flip when he heard Mavis's voice.

'Tommy, it's Mavis.'

'What's wrong? Has something happened?' he

asked anxiously. If that bastard Alec Pugh had found Mavis, if he'd laid a finger on her . . .

'No, everything's fine. I'm just ringing to let you know that we'll be moving out on Monday. You can have your flat back at last.'

'I see. Well, thanks for letting me know.'

'What shall I do with the keys?'

'I've got a spare set. Once you've locked up, just shove them back through the letterbox. Hang on though, do you need a hand? I've got my van.'

'No, it's all right. Pete's got a van too and he's picking us up.'

'OK, as long as you're sure,' he said, his thoughts all over the place. Mavis was leaving the area. She was going to Peckham, and he'd never see her again. 'Er . . . Mavis, I'll tell Jenny, but she might like to see you before you go. If that's the case, is it all right if I bring her over, perhaps tomorrow?'

'Yes, that's fine. I'd like to see her too.'

'What about me?' Tommy blurted out but could have kicked himself. Bloody hell, talk about making it obvious.

'Yes, Tommy, it'll be nice to see you too. I can't thank you enough for letting me stay in your flat.'

'It was nothing. Bye for now, Mavis,' Tommy said, hastily ringing off. God, he'd made a right fool of himself, but at last he admitted the truth. He liked Mavis, more than liked her, and, though

461

he hadn't thought of her in years, now he'd seen her again, he suspected that he always had.

It wasn't his ex-wife who'd been the girl of his dreams, it was Mavis, and he'd been unconsciously looking for her since she left Cullen Street. Belinda had just been a substitute, and maybe that's why the marriage hadn't worked. He'd never really loved her and she must have sensed that.

Jenny looked up as her cousin came home from work, saying, 'Stan's taken Greg to football practice. But why the long face, Willy?'

'Stop calling me that! My name is Tommy, Tom, or even Thomas, but not Willy.'

'All right, keep your hair on.'

'I'm sorry, Jenny, I didn't mean to snap. It's just that Mavis rang me this morning. She's moving out on Monday.'

'Well, that's good news, isn't it? You'll be getting your flat back.'

'Yes, I suppose so.'

'You don't sound too happy about it,' Jenny said, and as he sat down she moved to sit opposite, leaning forward to ask, 'Tommy, is there something going on between you and Mavis?'

'No, of course not,' he protested. 'She's your friend, that's all, and as I thought you'd like to see her before she moves out, I said I'd run you over there tomorrow.'

'Don't worry, I can get the bus.'

'There's no need,' he said quickly.

'I thought you'd say that, but why pretend, Tommy? I've seen the way you look at Mavis and I know you like her.'

'Yes, all right, Jenny, I like her, but I can't do anything about it. She's only just left her husband and the last thing she'll want is another bloke sniffing around.'

'Now, maybe, but all you've got to do is give her a bit of time. I've seen the way Mavis looks at you too, and even if she doesn't know it yet, I reckon she feels the same way.'

'Really?'

'Yes, really. Look, I know she isn't ready yet, but leave it until she settles and then you can find an excuse to go to see her.'

'What if she doesn't want to see me?'

'Trust me, she will.'

'I hope you're right, Jenny.'

So do I, Jenny thought. Tommy had been badly hurt by his ex-wife and the last thing she wanted was to put him in line for more heartbreak. Yet when she had seen Tommy and Mavis together, she had felt the sparks between them, even if Mavis wasn't aware of them yet. Surely she just needed some time?

CHAPTER FORTY-TWO

Mavis had decided to leave the packing until Sunday morning, but now, as she pulled a case from under the bed, she saw her son's eyes darken with fear. 'No, Mummy, I don't want to go home.'

Mavis hadn't wanted to tell them about their new home until it was assured, but now cursed herself for keeping up the pretence that this was just a holiday. Poor James, he looked terrified at the thought of returning to Ellington Avenue and, calling Grace, she sat down, pulling her daughter onto her lap. Grace may not understand, but hopefully James would. Patting the bed next to her, she said, 'James, come and sit next to me.'

With an arm around Grace, and one now around James, Mavis gently said, 'We're not going back to our old house. We've got a new one and it's next door to Granny, Pete, and Bobby.'

Grace clapped her hands, smiling with delight,

but James frowned. 'Is Daddy coming too?' he asked.

'No, darling, we're not going to live with your daddy any more. It'll just be us, you, me and Grace.'

'Just us?'

'Yes, darling.'

'We won't have to live with Daddy?'

'No, I promise, it'll be just us.'

At last James looked reassured, slumping against her as he said quietly, 'Good.'

Mavis could have cried. Her son was only six years old, punished too harshly by his father, and then had witnessed her own abuse. No wonder he didn't want to go home, and she hoped she would never have to see such deep fear in his eyes again.

'See Bobby now?' Grace asked.

'Not today, but tomorrow we'll be moving into our new house and you'll be able to see him every day. Now come on, you can both help me to pack.'

Grace scrambled from her lap and James was quick to follow, both dashing around madly to grab armfuls of toys. 'Whoa, there's no need to rush,' Mavis said as she found them a box. 'We've got all day so leave out some of your favourite toys to play with.'

Mavis left them to it as she began to put clothes into a suitcase. After the house in Ellington Avenue, and then this spacious flat, the children would find the new house rather cramped. Not only that, they would have to share a tiny bedroom, and that was sure to cause problems. Yet what did it matter? They'd be close to their gran, surrounded by love, and that was the most important thing.

Mavis paused. Edith Pugh had once said that she would grow to love Alec, but she never had. Instead all that had grown was hate; but at last she was free.

It was after three and, with his stomach full of Jenny's wonderful Sunday roast, Tommy was driving her to his flat to see Mavis. Greg was with them, the boy excited that he was going to see James again, and Tommy knew he was equally excited at the thought of seeing Mavis.

Everything Jenny had said made sense, Tommy thought as he drove around a corner. It would be hard, he knew that, but he would have to give Mavis space and time before he contacted her again.

For now he had to play it cool, and, as Tommy pulled up outside the flat, he turned to grin at Jenny. 'If I look like I'm drooling when I see Mavis, give me a dig in the ribs.'

'I'd love to,' she quipped. 'Can I make it two?'

'If you must,' he said before they climbed out of the van.

Tommy's stomach did a somersault when Mavis opened the door, and once again he marvelled at the effect she had on him. He'd noticed that she looked like his ex-wife, but now Belinda paled in comparison as Mavis's lovely, blue eyes met his.

'Hello, come on in,' she invited.

'He's seen her, Mummy. Is he drooling?' Greg asked.

'Shut up,' Tommy hissed, cursing that he'd said anything in front of Greg. He should have realised the boy would be all ears, and now he felt an absolute fool.

'Go and play with James,' Jenny ordered as she almost shoved the boy inside.

'But . . .'

'But nothing,' she said dismissively.

Mavis looked bemused, but led them into the living room, where Tommy was glad that Jenny led the conversation. 'I see you've been packing,' she said.

'Yes, and it's almost finished. Pete's picking us up first thing in the morning.'

'Greg, I'm going to live next to my granny,' James said, his face animated.

Jenny smiled softly. 'Bless him, he looks dead chuffed.'

'Me going too,' Grace cried.

'Yes, aren't you lucky?' Jenny said.

'Come on, Greg, let's play with my trains again,' James urged.

Grace wasn't going to be left out and joined the

467

two boys on the floor. For a moment Tommy watched them, but then Mavis spoke, her voice soft.

'Tommy, thanks again for letting us use your flat. I'm sorry it dragged on for two weeks.'

'No problem,' Tommy said as he and Jenny sat down. 'Anyway, look at this place, talk about a spring clean.'

'Once you move back in, I doubt it'll stay like this,' Jenny said. 'Men. They're hopeless without a woman to clean up after them. I bet Alec is finding that out too.'

'Have you seen him?' Mavis asked.

'Yes, but he ignored me. It's funny really. I sort of expected him to call round asking if I know where you are.'

'Oh, Jenny, I hadn't thought of that.'

'Don't worry, if he does get round to it, I'll tell the smarmy git that I haven't got a clue.'

'I've been frightened that he'll find me.'

'Well, he hasn't, and you're safe now. You've been safe here, and you'll be safe in Peckham too.'

'I know, but it won't be over until the divorce comes through and that could take ages.'

'Once you've seen a solicitor you'll be legally separated and that's a start.'

'Yes, it is, isn't it?' Mavis said, obviously brightened by the thought. 'Thanks, Jenny, you always manage to say the right thing.'

'I'll give you a chance to settle in and then, if it's all right with you, I'll get Tommy to run me over to see you.'

'Of course it's all right with me. I'd love to see you.'

Tommy had to hide a smile when Jenny turned to wink at him. Yes, he'd see Mavis again, but, as Jenny said, she needed time, and for now he had to be content with that.

It was two hours later when Jenny and Tommy left, and though Mavis could see that James was sad to see his friend leave with them, he soon brightened up when she suggested they finish the last of the packing.

With an early start in the morning, Mavis wanted the children to have an early night, and was relieved when she finally closed the last suitcase. There'd be so much to do once they were in Peckham. A new school to sort out for James, and with any luck a nursery for Grace, but none of this worried her.

From now on she'd be in charge of her own life, free to make her own decisions, and one thing Mavis was sure of, she'd never allow herself to be ruled by a man, or anyone, again. She'd been an idiot, a meek and biddable idiot, and though she had once tried to assert herself, to stand up to Alec, he'd used her fear for James against her.

Yes, Alec had won, but she was free of him now and her new life was beginning.

Mavis looked around the flat, satisfied that she had left it clean and tidy. With a wide yawn she turned out the lights before going into the bedroom, where she carefully climbed into bed. James was on the other side, Grace in the middle, but neither stirred as she laid her head on the pillow. Content, Mavis closed her eyes, almost immediately falling asleep.

It was early in the morning when Mavis woke up again, the dream still vivid in her mind. It was the same one that had haunted her for years, but this time it had been different. The man had still been there, and she had felt the same yearning as he reached out for her, but this time she had seen his face. No, no, it couldn't be him!

'Mummy,' Grace murmured.

Mavis reached out to pull her daughter into her arms. No, she didn't want him. She might have to rely on her mother for now, but one day she'd find a way to be independent. She would do it on her own too, run her own life, without any man taking control of her again.

CHAPTER FORTY-THREE

'I saw Mavis when she was taking James to school earlier. She looks as happy as a lark,' Marilyn said.

'Yes, she loves living here,' Lily agreed, and it was true. Mavis had been next door for six weeks now, and, despite the house being half the size of her home in Ellington Avenue, she was happier than ever. The children had been unsettled at first, and still hated sharing a bedroom, but thankfully James liked his new school. So far Mavis hadn't found a place in a local nursery for Grace, but her name was down and hopefully one would become available soon.

'My Rhona likes Mavis. It's nice they've become friends.'

Hardly that, Lily thought, but it was a thought she kept to herself. Almost from the day Mavis had moved in, Rhona had latched on to her but, at only seventeen, she doubted they had much in common. Rhona was boy, fashion and music mad, and Lily still thought she was allowed too much freedom. All right, things were changing nowadays, but unless Marilyn pulled Rhona's reins in, she was asking for trouble.

The door suddenly opened and Grace ran in, Mavis behind her. 'Hello, love,' Lily said, smiling at her daughter. 'Jenny rang earlier. She wants to pop over to see you again on Sunday. I said you'd ring her back.'

'I'll do it in a minute, but, first, what do you think of this?' Mavis asked, unrolling a sheet of paper.

'Gawd, blimey, Mavis, did you draw that?' Marilyn asked. 'It looks just like him.'

Lily had to agree. The sketch of Bobby was wonderful, her son's cheeky grin and the emergence of his first tooth captured perfectly. 'Mavis, it's great,' she said, once again feeling that familiar surge of guilt that she had, until now, refused to acknowledge Mavis's talent. 'Can I have it?'

'Of course you can,' Mavis said.

'Thanks, darling. I'll get Pete to frame it.'

'Here, Mavis, how much do you charge? I'd love one of my Rhona.'

'Er . . . I don't charge anything.'

'Well, you should,' Marilyn said. 'I can't afford much, but I could stretch to half a crown.'

'How about that, Mavis? It sounds like you've got your first commission,' Lily said, grinning broadly.

'No, Mum, I've only just started sketching again. I'm not good enough yet and need a lot more practice.'

'Practise on my Rhona then,' Marilyn suggested.

Mavis chewed her lower lip before saying, 'All right, but it may not be any good and I certainly won't accept payment for it.'

'Well, girl, if you're sure,' Marilyn said. 'Mind you, if it's good I'll make sure that a lot of people see it and, who knows, you might get orders for more.'

'I doubt that.'

'Mavis, don't put yourself down,' Lily said. 'If this sketch of Bobby is anything to go by, you could find yourself earning a few bob.'

'I don't know why you lack confidence in yourself,' Marilyn said. 'This drawing of Bobby is marvellous, and look at you, you're gorgeous. To top it all you speak so well, sort of posh.'

'I'm not posh.'

'You sound it to me, and I'm hoping it'll rub off on Rhona. If she learns to speak like you she could get out of that flaming factory. Find a better job.'

'Granny, look,' Grace said.

Lily turned to see that, using the edge of the sofa, Bobby had pulled himself to his feet. His legs wobbled, but at only seven months old he was standing. 'Who's a clever boy then?' she said, beaming with delight.

'James was walking at ten months and it looks like Bobby will too,' Mavis said.

Bobby flopped down onto his bottom, but, cushioned by his nappy, he just chuckled. 'Pooh, Granny, he smells,' Grace complained.

'He wants changing,' Lily said as she swooped Bobby into her arms.

Marilyn stood up. 'I'll be off, Lily. See you soon, Mavis.'

'Bye,' they both chorused and, as the door closed behind her, Mavis went to ring Jenny while Lily changed Bobby's nappy.

'It'll be nice for you to see Jenny again. Is Tommy bringing her in his van?' Lily asked as soon as her daughter finished the call.

'Yes,' Mavis said, her cheeks turning red.

'That's nice. I must admit Tommy's turned out all right. He's doing so well too, with his own business. You could do worse, my girl.'

'What's that supposed to mean?'

'I ain't blind, Mavis. The last time he came over, I saw the way he looked at you. I think you like him too, don't you?'

'Tommy's all right, but I'm not interested in him in that way, Mum.'

'Please yourself,' Lily said, 'but as I said, you could do worse.'

'No, thanks. I'm happy as I am. Anyway, it's time I was off. My place looks like a bomb's hit it.'

'Leave Grace with me. Bobby will only start screaming if you take her home.'

'Mum, she's more in your place than mine.'

'I don't mind. She's no trouble.'

'All right, but I'll take Bobby when I go to collect James from school.'

'Fine, see you later,' Lily said, and as her daughter left she relished the thought of preparing Pete's dinner without having to keep one eye on her son. Now that he was crawling, Bobby was into everything, and it'd be even worse when he started to walk. Mavis often took Bobby off her hands when she had housework, washing or ironing to do, and Lily marvelled at the difference it had made to her life now that her daughter was living next door.

Though she had pretended differently, Lily was pleased that Mavis wasn't interested in Tommy Wilson. He was a good-looking bloke and enough to turn any girl's head, but she wasn't ready to lose her daughter yet.

Of course, it wasn't easy for Mavis with Grace and James sharing a room, and she knew that it couldn't go on forever, but for now Lily was happier than she'd been in years. She'd been given a second chance with Mavis – a chance to be a proper mother and to make up for all her years of neglect. She wanted to keep Mavis close and the last thing she wanted was Tommy Wilson upsetting the apple cart.

CHAPTER FORTY-FOUR

On Sunday, Mavis looked around her small living room. The furniture was shabby, but she didn't care, and if it wasn't for the fact that Jenny was coming over she knew it wouldn't have been this tidy. Housework was done haphazardly these days, and Mavis loved being able to do as she pleased. All her married life she'd been given a list of daily tasks, ones that had to be completed, first to her mother-in-law's high standards, and then her husband's.

Never again, Mavis thought, cherishing her independence. Well, not quite, not yet. Financially she was still dependent on her mother, and remembered how loath she'd been to accept the tin box stuffed with money that had been shoved into her hands the day she moved in.

However, as soon as she could, Mavis had seen a solicitor, and now knew that there was no need to worry, the man insisting that she'd be entitled to a good settlement. It would take a while for the divorce to come through, but when it did Mavis knew she'd have the means to pay back all she owed her mother.

With a last look around the room, Mavis went next door. She was looking forward to seeing Jenny again, but couldn't feel the same about Tommy. He unsettled her, and, knowing now that he was the man who had haunted her dreams, she couldn't look at him without blushing.

'James, it's time to come home,' Mavis said as she walked into her mother's house. 'Greg will be here soon.'

Her son jumped to his feet, but Grace remained where she was. 'Come on, Grace, you too.'

'It's all right, Mavis, she can stay with us if she wants to,' said Lily.

'Mum, you've had her all morning.'

'It doesn't matter. Leave her with us,' Pete said.

Mavis smiled at the man she'd once been determined to hate. He was marvellous with the children and they loved him, both of them making a beeline for Pete as soon as they saw him. James was like a different boy already, more outgoing, with a ready smile always on his face. 'Well, if you're sure you don't mind,' she said, 'but, Grace, don't you want to see Jenny and Greg?'

'Yes, but take Bobby,' Grace appealed.

'All right,' Mavis agreed.

'Thank Gawd for that,' Lily said. 'You know what he's like when these two leave.'

Mavis picked Bobby up. 'Right, kids, let's go.'

'If he plays up, bring him back,' Pete called.

'He'll be fine,' Mavis assured him, and as she stepped outside the van was just turning the corner. Soon it pulled up beside her, Jenny and Greg tumbling out of the passenger side. 'Hello, you two, it's lovely to see you.'

'Mavis, you look even better than you did two weeks ago. You're blooming.'

'Hello, Mavis.'

She felt her heart skip a beat on hearing Tommy's voice, and, as she'd feared, Mavis felt the heat of a blush rising. 'Er . . . hello, Tommy,' she stammered, and avoiding his eyes she added, 'Come on in.'

'Let me hold him,' Jenny begged as soon as they were inside, her arms reaching out for Bobby.

'You'll be sorry. He weighs a ton.'

'I don't mind,' Jenny said as she took Bobby. 'Oh, dear, he's making me go all broody.'

'It's about time you had another nipper,' Tommy remarked. 'It ain't much fun being an only child and I should know.'

'Yes, me too, but do sit down,' Mavis urged.

'Greg seems happy enough,' Jenny said as they both took a seat.

'Yeah, I suppose he is.'

'Can we play in our bedroom?' James asked.

'Yes, all right,' Mavis agreed, though with the room so tiny she doubted they'd stay upstairs for long.

The children ran off, but Jenny continued to hold Bobby as she mused, 'I wonder what Stan would say if I tell him I want another baby.'

'I should think he'll enjoy the task,' Tommy said.

'Oh, you,' she chuckled. 'It's all right for men. They get all the pleasure, while we women get all the pain.'

'I didn't think a bit of nooky was that bad,' Tommy quipped.

'I'm not talking about that, you daft bugger. I'm talking about childbirth.'

Mavis smiled. Jenny and Tommy were always the same, bantering, but it was all in good fun and only her own awkwardness around Tommy spoiled her enjoyment of their company. 'Would you like a cup of tea or coffee?' she asked.

'Coffee for me,' Jenny said,

'Me too,' Tommy agreed, his smile warm as he met Mavis's eyes.

Mavis hurried from the room, fighting the feelings Tommy aroused, but as she placed the kettle onto a gas ring she almost jumped out of her skin when a voice spoke from behind her.

'Mavis, can I have a word? Oh, sorry, I didn't mean to make you jump.'

'It's all right. You just startled me,' she said, busying herself with spooning coffee into cups.

'Mavis, now that you're settled, I was wondering if you'd let me take you out. We could go for a meal, or to the pictures, in fact, anything you fancy.'

Mavis found her heart thumping in her chest. Tommy was asking her out and she didn't know how to respond. Yes, he aroused sexual feelings in her, but she'd never enjoyed lovemaking and doubted she ever would.

Why Tommy made her feel like this was beyond her, especially as nowadays she enjoyed the sheer pleasure of sleeping alone. For the first time in her life Mavis felt that she was her own woman, making her own decisions, and she wasn't ready to give that up. 'I'm sorry, Tommy, but no, I don't want to go out with you.'

'Fair enough,' he said, rapidly disappearing while Mavis carried on making the coffee.

When it was ready, she carried it through to her tiny living room, feeling tense, and she was relieved when Jenny spoke. 'James seems like a different boy, Mavis,' she said whilst bouncing Bobby on her lap.

'Yes, he is. He used to be so nervous around Alec, unnaturally quiet, but he's blossoming now.'

'Mavis, I think Alec might be moving soon. There's a sold sign outside the house now.'

'Is there? Goodness, I still can't believe he put it up for sale.'

'There's been a bit of gossip in the avenue, a few people saying that Alec has gone a bit funny.'

'Funny. What do you mean?'

'Well, like he's not right in the head.'

'What makes them think that?'

'It was the woman who lives the other side of me that started it off. Apparently, her friend works for the estate agent's and she said that when one of the chaps took someone round to view the house, he came back as white as a sheet. He said that when they went into the living room, Alec started talking to his mother as though she was still there. It really spooked him, and the buyer.'

Mavis frowned. It certainly sounded odd, but surely Alec hadn't lost his mind? 'Maybe he's still in a state, you know, still grieving,' she suggested.

'I don't know, perhaps, but you've got to admit it's strange. And that's not all. I haven't seen him leave for work for ages. I reckon he's lost his job.'

The children came running downstairs and Mavis held a finger to her lips in warning. They were both happy, hardly ever mentioning their father, and she didn't want them to hear anything about Alec that might unsettle them. Quickly she changed the subject to something mundane.

Tommy was quiet, hardly saying a word as she and Jenny talked about this and that, and too embarrassed to look at him, Mavis was glad when an hour later Jenny said it was time for them to go.

'It's been lovely to see you,' she said, showing them out.

'I'm sure Tommy won't mind bringing me over in another couple of weeks,' Jenny said, then lowering her voice she continued, 'If I hear any more about Alec, I'll let you know.'

'All right, and thanks,' Mavis said, and as Jenny climbed into the van she remained on the doorstep to wave her off, her eyes still avoiding Tommy's.

Alec was chuckling as he tore the solicitor's letter into pieces, and, throwing it onto the floor in a shower of paper, he started to pack. Mavis thought that she'd won, that she was going to get his money, but, no, she was going to lose.

To ensure that Mavis suffered, Alec was determined that there'd be no divorce, not for many, many years. They'd have to find him first, and he was determined to make that impossible. Once again, Alec chuckled. Mavis would have to work, probably as a skivvy to support herself and the children, and that suited Alec just fine. James and Grace might have to go without, but that didn't bother him. They'd been spoiled and James needed to toughen up, to find out that, thanks to women, life wasn't a bed of roses.

Alec paused to ponder. Would he miss the children? No, not really. If his mother hadn't manipulated him into marriage they would never have been born. Yes, his mother had caused all this, but he'd be free of her soon. Free of Mavis too.

His cases packed, Alec went downstairs and into his mother's room, smiling with satisfaction. 'It's nearly time for me to leave, Mother.

'What's that? I shouldn't have left my job? Don't make me laugh, Mother. It was you who chose my so-called career, who put me in that office, who forced me to work with all those silly girls, the ones who made my life a misery. They laughed at me, did you know that? They called me old fashioned, a stuffed shirt, and drove me mad with their incessant chatter.

'Yes, you may well ask what I'm going to do now, but I'm not going to tell you. I don't have to tell you anything, ever again. I'm free to do as I please.'

Alec went to the bookcase and pulled out his treasured stamp collection. 'Here's a clue, Mother,' he said, the albums in his arms.

He grinned at her puzzled expression, loving the thought of leaving her wondering. It was his love of stamp collecting that had given him the idea, and thanks to the sale of this house he would have ample money to follow his dream.

'Right, that's it, Mother. I'm off now, and good luck with the new owners. They've got four children, noisy little buggers, and I know you'll love that.'

Alec's high-pitched giggle filled the room, but

then he walked out, closing the door firmly behind him. It was time for his adventure to begin. He had his new identity in place and would no longer be known as Alec Pugh. That name had been his mother's choice, not his, and he refused to carry it with him.

He would find the perfect location, one that was miles and miles away from Battersea. He rather fancied a pretty village somewhere, with thatched cottages, deep in the countryside. Of course, there would have to be a shop for sale, and instead of collecting stamps, he would sell them.

Oh, it was going to be marvellous. He'd be able to spend his life talking to fellow enthusiasts, buying stamps from around the world to offer his customers. He'd be his own man, unencumbered by women, and if one dared to come into his shop, he'd kick the bitch out.

CHAPTER FORTY-FIVE

Tommy stood in the yard and watched as his men drove off. They were decent signwriters and he was glad to have found them. Ed was doing a shop sign for a new greengrocer that was about to open a few streets away, and Bill just had the finishing touches to do before his job was complete and he could start the next. The business was flourishing and he'd have to employ another bloke soon, but in the meantime, rather than turn work away, Tommy would do the latest job himself. Not that he minded. It was good to keep his hand in and it got him away from the office for a while, even if it meant leaving the telephone and the yard unattended. Maybe he should think about taking a girl on, a school leaver perhaps, who could at least man the telephone and do a little to keep his ever-growing files in order.

Tommy's heart sunk when his mother walked into the yard. Bloody hell, five minutes later and he'd have been gone, the gate locked, but now he had to put up with another barrage as she marched up to him.

'I rang Belinda this morning and she told me that you've only been to see Davie once since you left her.'

'What's the point? I've told you before, I'm sure he isn't mine, and Belinda should think herself lucky that I still support him. I was hoping she'd marry the latest mug who has taken her on, and then I wouldn't have to support her too.'

'What are you talking about? What mug?'

'The latest bloke she's got living with her.'

'Belinda didn't mention another man.'

'Well, believe me, she's got one and I wish him the best of luck.'

'You should never have left her and I still dread to think what my neighbours will say if they find out you're divorced. The least you can do is find a yard out of this area.'

'Mum, please, not this again.'

'Now you listen to me. Unlike Lily Jackson, I won't be the subject of gossip. It was bad enough that she left Cullen Street to live with another man, but from what I've heard her daughter has turned out to be just as bad.'

'What are you on about?'

'They're saying that Mavis has left her husband. Apparently she's gone off with another man.'

'That's rubbish. Yes, Mavis has left her husband, but she had good reason.'

He saw his mother frown, the puzzlement on her face as she asked, 'How do you know that? Have you seen her?'

'Oh, yes, Mum, I've seen her. In fact, she stayed in my flat for a while.'

'Stayed with you! You're . . . you're the other man! No, Tommy, no! You can't do this to me. What will people say? Mavis is backward, an idiot. You can't take up with her – you just can't.'

'My God, listen to yourself. Mavis isn't an idiot, and I know that now. Her husband was knocking her about and she's been through hell, but what's the point in telling you about it? All you care about is yourself and your own reputation.'

'That isn't true. I . . . I'm thinking about you,' she blustered, 'about what people will say when they find out.'

'Yeah, if you say so, but you can relax, Mum. Unfortunately, Mavis isn't interested in me.'

'I'm glad to hear it. If you took up with her I'd never live it down, and I'd never forgive you, Tommy.'

'Just go, Mum. I've got work to do.'

'All right, I'm going, but keep away from Mavis,' she warned.

Tommy shook his head in disgust as his mother left the yard. She'd never change and he was regretting moving back to Battersea. As long as he remained she'd keep on nagging him to leave again, but that was nothing compared to the hell she'd put him through if he took up with Mavis.

Tommy loaded the van. If Mavis had agreed to go out with him he wouldn't have given a fig about what his mother said, but she had turned him down. Jenny was wrong, Mavis wasn't interested in him, and somehow he had to face that.

CHAPTER FORTY-SIX

It was now June and Alec had disappeared four months ago. Mavis was worried and her voice echoed her concern. 'What am I going to do, Mum?'

'I dunno, love,' Lily told her daughter.

'Alec seems to have disappeared off the face of the earth.'

'Yeah, well, I know how that feels. Your father did the same.'

'But unless Alec's found, I won't get my settlement.'

'You've still got the money I gave you and that should last you for a good while. There's your sketching too and you've got three more orders.'

'That won't bring in enough to pay you back.'

'I told you, the money's yours and I wouldn't have taken it even if you'd tried to repay me.'

Mavis rubbed a hand across her forehead, worried about what was now an uncertain future.

As it was warm now, at least she wouldn't have to buy coal, but the children needed new clothes, shoes, and the money her mother had given her wouldn't last forever. She had a little income from her sketches to replenish some of it, but what if the orders dried up?

'I'd best get back,' Lily said. 'Bobby's gone down for the night, but he's teething again. If he wakes up screaming, well, you know what Pete's like. He'd bring him downstairs in a jiffy and it'll be murder to settle him down again.'

'All right, Mum. I'll see you in the morning.'

'Try to stop worrying, Mavis. Things will work out, you'll see.'

Mavis managed a small smile, but her face straightened as soon as the door closed behind her mother. For a while Mavis sat deep in thought, wondering how she could increase her income, and finally coming up with an idea.

If more people saw her sketches, perhaps the orders would increase. She could start by showing a sample of her work to the other mothers at Grace's nursery. After that she could widen the area, try others, even schools. It could work, surely it could. Feeling uplifted, Mavis decided to start a new sketch to use as a sample, using Grace as her subject.

Deep in concentration as she sketched, Mavis was startled by a knock on her door at eight thirty.

She put down her pencil and opened the door, smiling when she saw Rhona. 'What's this? Saturday night and you haven't gone out?'

'I did, but I got stood up. I hung around for half an hour, but then thought, sod it, and came home. There's plenty more where he came from.'

'I only ever had one boyfriend and we married very quickly,' Mavis mused.

'Blimey, fancy that. What was it? Were you in the club?'

'No, of course not, and before you ask, I hadn't slept with him either,' Mavis said, and though Rhona was unabashed, unembarrassed by the mention of sex, Mavis still found herself reticent.

'Sod that. You should have sampled the goods before you married him.'

'Rhona,' Mavis admonished, trying her best not to smile.

'You should see your face,' Rhona giggled, 'you're trying to look like a shocked virgin, but I can see you're trying not to laugh.'

'I *was* married, so I'm hardly a virgin,' Mavis said.

'You still act like one. What's the matter? Wasn't your old man any good in bed?'

'Er . . . er . . .'

'All right, it was a daft question. If your husband was the only man you slept with, how would you know?'

'I don't, but most girls are probably in the same position when they marry.'

'Leave it out, Mavis. This is the 1960s and we know better than to lie back and think of England. As for you, do you mind if I ask you a very personal question?'

'It depends. Ask me and we'll see.'

'Did you enjoy sex?'

Mavis flushed. It wasn't a subject she'd ever discussed with anyone and Rhona was only seventeen. Yet she'd been younger, sixteen when she married Alec, and had gone to bed with him with no idea what to expect. She knew that Rhona was on the pill, that she wasn't a virgin, and, in fact, according to Lily, she was sex mad. But why? She countered the question with one of her own. 'Do you?'

'Enjoy sex? Yeah, with the right bloke it's great.'

'I just don't see what there is to enjoy.'

'Was your husband a virgin too?'

'Well, yes, I think so.'

'They're the worst. They ain't got a clue and it's over before you can say bingo. There's the selfish ones too, who although they aren't virgins, are only interested in their own enjoyment and leave you wanting more.'

'My . . . my husband was like that.'

'You poor cow, but honestly, Mavis, you don't know what you're missing. You should get yourself another bloke, and with any luck he'll be good in bed.'

'No, thanks. I'm happy as I am.'

'For now, maybe, but you're only in your twenties. A bloke is sure to come along, one that you'll fancy something rotten and then you'll change your mind.'

'No, I won't,' Mavis insisted. A man *had* come along, one who had haunted her dreams for years – Tommy. Yet she didn't want him, or any other man in her life.

Rhona had said that sex was wonderful, but Mavis was sure that, despite the feelings Tommy aroused, it was something she could do without. She relished her independence, still loved making her own decisions, doing what she wanted, when she wanted.

The barriers she had managed to put in place whenever she saw Tommy would remain. The more Mavis lived alone, the more Mavis liked it, and there was no way on earth she was going to place her trust in a man again.

'Pete, I've been thinking,' Lily said.

'Oh, yeah, about what?'

'The future and what's going to happen to Mavis if she doesn't get her settlement.'

'I know what you're going to say, Lily.'

'You do?' she said, surprised by his foresight.

'It's obvious. Mavis will have to get a job to support them and you're going to offer to have the kids.'

'Would you mind?'

'No, of course not.'

'I'm worried about the house too. It isn't big enough and though I suppose James and Grace can share that tiny bedroom for a while longer, there'll come a time when they'll need their own rooms again.'

'Lots of kids have to share. It won't do them any harm.'

'Maybe not, but one day Mavis is going to want a bigger house. I dread the thought of her moving away from us.'

'Blimey, Lily, talk about a worry guts. If Mavis doesn't get her settlement she's gonna find it hard enough to find the rent for a two bedroom house, let alone three. It'll be years before she can think about moving.'

'With a job and the money she earns from her sketches, it might not be out of reach.'

'Yeah, maybe, but if you're gonna look after the kids, she'll have to stay in this area.'

Yes, Pete was right, Lily thought. Maybe she was worrying about nothing, but she loved having Mavis living next door and it wouldn't be the same, even if she stayed in the same area.

'It's daft to worry about the future all the time,

Lily. I mean, what's to say that we won't move one day?'

'Move – but why would we?'

'Peckham is changing, with lots of demolition and development going on. It means plenty of work for me, but who knows, one day it could be the houses in this street that are coming down.'

'Pete, don't say that. I love it here. I like this house, and it's smashing to have a back garden instead of the concrete yard I had in Cullen Street.'

'Sod it, now I've given you something else to worry about, and I wish I'd kept my mouth shut.'

'Have you heard something? Is that it?'

'No, Lily, it was just a passing thought, that's all, but listen, if it'll stop you worrying I'll make you a promise. If the day ever comes that we have to move, I'll do everything I can to make sure that I find two houses side by side, one for us and one for Mavis.'

'Oh, Pete, I love you,' Lily cried, and as the words left her mouth she knew that this time she meant them. She did love Pete, really loved him, and at last she could let Ron go.

CHAPTER FORTY-SEVEN

At one time, on her mother's suggestion, Mavis had considered getting a full-time job, but, without any skills, cleaning was the only option open to her, and the pay would be hardly enough to pay the rent.

It was now August, and thankfully her ideas had paid off and Mavis was happy as she fulfilled yet another order. Her sketch of Grace had captured the child perfectly, the chubby cheeks and cheeky grin endearing. When she had shown it to the other mothers at nursery last month, she'd received a flood of orders, and thanks to Pete she could now offer a framing service too. He had found a company that sold frames in bulk, and though it had bitten into her funds they were proving popular, giving her a good profit on the investment.

There was still no news of Alec, but now that her worries about the future had eased, Mavis didn't care. He was gone, out of their lives, and she was earning enough to support them. She never wanted to see Alec again, in court or anywhere else, and soon hoped to replace the money she had taken from her mother's tin box. Despite her mother insisting that she wouldn't take it back, Mavis had never really felt it was hers. She had hated feeling dependent, hated spending what she would always feel was her mother's money, but at last she was living off her own earnings.

Mavis was hot, her face beaded with perspiration as she held up the latest order. She was pleased with it – pleased that somehow she always managed to capture the essence of every child she sketched.

A glance at the clock surprised her. It was time to collect the children from her mother's. Mavis didn't know what she would have done without her mother during the school summer holidays. She took the children off her hands every day from ten in the morning until three in the afternoon, giving her plenty of time to work.

'Hello, Mum, have they behaved themselves?' Mavis asked as she walked into her mother's house.

'Yeah, they've been in the garden most of the day, and it's only this one who gives me any trouble,' Lily said, though she was grinning as she looked at Bobby.

He chuckled, arms out as he toddled over to

Mavis. She picked him up, planted a kiss on his cheek, and then hugged him to her. 'Hello, you bruiser, and what have you been up to this time?'

'He broke my doll,' Grace complained, but then she said confidently, 'Granddad will mend it.'

Mavis smiled. It hadn't taken the children long to call Pete Granddad, but she didn't mind. He was wonderful with them, the perfect man to have in their lives, and, yes, no doubt he'd be able to mend Grace's doll. 'Come on, let's go,' she said. 'It's time to give your gran a bit of peace.'

'Yeah, and it'll give me a chance to clear this lot and the garden up,' Lily said, smiling ruefully at the toys strewn all over the living room floor.

'I'll do it if you like,' Mavis offered.

'No, just take Bobby as usual and without him around I'll get it done in a jiffy.'

'All right. I'll bring him back in a couple of hours. See you later, Mum.'

'See you, pet.'

With Bobby still in her arms, Mavis returned home. Like her mother's, the house was stifling when she walked inside. 'Why don't you two play in the garden?' she suggested to James and Grace.

'And Bobby,' Grace said.

'Yes, all right, but let me get a chair and then I'll sit outside too.'

It wasn't much cooler in the garden, the heat making Mavis feel somnolent as she forced her eyes to remain open. Jenny was coming over again on Sunday, and Mavis loved it that they had remained friends.

She had a surprise waiting for Jenny when she arrived. In a spare moment she had done a sketch of Greg; and though she still loved pencil art, there were times when she longed to use another medium, especially oils.

Though still watching the children, Mavis found her mind wandering to the past and the portrait of her grandmother she had painted at school. It was the only oil on canvas she had painted, but Tommy had ruined it. Despite all this time, the memory of that day still had the power to upset her, and she wondered if that was why she still found it difficult to relax in Tommy's company.

Thankfully he no longer pestered her for a date, but even that left her wondering. Had someone else caught his eye – yes, probably. A good-looking man like Tommy would have his pick.

Alec knew he was considered eccentric by most of the villagers, but he didn't care. He loved living in the heart of Devon, loved the countryside, the long walks, his dog by his side. The Labrador was obedient, faithful, his constant companion and all the company he needed.

'Morning, Mr Collier,' someone called.

Alec just nodded as he continued on his way,

leaving the village to climb Ham Hill. He was Charles Collier now, choosing initials that held no clue to his parentage. The shop brought in little money, but he didn't care about that either. He had purchased the premises with living accommodation on the top floor, the price reasonable and leaving him sufficient funds from the sale of his mother's house. There were also her investments, of course, ones that had passed to him and that provided a monthly income.

'Hunter, fetch,' Alec called as he threw a stick. The dog bounded off, soon returning with the stick in his mouth, which he dropped at Alec's feet.

Alec threw it again, his mind still on his business. The location of the shop was wrong, he knew that, but what little custom he had was enough. He only opened the premises from ten till four, and the few customers who crossed the threshold were like-minded, fellow stamp enthusiasts, men like him who could talk for hours about their latest finds.

Yes, men, no women, and the first one who had dared to venture into his shop had soon found out that he didn't welcome female customers, whether she wanted to purchase stamps for her husband's collection or not. He had chased her out and word had soon spread in the small village, but that suited him just fine.

What did he care if there was gossip – if some villagers thought him mad? He didn't need people, especially not women. He had his dog, his stamps and the comfort of his flat above the shop. His life was all he wanted now; unencumbered, and the only things that still had the power to unsettle him were thoughts of his wife and mother.

Hunter dropped the stick at Alec's feet again and this time when he picked it up, Alec flung it in anger. He hoped Mavis was suffering, that she was back to living in the poverty she had come from.

Alec reached the top of the hill, where he stood for a while, his mind calming at last as he drank in the wonderful view, thoughts of his wife and mother safely tucked away again.

'Hello, love,' Lily greeted when Pete came home from work, but as he wrapped his arms around her she pulled a face. 'Blimey, you stink.'

'Working in this heat, what do you expect?' he asked, then released her to swing Bobby up into his arms. 'You're not going to complain too, are you?'

As always when he saw his father, Bobby chuckled, and when he was then thrown up into the air to be caught in strong arms, he giggled with delight. 'Your daddy has got some good news.'

'Oh, yeah, and what's that?' Lily asked.

'I've got a new contract, a big one.'

'Have you now, and is it local?'

'Yes, and you and me are gonna be in clover. In another year, maybe less, we should be able to think about buying our own house.'

'But I can't leave Mavis!' Lily said, recoiling at the thought.

'Who said anything about leaving her? I've got it all planned. We could find a big old house and divide it into two flats. Three bedrooms for Mavis, two for us. How would that suit you?'

'I said I didn't want to move from here – but our own house, that'd be smashing,' Lily said, but then she sobered. 'A place that size would cost a lot of money.'

'I know, but I've looked at the profit margins and I reckon we can do it.'

'Less than a year,' Lily mused.

'Yes, but don't count your chickens yet. A lot can happen in a year. Tommy Wilson is still sniffing around Mavis, and eventually she might give in.'

'No, Pete, he hasn't asked her out for ages.'

'Well, if not him, someone else might come along.'

'I doubt it,' Lily said confidently. 'I know that Mavis is happy as she is, and she's told me herself that she isn't interested in having another man in her life. Not only that, even if she did meet someone, she can't marry again, not until she can divorce Alec and, unless he's found, she'll have to wait seven years.'

'Lily, *we* lived together and there's nothing to stop Mavis from doing the same.'

'It's different for Mavis. She's got the kids to think about and living with a man is still frowned on.'

'If you say so. But for now, if I want another cuddle I'd better get cleaned up.'

'Yes, do that,' Lily said as Pete put Bobby onto the floor again. Their own house! All of them living under the same roof. It sounded wonderful and Lily couldn't wait to tell Mavis.

CHAPTER FORTY-EIGHT

'Tommy, you don't seem keen about taking me to see Mavis again today.'

'What do you expect, Jenny?'

'Don't give up. Mavis likes you. It's been a while now since you asked her out, and you never know, she may feel differently now.'

'All right, I'll try again and if she says no, then that's it, Jenny. I'm walking away.'

'I don't think you'll have to.'

'I hope you're right, but somehow I doubt it,' Tommy said, yet maybe Jenny was right. Maybe he'd been too impatient and had frightened Mavis off. He'd stepped back, given her more time, and hopefully that had done the trick.

Mavis was once again dwelling on her future. Her mother had said that in less than a year's time she and Pete could be buying a house, and one in which there would be a flat for her and the children.

It sounded ideal, and with three bedrooms James and Grace would have their own rooms again.

Of course, she'd be living under her mother's roof again, but she could remain independent by insisting on paying rent. Her mother said that they intended to stay in Peckham and if they were close to where they were now that would be wonderful too. It would mean that James could stay in the same school, and by then Grace would be five, ready to start in the infant section.

The children were in the garden and after tidying up Mavis was taking a rare moment to relax before Jenny arrived with Greg and Tommy. It was hot and humid, and even though she had put on a clean cotton dress, it was already clinging damply to her body.

Mavis heard the van when it pulled up outside and, eager to see them, she quickly went to open the door. 'Come on in,' she greeted while swiftly wiping beads of perspiration from her forehead. 'You all look as hot as me.'

'Yes, it's a scorcher,' Jenny said as they all trooped inside.

'James is in the garden,' Mavis told Greg, smiling when the boy scooted off. She then turned to Tommy and Jenny again, saying, 'Sit down and I'll get us a cold drink.'

'Smashing,' Jenny said as she flopped onto the sofa.

505

When Mavis returned it was to find that Tommy was still on his feet and looking at an unfinished sketch. 'It's going to be good,' he said.

'That one you gave me of Greg is bloody marvellous,' Jenny said as she took a glass of squash from the tray. 'It's got pride of place on my living room wall.'

'Mavis, I know it was a long time ago,' Tommy said, 'but I can still remember a portrait you did of your gran.'

'Yes, the one that you ruined,' Mavis found herself saying sharply, the anger rising up and surprising her.

'It sounds like you still haven't forgiven me.'

Mavis tried to sound dismissive. 'Of course I have. It was a long time ago and we were just kids.'

'And as I've said before, I was a little sod,' Tommy commented as he too took a glass before sitting on the sofa. 'In fact, I can still recall how devastated you looked. It made me feel like a little shit and it was then I started to grow up. It might be a bit late, but I'm sorry, Mavis, sorry for ruining your painting.'

'Tommy, if I remember rightly, you apologised when we were younger. Now I'll just pop outside to give the children their drinks. I'll be back in a tick,' she said, surprised at the turn in the conversation. Only a couple of days ago she had been thinking about her gran's portrait, and now

Tommy had brought up the same subject. It was nice that he'd apologised again. As he said, they had just been kids and it was silly of her to still hold it against him.

'You should get back to it, Mavis, painting with oils, I mean,' Tommy said when she returned to the living room.

'It isn't that easy. I think the portrait was good, but in all honesty I doubt it was anything special. I was untrained then and still am, with an awful lot to learn.'

'I think you're a natural,' Tommy said.

'Thanks, and who knows, one day I might take up oils again,' Mavis told him. 'At the moment I haven't got the time or the money.'

'How are you doing for orders?' Jenny asked.

'Fine, but I've got a bit of news. It isn't definite yet, but in less than a year I could be moving.'

'Where to?'

'I'll still be in Peckham, hopefully sharing a house with my mother and Pete.'

Jenny pursed her lips. 'Sharing? Are you sure that's a good idea?'

'I'll have a separate flat, and to be honest, Jenny, it'll be a godsend. I need an extra bedroom and this is the only way I'll be able to afford it,' Mavis told her.

'It'd be nice if you had someone to look after you. A good man – a decent man.'

Mavis wasn't daft. She knew who Jenny was alluding to, and if she ever did want a man in her life again it would be someone like Tommy. He'd asked her out several times and sometimes she'd been tempted, but the thought of being under a man's dominance and control again always made her shy away. Not only that, she had the children to think about, and though so young they had seen too much. She would never put them at risk again, but maybe one day she'd find the courage to put a toe in the water. She doubted Tommy would wait that long. He was so good looking and, as Jenny said, a decent bloke. He'd be snapped up soon, and Mavis was just surprised that he hadn't been already.

'I don't need looking after, Jenny. I like being on my own and I'm fine,' Mavis now said, and as she and Jenny continued to chat, Mavis was unaware of the plans someone just a few doors away was making.

CHAPTER FORTY-NINE

Rhona had been keeping her eye out and had seen Mavis's friend arrive, but it wasn't her she was interested in. It was the bloke with her – the one who Mavis had said was her friend's cousin. Gawd, he was gorgeous, a bit older than the blokes she usually went for, but she was sick of going out with fellers of her own age. They were useless, leaving her unsatisfied, and she was desperate for a man of experience. Rhona knew that her cravings were unnatural, but she couldn't hold them in check. Anyway, why should she? With the birth control pill she didn't have to worry, and as this bloke wasn't local there wouldn't be any danger of more gossip.

With a sly smile, Rhona patted her hair into place and then left the house to knock on Mavis's door. 'Oh, sorry,' she said, walking straight in when Mavis opened it. 'I didn't know you had company.'

'Er . . . hello, Rhona. This is my friend Jenny and that's Tommy.'

Rhona nodded briefly at Jenny before her eyes fixed on Tommy. He was even better looking close up, and with what she hoped was a sexy voice she drawled, 'Well, hello. It's nice to meet you.'

'You too,' he said, an amused smile on his face.

Without invitation, Rhona sat next to him on the sofa, and crossing her legs she made sure her skirt rode up over her knees. 'My, you smell nice. What is it, Brut?'

'No, love, it's Old Spice.'

'Spice, spicy, yes, I like that.'

'Rhona,' Mavis said. 'I'm sorry, but would you mind coming back later?'

'Oh, do I have to? I was just starting to enjoy myself.' And then imitating a Brigitte Bardot pout she said to Tommy, 'You don't want me to go, do you?'

'Well, love, nice as it is to have your company, I'm afraid that Jenny and I have things we need to discuss with Mavis. In private.'

As Tommy said this, Rhona didn't miss the grateful smile on Mavis's face. In fact, when looking at him, Mavis looked doe-eyed. Right, so much for her not being interested in men. Oh, well, if she wanted this one, good luck to her – after all, there were plenty more fish in the sea.

Rhona stood up, saying, 'Fair enough. See you,' and with a brief wave she walked out.

'Honestly, that girl,' Mavis said as the door closed behind Rhona. 'Talk about making herself obvious.'

'Well, Tommy, she certainly made it clear that she liked you,' Jenny said with a wide smile on her face.

'She's a bit young for me.'

'Tommy, thanks for your quick thinking,' Mavis said, smiling warmly.

'That's all right,' he said, pleased that there might be a glimmer of hope. He may have been mistaken, but he was sure that Mavis hadn't looked pleased to see Rhona flirting with him. As Jenny had suggested, for over two months he had stood back, just being friendly, but now he wanted to ask Mavis out again and maybe this was a good sign.

'Can I get you both another drink?' she asked.

'Yes, please,' Jenny said. 'What about you, Tommy?'

'Thanks,' he said, unable to miss the way Mavis's dress clung to her body as she walked from the room, but unaware that though she seemed composed, Mavis's thoughts were raging.

Mavis poured the drinks, her emotions all over the place. Jealous! She'd been jealous when Rhona had flirted with Tommy. What was the matter with her? She didn't want Tommy Wilson, and if he asked her out again, she'd still say no. She was content on her own, but her earlier thoughts returned. Maybe she would find the courage to go out with a man again, but if she did it would have to be with one who wouldn't control her life, a gentle sort of chap, perhaps someone like Pete. He didn't try to rule her mother, the marriage more like a partnership, and it was wonderful to see how happy they were. Would she ever find such happiness? Mavis doubted it.

'Tommy, did you see Mavis's face?' Jenny said. 'I don't think she liked it when that girl was all over you.'

'Yes, I know,' he said hurriedly. 'If you get the chance, can you leave me alone with Mavis?'

'Good luck, Tommy – let's hope she says yes this time.'

'If she doesn't, I can't go on like this, Jenny, waiting, hoping. Yes, I'll ask her out again, but it'll be for the last time. If Mavis says no, then that's it and I'll know it's time for me to move on.'

'Fingers crossed then,' she said, 'but I don't think you'll need it. As I said, she looked jealous.'

'That's what I thought.'

Tommy sat back, hoping that Jenny would be able to give him the opportunity he needed. Mavis had everything. She had looks to die for, a soft, kind personality and, to top it all, an incredible talent for art. Mavis should be using oils again, extending her talent, but she was too busy making a living from her sketches. One day Tommy wanted to change all that. He wanted to cherish Mavis and her children, to take her away from the life of hardship she now had.

'What do you think about Mavis sharing a house with her mother?'

Just then, Mavis came back into the room leaving Tommy no chance to answer. Sharing with her mother was hardly ideal, he thought, and little better than living in this poky house. He had a better idea. The business was going great and he could even afford to take out a mortgage on another house. He'd take the financial burden away from Mavis – make sure that she and the children wanted for nothing, leaving her to concentrate on art, without having to worry about selling it. She could use oils again, and, who knows, one day she might even have an exhibition. Surely that was what Mavis wanted? Surely that was better than wasting her talent on sketches?

He heard what sounded like Greg yelling in the garden and quickly looked at Jenny.

'It's all right, Mavis. You've got your hands full. I'll go,' she said, giving him a swift wink before she went outside.

Mavis placed the tray of drinks on the table, about to go outside too, but Tommy quickly said, 'Mavis, wait. Don't go. I need to talk to you.'

'You do? What about?'

'Sit down . . . please,' Tommy urged. This was it, he thought. It was now or never, and as she sat down he leaned forward, saying urgently, 'Mavis, I'd like to help you.'

'Help me. What do you mean?'

'I'm not hard up and . . . and I'd like to look after you. Is there a chance for me? Is there a chance that we could have a future together?'

Mavis looked stunned. Her mouth opened, but no words came out.

'All right,' he said, 'don't look at me like that. I know I'm jumping the gun, but at least for a start, let me take you out. If it works out between us, it'd be great, and I know it's a bit previous, but I've already been planning your future. With your painting for instance, I'll tell you what you can do . . .'

'You . . . you've been planning my future?' Mavis interrupted, indignation colouring her cheeks. 'How dare you? And how dare you think you can tell me what to do?'

'No, no, you've got it wrong,' Tommy protested. 'I'm not trying to tell you what to do.'

'It sounds like you are to me,' Mavis shouted as she jumped to her feet. 'My God, I've spent my life being told what to do and the last thing I want is to go through that again.'

'Mavis, what's going on?' Jenny asked as she marched back into the room. 'I could hear you shouting from the garden.'

'Ask him. He's the one who wants to run my life.'

'Tommy, what on earth did you say to her?'

'I asked her out, that's all, and all right, I might have been a bit previous talking about our future.'

'Our future! We have no future,' Mavis snapped.

'Please, Mavis, calm down,' Jenny urged, and obviously trying to defuse the situation further she feigned exasperation. 'Honestly, Tommy, you haven't got a clue. I don't know what you said to Mavis, but you've certainly upset her and I think she needs a bit of time on her own to cool down. Come on, we'll go into the garden.'

Mavis still looked stiff with indignation, and shaking his head Tommy rose to his feet. 'Fine,' he said, following Jenny outside.

The children were engrossed, hardly sparing them a glance as they continued to make some sort of den. 'Well, Tommy, that obviously didn't go down well,' Jenny said wryly.

'That's it, I'm finished. I'm never going to ask her out again.'

'Don't say that. You two are made for each other, I know you are.'

'No, Jenny, we aren't. I've got to accept that now and you have, too.'

'Can't you at least apologise to Mavis for upsetting her?'

'Why should I apologise? Bloody hell, Jenny, all I said to Mavis was that I wanted to look after her. What's wrong with that?'

'I don't know, I wish I did, but at least if you say you're sorry, you can remain friends.'

'Yes, that would suit you, wouldn't it? It would mean you'd still get a lift over here every fortnight. But have you given a thought to how I'm feeling?'

Jenny had the grace to look ashamed. 'Tommy, I'm sorry, really I am. I wasn't even thinking about a lift, honestly I wasn't. It's just that if you two can remain friends, who knows, one day it might develop into more.'

'No, I told you, I'm finished,' he said, yet even as he said these words again, Tommy knew it wasn't the truth. The last few months had made him realise that Mavis was the only girl for him, and even if he met someone else she would only be second best, just as his ex-wife had been. 'All right, Jenny, if it makes you happy, I'll apologise. Come on, let's go back inside and hopefully Mavis will have calmed down by now.'

'You go ahead. I'll check on the kids first.'

He took a deep breath, saying as soon as he stepped into the room, 'Mavis, I'm sorry, and please, don't look so nervous. I promise, I won't ask you out again.'

'Tommy, I'm sorry too. I know I overreacted, but . . . but it's just that I don't want to go out with you, or anyone. Alec was violent and I lived in fear that he would turn on the children. He ruled me, ruled them, and I can't face that again.'

'I'm not Alec, and I hope one day you'll realise that. I would never lay a hand on you or your children.'

'No, I don't think you would,' Mavis said, and for a moment Tommy dared to hope, but then she shook her head. 'I'm sorry, Tommy, really I am, but I'm just not ready to go out with anyone.'

'All right, Mavis, but can we at least stay friends?'

'Yes, of course we can. You were so kind to me when you let me have your flat, and I'll always be grateful to you for that.'

'There's no need. I'd have done the same for anyone or are you forgetting that, at the time, I didn't know the flat was for you?'

'No, I hadn't forgotten and you should have seen your face the first time you came to collect your things.'

'Talking about faces,' Tommy said, pleased that the atmosphere had relaxed between them, 'that Rhona can certainly pull a few, especially that Bardot pout. Still, she isn't a bad-looking bird and young for me or not, I might just ask her out.'

'Rhona's man mad,' Mavis said brusquely. 'She'll eat you alive.'

Tommy hid a smile. He wasn't really interested in Rhona, but had wanted to gauge Mavis's reaction. He hoped he hadn't got it wrong again, but for a moment he thought he'd seen another spark of jealousy in her eyes. All right, for now she was only willing to offer friendship, but as Jenny said, one day it might develop into more.

Only time would tell, and yet no matter how long it took, Tommy knew he would never give up. Mavis was the girl for him and somehow he felt that they were meant to be together. He just had to convince Mavis of that.

Mavis waved as Jenny and Tommy drove off, but seconds later Rhona appeared, tripping towards her on stiletto heels.

'Sorry, Mavis,' she chirped. 'I didn't realise I was treading on your toes.'

'What on earth are you talking about?'

'Come on, don't give me that. You said you're not interested in blokes, but I saw the way you reacted when I tried to give that Tommy the eye.'

'I don't know what you mean. I just felt he was too old for you, that's all.'

'If you say so, but if you ask me you're nuts. He's a bit of all right and I reckon he's got his eye on you.'

Mavis sighed. 'All right, I'll admit he's asked me out a few times, but I'm not interested.'

Rhona's eyebrows rose. 'Are you sure about that?'

'Yes, I'm sure.'

'In that case I might just give him another try.'

'That's up to you, but are you coming in?'

'Yeah, why not? I ain't got anything else planned.'

Mavis hid her feelings as Rhona flopped onto a chair. Why did the thought of Tommy and Rhona going out together make her feel sick? Why was she feeling like this? Mavis knew the answer but did her best to deny it. She liked Tommy, perhaps more than liked him.

'Blimey, you should see your face,' Rhona said, 'but don't worry, I'm only kidding. I could see that Tommy wasn't interested in me. I reckon he only flirted a bit to make you jealous.'

Without thinking, Mavis blurted out, 'Well, he succeeded.'

'See, I was right, you do fancy him.'

Mavis walked to the back door and seeing that the children were playing happily, she returned to sit opposite Rhona. 'All right, I'll admit it. I do like Tommy, but I don't want to go out with him.'

'Why not?'

'I don't ever want a man, or anyone, to control my life again.'

'You daft mare. A bloke can only control you if

519

you let him, and, anyway, he's only asked you out on a date.'

'Tommy wants more than that, Rhona. He talked about his plans for our future.'

'Surely that shows that he just wants to look after you?'

'I can look after myself,' Mavis said, her voice clipped.

'Yes, and you've proved that now. Look how far you've come. You're stronger, self-reliant, but surely you don't want to live like a bleedin' nun for the rest of your life?'

'Rhona, I'm scared,' Mavis admitted at last. 'I'm a useless judge of character. I thought a woman called Edith Pugh was a wonderful woman and ran to her with my problems. She was the first person who treated me as if I had any intelligence, but all the time she was manipulating me into marrying her son.'

'We all make mistakes about people and she was probably good at hiding her true colours, that's all.'

'Yes, but I thought her son was nice too, and though I didn't love him, I tried to be a good wife. He turned out to be even worse, dominant, and then violent.'

'Maybe he was just a product of his mother.'

'Perhaps, but I misjudged Pete too. I was awful to him, blamed him for my father's disappearance, yet I was so wrong. He's a wonderful man who has taken us all under his wing.'

'Yes, and Tommy is probably a smashing bloke too, but you won't even give him a chance. Why not risk it, Mavis? A date doesn't commit you to anything. If it doesn't work out you can tell him to bugger off.'

Rhona's words sunk in and at last Mavis smiled. There hadn't been any dates with Alec, hardly any chance to get to know him before they married. If she went out with Tommy it would have to be different. She would want them to take things slowly, to get to know each other first, and then maybe, just maybe . . .

'So, what are you going to do?' Rhona asked.

Mavis had come to a decision and felt a surge of excitement. Yes, she'd do it, but it would be on her terms.

'I'm going to ring Tommy, and he's going to get the shock of his life. This time it's going to be *me* asking *him* out.'

Read on for an exclusive extract of Kitty Neale's
new book, coming in Winter 2009.

CHAPTER ONE

PART ONE
Battersea, South London, September 1940

Ten-year-old Ellen Stone woke to the incessant wail of the air-raid siren. Neighbourhood dogs were already howling and Ellen's stomach churned with fear as she flung back the blankets.

'Come on, get a move on,' her mother, Hilda, shouted, 'and don't forget your gas mask.'

Ellen's thin legs wobbled as she reached out in total darkness to fumble for the light switch. With the blackout in force and the windows covered to prevent even a chink of light escaping, her bedroom looked gloomy in the dim glow of a bare light bulb. Ellen pushed her shoulder-length, dark wavy hair aside as she thrust bare feet into her shoes and then grabbing the hated gas mask, she ran downstairs.

'Hurry up,' her mother urged as she flung open the back door.

They stumbled down the garden to the Anderson shelter, but could already hear the heavy, uneven throb of bombers flying across London.

'Oh, Mum,' cried Ellen as her mother closed the door behind them.

'I know, love, I know,' Hilda murmured, urging her to sit on the camp bed, 'but don't worry. They're probably going for the Surrey Docks again. Now hold the torch so I can light the oil lamp.'

With hands shaking, Ellen did as she was told and though her mother was a tiny woman, less than five feet tall, she leaned on her strength. With light brown hair, small dark eyes and a thin face, her mother was mouse-like in appearance, but there was nothing meek in her demeanour. She could be soft and kind, but woe betide anyone who crossed her.

'There, that's better,' Hilda said in the dim glow from the oil lamp.

Ellen almost jumped out of her skin when a loud barrage of anti-aircraft fire started up from the direction of Battersea Park, where huge banks of guns had been put in place.

'Listen, love,' Hilda said above the noise as she sat down to place a protective arm around Ellen's shoulders, 'this can't go on. We need to get you out of London, but I don't fancy this evacuation lark where you'd be sent off to strangers.

I've written to Gertie, asking if you can stay with her for a while, and she's agreed.'

'But . . . but what about you? I don't want to go without you.'

'Your grandparents won't shift and with your gran so ill, I can't leave them. You'll be fine with Gertie and you'll love it on her smallholding. She's even got chickens.'

There was the sudden scream of high explosives, along with the clatter of incendiaries as they fell on roofs and pavements. This was followed almost immediately by a loud boom, then another as the ground shook beneath them. Ellen was deafened by the noise and terrified, she burrowed into her mum's chest. The barrage went on and on, the bombs so close that Ellen suddenly found herself pushed down onto the camp bed, her mother hunched over her like a shield.

All sense of time was lost, but then came a strange stillness, a hush before more noise, this time the dull thud of walls collapsing. 'Mum, something's on fire,' Ellen said when the smell of burning pervaded the shelter.

Slowly, dazedly, they sat up to hear the crackle of flames. 'It's all right, we're safe here,' Hilda assured, though there was a tremor in her voice. 'I . . . I'll make us both a nice hot drink.'

Trembling, Ellen watched her mother as she lit the primus stove and then set an old metal kettle onto it. Slowly steam rose from the spout and then spooning cocoa into tin mugs, followed by a large spoonful of sweet, condensed milk, Hilda stirred the mixture vigorously before holding one out. Ellen took it, her voice a croak as she said, 'Thanks, Mum.'

'I think the raid's over, love, but we'll have to wait for the all clear.'

They sat sipping their drinks, ears alert and dreading another wave of bombers, but at last, after what felt like another hour, the all clear siren sounded.

Tentatively they left the shelter, only to stand almost paralysed with shock at the sight that greeted them. Their house, along with every one in the street had been destroyed, crushed, and all that remained were piles of rubble.

'Oh no, no,' Hilda gasped.

The landscape appeared vast, alien, and at first beyond Ellen's comprehension, but then she realised why. It wasn't just their street that had been hit; it was the next one and the one beyond that, the area now an open mass of destruction. Dust was thick in the air, along with the acrid smell of smoke. Small fires burned and Ellen was dimly aware of the distant sound of bells clanging as fire engines rushed to the scene. Yet still she and her mother stood, dazed and unmoving.

Gradually more people appeared, like them,

covered in dust, and it was only then that Ellen's mother seemed to come to life. 'Mum! Dad,' she cried, grabbing Ellen's hand to drag her forward.

They stumbled over rubble, disorientated, both now coated in filth, until at last Ellen thought they might be in what was once the next street. Even though she knew what to expect, a sob caught in her throat. It was gone, like theirs. Her grandparents' house was gone.

'Mum! Dad!' Hilda yelled, falling to her knees as she frantically dug at the rubble.

Ellen ran to help, their hands and fingers soon bleeding, yet still they dug. 'I told them,' Hilda sobbed. 'I told them to use their shelter, but they just wouldn't listen and preferred to crawl under the table. Mum! Dad! Can you hear me?'

For a moment they paused, listening, praying to hear voices, but there was nothing. They began to pull at the rubble again, but then hands reached out to drag them away.

'Come on, you've got to stand back,' an ARP warden said. 'It's too dangerous for you and the heavy rescue teams are here now.'

Exhausted, they were led away and not long after a mobile canteen arrived. They were given cups of tea, a woman saying sympathetically, 'Are you all right, my dear?'

'My parents, they're under that lot. I've got to help,' Hilda gasped, about to move forward again.

'No, leave it to the rescue teams. They know how to assess the risks; how to find people buried under rubble and it's best if you stay out of the way.'

The vast area was a hive of activity now, firemen, policemen, ambulances, heavy rescue teams, ARP wardens, but all Ellen could think about was her beloved gran and granddad. She was aware of other people around them, women and children crying, but she felt strange, remote, sounds coming as though from a distance. She swayed, a rushing sound in her ears, and then as her knees caved beneath her, Ellen sank into a pit of darkness.

Hilda was reeling with grief. It had been a dreadful twenty-four hours and she was almost on the point of collapse, yet she had to hold herself together for her daughter's sake. Her only relief was that Ellen wasn't hurt, her fainting fit a combination of shock and nervous exhaustion, but she was still whey-faced and like her, grieving.

It had been hours before her parents were pulled from the rubble, both dead, and for the rest of her life Hilda knew she would never forget the nightmare of seeing their broken bodies. Now she had the funeral to arrange and though her friend, Mabel Johnson, who lived just outside the bomb-damaged area, had taken them in, Hilda felt so alone. If only Doug was here, but at the outset of war her husband had enlisted in the navy. He was on a ship, somewhere at sea, and with so many shipping losses she feared for his safety.

'Here, get that down you,' Mabel said as she handed Hilda a cup of tea.

'Mabel, I've lost everything. My home, furniture, and until you all rallied round, we only had the filthy clothes we stood in.'

'You'll find somewhere else to live, but until you do you're welcome to stay here. With both my boys evacuated to Devon, I've got plenty of room.'

'Thanks, it's good of you, but you've seen the state Ellen's in. Once the funeral is over, I'm taking her out of London.'

'Where to?'

'I've got a friend with a smallholding in Somerset.'

'Blimey, girl, you're a Londoner. You'd go potty living in the sticks. Ellen can be evacuated, but you should stay here.'

Hilda shook her head against her friend's words. Since autumn, living in London had been hell. They were calling the continuous bombing raids, the blitz, and now that her parents were gone, all Hilda wanted was to get away from this devastated area and the dreadful memories. Gertie would take them in and in Somerset they'd be safe, her friend's home a haven until this dreadful war was over.

CHAPTER TWO

Ellen was shaken awake when the train pulled into Crewkerne station and she climbed bleary-eyed out of the carriage. It was past four-thirty in the afternoon as they stood on the platform, the bitter cold biting through their clothes, but only moments later a tall, big-boned woman appeared. Ellen was amazed to see that she was wearing scruffy, brown, corduroy trousers that were tucked into wellington boots, along with a dirty, navy duffel coat. Not only that, she was wearing a brown flat cap with dark blonde hair tucked up beneath it.

'Hilda,' she cried, striding up to them, her strong features softened by a wide smile.

'Hello, Gertie.'

'You look exhausted. Come on, let's get you home,' Gertrude Forbes said as she grabbed both suitcases.

'It was a bugger of a journey with delay after delay.'

'My goodness, is that Ellen? I can't believe it.'

'Of course it's Ellen. She's ten now.'

'She's so pretty, but has it been that long since I've seen you?'

'Yes, all of seven years.'

'Where does the time go? Come on, follow me,' said Gertie, striding ahead of them now.

'Blimey, is that yours?' Hilda asked when she saw a small horse and cart.

'Yes and as Ned's the only transport I have, I'd be lost without him.'

Hilda eyed the horse warily, but Gertie urged them to climb onto a bench-like seat at the front of the flat cart. She then stowed their cases on the back before heaving herself up beside them. 'Right, we're off,' she said, taking the reins and with a gentle click of her tongue, the horse moved forward.

Ellen had never been on a horse and cart before and found it strange; the gentle sway, the clip, clop of hooves as they rode along a narrow cobbled street. Soon they were passing through a small town and she listened as her mother spoke to Gertie.

'Thanks for this. Thanks for taking us in.'

'It's nothing, but I was sorry to hear about your parents.'

'I still can't believe they're gone.'

Ellen leaned against her mother, shivering, and

her teeth beginning to chatter. 'Mum . . . I . . . I'm cold.'

'Here,' Gertie said as a tarpaulin-like cover was thrown over them. 'Tuck that in around you.'

'How far is it to your place?' Hilda asked.

'It's a fair trot, and don't expect much. By the time we get there you'll find yourself in the middle of nowhere, and as for those daft shoes, forget it. Like me, you'll need boots and the same goes for Ellen.'

'Gertie, I can't believe how different you look. In London you always loved to dress up and I never thought I'd see the day when you'd wear trousers and wellies.'

'Needs must,' she said dismissively, 'and anyway, I prefer them.'

'You said in your letters that you're fine, but it's been years since Susan left. Have you found anyone else?'

'No, and I don't want to.'

'Aren't you lonely?'

'Not really. I have my animals and, unlike people, they don't let you down.'

'Oh Gertie, you sound so bitter.'

'What do you expect?' she replied, her blue eyes flashing. 'I lost everything for Susan, my reputation, my career, but after moving here she left me.'

'You could have returned to London.'

'At first I wanted to lick my wounds in private,

then as time passed, I became used to the seclusion. I love it now. I'm self-sufficient and doubt I'll ever leave.'

'Yeah, well, at the moment you're better off here.'

'London sounds like hell. No wonder you wanted to leave.'

'Since September we've had bombing raids day and night, but mostly at night now.'

'Well, you'll be safe here.'

'Have you heard from your father?' Hilda asked. 'Is he still in London?'

'No, I haven't heard from him and don't expect to. When he found out he almost had an apoplectic fit. I've disgraced the family name and he'll never forgive me.'

Ellen was at a loss to understand this strange conversation. Why was Gertie talking about licking wounds and what on earth was an apoplectic fit? She wanted to ask, but knew better than to interrupt adults when they were talking. They had left the town behind now, the countryside they were passing through, winter-bleak. Yet it was so quiet, so peaceful, and Ellen found her eyes closing.

Hilda saw that Ellen had fallen asleep again and held her close. After her parents' death there hadn't been a lull in the bombing and she'd lost count of the times they'd been forced to flee into Mabel's shelter. During lulls, as though shutting out her fears, Ellen would sleep, yet when awake her nerves seemed at breaking point. Hilda sighed heavily, the tension in her neck easing. Gertie had welcomed them and at last they were away from the bombings. Surely here in the peace of the countryside Ellen's nerves would heal.

'I know it's been yonks since I've seen you,' Gertie said, 'but just how long have we been friends?'

'Blimey, let me think. I was about eight years old when my mum started work as a domestic in your father's house. I think we saw each other a few times, though at that time I'd hardly call us friends.'

Gertie chuckled. 'Yes, I remember now and my goodness, I was such a stuck-up little bitch.'

'Don't remind me,' Hilda said ruefully.

'When my mother died and I was sent to boarding school, I had a rude awakening. I hated it, yet it was worse when I came home during the school holidays. My father used to ignore me, and if it wasn't for your mother's kindness, my life would have been very bleak.'

'My mum was a good woman, but even then you and I rarely saw each other. I think it all changed when you were expelled and by then we must have been around twelve years old.'

'I wasn't sorry to be expelled, in fact I think I pushed for it by behaving so badly, but I came unstuck. It was worse being tutored at home and

I was so bloody lonely. My father was never in and after lessons I just rattled around in that huge house, with just your mother and the cook for company.'

'That was when my mum started dragging me to your house every weekend and during school holidays.'

'She dragged you! Was it that bad?'

'Gertie, I hate to say it, but it was at first. I hardly knew you and let's face it you were a lot different from my usual friends. To me you sounded posh, upper class, and in fact, you still do.'

'It certainly didn't rub off on you though,' Gertie said, but the sting was taken out of her words by her warm smile. 'I'm only joking, but though you've never mentioned it before, you must have resented having to come to Kensington.'

'I haven't said anything before because, despite our different upbringing, we soon became fast friends.'

'I envied you your family; the closeness you shared.'

'Blimey, I don't know why. Compared to mine, your home was like a palace.'

'My life was so restricted that it was more like a prison. Thank goodness you came along and we became more than just friends. To me you were like a sister, one who stood by me through thick and thin.'

'Now don't exaggerate,' Hilda protested. 'As adults we went our separate ways. You for teacher training, and me, well, until I met Doug, I only worked in a local shop.'

'Maybe, but we've always stayed in touch. I can't tell you how much it meant to me when, unlike everyone else, you didn't judge me, or ostracise me.'

'Why should I? You're still the same person and a good one at that. Take now for instance. If it wasn't for you I'd have been forced to have Ellen evacuated to strangers.'

'When the school found out about me, they couldn't get rid of me quickly enough. I was treated like a monster, a bad influence and unsafe to be around children. I was thrilled to get your letter and it meant a lot that you were going to trust Ellen to me.'

Hilda felt anger on Gertie's behalf. It would be strange staying with her, but she had no fear of her preferences. As Gertie had said, they were more like sisters, Hilda's voice gentle as she said, 'You're not a monster. You love kids and there's nobody I'd trust more with my daughter.'

'It's nice that you've arrived just before Christmas.'

Hilda's throat tightened. She didn't want to think about Christmas, her first one without her parents, but then Ellen stirred.

'Ain't we there yet?' she asked tetchily.

It was Gertie who answered. 'We haven't got far to go now, and I've left a beef casserole braising in the range.'

'Cor,' Ellen said, brightening as she sat upright.

'How do you get on with rationing?' Hilda asked.

'So far, it isn't a problem, and the butcher doesn't even ask for a coupon.'

'Blimey, you're lucky. In London we only get our rationed amounts and there's talk of it getting worse with food in really short supply.'

Soon a tiny village loomed in front of them and Hilda heaved a sigh of relief, but Gertie just drove through it and out the other side. On and on they went, until finally, after about twenty minutes, Gertie eased the horse and cart left into a narrow lane. At the end she finally pulled on the reins, saying as the horse drew to a halt and she hopped down, 'I'll just open the gates.'

It was almost dark now and Hilda could see little as her eyes tried to pierce the gloom. Gertie didn't get onto the carriage again, instead she gripped the bridle to lead the horse through the wooden gates. She could now see a small cottage but as Gertie tethered the horse and Hilda climbed down, her shoes sank into thick, heavy, mud. 'Yeah, I can see what you mean about boots,' she complained, feeling the suck and squelch as she ruefully lifted a foot.

Gertie reached her arms up to Ellen. 'Come on, down you get, but watch your step.'

Tentatively Hilda and Ellen squelched to the front door, both taking off their mud-caked shoes before stepping inside. It was dark, but they felt a welcome blast of warm air, along with a low growl. 'Oh Gawd, what's that?' Hilda gasped.

'It's only Kipper,' Gertie said as she lit an oil lamp.

'Kipper?' yelped Hilda as the growls turned to yaps.

'He won't hurt you,' Gertie assured and as light pierced the gloom, a small white dog, with a blaze of black on his face, was now in view.

The dog ran up to Ellen, barking with excitement now and she smiled, crouching down to stroke him. 'He's so cute.'

'He's a Jack Russell terrier and perfect for ratting.'

'Rats,' Hilda squeaked. 'Oh, blimey.'

'There are rats in London, and in fact probably more than around here. Now I must see to the horse. Make yourself at home, Hilda, and to start with you can put the kettle on the range to boil.'

'Yeah, all right, but why the oil lamps? Ain't you got electricity?'

'No, Hilda, but at least I've got running water.'

'Mum, I need the toilet,' Ellen said.

'Go through the scullery and you'll find it outside the back door,' Gertie told her.

Ellen hurried out the back, whilst Gertie, with the dog at her heels, left at the front, leaving Hilda to look around the room. The ceiling was low, crossed with heavy, dark beams, the room dominated by a huge, black cooking range. A small, scruffy wooden table stood in the centre, and on each side of the range she saw a wingback chair, one with horsehair stuffing poking through the upholstery. Other than that there was a dresser, the shelves packed with a mishmash of china.

Gertie was right, this place wasn't much, but nevertheless Hilda was charmed by the cosy atmosphere. Gertie had done her best, the tiny, deep-set, lead-paned window dressed with chintzy curtains, the wide sill sporting a jug of dried flowers. Hilda found herself sniffing the air, her mouth salivating at the rich aroma of beef casserole.

'It's a funny toilet,' Ellen said as she came back inside. 'There isn't a proper seat, just a long wooden bench with a hole in it.'

'I never thought I'd see the day when I thought our little house was luxurious, but compared to this . . .' Hilda had to pause, a lump in her throat. There was no house now, her home just a pile of rubble. Hilda managed to swallow her emotions. They were here now, safe, and that was the most important thing. 'We'll be eating soon, but in the meantime I'll make us all a drink.'

'Mum, why does Gertie wear men's clothes?'

Hilda paused as she wondered how to answer her daughter's question. Ellen was too young to understand, so grasping she said, 'I expect it's because it's sensible to wear trousers when you're working outdoors, and warmer too.'

'Can I wear trousers?'

'Well, yes, I suppose so, but I don't know how we'll get hold of any in your size.'

'Get hold of what?' Gertie asked, catching the tail end of the conversation as she stepped inside.

'Like you, Ellen wants to wear trousers.'

'That won't be a problem. I've got a sewing machine and we can soon knock her up a couple of pairs. You'll need some too, Ellen.'

'Me! Me in trousers! No, I don't think so.'

'Huh, we'll see about that. Now, is the kettle on?' Gertie asked brusquely.

'I was just about to do it.'

'Get a move on and you, Ellen, can lay the table for dinner.'

'Oh, Gertie, you haven't changed and sound as bossy as ever,' Hilda said, giggling as she added, 'Gawd, talk about a school mistress. What next? If we don't behave, will you give us the cane?'

Gertie at first looked shocked, but then she too began to laugh. 'Oh, Hilda, I'm so glad you're here.'

'Can we have our dinner now?' a small voice said.

'We certainly can,' Gertie said, 'and tomorrow I'll show you how to collect eggs for our breakfast.'

'Cor,' Ellen said. 'I like it here. Where's your dog?'

'He's been cooped up in here while I went to fetch you, but once we've eaten you can call him in again. I've a cat too, but Wilfred's a tom and is mostly off roaming.'

'What else have you got?' Ellen asked eagerly.

'Two pigs and a goat.'

Hilda smiled as she saw her daughter's delight. It was going to be all right, and she was sure that bringing Ellen here was the right decision. Ellen would recover and she was sure to enjoy exploring the countryside. And I'll be fine too, Hilda decided, yet there was no way that Gertie was going to get her into trousers.

CHAPTER THREE

During the next four months Hilda saw a huge change in her daughter. They were still grieving, but for both of them the horrors of living in London during the blitz seemed far away. Instead of the air-raid warning siren, they woke up to the sound of Gertie's cockerel and birdsong. Christmas had passed with just the three of them, their presents to each other homemade and somehow, Hilda had got through it with only a few private tears.

The only school was on the other side of the village and as it was a long way to go, Gertie was tutoring Ellen at home. At first she had seemed to miss the company of other children, but as spring arrived and trees that had been skeletal burst into new growth, Ellen had become totally enamoured with the countryside. When not having lessons or helping out on the smallholding, she spent hours roaming the woods, bringing home all sorts of things, bugs, bluebells and other wild flowers, all of which Gertie would identify for her. Gertie showed her how to press the flowers and leaves before carefully placing them in albums, and for Ellen, a love of nature was born.

Hilda's smile was wry. She couldn't feel the same. Yes, it was safe here, but she hated living in such total isolation. Gertie didn't have a wireless, so the only news they got was when they made a trip to the village. She had kept in touch by letter with Mabel and had heard from her how things were in Battersea, thankful that her friend had decided to move to Clapham where she insisted it was safe.

Hilda wasn't keen on working outdoors either, especially mucking out the two pigs, or the back-breaking digging for spring planting that had become a nightmare. If she had news of Doug it would be something, but though she'd sent him a letter with her new address, so far there hadn't been a reply. God, she missed him so much, prayed he was safe, and for a moment tears stung her eyes. They'd lost so many vessels, so many seamen, and she lived in constant fear of hearing that his ship had been sunk.

'Are you all right, Hilda?'

'Can we go to the village today?'

'There's no need to go twice a week and I'd rather get the rest of the potatoes in, along with cabbage and carrots. There's the salad crop too and tomatoes to bring on in the greenhouse.'

'Oh for God's sake, Gertie, give it a break.'

'This is a busy time of year and if I don't plant, I don't eat. I know I've preserved fruit from last year, made jam and pickles, but I need to sell produce to buy flour, meat, and anything else I can't grow.'

'It still seems strange to think of you making jam and before we came I had no idea how much land you had. How on earth have you managed on your own?'

'I had a lad of fifteen working for me, but once conscription started labour became short. He found a job earning more than I could possibly pay him, and since then it's been impossible to find hired help. I had to cut down on planting, but with you here we can get more in.'

'Yeah, and I've done my best to muck in, but I'm really worried about Doug. I haven't heard from him yet, and if you take me to the village, I promise I'll really get stuck in again when we get back.'

'If you'd only learn to handle Ned you could go on your own.'

'He hates me.'

'Hilda, he's a horse and just needs firm hands on the reins.'

'I was firm, but the sod wouldn't move.'

Gertie shook her head with obvious disgust, but Hilda tried a winning smile. It was all right for

Gertie. She was happy living like a virtual recluse, but for Hilda it was becoming more and more difficult. She missed her friends, the bustle of London, and if only the Luftwaffe would stop dropping bombs, she'd go back like a shot. 'Please, Gertie,' she appealed again.

'Oh, all right. I need to see the butcher so might as well do that, but I'm not hanging about while you waste time gossiping to the locals again.'

'Thanks, Gertie,' Hilda said, smiling with delight as she went to the bottom of the stairs to call Ellen. They shared a bedroom under the eaves, snuggled up in a huge, lumpy, iron-framed bed. 'Ellen, Ellen, come on, get up.'

'Another one,' Ellen said when she finally appeared, her hands cupped around a catch.

Hilda shuddered as she backed away. This was another thing she hated, the huge spiders that regularly appeared in their bedroom and the rest of the cottage. 'Is it one of them whoppers?'

'Yes, a tree spider,' Ellen said as she walked over to the back door.

'Hurry up! Get it out of here before you drop it,' Hilda urged.

'Honestly, Hilda,' said Gertie. 'Anyone would think you've never seen a spider before. You should be used to them by now and there are plenty of spiders in London.'

'Yeah, but not those bloody great hairy things.'

'They won't hurt you,' Gertie said as she opened the back door for Ellen, the spider now dispatched.

Hilda's cheeks puffed with relief, the insect soon forgotten as she began to boil eggs for their breakfast. She was anxious to go and as soon as they'd eaten she chivvied Ellen to get ready, whilst Gertie went to get the horse from the small field. Just getting Ned to the cart and harnessed took so long and it drove Hilda mad, but knowing better than to complain she just smiled gratefully at Gertie when at last they set off.

It was a nice morning with hardly a cloud in the sky and just a slight nip in the air. 'Oh, Gertie, I hope there's a letter.'

'Stop worrying. If anything had happened to Doug you'd have heard.'

'I haven't got a clue where he is, where he's headed, what ocean. I think he tried to tell me in his last letter, but it was so heavily censored with line after line blacked out and unreadable.'

'How did he end up in the navy?'

'As soon as the war started he couldn't wait to get to a recruitment office. He said he didn't fancy the army with all the foot slogging, so volunteered for the navy.'

'What does he do?'

'He's in the engine room, but I don't why the silly bugger was so quick to enlist.'

'Mum, you sweared,' Ellen protested.

'Swore,' Gertie corrected.

Hilda smiled ruefully as she ruffled her daughter's hair. 'Yeah, well, this war is enough to make a saint swear, not that I want to hear you using bad language.'

Ellen leaned against her whilst Hilda's mind was full of her husband. Letters had been fairly regular until now and despite Gertie's reassurance, Hilda couldn't help worrying.

At last the village came into view, and soon they were pulling up outside the village general store-cum-post office. Gertie had hardly tethered the horse before Hilda was hurrying inside, thankful to find she was the only customer. 'Is there any mail for me?' she asked eagerly.

'No, I'm sorry, there's nothing,' Mrs Brannon, the elderly postmistress said.

Hilda sagged with disappointment, but as Ellen rushed into the shop she managed to hide her feelings.

'Is there a letter, Mum?'

'No, pet, but don't worry,' Hilda said. 'Your dad's sure to write soon.'

'Can I have some sweets?'

'Yes, all right, and I might as well get a few things in.' There was still no evidence of food shortages as Hilda pulled out their ration books, glad that at least she had always taken these, along with their birth certificates and marriage lines to

549

the shelter. Amongst other things she asked for butter, sugar, flour and yeast, along with a newspaper. Ellen chose a gobstopper and some barley sugar, Mrs Brannon totting up the bill as Gertie stepped inside.

'Come on, Hilda, get a move on,' she chided.

'Morning, Miss Frost,' the postmistress said pointedly.

'Good morning, Mrs Brannon,' she replied, her tone clipped.

'I was only saying to Mrs Cook earlier that it must be nice for you having a friend to stay.'

Gertie didn't answer the woman, only saying to Hilda as she marched out of the shop again, 'I'll wait for you outside.'

Mrs Brannon's neck stretched as she said indignantly, 'Well I never.'

'Sorry,' Hilda said as she hurriedly paid for her goods before leaving the shop.

'Look, I've got a gobstopper,' Ellen said as she ran to Gertie's side.

'That'll keep you quiet for all of five minutes.'

'Blimey, Gertie, you were a bit short with Mrs Brannon.'

'She was just after gossip and I won't give her, or anyone else in the village, the satisfaction of knowing my business. Now let's get to the butchers and then we can go home.'

Hilda sighed. Unlike Gertie, she missed chatting

to people, all right, gossiping if that's what Gertie chose to call it, but nowadays she didn't get the chance. 'While we're there I'll get some sausages and a bit of bacon, but why do you need to talk to him?'

'Until I get new crops to sell, money will be a bit tight, so at this time of year I take him one of my pigs for slaughter.'

'No! No!' Ellen yelped.

'Oh, darn, I shouldn't have said anything in front of her.'

'Yeah, well it's a bit late now,' Hilda snapped as Ellen flung herself against her.

Gertie crouched down. 'Listen, Ellen, you like eating roast pork, sausages, and bacon don't you? I raise pigs for food, not as pets, but I'm sorry, I should have warned you.'

'Wh . . . what about the other one?'

'She'll be having a litter soon, and once weaned I'll sell all the piglets but one which I'll fatten up for next year. I know it all sounds awful to you, but it's the way of life on farms and smallholdings.'

Ellen wasn't mollified, but then they were all distracted by the roar of an engine as a motor-bike drove into the village. At first Hilda thought the driver was going to pass straight through, but he suddenly braked, his legs then straddling the road whilst he lifted his goggles.

Hilda was puzzled as his eyes turned towards her, but then the bag of shopping left her hand in shock. Groceries spilled onto the pavement, unheeded as she dashed towards him. 'Doug! Ohhh . . . Doug,' she cried, her face alight with joy.